Cornish Short Stories

The Francis Boutle Book of
Cornish Short Stories

Selected by
Alan M. Kent and Derek R. Williams

Francis
Boutle
Publishers

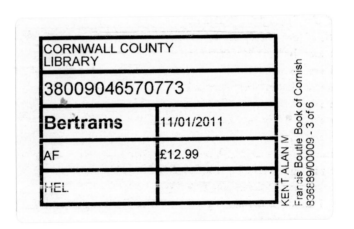
First published by
Francis Boutle Publishers
272 Alexandra Park Road
London N22 7BG
Tel/Fax: (020) 8889 7744
Email: info@francisboutle.co.uk
www.francisboutle.co.uk

ISBN 978 1 903427 55 2

Contents

Acknowledgements

The Black Letter Pamphlet: News from Perin in Cornwall of a most Bloody and un-exampled Murder. Quarto. Bodley, 4, M G29(2), Oxford; Edward Lhuyd, *Archaeologica Britannica*, Oxford: Oxford University Press, 1707; Robert Hunt (ed.), *Popular Romances of the West of England: Second Series*, London: J.C. Hotten, 1865; Anthony Trollope, *Lotta Schmidt and Other Stories*, London: Strahan, 1867; William Bottrell (ed.), *Traditions and Hearthside Stories of West Cornwall: First Series*, Penzance: W. Cornish, 1870; Thomas Hardy, *A Changed Man, The Waiting Supper and other tales*, London: Macmillan, 1966 [1913]; Mark Guy Pearse, *A Village Down West*, London: Epworth Press, 1924; J. H. Pearce, *Drolls from Shadowland*, London: Lawrence & Bullen, 1893; J. Henry Harris, *The Luck of Wheal Veor and other stories of The Mine, Moor, and Sea*, Truro: Pollard, 1901; Sir Arthur Quiller-Couch, *Noughts and Crosses*, London: Dent, 1928 [1891]; John Baragwanath King, 'The Laughing Cornishman' in Trelawney Roberts and Charles Henderson (eds.), *Tre Pol and Pen: The Cornish Annual 1928*, London: Dodsworth, 1928; C. A. Dawson Scott, *The Vampire: A book of Cornish and other stories*, London: Robert Holden, 1925; H. D. Lowry, *Wreckers and Methodists and other stories*, London: Heineman, 1893; Charles Lee, *Cornish Tales*, London: Dent, 1941; Phyllis Bottome, *The Derelict*, New York: The Century Co., 1917; D. H. Lawrence, *England, My England*, London: Martin Secker, 1924 [1922]; Anne Treneer, *Happy Button and other stories*, London: Westaway Books, 1950; A. L. Rowse, *West Country Stories*, London: Macmillan, 1946; Mary Williams, 'No Ticket' was first published in Peter C. Smith (ed.), *The Phantom Coach*, London: William Kimber, 1979; Daphne du Maurier, *The Birds and other stories*, Arrow, 1992 [*The Apple Tree: a short novel and some stories*, London: Gollancz, 1952]; 'Window in the Attic' by J. C. Trewin © J. C. Trewin 1973. Reprinted with permission of the estate of J. C. Trewin; Winston Graham, 'Jack's Fight' in *Argosy*, 1971; Jack Clemo, *The Bouncing Hills*, Redruth: Dyllansow Truran, 1983; Denys Val Baker, 'The Outcast' in Denys Val Baker (ed), *The Cornish Review*, No. 9, Winter, 1951; Charles Causley, *Hands to Dance and Skylark*, London: Robson Books, 1979 [1951]; Phyllis M. Jones, *New People In An Old World*, Pontyberem: Kenwyn Publishers, 2009; Kenneth Moss, *Encounter in St Ives and other stories of Cornwall*, London: Kimber, 1980; Donald R. Rawe, 'The Deep Sea Dream' in Denys Val Baker (ed.), *Cornish Short Stories*, Harmondsworth: Penguin, 1976; N. R. Phillips, 'Bella Vista' in John T. Wilson (ed.), *The Ebb Tide and other stories from Cornwall*, Zennor: Weavers Press Publishing, 1991; John Branfield, *The Day I Shot My*

Dad And Other Stories, London: Gollancz, 1989; Liz Harman, *Now 'Ark To Me: Cornish Tales*, Linkinhorne: Giss 'On Books, 2006; E. V. Thompson, 'The Day the Cup Came to Trescoppa' in Simon Parker (ed.), *Scryfa* vol. 4, Linkinhorne: Giss 'On Books, 2004; Michael Morpurgo, 'Gone to Sea' from *The White Horse of Zennor* © Michael Morpurgo 1982. Published by Egmont UK Ltd London and used with permission; Les Merton, *Dark Corners: a return to Cornish noir*, Bristol: Boho Press, 2005; Myrna Combellack, *Cuts in the Face: Stories from Cornwall*, Carharrack: Cornish Fiction, 2004; 'The Lighthouse Keeper's' Wife by Helen Dunmore. Reprinted with permission of A. P. Watt Ltd. on behalf of Helen Dunmore; Tim Saunders, 'Blue Murder' in Simon Parker (ed.), *Scryfa*, vol. 6, Linkinhorne: Giss 'On Books, 2005; Simon Parker, *Full As An Egg*, Mount Hawke: Truran, 2006; Annamaria Murphy, 'Below' in Simon Parker (ed.), *Scryfa*, vol. 2, Linkinhorne: Giss 'On Books, 2003; Stacey Guthrie, 'Doubled Up And Baked Like Fate' in Simon Parker (ed.), *Scryfa*, vol. 8, Linkinhorne: Giss 'On Books, 2006.

The authors would like to acknowledge the help and assistance of Simon Parker, Shirley Brown, Jackie Fergus, Christine Faunch, the Special Collections, University of Exeter Library and the Cornish Studies Library, Redruth, in the preparation of this volume.

Introduction

This collection anthologises forty short stories written about Cornwall and the Cornish. It begins with an anonymous short story – now commonly known as *The Bohelland Tragedy* – from 1618, and ends with Stacey Guthrie's *Doubled Up And Baked Like Fate*, a story conceived at the start of the third millennium. In this four hundred year period, we witness the development of the short-story form, and its significance within the Cornish and Anglo-Cornish literary continuum. The last ten years have seen a remarkable flowering of literature in Cornwall, not only by new writers (in both Cornish and English), but also the gathering together of the traditions of writing inherent in the territory. From this, we have been able to better document what has been written in the past, and what still needs to be said. The purpose of this collection is to show what the short story has had to say so far.

Many of the writers here will be familiar names, who have been anthologised in previous collections such as Denys Val Baker's *Cornish Short Stories*, but we have tried in the *Francis Boutle Book of Cornish Short Stories* to balance this with some new and less well-known voices. Some of the writers come from elsewhere, but many others were born and bred in Cornwall. Different styles are to be found within the collection. A number of writers develop their narratives in Standard English, while others use genuine Cornu-English dialect. As editors, we have, however, noted that many of the writers included in previous collections were not Cornish. We have attempted to redress the balance here, with a generous selection from indigenous writers who have often been dismissed as either second class or not canonical.

As can be seen from the four hundred years of its development, the short story has had a relatively long pedigree in Cornwall. Although Nicholas Boson's *John of Chyanhor* is the only surviving short story originally written in Cornish, there were perhaps other narratives from the later phase of Cornish which have not survived. Compared to other European territories, where prose narrative seems to have developed comparatively late, in Cornwall there occurred an early engagement with the form. The continuity of this form, throughout the nineteenth and twentieth centuries in particular, shows that it has been highly successful in imagining the Cornish experience both at home and abroad.

As we progress through literary history, we see the folk or morality tale as the starting point for the development of narrative, and curiously, it is often folklore which remains significant within the genre. As the nineteenth century unfolded, and

Cornwall became an industrial Celtic territory, we certainly see an engagement with the development of engineering and mining. As the nineteenth century gave way to the twentieth, it was the advent of tourism which shaped much literary production, as well as a new engagement with Celtic Revivalism and the revival of the Cornish language. The collapse of the industrial infrastructure in post-war Cornwall has facilitated yet another re-engagement with Cornish identity, and perhaps a stronger resilience to incorporation within England. The debate over 'English county' or 'Celtic nation' is found in many of these narratives. Although it is a debate which is unlikely to be resolved in the near future, it is one which makes these narratives so compelling to us as readers.

Thematically, it seems the short story in Cornwall displays an obsession with place, and with certain generic themes which we might expect in the land of the 'West Britons'. Mining, fishing, Methodism, tourism, and superstition and the supernatural all feature prominently in this latest collection, as does the age-old relationship between the sexes. Celticity is all pervasive, as nearly all the writers examine the identity and difference of the Cornish in the island of Britain and how they operated globally and internationally. Very often, the stories deal with the difficulties and inherent problems of being Cornish, and of having to exist in a sometimes extreme and isolated environment. Increasingly, modern writers are using humour to leaven their depictions of what we might call the Cornish condition. The stories respond to changes in society, religion, economics and politics across the centuries both in Cornwall, and in a wider Britain, yet also depict resilience to change and how the Cornish 'd' belong to be'.

There have been inherent difficulties for the development of the novel in Cornwall. It has been hard for some writers to develop a readership base, which allows longer prose fiction to be viable. Cornwall is still seen as a vehicle for historical romance, which in itself is perfectly valid, though sometimes this appears to have restricted the development of more socially-realist fiction. The short story offers an alternative method of literary production, because it is efficient and easier to shape for smaller, alternative readerships. In this way, both anti-metropolitan and peripheral communities can be explored. For contemporary writers, this agenda comes in the wake of devolutionary trends within writing across Britain, where the voice is more radical and fiercely pro-Cornish. In this way, writers are renegotiating their relationship with the communities they represent, and with those which they resist.

The short story is not an easy genre for the writer. In his introduction to Charles Lee's *Cornish Tales* (1941), that doyen of Anglo-Cornish literature, Arthur Quiller-Couch, described the difficulties of composition. He noted that the short story was 'a difficult art' because 'the aim was to compress into small room men and women "doing things" at a crisis, which of itself... cunningly suggests what came before, maybe what is to come...' One hope is that this collection of cautionary tales will make readers aware of what has been achieved in the past – often by writers who have been overlooked as practitioners of the 'difficult art' of teasing out the nuances of human behaviour. Another hope is that the collection will continue to inspire a new generation to use the genre to both inform and entertain. Quiller-Couch again, wrote of how he approached the short story. It is a method that is still profoundly relevant. He said:

'[M]y way... has always been to tell a stark tale and leave it, whether for deeper mood, to the reader's own understanding. It is his to catch in his mind and remember...'

Alan M. Kent and Derek R. Williams
Golowan Eve 2010

Anon

The Bohelland Tragedy

(News from Perin [Penryn] in Cornwall: A most bloody and unexampled murder very lately committed by a father on his own son (who was lately returned from the Indies) at the instigation of a merciless stepmother, together with their general most wretched ends, being all performed during the month of September last. Anno 1618).

An unfortunate murder lately committed near Perin [Penryn] in Cornwall.

At Perin [Penryn], a town in Cornwall, lived a man of honest life and ample possessions, being in his youth blest with a virtuous wife, who brought him many sweet and toward [docile] children that stood like so many olive branches about his table. And thus was he a long time blest, only because he feared the Lord.

But as there is no day so bright and glorious in which one cloud or other interposes not itself, and no estate so firm but it is subject to alteration, so it fell out with him. For amongst the rest, one of his children, and (which augmented his grief the more) the youngest, proved so wild and misgoverned as neither gentle admonitions of his parents, nor severe correction of master or tutor, could any way work to good purpose upon him. So wild and rank grew the weeds of disobedient stubbornness in him that [he] consorted with a crew of his own condition, [and] having made what spoil they could ashore, they determined a voyage to sea, and made what havoc they could there also.

Which took effect [happened thus]. Being once at Sea (Dux omnium malorum as we term it) they spare neither Spanish, French, Dutch, Scots or English, but make good the proverb, and count all fish that come to the net. And having (after many petty ones) taken one rich prize, thinking with the fools in their hearts that there was no God but their gold, they determined to put ashore in Turkey, and there lewdly spend what was unlawfully got.

But mark the judgement of God upon such; being within ken [sight] of shore, they were suddenly becalmed, and set upon by the Turkish galleys, who after [a] long and sharp fight of both sides, got the better : yet such was their resolution, they fought it out to the last man, [and] our English gallant, seeing no way to safety, took some of the best and wealthiest jewels he had about him, and with his sword in his hand leapt into the sea.

The Turkish men minding the booty, then our naked men boarded and fell to rifling, where they found much wealth, and accordingly enjoyed it.

In the meantime our English cavalier, with much difficulty recovers [reaches] the shore, where with cold comfort (we may imagine) seeing he could not save those things for which his soul and body were (without God's great mercy) quite lost, he began to look back into the past course of his life; where finding much matter of grief, but little or none of any comfort, he began to fall into serious meditation with himself, that if he with the rest of his comforts had been cast away at sea, with all his bloody and unrepented sins about him – viz theft, piracy, murder, drunkenness, swearing, lust, blasphemy and the like – in what a miserable and desperate estate his poor forlorn soul should have stood at the last great and terrible day, when the sentence of dreadful *Ite* [Go] and comfortable *Venite* [Come], shall (by the great and most high Judge and chief justice of all flesh) be pronounced.

But withal, hoping and confessing it was God's mercy to give him longer time for repentance that the sea had not swallowed him with the rest, he began to gather comfort, and make a Christian use of his preservation: in this manner determining to change those jewels and diamonds he had, into gold, and with them turn petty merchant, or some like [such] honest and thriving course.

But going to sell his jewels, it happened that one of the richest was known to have belonged to the governor of the town, under whose command he then was. The truth of the business [being] examined, it fell out that the ship which he and his company had taken and rifled at sea, (and in which that jewel with others were found) belonged to the governor of Algiers.

In regard whereof, he was presently apprehended as a pirate and so sentenced [as] a slave to the galleys. To plead excuse, or beg for mercy was in vain; into a galley was our gallant conducted, where chained amongst other Christians to the Bogaban't [solid block], he was enjoined [ordered] to tug at an oar, his dinner and supper coarse bran and water, his morning breakfast and afternoon bever[age], the bull's pizzle [a flogging instrument made from a bull's penis] and the bastinado [punishment consisting of striking the soles of the feet]. A good caveat for our fierce heads, whose running wits are some[times] at Rome, some[times] in Venice, and some[times] in Spain, before their heads be out of the shell.

Now he begins to call to mind his disobedience to his parents and [to] think what a quiet life and full of pleasure it had been for him, to have sit [sat] in his furred gown at his study in the university, or warm and dry at some honest tradesman's shop in the city; to have had [a] warm diet twice a day and welcome, and not have begged coarse bran and water, and have gone without it.

These and the like considerations were his familiar discourse. Having continued some while in the galley, coming one day ashore, whilst the captain and other officers fell to quaffing, he and other Christians with him (slaves) to the number of some ten, by their industry filed off their irons, and hiding their legs in short straw that was allowed them in the night, their captain and officers drunk so ashore and others in the galley, they made a desperate and yet happy escape, and got ashore, where such lucky success crowned their attempts, that in few months after (assisted by the charitable bounty of well-disposed merchants) they arrived upon the coast of England.

In all this time his father and mother hearing no news of him, imagined him to be dead, which was such a grief to his mother, that it brought her (as was imagined) before her time to her end.

On the other side he, calling to mind his stubborn carriage and willful disobedience, was ashamed to be known for their son, but altogether loathing his former courses, bound himself [ap]prentice to a barber surgeon far off in the west, with whom having served most of his time, and well profited in his profession, his master sent him [as] surgeon in a ship to the Indies.

Where such good liking was conceited [conceived] of him, that after a voyage or two for his master, his time expired, and some gratuity received of [from] his master for his true and faithful service, he went out again for himself. Having thus wrought himself an estate of some two hundred pound[s] and better, coming this last voyage from the Indies, and longing as 'tis the nature of all men, at last to see and visit his father, country and acquaintance[s], from whom he had now for the space of fifteen or sixteen years been a stranger. And the ship which he came in, staying in the river being unladen, and every man honestly paid his wages and what he had in venter [in his belly, ie what he had eaten and was charged for], a ship being ready bound for Cornwall, he became a passenger in her, and no sooner put to sea, but a gentle calm ushered [attended] the ship, that seemed to dally and play the wanton on the curled bosom of the waves; a shoal of porpoises that like active tumblers vaulted in their watery progress, made them such variety of present pastime, they seemed secure and free from all danger that misfortune could [in] any way threaten.

But note the event [outcome]: being within ken [sight] of the English shore, a pitchy [black] cloud so dark and palpable as day and night were indistinguishable, enveloped the sun; unto this the winds like great men bowed to one another. Rain brawled loud and talked roughly. In this night of horror now was the ship banded like a ball against the roughest heaven, and in the same instant thrown down as low as the centre. Billow cuffs billow, and one wave buffets another, so full of disordered rudeness grew the elements, as the world seemed nothing else but like an image of the first general chaos. In conclusion, so gross and palpable grew this confusion, as had not the tongue of eternity cried *fiat dies* [let it be day] a second time, it had [would have] been eternal night. During this mutinous insurrection of the waves, the master being a stranger, and unacquainted with the coast, split his ship against a rock; at which, imagine in what a confused clamour they were: some praying, some cursing, and others exclaiming, which would have rent a man's heart harder then the rock they ran against. But in vain, the storm like a cruel tyrant having predestined all their ruins, spared neither young nor old, but made a general massacre of them all.

This young factor [merchant] only except[ed], who with many other the terrible tempests in action, cast divers [several] plots for safety, and withal, as they were mindful of their hues, so did they not altogether forget the means, and divers jewels they had aboard, especially our young English factor who, well experienced in swimming, loaded himself with so much gold, as he thought might be no way [be] prejudicial to his safety.

Thus laden with jewels and gold, by the will of heaven and his own careful and painful industry, sometimes swimming, and other whiles [times] catching hold of rent planks and the like. For the ship once wrecked, the sea grew calm, and the winds (like tyrants) having done what havoc they could, flew raging to the shore, and there sat smiling at the ruins and spoil they had made.

Our young gallant ashore, wet, and unacquainted by reason of his discontinuance [interruption to his life], enquired of the next passenger he met the way to Perin [Penryn], who accordingly directed him.

Being entered the town, he (without acquainting any man with his name or business) repairs to the house where some sixteen years since, being an inn, he had left his own father dwelling. Where enquiring as a stranger for such a man, he heard that his first wife being dead, he had married a second, and given that house (being a well [ac]customed inn) to the master of it, in [by] way of dowry with one of his daughters, being sister to this our distressed traveller.

This woman he desired to see and consort [with] withal, who by reason of his long absence, had altogether forgot[ten] him. He notwithstanding asked if she never had a wild youth (concealing his own name) to [as] her brother. She answered yes, and one that above all the rest her father and mother cockered [indulged] and loved, but he was long since taken by the Turks and died (as they were informed) a galley slave. He laboured to persuade the contrary, and gave many and certain likelihoods, that he was the same party, telling the name of his godfathers, and where they dwelt, as also with whom, and in what place he went to school; but all to no purpose, so thoroughly was she grounded in the report of his death, as nothing could persuade the contrary.

Till at last she called to mind an infallible token, which was this: that if he were her brother, he had a great red mole growing in the bent [bend] of his left arm, by which, she had often heard her mother say, especially on her death bed, that if ever it were his fortune to come again, they might easily know him amongst a thousand. And except he could show her that, all other proofs in the world should never persuade her that he was her brother, but some cunning imposter. Whereupon, not willing to hold her longer in suspense, he opened his bosom, and gave her certain testimony of the truth.

At sight whereof she fell about his neck and kissed him, not being able (for the violence of instant joy) to refrain from shedding of tears. The young man demanded how his father, mother, and the rest of their kindred did; but when he heard that his mother was dead, and the chief cause of it proceeded from his disobedient stubbornness and obstinate course, he fell into such weeping, she had much labour to comfort him, requesting him to come in, and take such entertainment as her house could of the sudden afford [offer] him.

To which he would in no wise [way] consent, till [he] had seen, done his duty to, and craved pardon of his father, who dwelt at a country house of his young wife's, some three or four miles distant.

From which by many forceable [forceful] reasons she laboured to dissuade him, viz. that their mother-in-law might have no just cause to hit their father in the teeth with his son's baseness, being poorly apparelled and newly sea-wrecked, nor think he came for a stock to set up his trade with, especially considering that by the marriages and great portions given with his children, his quiet life was much disturbed, and his estate more impoverished. His answer was that his coming should be a hindrance neither to her nor his father, for though in that poor and thin habit, he brought enough for himself, and if need were [be], to be a help and supply to them, and the rest of their poor family.

Only his request was, that she would conceal his name and coming, not only from the household, but [from] her husband, to try [to see] if his father (as she already had been) could be deceived in his acquaintance, or not. And if he were, that then the next morning she would meet him there at breakfast, with as many of their kindred as was possible, because that besides his presence, he had brought that home, that being seen and known, 'twould make their joy a great deal the more full; when the good old man should not only find of a stubborn and disobedient, a dutiful and penitent child, and not so only, but one that by his painful industry got that in his youth which should relieve and comfort his father in his declining estate.

These premises considered, she condescended [consented] to his request, and only tasting a cup of beer, for that time parted: He journeying towards his father, and she to meditate upon the passionate joy [that] would befall their whole family the next day at breakfast. So leave we them and speak a word or two of the good old man their father.

Who by good house keeping, associating himself with knights and gentlemen somewhat above his estate, as also by preferring his own, and his second wife's kindred to great and wealthy marriages, had brought himself much behind hand in the world. To all this his wife being somewhat churlish, and more respecting her own future estate, then [than] his present welfare; and as it is common with all mothers, to prefer the good of their own children before them, to whom they are but mothers-in-law. All these things put together, but especially seeing his supposed friends, and ancient company keepers, begin to think and draw their necks out of the collars as the proverb is, was no little grief to the heart of the good old man.

To this a friend gave him notice, of an execution [warrant] of three hundred pound[s] come out against him, that much disquieted him. His son comes to the woman, demanding lodging and meat, being a poor sea-faring man, and their ship and all their goods lost at sea.

She answered, she would ask her husband's consent, which she did.

He entreats her of all love she would use him well, urging he had a son at sea himself (if alive at least) and knew not what want he might stand in. She says he is a poor knave. So much more needy of relief, answered her husband. She rails at him, and tells him such prodigality hath brought him so low. And such charity, he hopes, will be a means to raise him as high as ever he was, [he] sent for him in, gets him a warm candle, caused a pullet to be killed, and such fare as his present estate afforded, provided he.

Supper being ended, the good old man was desirous of news, (and rather if he could hear any of his son), yet in regard of the young man's late sea wreck, and sharp travail [trouble], he put off their discourse till the next morning, and so taking leave, betook him to his bed, requesting his wife (for other servants all that time were not in their house) to light the young man to his lodging.

The old man gone, his wife (as the custom of most women is) desirous of news, fell into a serious discourse with him, of money, and (as the young man thought) frivolous matters. And imagining (perhaps justly) that she feared he might in the night steal somewhat [something], or offer them, being lean [poor] people, some discourtesy, to clear all manner of suspect [suspicion], he plucked out divers [several] bags of gold, to the value of some four hundred pound[s], using these or the like words: Mrs, that you may know your kindnesses are not cast away upon some base or ungrateful peasant, ill-nurtured in the rules of requital [repayment], keep this for me till tomorrow, when before some good friends of mine, which I purpose [propose] to send for, I will show myself a willing and bountiful debtor, and acquaint them and you with the discourse [story] of my whole travails, which I make no doubt will be both pleasing and acceptable to all. With these or the like words, giving her the gold to lay by till morning, she lighted him up to bed, where we leave him to his rest, and return to the covetous stepmother.

Who thinking of her present wants, and looking of [at] the gold, cast about twenty ways how to enjoy it for her own, when presently the devil, that is always ready to take hold of the least advantage that may be to increase his kingdom, whispered this comfort in her ear, showing her the golden temptation, saying: all this will I give thee, if thou wilt but make away a poor stranger that sleeps under thy mercy.

She, like her first grandam [Eve], seeing the gold fair to look to [at], and the task easily and without much danger to be affected [effected], took the devil at his word, and tied herself to him with an oath, that if she might peaceably enjoy the gold, the true owner of it should never wake.

Here now were fit occasion to talk of gold: the pain, labour and danger a man takes to compass [possess] it, and the infinite vexations, troubles, and casualties a man undergoes to keep it; so that I may speak of gold, as the Macedon did of a kingdom, it is more difficult to keep then conquer; but of that at some other time and in fitter place. She resolved to keep the gold, tho[ugh] for it she lose her life, and forfeits her soul, for where the devil plays the lawyer, that's his ordinary fee.

First, therefore, she goes up to her husband, whom after she had waked, she questions how and what course he will take to annoy [counter] the execution [warrant] come out against him: He requests her to be quiet, and that it was now no fit time of night to dispute of such business. If the worst came that could, he had friends and children [who] would not see him sink under so slight a burden.

She answered [that] trusting to friends and relying upon children, (into whose hands he had put his whole estate), had brought them so much behind hand as they were; telling him that if he would be ruled by her, he should [would] rid himself of all debt and danger, without help either of friends or children, to [in] whom, whosoever trusteth, shall find that he leans on a broken staff, or a shivered [withered] reed. He requests to know how. She tells him by means of the poor sailor that lodged there, acquainting him with what store of gold he had about him, and how easily without danger (coming in late and unseen the same night) they might make it all theirs.

He, seeing her thoughts set all on murder, mildly dissuaded her, laying before her the inevitable dangers, and strange judgments of God showed upon [to] people in the like kind of offending. But when all that prevailed not, he concluded his speech with that part of Scripture: What will it avail a man or a woman to get the whole world, and lose his own soul; and so settled himself to sleep.

But all in vain, for such deep impression of gain, and palpable reasons of safety [security], had the devil granted [instilled] in her thoughts, 'twas impossible to rub them out; and therefore instead of desisting from her [in]tended practice, she began to make it good, and show devilish arguments to approve [prove] the lawfulness of it.

Insomuch, that to conclude her devilish persuasions, [she] drew the good old man out of his bed, with an intent to do a murder, which murder itself would have blushed to have committed. Twice by her devilish enticements did he attempt it, and twice his better genius [inner self] counselled him to the contrary. At last, the devil, (for the more valiantly he is resisted grows the more malicious) by whose persuasion, the old man the second time in bed, having bitterly denied the bloody act and given her and the devil (whose advocate she was) their answer as he well hoped, she comes the third time to his bedside, and to make her temptation the more forcible, pours out the gold, fetching her hellish argument *a minore ad maius* [literally, from smaller to bigger], thus: how easily and with what little or no danger such a huge mass of wealth might be purchased; which when he refeld [refuted] by urging the unlawfulness of it, she burst out into bitter execrations and cursings, calling him [a] faint-hearted coward, and wished, that if he did let slip that occasion, he might lie and rot in a gaol, vowing that she would not only animate and set on all his creditors to his utter undoing, but dishearten and draw all her and his friends from helping and relieving him.

In conclusion, the devil and she prevailed, and on he goes the third time to attempt this deed of darkness, and entered the chamber; so deadly was her intent, she thrust the knife in his hand, and stood heartening of [spurring] him on at the door. He, coming to the bedside, found him fast asleep, and looking steadfastly upon him, a drop of blood fell from his nose upon the young man's breast, and seemed to blush and look red, as if it had in dumb sign dissuaded him from that devilish intent. To conclude, the bloody deed is done, an innocent son slain by a guilty father, his life blood shed by him from whom both life and blood were received. A cruel murder, and so unnatural, as time hath not in all his records one more horrid and detestable; to see what a piteous groan and rueful look the dying son cast upon the murderous father, I leave to their considerations, that either knew the love of a father to [for] a son, or a son to [for] the father. Only this one noteworthy remembrance I here credibly recite, that just as the knife was entering his throat, the screech owl beat her pineons [wings] against the window, and gave a fearful shriek at the bed's head, as if she had said, Awake young man awake; but all in vain, the innocent is dead, and the guilty possessed his gold.

The next morning very early, the sister, according to [her] promise, [a]lights at the gate, and after her duty done to her father, desires to see and speak with her brother. The old man amazed at this kind of visitation, asks what brother she meant. She replies: the young man that in the habit of a poor sailor came the last night, to demand lodging, promised as that morning to meet her and divers [several] other[s] of their kindred, which she had brought to breakfast, and that he had brought home store of gold, with which he purposed [proposed] to pay his father's debts. The old man hearing this discourse, betwixt [between] fear and horror, looked pale and trembled, yet seeing no remedy, he demanded how she knew that young man to be her brother. After many other probable likelihoods, she named the mole in the bent [bend] of his left arm. At hearing of which, without further words, as if he had been struck with a sudden ecstasy, he runs up to the chamber where this heinous murder was committed, and finding the token true, with the same knife he had killed his son, he murdered himself. His wife, seeing her husband stay somewhat longer than she expected, runs up after him to see the event, where finding her husband dead in his son's arms, the devil on one side, and her own guilty conscience on the other, telling and urging her to be the cause of all this; her conscience persuading she had deserved death of body in this world, and the devil assuring her she could not escape damnation in the world to come, took the same knife (yet reeking with the blood of her breathless [dead] husband) and with it ripped up her own bosom. The daughter staying below, wondering neither father, brother nor mother came down (great with child as she was), went by [up] the stairs, where she became a witness to the most lamentable (and worthiest to be pitied) spectacle that ever eye saw.

The covetous stepmother not yet altogether dead, as well as she could in broken accents excused her husband, and acknowledged herself the ground[s] and author of all this, which hindered the good woman from doing instant violence upon herself. But such was her extreme grief, to see a father murder his own son first, then himself, and a covetous stepmother [the] author of all this, she grew frantic, and threw herself first into the arms of her father, then of her brother, kissing the one, and showering tears upon the other, with such ardour of affection and violence of passion, it made all the standers by with a general voice cry out: It was the bloodiest and most inhuman murder, the country was ever guilty of.

And so to the end it may be a warning, to all covetous stepmothers and a content for all easy fathers to avoid the like hereafter: At the entreaty of divers [several] gentlemen in the country, it is as near the life [truth] as pen and ink could draw it out, thus put in print.

FINIS

Nicholas Boson

JOHN OF CHYANHOR

Translated from Cornish by Alan M. Kent and Tim Saunders

In the time that is past, there were living in St Levan a man and a woman in the place called Chyanhor.

And the work fell scarce. And the man said to his wife, 'I will go to seek work and you can earn your living here.'

He took fair leave, and far to the east he travelled, and at last he came to the house of a farmer, and sought work there.

'What work can you do?' said the farmer. 'Every kind of work,' said John. And they bargained for three pounds a year wages.

And when it came to the end to the year, his master said, 'Here are your wages. But if you will give them back to me I shall teach you a point of knowledge.'

'What is it?' said John. 'No,' said his master, 'give them to me, and then I will tell you.' 'Take them then,' said John. Then his master said, 'Take care not to leave the old road for a new road.'

And they bargained for another year for similar wages. And when it came to the end of the year his master brought him the three pounds. 'Look, John,' said his master, 'here are your wages. But if you give them back to me I will teach you another point of knowledge.'

'What is it?' said John, 'No,' said his master, 'give them to me and I will tell you.' 'Take them, then,' said John. Then his master said, 'Take care not to lodge in the house of an old man married to a young woman.'

And they bargained for another year. And when it came to the end of the year his master brought him the three pounds. 'Look, John,' said his master, 'here are your wages. But if you will give them back to me I will teach you the best point of knowledge of all.'

'What is it?' said John. 'No,' said his master, give them to me, and I will tell you.' 'Take them then,' said John. Then his master said, 'Be struck twice before striking once, and that is the best point of knowledge of all.'

Now John would not serve any longer, but wanted to go home to his wife. 'Do not,' said his master, 'go home today. My wife is baking this morning and she will make a cake for you for your wife.'

And they put the nine pounds in the cake. And when John took his leave, his master said, 'Here is a cake for you to bring home to your wife. And when you and your wife are most happy together then break the cake and not before.'

He took fair leave, and travelled homewards, and at last he came to St Hilary Down. There he met with three merchants of Treen (fellow parishioners) coming home from Exeter fair.

'Oh John,' said the three, 'come with us. We are glad to see you. Where have you been so long?'

Said John, 'I was serving, and now I am going home to my wife.' And said they, 'Go with us, and welcome you will be.'

They took the new road, and John kept to the old road.

And he went by the hedges of Choon. And the merchants were not long gone from John, when thieves seized them.

And they started to cry out. And with the cry that the merchants made John cried also, 'Thieves! Thieves!'

And with the cry that John made the thieves let the merchants go. And when they came to Marazion, then they met once more.

'O John,' said they, 'we are beholden to you. If it weren't for you we should all be murdered. Come with us, and welcome you will be.'

And when they came to the inn where they should lodge, said John, 'I ought to see the host of the house.'

'The host of the house?' they said. 'What do you want with the host of the house? Here is our hostess, and she is young. If you want to see the host of the house, go to the kitchen, and there you will find him.'

And when he came to the kitchen, he saw the host of the house, and he was an old man, weak, and turning the spit.

And John said, 'I will not lodge here but in the next house.' 'Not yet,' they said. 'Have supper with us and welcome you will be.'

Now the hostess of the house, she planned with a certain monk in the house, to destroy the old man in bed at night, and to put the blame on the merchants.

And when John was in bed, there was a hole in the gable of the house and he saw a light. He stood up in his bed, and he listened, and he heard the monk speaking. Turning his back to the wall, he said, 'Perhaps there is somebody in the next house to see our dirty deed.' And with that the bad wife and her companion murdered the old man in the bed.

And with that John with his knife cut (through the hole) a fair-sized round piece from the back of the monk's gown.

And the next morning the bad wife started to cry that her good man had been murdered. And as there was neither a man nor a child in the house except the merchants, they should hang for it.

Then they were taken and led to the gallows. And at last John met them.

'O John,' they said, 'we have had hard luck. Our host was murdered last night and we must hang for it.'

'All of you? Look to the justices,' said John, 'to bring before them those who did the evil deed.'

'Who knows,' they said, 'who did the evil deed?' 'Who did the evil deed?' said John. 'If I cannot prove who did it, I will hang for it.'

'Say then,' they said. 'Last night,' said John, 'when I was there in my bed I saw a light and I stood up and there was a hole in the gable of the house.'

'And a certain monk turned his back against the hole. "Perhaps," he said, "there is somebody in the next house who will see our dirty deed." '

'And with that I cut with my knife through the hole a fair-sized piece from the back of the monk's gown. And to prove it, I can show you the piece in my pocket.'

And with that the merchants were released, and the woman and the monk were taken and hanged.

Then they all came together to Marazion, and at last they came to Coose Cornwilly in Buryan.

There was a forked road, and the merchants wanted John to go home with them again. But for the time being he would not, but would rather go home to his wife.

And when he had left the merchants he span out the time so that he might see whether his wife was staying faithful to him, was she or was she not.

And when he came to the door, he thought he heard another man in the bed. He pressed his fist on his dagger to murder them both. But he remembered that he had been warned before striking once.

And he went outside again and knocked. 'Who is it in God's name?' she said.

'I am here,' said John. 'By Mary, who do I hear?' said she. 'If you are John, come in.' 'Bring the light then,' said John. And she brought the light.

And when John came in he said, 'When I came to the door, I thought I heard another man in the bed.'

'Oh John,' said she, 'when you set off, I was three months gone with child; and now we have a sweet little son in the bed, thanks be to God.'

Said John, 'I will tell you. My master and mistress gave me a cake and said to me, "Break the cake when you and your wife are most happy together and not before." And now we have cause to be happy.'

They broke the cake, and there were the nine pounds in the cake. And the money they kept, and the cake they ate. And there was no quarrelsomeness or spite between them in the world. And this is an end to my story about them.

Robert Hunt

THE WITCH AND THE TOAD

An old woman called Alsey – usually Aunt Alsey – occupied a small cottage in Anthony, one of a row which belonged to a tradesman living in Dock – as Devonport was then designated to distinguish it from Plymouth. The old woman possessed a very violent temper, and this, more than anything else, fixed upon her the character of being a witch. Her landlord had frequently sought his rent, and as frequently he received nothing but abuse. He had, on the special occasion to which our narrative refers, crossed the Tamar and walked to Anthony, with the firm resolve of securing his rent, now long in arrear, and of turning the old termagant out of the cottage. A violent scene ensued, and the vicious old woman, more than a match for a really kind-hearted and quiet man, remained the mistress of the situation. She seated herself in the door of her cottage and cursed her landlord's wife, 'the child she was carrying,' and all belonging to him, with so devilish a spite that Mr— owned he was fairly driven away in terror.

On returning home, he, of course, told his wife all the circumstances; and while they were discoursing on the subject, – the whole story being attentively listened to by their daughter, then a young girl, who is my informant, – a woman came into the shop requiring some articles which they sold.

'Sit still, father,' said Mrs— to her husband; 'you must be tired. I will see to the shop.'

So she went from the parlour into the shop, and, hearing the wants of her customer, proceeded to supply them; gossiping gaily, as was her wont, to interest the buyer.

Mrs— was weighing one of the articles required, when something falling heavily from the ceiling of the shop, struck the beam out of her hand, and both – the falling body and the scales – came together with much noise on to the counter. At the same instant both women screamed; – the shopkeeper calling also 'Father! father!' – meaning her husband thereby – with great energy.

Mr— and his daughter were in the shop instantly, and there, on the counter, they saw an enormous and most ugly toad sprawling amidst the chains of the scales. The first action of the man was to run back to the parlour, seize the tongs, and return to the shop. He grasped the swollen toad with the tongs, the vicious creature spitting all the time, and, without a word, he went back and flung it behind the block of wood which was burning in the grate. The object of terror being removed, the wife, who was shortly to become the mother of another child, though usually a woman who had great command over her feelings, fainted.

This circumstance demanding all their attention, the toad was forgotten. The shock was a severe one; and although Mrs— was restored in a little time to her senses, she again and again became faint. Those fits continuing, her medical attendant, Dr— was sent for, and on his arrival he ordered that his patient should be immediately placed in bed, and the husband was informed that he must be prepared for a premature birth.

The anxiety occasioned by these circumstances, and the desire to afford every relief to his wife, so fully occupied Mr—, that for an hour or two he entirely forgot the cause of all this mischief; or, perhaps satisfying himself that the toad was burnt to ashes, he had no curiosity to look after it. He was, however, suddenly summoned from the bed-room, in which he was with his wife, by his daughter calling to him, in a voice of ter-ror –

'O father, the toad, the toad!'

Mr— rushed down-stairs, and he then discovered that the toad, though severely burnt, had escaped destruction. It must have crawled up over the log of wood, and from it have fallen down amongst the ashes. There it was now making useless struggles to escape, by climbing over the fender.

The tongs were again put in requisition, with the intention this time of carrying the reptile out of the house. Before, however, he had time to do so, a man from Anthony came hastily into the shop with the information that Aunt Alsey had fallen into the fire, as the people supposed, in a fit, and that she was nearly burnt to death. This man had been sent off with two commissions – one to fetch the doctor, and the other to bring Mr— with him, as much of the cottage had been injured by fire, communicated to it by the old woman's dress.

In as short a time as possible the parish surgeon and Mr— were at Anthony, and too truly they found the old woman most severely burnt – so seriously, indeed, there was no chance that one so aged could rally from the shock which her system must have received. However, a litter was carefully prepared, the old woman was placed in it, and carried to the workhouse. Every attention was given to her situation, but she never recovered perfect consciousness, and during the night she died.

The toad, which we left inside the fender in front of a blazing fire, was removed from a position so trying to any cold-blooded animal, by the servant, and thrown, with a 'hugh' and a shudder, upon one of the flower-beds in the small garden behind the house.

There it lay the next morning dead, and when examined by Mr—, it was found that all the injuries sustained by the toad corresponded with those received by the poor old wretch, who had no doubt fallen a victim to passion.

As we have only to deal with the mysterious relation which existed between the witch and the toad, it is not necessary that we should attend further to the innocent victim of an old woman's vengeance, than to say that eventually a babe was born – that that babe grew to be a handsome man, was an officer in the navy, and having married, went to sea, and perished, leaving a widow with an unborn child to lament his loss. Whether this was a result of the witch's curse, those who are more deeply skilled in witchcraft than I am may perhaps tell.

Anthony Trollope

MALACHI'S COVE

On the northern coast of Cornwall, between Tintagel and Bossiney, down on the very margin of the sea, there lived not long since an old man who got his living by saving sea-weed from the waves, and selling it for manure. The cliffs there are bold and fine, and the sea beats in upon them from the north with a grand violence. I doubt whether it be not the finest morsel of cliff scenery in England, though it is beaten by many portions of the west coast of Ireland, and perhaps also by spots in Wales and Scotland. Cliffs should be nearly precipitous, they should be broken in their outlines, and should barely admit here and there of an insecure passage from their summit to the sand at their feet. The sea should come, if not up to them, at least very near to them, and then, above all things, the water below them should be blue, and not of that dead leaden colour which is so familiar to us in England. At Tintagel all these requisites are there, except that bright blue colour which is so lovely. But the cliffs themselves are bold and well broken, and the margin of sand at high water is very narrow, – and so narrow that at spring-tides there is barely a footing there.

Close upon this margin was the cottage or hovel of Malachi Trenglos, the old man of whom I have spoken. But Malachi, or old Glos, as he was commonly called by the people around him, had not built his house absolutely upon the sand. There was a fissure in the rock so great that at the top it formed a narrow ravine, and so complete from the summit to the base that it afforded an opening for a steep and rugged track from the top of the rock to the bottom. This fissure was so wide at the bottom that it had afforded space for Trenglos to fix his habitation on a foundation of rock, and here he had lived for many years. It was told of him that in the early days of his trade he had always carried the weed in a basket on his back to the top, but latterly he had been possessed of a donkey which had been trained to go up and down the steep track with a single pannier over his loins, for the rocks would not admit of panniers hanging by his side; and for this assistant he had built a shed adjoining his own, and almost as large as that in which he himself resided.

But, as years went on, old Glos procured other assistance than that of the donkey, or, as I should rather say, Providence supplied him with other help; and, indeed had it not been so, the old man must have given up his cabin and his independence and gone into the workhouse at Camelford. For rheumatism had afflicted him, old age had bowed him till he was nearly double, and by degrees he became unable to attend the donkey on its upward passage to the world above, or even to assist in rescuing the coveted weed from the waves.

At the time to which our story refers Trenglos had not been up the cliff for twelve months, and for the last six months he had done nothing towards the furtherance of his trade, except to take the money and keep it, if any of it was kept, and occasionally to shake down a bundle of fodder for the donkey. The real work of the business was done altogether by Mahala Trenglos, his granddaughter.

Mally Trenglos was known to all the farmers round the coast, and to all the small tradespeople in Camelford. She was a wild-looking, almost unearthly creature, with wild-flowing, black, uncombed hair, small in stature, with small hands and bright black eyes; but people said that she was very strong, and the children around declared that she worked day and night, and knew nothing of fatigue. As to her age there were many doubts. Some said she was ten, and others five-and-twenty, but the reader may be allowed to know that at this time she had in truth passed her twentieth birthday. The old people spoke well of Mally, because she was so good to her grandfather; and it was said of her that though she carried to him a little gin and tobacco almost daily, she bought nothing for herself; – and as to the gin, no one who looked at her would accuse her of meddling with that. But she had no friends, and but few acquaintances among people of her own age. They said that she was fierce and ill-natured, that she had not a good word for any one, and that she was, complete at all points, a thorough little vixen. The young men did not care for her; for, as regarded dress, all days were alike with her. She never made herself smart on Sundays. She was generally without stockings, and seemed to care not at all to exercise any of those feminine attractions which might have been hers had she studied to attain them. All days were the same to her in regard to dress; and, indeed, till lately, all days had, I fear, been the same to her in other respects. Old Malachi had never been seen inside a place of worship since he had taken to live under the cliff.

But within the last two years Mally had submitted herself to the teaching of the clergyman at Tintagel, and had appeared at church on Sundays, if not absolutely with punctuality, at any rate so often that no one who knew the peculiarity of her residence was disposed to quarrel with her on that subject. But she made no difference in her dress on these occasions. She took her place on a low stone seat just inside the church door, clothed as usual in her thick red serge petticoat and loose brown serge jacket, such being the apparel which she had found to be best adapted for her hard and perilous work among the waters. She had pleaded to the clergyman when he attacked her on the subject of church attendance with vigour that she had got no church-going clothes. He had explained to her that she would be received there without distinction to her clothing. Mally had taken him at his word, and had gone, with a courage which certainly deserved admiration, though I doubt whether there was not mingled with it an obstinacy which was less admirable.

For people said that old Glos was rich, and that Mally might have proper clothes if she chose to buy them. Mr Polwarth, the clergyman, who, as the old man could not come to him, went down the rocks to the old man, did make some hint on the matter in Mally's absence. But old Glos, who had been patient with him on other matters, turned upon him so angrily when he made an allusion to money, that Mr Polwarth found himself obliged to give that matter up, and Mally continued to sit upon the stone bench in her short serge petticoat, with her long hair streaming down her face. She did so far sacrifice to decency as on such occasions to tie up her black hair with an old shoe-string. So tied it would remain through the Monday and Tuesday, but by Wednesday afternoon Mally's hair had generally managed to escape.

As to Mally's indefatigable industry there could be no manner of doubt, for the quantity of seaweed which she and the donkey amassed between them was very surprising. Old Glos, it was declared, had never collected half what Mally gathered together; but then the article was becoming cheaper, and it was necessary that the exertion should be greater. So Mally and the donkey toiled and toiled, and the seaweed came up in heaps which surprised those who looked at her little hands and light form. Was there not some one who helped her at nights, some fairy, or demon, or the like? Mally was so snappish in her answers to people that she had no right to be surprised if ill-natured things were said of her.

No one ever heard Mally Trenglos complain of her work, but about this time she was heard to make great and loud complaints of the treatment she received from some of her neighbours. It was known that she went with her plaints to Mr Polwarth; and when he could not help her, or did not give her such instant help as she needed, she went – ah, so foolishly! to the office of a certain attorney at Camelford, who was not likely to prove himself a better friend than Mr Polwarth.

Now the nature of her injury was as follows. The place in which she collected her seaweed was a little cove; the people had come to call it Malachi's Cove from the name of the old man who lived there; – which was so formed, that the margin of the sea therein could only be reached by the passage from the top down to Trenglos's hut. The breadth of the cove when the sea was out might perhaps be two hundred yards, and on each side the rocks ran out in such a way that both from north and south the domain of Trenglos was guarded from intruders. And this locality had been well chosen for its intended purpose.

There was a rush of the sea into the cover, which carried there large, drifting masses of seaweed, leaving them among the rocks when the tide was out. During the equinoctial winds of the spring and autumn the supply would never fail; and even when the sea was calm, the long, soft, salt-bedewed, trailing masses of the weed, could be gathered there when they could not be found elsewhere for miles along the coast. The task of getting the weed from the breakers was often difficult and dangerous, – so difficult that much of it was left to be carried away by the next incoming tide.

Mally doubtless did not gather half the crop that was there at her feet. What was taken by the returning waves she did not regret; but when interlopers came upon her cove, and gathered her wealth, – her grandfather's wealth, beneath her eyes, then her heart was broken. It was this interloping, this intrusion, that drove poor Mally to the Camelford attorney. But, alas, though the Camelford attorney took Mally's money, he could do nothing for her, and her heart was broken!

She had an idea, in which no doubt her grandfather shared, that the path to the cove was, at any rate, their property. When she was told that the cove, and sea running into the cove, were not the freeholds of her grandfather, she understood that the statement might be true. But what then as to the use of the path? Who had made the path what it was? Had she not painfully, wearily, with exceeding toil, carried up bits of rock with her own hands, that her grandfather's donkey might have footing for his feet? Had she not scraped together crumbs of earth along the face of the cliff that she might make easier to the animal the track of that rugged way? And now, when she saw big farmers' lads coming down with other donkeys, – and, indeed, there was one who came with a pony; no boy, but a young man, old enough to know better than rob a poor old man and a young girl, – she reviled the whole human race, and swore that the Camelford attorney was a fool.

Any attempt to explain to her that there was still weed enough for her was worse than useless. Was it not all hers and his, or, at any rate, was not the sole way to it his and hers? And was not her trade stopped and impeded? Had she not been forced to back her laden donkey down, twenty yards she said, but it had, in truth, been five, because Farmer Gunliffe's son had been in the way with his thieving pony? Farmer Gunliffe had wanted to buy her weed at his own price, and because she had refused he had set on his thieving son to destroy her in this wicked way.

'I'll hamstring the beast the next time as he's down here!' said Mally to old Glos, while the angry fire literally streamed from her eyes.

Farmer Gunliffe's small homestead – he held about fifty acres of land – was close by the village of Tintagel, and not a mile from the cliff. The sea-wrack, as they call it, was pretty well the only manure within his reach, and no doubt he thought it hard that he should be kept from using it by Mally Trenglos and her obstinacy.

'There's heaps of other coves, Barty,' said Mally to Barty Gunliffe, the farmer's son.

'But none so nigh, Mally, nor yet none that fills 'emselves as this place.'

Then he explained to her that he would not take the weed that came up close to hand. He was bigger than she was, and stronger, and would get it from the outer rocks, with which she never meddled. Then, with scorn in her eye, she swore that she could get it where he durst not venture, and repeated her threat of hamstringing the pony. Barty laughed at her wrath, jeered her because of her wild hair, and called her a mermaid.

'I'll mermaid you!' she cried. 'Mermaid, indeed! I wouldn't be a man to come and rob a poor girl and an old cripple. But you're no man, Barty Gunliffe! You're not half a man.'

Nevertheless, Bartholomew Gunliffe was a very fine young fellow, as far as the eye went. He was about five feet eight inches high, with strong arms and legs, with light curly brown hair and blue eyes. His father was but in a small way as a farmer, but, nevertheless, Barty Gunliffe was well thought of among the girls around. Everybody liked Barty, – excepting only Mally Trenglos, and she hated him like poison.

Barty, when he was asked why so good-natured a lad as he persecuted a poor girl and an old man, threw himself upon the justice of the thing. It wouldn't do at all, according to his view, that any single person should take upon himself to own that which God Almighty sent as the common property of all. He would do Mally no harm, and so he had told her. But Mally was a vixen, – a wicked little vixen; and she must be taught to have a civil tongue in her head. When once Mally would speak him civil as he went for weed, he would get his father to pay the old man some sort of toll for the use of the path.

'Speak him civil?' said Mally. 'Never; not while I have a tongue in my mouth!' And

I fear old Glos encouraged her rather than otherwise in her view of the matter.

But her grandfather did not encourage her to hamstring the pony. Hamstringing a pony would be a serious thing, and old Glos thought it might be very awkward for both of them if Mally were put into prison. He suggested, therefore, that all manner of impediments should be put in the way of the pony's feet, surmising that the well-trained donkey might be able to work in spite of them. And Barty Gunliffe, on his next descent, did find the passage very awkward when he came near to Malachi's hut, but he made his way down, and poor Mally saw the lumps of rock at which she had laboured so hard pushed on one side or rolled out of the way with a steady persistency of injury towards herself that almost drove her frantic.

'Well, Barty, you're a nice boy,' said old Glos, sitting in the doorway of the hut, as he watched the intruder.

'I ain't a doing no harm to none as doesn't harm me,' said Barty. 'The sea's free to all, Malachi.'

'And the sky's free to all, but I mustn't get up on the top of your big barn to look at it,' said Mally, who was standing among the rocks with a long hook in her hand. The long hook was the tool with which she worked in dragging the weed from the waves. 'But you ain't got no justice nor yet no sperrit, or you wouldn't come here to vex an old man like he.'

'I didn't want to vex him, nor yet to vex you, Mally. You let me be for a while, and we'll be friends yet.'

'Friends!' exclaimed Mally. 'Who'd have the likes of you for a friend? What are you moving them stones for? Them stones belongs to grandfather.' And in her wrath she made a movement as though she were going to fly at him,

'Let him be, Mally,' said the old man; 'let him be. He'll get his punishment. He'll come to be drowned some day if he comes down here when the wind is in shore.'

'That he may be drowned then!' said Mally, in her anger. 'If he was in the big hole there among the rocks, and the sea running in at half tide, I wouldn't lift a hand to help him out.'

'Yes, you would, Mally; you'd fish me up with your hook like a big stick of seaweed.'

She turned from him with scorn as he said this, and went into the hut. It was time for her to get ready for her work, and one of the great injuries done her lay in this, – that such a one as Barty Gunliffe should come and look at her during her toil among the breakers.

It was an afternoon in April, and the hour was something after four o'clock. There had been a heavy wind from the north-west all the morning, with gusts of rain, and the sea-gulls had been in and out of the cove all the day, which was a sure sign to Mally that the incoming tide would cover the rocks with weed.

The quick waves were now returning with wonderful celerity over the low reefs, and the time had come at which the treasure must be seized, if it was to be garnered on that day. By seven o' clock it would be growing dark, at nine it would be high water, and before daylight the crop would be carried out again if not collected. All this Mally understood very well, and some of this Barty was beginning to understand also.

As Mally came down with her bare feet, bearing her long hook in her hand, she saw

Barty's pony standing patiently on the sand, and in her heart she longed to attack the brute. Barty at this moment, with a common three-pronged fork in his hand, was standing down on a large rock, gazing forth towards the waters. He had declared that he would gather the weed only at places which were inaccessible to Mally, and he was looking out that he might settle where he would begin.

'Let 'un be, let 'un be,' shouted the old man to Mally, as he saw her take a step towards the beast, which she hated almost as much as she hated the man.

Hearing her grandfather's voice through the wind, she desisted from her purpose, if any purpose she had had, and went forth to her work. As she passed down the cove, and scrambled in among the rocks, she saw Barty still standing on his perch; out beyond, the white-curling waves were cresting and breaking themselves with violence, and the wind was howling among the caverns and abutments of the cliff.

Every now and then there came a squall of rain, and though there was sufficient light, the heavens were black with clouds. A scene more beautiful might hardly be found by those who love the glories of the coast. The light for such objects was perfect. Nothing could exceed the grandeur of the colours, – the blue of the open sea, the white of the breaking waves, the yellow sands, or the streaks of red and brown which gave such richness to the cliff.

But neither Mally nor Barty were thinking of such things as these. Indeed they were hardly thinking of their trade after its ordinary forms. Barty was meditating how he might best accomplish his purpose of working beyond the reach of Mally's feminine powers, and Mally was resolving that wherever Barty went she would go farther.

And, in many respects, Mally had the advantage. She knew ever rock in the spot, and was sure of those which gave a good foothold, and sure also of those which did not. And then her activity had been made perfect by practice for the purpose to which it was to be devoted. Barty, no doubt, was stronger than she, and quite as active. But Barty could not jump among the waves from one stone to another as she could do, nor was he as yet able to get aid in his work from the very force of the water as she could get it. She had been hunting seaweed in that cove since she had been an urchin of six years old, and she knew every hole and corner and every spot of vantage. The waves were her friends, and she could use them. She could measure their strength, and knew when and where it would cease.

Mally was great down in the salt pools of her own cove, – great, and very fearless. As she watched Barty make his way forward from rock to rock, she told herself, gleefully, that he was going astray. The curl of the wind as it blew into the cover would not carry the weed up to the northern buttresses of the cove; and then there was the great hole just there, – the great hole of which she had spoken when she wished him evil.

And now she went to work, hooking up the dishevelled hairs of the ocean, and landing many a cargo on the extreme margin of the sand, from whence she would be able in the evening to drag it back before the invading waters would return to reclaim the spoil.

And on his side also Barty made his heap up against the northern buttresses of which I have spoken. Barty's heap became big and still bigger, so that he knew, let the pony work as he might, he could not take it all up that evening. But still it was not as large as Mally's heap. Mally's hook was better than his fork, and Mally's skill was better than his strength. And when he failed in some haul Mally would jeer him with a wild, weird laughter, and shriek to him through the wind that he was not half a man. At first he answered her with laughing words, but before long, as she boasted of her success and pointed to his failure, he became angry, and then he answered her no more. He became angry with himself, in that he missed so much of the plunder before him.

The broken sea was full of the long straggling growth which the waves had torn up from the bottom of the ocean, but the masses were carried past him, away from him, – nay, once or twice over him; and then Mally's weird voice would sound in his ear, jeering him. The gloom among the rocks was now becoming thicker and thicker, the tide was beating in with increased strength, and the gusts of wind came with quicker and greater violence. But still he worked on. While Mally worked he would work, and he would work for some time after she was driven in. He would not be beaten by a girl.

The great hole was now full of water, but of water which seemed to be boiling as though in a pot. And the pot was full of floating masses, – large treasures of seaweed which were thrown to and fro upon its surface, but lying there so thick that one would seem almost able to rest upon it without sinking.

Mally knew well how useless it was to attempt to rescue aught from the fury of that boiling cauldron. The hole went in under the rocks, and the side of it towards the shore lay high, slippery, and steep. The hole, even at low water, was never empty; and Mally believed that there was no bottom to it. Fish thrown in there could escape out to the ocean, miles away, – so Mally in her softer moods would tell the visitors to the cove. She knew the hole well. Poulnadioul she was accustomed to call it; which was supposed, when translated, to mean that this was the hole of the Evil One. Never did Mally attempt to make her own of weed which had found its way into that pot.

But Barty Gunliffe knew no better, and she watched him as he endeavoured to steady himself on the treacherously slippery edge of the pool. He fixed himself there and made a haul, with some small success. How he managed it she hardly knew, but she stood still for a while watching him anxiously, and then she saw him slip. He slipped, and recovered himself; – slipped again, and again recovered himself.

'Barty, you fool!' she screamed; 'if you get yourself pitched in there, you'll never come out no more'.

Whether she simply wished to frighten him, or whether her heart relented and she thought of his danger with dismay, who shall say? She could not have told herself. She hated him as much as ever, – but she could hardly have wished to see him drowned before her eyes.

'You go on, and don't mind me,' he said, speaking in a hoarse, angry tone.

'Mind you! – who minds you?' retorted the girl. And then she again prepared herself for her work.

But as she went down over the rocks with her long hook balanced in her hands, she suddenly heard a splash, and turning quickly round, saw the body of her enemy tumbling amidst the eddying waves in the pool. The tide had now come up so far that every succeeding wave washed into it and over it from the side nearest to the sea, and then ran down again back from the rocks, as the rolling wave receded, with a noise like the fall of a cataract. And then, when the surplus water had retreated for a moment, the surface of the pool would be partly calm, though the fretting bubbles would still boil up and down, and there was ever a simmer on the surface, as though, in truth, the cauldron were heated. But this time of comparative rest was but a moment, for the succeeding breaker would come up almost as soon as the foam of the preceding one had gone, and then again the waters would be dashed upon the rocks, and the sides would echo with the roar of the angry wave.

Instantly Mally hurried across to the edge of the pool, crouching down upon her hands and knees for security as she did so. As a wave receded, Barty's head and face was carried round near to her, and she could see that his forehead was covered with blood. Whether he were alive or dead she did not know. She had seen nothing but his blood, and the light-coloured hair of his head lying amidst the foam. Then his body was drawn along by the suction of the retreating wave; but the mass of water that escaped was not on this occasion large enough to carry the man out with it.

Instantly Mally was at work with her hook, and getting it fixed into his coat, dragged him towards the spot on which she was kneeling. During the half minute of repose she got him so close that she could touch his shoulder. Straining herself down, laying herself over the long bending handle of the hook, she strove to grasp him with her right hand. But she could not do it; she could only touch him.

Then came the next breaker, forcing itself on with a roar, looking to Mally as though it must certainly knock her from her resting-place, and destroy them both. But she had nothing for it but to kneel, and hold by her hook.

What prayer passed through her mind at that moment for herself or for him, or for that old man who was sitting unconsciously up at the cabin, who can say? The great wave came and rushed over her as she lay almost prostrate, and when the water was gone from her eyes, and the tumult of the foam, and the violence of the roaring breaker had passed by her, she found herself at her length upon the rock, while his body had been lifted up, free from her hook, and was lying upon the slippery ledge, half in the water and half out of it. As she looked at him, in that instant, she could see that his eyes were open and that he was struggling with his hands.

'Hold by the hook, Barty,' she cried, pushing the stick of it before him, while she seized the collar of his coat in her hands.

Had he been her brother, her lover, her father, she could not have clung to him with more of the energy of despair. He did contrive to hold by the stick which she had given him, and when the succeeding wave had passed by, he was still on the ledge. In the next moment she was seated a yard or two above the hole, in comparative safety, while Barty lay upon the rocks with his still bleeding head resting upon her lap.

What could she do now? She could not carry him; and in fifteen minutes the sea would be up where she was sitting. He was quite insensible and very pale, and the blood was coming slowly, – very slowly, – from the wound on his forehead. Ever so gently she put her hand upon his hair to move it back from his face; and then she bent over his mouth to see if he breathed, and as she looked at him she knew that he was beautiful.

What would she not give that he might live? Nothing now was so precious to her as his life, – as this life which she had so far rescued from the waters. But what could she do? Her grandfather could scarcely get himself down over the rocks, if indeed he could succeed in doing so much as that. Could she drag the wounded man backwards, if it were only a few feet, so that he might lie above the reach of the waves till further assistance could be procured?

She set herself to work and she moved him, almost lifting him. As she did so she wondered at her own strength, but she was very strong at that moment. Slowly, tenderly, falling on the rocks herself so that he might fall on her, she got him back to the margin of the sand, to a spot which the waters would not reach for the next two hours.

Here her grandfather met them, having seen at last what had happened from the door.

'Dada,' she said, 'he fell into the pool yonder, and was battered against the rocks. See there at his forehead.'

'Mally, I'm thinking that he's dead already,' said old Glos, peering down over the body.

'No, dada; he is not dead; but mayhap he's dying. But I'll go at once up to the farm.'

'Mally,' said the old man, 'look at his head. They'll say we murdered him.'

'Who'll say so? Who'll lie like that? Didn't I pull him out of the hole?'

'What matters that? His father'll say we killed him.'

It was manifest to Mally that whatever any one might say hereafter, her present course was plain before her. She must run up the path to Gunliffe's farm and get necessary assistance. If the world were as bad as her grandfather said, it would be so bad that she would not care to live longer in it. But be that as it might, there was no doubt as to what she must do now.

So away she went as fast as her naked feet could carry her up the cliff. When at the top she looked round to see if any person might be within ken, but she saw no one. So she ran with all her speed along the headland of the corn-field which led in the direction of old Gunliffe's house, and as she drew near to the homestead she saw that Barty's mother was leaning on the gate. As she approached, she attempted to call, but her breath failed her for any purpose of loud speech, so she ran on till she able to grasp Mrs Gunliffe by the arm.

'Where's himself?' she said, holding her hand upon her beating heart that she might husband her breath.

'Who is it you mean?' Mrs Gunliffe, who participated in the family feud against Trenglos and his granddaughter. 'What does the girl clutch me for in that way?'

'He's dying then, that's all.'

'Who is dying? Is it old Malachi? If the old man's bad, we'll send some one down.'

'It ain't dada, it's Barty! Where's himself? Where's the master?' But by this time Mrs Gunliffe was in an agony of despair, and was calling out for assistance lustily. Happily Gunliffe, the father, was at hand, and with him a man from the neighbouring village.

'Will you not send for the doctor?' said Mally. 'Oh, man, you should send for the doctor!'

Whether any orders were given for the doctor she did not know, but in a very few minutes she was hurrying across the field again towards the path to the cove, and Gunliffe with the other man and his wife were following her.

As Mally went along she recovered her voice, for their step was not so quick as hers, and that which to them was a hurried movement, allowed her to get her breath again. And as she went she tried to explain to the father what had happened, saying but little, however, of her own doings in the matter. The wife hung behind listening, exclaiming every now and again that her boy was killed, and then asking wild questions as to his being yet alive. The father, as he went, said little. He was known as a silent, sober man, well spoken of for diligence and general conduct, but supposed to be stern and very hard when angered.

As they drew near to the top of the path, the other man whispered something to him, and then he turned round upon Mally and stopped her.

'If he has come by his death between you, your blood shall be taken for his,' said he.

Then the wife shrieked out that her child had been murdered, and Mally, looking round into the faces of the three, saw that her grandfather's words had come true. They suspected her of having taken the life, in saving which she had nearly lost her own.

She looked round at them with awe in her face, and then, without saying a word, preceded them down the path. What had she to answer when such a charge as that was made against her? If they chose to say that she pushed him into the pool, and hit him with her hook as he lay amidst the waters, how could she show that it was not so?

Poor Mally new little of the law of evidence, and it seemed to her that she was in their hands. But as she went down the steep track with a hurried step, – a step so quick that they could not keep up with her, – her heart was very full, – very full and very high. She had striven for the man's life as though he had been her brother. The blood was yet not dry on her own legs and arms, where she had torn them in his service. At one moment she had felt sure that she would die with him in that pool. And now they said that she had murdered him! It may be that he was not dead, and what would he say if ever he should speak again? Then she thought of that moment when his eyes had opened, and he had seemed to see her. She had no fear for herself, for her heart was very high. But it was full also, – full of scorn, disdain, and wrath.

When she had reached the bottom, she stood close to the door of the hut waiting for them, so that they might precede her to the other group, which was there in front of them, at a little distance on the sand.

'He is there, and dada is with him. Go and look at him,' said Mally.

The father and mother ran on stumbling over the stones, but Mally remained behind by the door of the hut.

Barty Gunliffe was lying on the sand where Mally had left him, and old Malachi Trenglos was standing over him, resting himself with difficulty upon a stick.

'Not a move he's moved since she left him,' said he, 'not a move. I put his head on the old rug as you see, and I tried 'un with a drop of gin, but he wouldn't take it, – he wouldn't take it.'

'Oh, my boy! my boy!' said the mother, throwing herself beside her son upon the sand.

'Haud your tongue, woman,' said the father, kneeling down slowly by the lad's head, 'whimpering that way will do 'un no good.'

Then having gazed for a minute or two upon the pale face beneath him, he looked up sternly into that of Malachi Trenglos.

The old man hardly knew how to bear this terrible inquisition.

'He would come,' said Malachi; 'he brought it all upon hisself.'

'Who was it struck him?' said the father.

'Sure he struck hisself, as he fell among the breakers.'

'Liar!' said the father, looking up at the old man.

'They have murdered him! – they have murdered him!' shrieked the mother.

'Haud your peace, woman!' said the husband again. 'They shall give us blood for blood.'

Mally, leaning against the corner of the hovel, heard it all, but did not stir. They might say what they liked. They might make it out to be murder. They might drag her and her grandfather to Camelford Gaol, and then to Bodmin, and the gallows; but they could not take from her the conscious feeling that was her own. She had done her best to save him, – her very best. And she had saved him!

She remembered her threat to him before they had gone down on the rocks together, and her evil wish. Those words had been very wicked; but since that she had risked her life to save his. They might say what they pleased of her, and do what they pleased. She knew what she knew.

Then the father raised his son's head and shoulders in his arms, and called on the others to assist him in carrying Barty towards the path. They raised him between them carefully and tenderly, and lifted their burden on towards the spot at which Mally was standing. She never moved, but watched them at their work; and the old man followed them, hobbling after them with his crutch.

When they had reached the end of the hut she looked upon Barty's face, and saw that it was very pale. There was no longer blood upon the forehead, but the great gash was to be seen there plainly, with its jagged cut, and the skin livid and blue round the orifice. His light brown hair was hanging back, as she had made it to hang when she had gathered it with her hand after the big wave had passed over them. Ah, how beautiful he was in Mally's eyes with that pale face, and the sad scar upon his brow! She turned her face away, that they might not see her tears; but she did not move, nor did she speak.

But now, when they had passed the end of the hut, shuffling along with their burden, she heard a sound which stirred her. She roused herself quickly from her leaning posture, and stretched forth her head as though to listen; then she moved to follow them. Yes, they had stopped at the bottom of the path, and had again laid the body on the rocks. She heard that sound again, as of a long, long sigh, and then, regardless of any of them, she ran to the wounded man's head.

'He is not dead,' she said. 'There; he is not dead.'

As she spoke Barty's eyes opened, and he looked about him.

'Barty, my boy, speak to me,' said the mother.

Barty turned his face upon his mother, smiled, and then stared about him wildly.

'How is it with thee, lad?' said his father. Then Barty turned his face again to the latter voiced, and as he did so his eyes fell upon Mally.

'Mally!' he said, 'Mally!'

It could have wanted nothing further to any of these present to teach them that, according to Barty's own view of the case, Mally had not been his enemy; and, in truth,

Mally herself wanted no further triumph. That word had vindicated her, and she withdrew back to the hut.

'Dada,' she said, 'Barty is not dead, and I'm thinking they won't say anything more about our hurting him.'

Old Glos shook his head. He was glad the lad hadn't met his death there; he didn't want the young man's blood, but he knew what folk would say. The poorer he was the more sure the world would be to trample on him. Mally said what she could to comfort him, being full of comfort herself.

She would have crept up to the farm if she dared, to ask how Barty was. But her courage failed her when she thought of that, so she went to work again, dragging back the weed she had saved to the spot at which on the morrow she would load the donkey. As she did this she saw Barty's pony still standing patiently under the rock, so she got a lock of fodder and threw it down before the beast.

It had become dark down in the cove, but she was still dragging back the sea-weed, when she saw the glimmer of a lantern coming down the pathway. It was a most unusual sight, for lanterns were not common down in Malachi's Cove. Down came the lantern rather slowly, – much more slowly than she was in the habit of descending, and then through the gloom she saw the figure of a man standing at the bottom of the path. She went up to him, and saw that it was Mr Gunliffe, the father.

'Is that Mally?' said Gunliffe.

'Yes, it is Mally; and how is Barty, Mr Gunliffe?'

'You must come to 'un yourself, now at once,' said the farmer. 'He won't sleep a wink till he's seed you. You must not say but you'll come.'

'Sure I'll come if I'm wanted,' said Mally.

Gunliffe waited a moment, thinking that Mally might have to prepare herself, but Mally needed no preparation. She was dripping with salt water from the weed which she had been dragging, and her elfin locks were streaming wildly from her head; but, such as she was, she was ready.

'Dada's in bed,' she said, 'and I can go now if you please.'

Then Gunliffe turned round and followed her up the path, wondering at the life which this girl led so far away from all her sex. It was now dark night, and he had found her working at the very edge of the rolling waves by herself, in the darkness, while the only human being who might seem to be her protector had already gone to his bed.

When they were at the top of the cliff Gunliffe took her by her hand, and led her along. She did not comprehend this, but she made no attempt to take her hand from his. Something he said about falling on the cliffs, but it was muttered so lowly that Mally hardly understood him. But, in truth, the man knew that she had saved his boy's life, and that he had injured her instead of thanking her. He was now taking her to his heart, and as words were wanting to him, he was showing his love after this silent fashion. He held her by the hand as though she were a child, and Mally tripped along at his side asking him no questions.

When they were at the farm-yard gate, he stopped there for a moment.

'Mally, my girl,' he said, 'he'll not be content till he sees thee, but thou must not stay long wi' him, lass. Doctor says he's weak like, and wants sleep badly.'

Mally merely nodded her head, and then they entered the house. Mally had never been within it before, and looked about with wondering eyes at the furniture of the big kitchen. Did any idea of her future destiny flash upon her then, I wonder? But she did not pause here a moment, but was led up to the bedroom above the stairs, where Barty was lying on his mother's bed.

'Is it Mally herself?' said the voice of the weak youth.

'It's Mally herself,' said the mother, 'so now you can say what you please.'

'Mally,' said he, 'Mally, it's along of you that I'm alive this moment.'

'I'll not forget it on her,' said the father, with his eyes turned away from her. 'I'll never forget it on her.'

'We hadn't a one but only him,' said the mother, with her apron up to her face.

'Mally, you'll be friends with me now?' said Barty.

To have been made a lady of the manor of the cove for ever, Mally couldn't have spoken a word now. It was not only that the words and presence of the people there cowed her and made her speechless, but the big bed, and the looking-glass, and the unheard-of wonders of the chamber, made her feel her own insignificance. But she crept up to Barty's side, and put her hand upon his.

'I'll come and get the weed, Mally; but it shall all be for you,' said Barty.

'Indeed, you won't then, Barty dear,' said the mother; 'you'll never go near the awesome place again. What would we do if you were took from us?'

'He mustn't go near the hole if he does,' said Mally, speaking at last in a solemn voice, and imparting the knowledge which she had kept to herself while Barty was her enemy; ''specially not if the wind's any way from the nor'ard.'

'She'd better go down now,' said the father.

Barty kissed the hand which he held, and Mally, looking at him as he did so, thought that he was like an angel.

'You'll come and see us to-morrow, Mally' said he.

To this she made no answer, but followed Mrs Gunliffe out of the room. When they were down in the kitchen, the mother had tea for her, and thick milk, and a hot cake, – all the delicacies which the farm could afford. I don't know that Mally cared much for the eating and drinking that night, but she began to think that the Gunliffes were good people, – very good people. It was better thus, at any rate, than being accused of murder and carried off to Camelford prison.

'I'll never forget it on her – never,' the father had said.

Those words stuck to her from that moment, and seemed to sound in her ears all the night. How glad she was that Barty had come down to the cove, – oh, yes, how glad! There was no question of his dying now, and as for the blow on his forehead, what harm was that to a lad like him?

'But father shall go with you,' said Mrs Gunliffe, when Mally prepared to start for the cove by herself. Mally, however, would not hear of this. She could find her way to the cove whether it was light or dark.

'Mally, thou art my child now, and I shall think of thee so,' said the mother, as the girl went off by herself.

Mally thought of this, too, as she walked home. How could she become Mrs Gunliffe's child; ah, how?

I need not, I think, tell the tale any further. That Mally did become Mrs Gunliffe's child, and how she became so the reader will understand; and in process of time the big kitchen and all the wonders of the farm-house were her own. The people said that Barty Gunliffe had married a mermaid out of the sea; but when it was said in Mally's hearing I doubt whether she liked it; and when Barty himself would call her a mermaid she would frown at him, and throw about her black hair, and pretend to cuff him with her little hand.

Old Glos was brought up to the top of the cliff, and lived his few remaining days under the roof of Mr Gunliffe's house; and as for the cove and the right of sea-weed, from that time forth all that has been supposed to attach itself to Gunliffe's farm, and I do not know that any of the neighbours are prepared to dispute the right.

William Bottrell

The Pisky-led Commercial Traveller's Ride over the Hills

'I hate the man who can travel from Dan to Beersheba, and say, " 'Tis all barren." '
– STERNE.

'How low soever the matter, I trust in God for high words.' – Love's Labour Lost.

Not so very long ago, a traveller was staying at one of the three or four commercials'
favourite resorts at Penzance. The gentleman had often been to that town, but had not
visited St Ives, although he was curious to see the place, with the name of which he had
been familiar from the time he could lisp the old nursery rhymes about 'The man of St
Ives, who had seven wives,' &c. Our traveller started on horseback from Penzance early
in the morning, that he might have plenty of time to explore the famous old place, and
to visit some of the Lelant mines lying near his road. After visiting Providence mine,
and having a long chat with that intelligent and amiable old patriarch, Captain John
Anthony, he arrived, about three o'clock, very sore and very hungry, 'at the town that
went down on the sea-shore to get washed, and hadn't the strength to get back again.'
After satisfying his stomach with a splendid fish dinner and other good things, readily
served at the 'Western' Hotel, he sallied out to view the new pier, of which the men of
St Ives are so proud. From seeing many quaint, picturesque old houses around the
Market-place, he was induced to wander through the labyrinth of alleys and lanes into
the back settlements, hoping to find some structure ancient enough to pass for the
habitation of the mythical personage of the seven wives. He found some dwellings
which he thought (reasonably enough) must have been built before Noah's time, when
it might have been thoroughly washed, but the traveller did not think it could ever
have been cleansed since, from the sickening smells, and stunning odours of the very
essence of stench, which saluted him at every turn, as he picked his way through the
Dijey, and leaped the gutters about Charn Chy. It was in the midst of a busy fishery
season, and he saw enough, and smelt too much, to satisfy his curiosity, without proceeding any further quayward. As soon as he got back to the 'Western,' he fortified his
rebellious stomach (that now detested fish) with good store of Mr Hodge's best brandy.
Then he was got on board his nag, and took his course up the Stennack, intending to
return to Penzance by the old road, and examine the works and machinery at Wheal
Reeth mine on the way.

I expect he must have reached Cripple's Ease, as he said that he stopped at a road-side inn to make more particular enquiries about the nearest way to the mine; then, after wandering through miles of lanes, that seem to lead to no place in particular (always, he would swear, following exactly the directions given him) without coming to Wheal Reeth, he found himself, at ten o'clock on a dark foggy night, he didn't know where.

From all I could make out, by his description of the place and people he next encountered, he must have rambled through the intricate bye-lanes to some place on Lelant Downs, when, seeing a light shining from the bedroom window of a cottage, he rode up to the gate of the small enclosure before the dwelling, pushed open the wicket, rode into the garden, and tapped at the window (whence the light shone) two or three times with his whip; then he heard a woman's voice just inside the curtained casement: 'Jan, art a sleepan Jan? dedst thee hear that nackan?' 'Iss,' replied Jan from the bed, 'open the winder and see what's there.' 'No I weddent for the world, I am sure a es a sperat, or a token; what else can ever come to this out-of-the-way place this time of night, I should be glad to know: I tell thee Jan, a as a warnan for to make thee think of thy latter end, for thee to turn from thy evil ways and mend, for thee art a great sinner and most abominable liar (as thee dost know as well as I can tell thee), but thee art too proud to own at. May the Lord break that stony heart of thine.'

'Hold thy tongue thou fool, and open the winder,' says Jan, 'or I'll get out of bed and see.'

'No thee shusen't, for a es the old one come for thee; I'll put out the light and come into bed to thee.'

The traveller, getting tired of hearing the woman's sermon or banter (hard to say which) tapped the window again, at the same time he happened to cough. 'There Molly,' says Jan, 'dost a think thy sperat have catched a cold. Thee cust hear'n coughan 'spose. I have heard of the sperats, as well as the knackers in the bals, making all sorts of queer noises, yet I never heard of a sperat to cough, or sneeze before; must be some of the boys up the hill, going home from bal, who want a light for their pipes; I'll get up and see.' Suiting the action to the word, Jan sprang out of bed, drew back the curtain, and opened the windows. Though the man in the fog was within three or four feet of the window, Jan not being able to see him, when he first came from the glare of the candle-light, called out, 'Hallo, what cheer, where are 'e, and who are 'e an? what do 'e want?'

'I took the liberty of calling to enquire the way to Penzance.'

'Ha! I'm beginnan to see thee now: a man and hoss! I do declare, but what dost a do here? but dus'na move an inch for what thee dust do, nor thy hoss nether: whatever made the bufflehead to ride into my garn (garden)? thee west destroy my bed of leeks, but I can't understand thy lingo at all, thee art speaken like a forraner to me: what do 'e mean to say at all! speak plain: what dost a want here this time of night?' 'Tell me the road to Penzance if you please?' 'The road to Penzance! why there's scores of roads from here to Penzance, take whichever thee hast got a mind to ef one es'nt annuf for thee, take two ef thee west, but dosna move an inch tell I come down.' 'My good man, only have patience to hear me, and I'll pay for your bed of leeks. I lost my way in trying to get from St Ives to Wheal Reeth. If I am near the mine now I shall be glad to stop in the count house, stable, or any place, over night. I am so sore I can scarcely sit on horse-back.' 'The Lord bless 'e sir. I'll be down to 'e in a minute: you are one of the venturars I spose? how sorry I am that I didn't know 'e before: lev me put on a few rags and I'll be down in a crack: excuse me sir, please. I'll be down in a jiffey, quick as a wink, and put 'e in the road to the town or the bal.'

'No, my good man, don't come down by any means; besides, I've nothing whatever to do with mines.' 'Ha! arn't 'e a venturar, an? who or what are 'e, an? and where ded 'e come from?' Here the man, who was preparing to dress, stooped down again, with nothing on but his shirt and night-cap, and stretched himself halfways out of the win-dow, the better to see the night-rider. The fog had now become a slag (half mist, half rain), when the traveller replied, 'I'm a pin-maker from Birmingham.' 'A pin-maker! A pin-maker! Why a great man like you don't make the things the women fasten their rags with, do 'e? And you are come from the place we cale Brummagam, where the but-tons come from: that's an outlandish place a long way off, es'na? but lord, you can never get a living making pins, ef you make niddles too. And the hoss thee hast picked up upon the road I spose? Now, don't 'e move an inch. A poor pin-maker! Why, don't 'e do anything else but that to get your living, an?'

'Why no, and get a very good living too.'

'Why, hast a got a wife, an?' 'Yes, a wife and family.' 'Why, thee doesn't maintain thyself, wife, and family, makan pins and niddles, dost a? What can they have to eat, an? Molly, dost a hear what the man es tellan of? A will take thee to believe 'n, for thee west believe anthing that any fool may tell thee.' Now the woman came, and poked her head, covered with her petticoat, out of the window, over the man's back; so great was their curiosity to hear his story. When the commercial explained to the astonished cou-ple how he belonged to a manufactory where pins and needles were made by machin-ery, and where hundreds of hands, of all ages, were employed, Jan, without stopping to put on much clothing, came down, brought the traveller in, slipped the bridle from the head of the tired and hungry horse, and let it graze along the road (no fear of the horse straying far). In the meantime the good wife got a comfortable cup of tea for the weary, piskey-led, traveller.

The worthy couple were quite sure that the pin-maker was piskey-led, because, when they went over-stairs, a few minutes before his arrival, there was no appearance of the fog, which they both assured him was raised by the mischievous, laughing gob-lin, as well as the many other strange appearances that beguiled him, such as making narrow lanes and by-paths look like broad turnpike roads; what seemed to him to be candles, or blazing fire-light, seen through cottage-windows, when approached were found to be nothing but glowworms shining in the hedges; and to prevent the piskey having any more power over him, they persuaded him to turn his coat inside out. As our good couple kept a cow, the pin-maker was regaled with many dainties from the dairy, besides a treat of blackberry cake, thickly spread with delicious scalded cream. Notwithstanding the simplicity of the couple, whom the traveller at first thought to be a very uncouth pair, he remained with them three or four hours, well pleased with their frankness and cordiality.

The tinner, in his quaint way, gave much curious information about mining affairs and miners' tricks – much that the traveller would never have heard from the officials of the count-house or mine-brokers, who were not all favourably spoken of, any more than the smelters, who the miner said still try to squeeze out the same profits from the poor tinner's labour as when he gained just sufficient to enable him and his family to live comfortably, and which was more then than double as much as they all (children big and small, who ought to be at school, and the mothers who have more than enough to do in the house) can now contrive to scrape together. Much he said in praise of the owners of some mines, who are keeping on the works (merely that the people may have employment), without any hopes of present profit, and great risk of ultimate loss to themselves.

After many mutual good wishes, and the absolute refusal of the proffered payment for leeks, tea, and trouble, and – what the stranger valued most – the hearty good will with which they entertained him, the traveller left, with his coat turned inside out, and accompanied by Jan as far as the bottom of Nut Lane, where he was glad enough to find himself out of the land of mist, and once more on the turnpike-road, about day-break. Having to go slowly, very slowly, on account of the soreness he felt from having been so long in the saddle (to which he was not much accustomed), it was after sunrise when he hailed with heartfelt joy the first sight of the Mount, from Tregender hill, and returned to his inn about the same hour he had left it the previous morning, much to the satisfaction of his host, who had been rather uneasy about the long absence of man and horse, knowing that the traveller intended to return early in the afternoon of the day he went to visit St Ives. The anxiety of mine host did not proceed from any fears that the jolly traveller would be enticed into grief by the blandishments of the mermaids of St Ives, who are sure to be seen staring from the openings of their caverns (all the way from their Green Court to Charn Chy), with eyes and open mouths strained to unnatural dimensions at any stranger who may chance to pass by, roaring out to each other, 'Who is that, you?' 'Where ded he come from, an?' 'Drag in the cheeld, you! There's a cow comean, or she's a mad bull, esn't she? Waen't she bite, you?' No, no; the host was well enough acquainted with the place, to know that all the fascinations of the Sirens of the Dijey would be powerless when smothered in such a malodorous atmosphere, to all but those who are 'to the manner born.' He rather feared that man and horse might have found their way into some deserted tin-work, or unfenced shaft on the moors.

The weary explorer of back-settlements and bye-lanes (wanting sleep more than breakfast) was glad to lay himself on the comfortable bed he left four-and-twenty hours before, to have a little rest before he started for Birmingham. We hope that when he comes this way again, he will bring down good store of pins and needles for our Molly, and another story of his adventures for us.

Thomas Hardy

A MERE INTERLUDE

I

The traveller in school-books, who vouched in dryest tones for the fidelity to fact of the following narrative, used to add a ring of truth to it by opening with a nicety of criticism on the heroine's personality. People were wrong, he declared, when they surmised that Baptista Trewthen was a young woman with scarcely emotions or character. There was nothing in her to love, and nothing to hate – so ran the general opinion. That she showed few positive qualities was true. The colours and tones which changing events paint on the faces of active womankind were looked for in vain upon hers. But still waters run deep; and no crisis had come in the years of her early maidenhood to demonstrate what lay hidden within her, like metal in a mine.

She was the daughter of a small farmer in St Maria's, one of the Isles of Lyonesse beyond Off-Wessex, who had spent a large sum, as there understood, on her education, by sending her to the mainland for two years. At nineteen she was entered at the Training College for Teachers, and at twenty-one nominated to a school in the country, near Tor-upon-Sea, whither she proceeded after the Christmas examination and holidays.

The months passed by from winter to spring and summer, and Baptista applied herself to her new duties as best she could, till an uneventful year had elapsed. Then an air of abstraction pervaded her bearing as she walked to and fro, twice a day, and she showed the traits of a person who had something on her mind. A widow, by name Mrs Wace, in whose house Baptista Trewthen had been provided with a sitting-room and bedroom till the schoolhouse should be built, noticed this change in her youthful tenant's manner, and at last ventured to press her with a few questions.

'It has nothing to do with the place, nor with you,' said Miss Trewthen.

'Then it is the salary?'

'No, nor the salary.'

'Then it is something you have heard from home, my dear.'

Baptista was silent for a few moments. 'It is Mr Heddegan,' she murmured. 'Him they used to call David Heddegan before he got his money.'

'And who is the Mr Heddegan they used to call David?'

'An old bachelor at Giant's Town, St Maria's, with no relations whatever, who lives about a stone's throw from father's. When I was a child he used to take me on his knee and say he'd marry me some day. Now I am a woman the jest has turned earnest, and he is anxious to do it. And father and mother say I can't do better than have him.'

'He's well off?'

'Yes – he's the richest man we know – as a friend and neighbour.'

'How much older did you say he was than yourself?'

'I didn't say. Twenty years at least.'

'And an unpleasant man in the bargain perhaps?'

'No – he's not unpleasant.'

'Well, child, all I can say is that I'd resist any such engagement if it's not palatable to 'ee. You are comfortable here, in my little house, I hope. All the parish like 'ee: and I've never been so cheerful, since my poor husband left me to wear his wings, as I've been here with 'ee as my lodger.'

The schoolmistress assured her landlady that she could return the sentiment. 'But here comes my perplexity,' she said. 'I don't like keeping school. Ah, you are surprised – you didn't suspect it. That's because I've concealed my feeling. Well, I simply hate school. I don't care for children – they are unpleasant, troublesome little things, whom nothing would delight so much as to hear that you had fallen down dead. Yet I would even put up with them if it was not for the inspector. For three months before his visit I didn't sleep soundly. And the Committee of Council are always changing the Code, so that you don't know what to teach, and what to leave untaught. I think father and mother are right. They say I shall never excel as a schoolmistress if I dislike the work so, and that therefore I ought to get settled by marrying Mr Heddegan. Between us two, I like him better than school; but I don't like him quite so much as to wish to marry him.'

These conversations, once begun, were continued from day to day; till at length the young girl's elderly friend and landlady threw in her opinion on the side of Miss Trewthen's parents. All things considered, she declared, the uncertainty of the school, the labour, Baptista's natural dislike for teaching, it would be as well to take what fate offered, and make the best of matters by wedding her father's old neighbour and prosperous friend.

The Easter holidays came round, and Baptista went to spend them as usual in her native isle, going by train into Off-Wessex and crossing by packet from Pen-zephyr. When she returned in the middle of April her face wore a more settled aspect.

'Well?' said the expectant Mrs Wace.

'I have agreed to have him as my husband,' said Baptista, in an off-hand way. 'Heaven knows if it will be for the best or not. But I have agreed to do it, and so the matter is settled.'

Mrs Wace commended her; but Baptista did not care to dwell on the subject; so that allusion to it was very infrequent between them. Nevertheless, among other things, she repeated to the widow from time to time in monosyllabic remarks that the wedding was really impending; that it was arranged for the summer, and that she had given notice of leaving the school at the August holidays. Later on she announced more specifically that her marriage was to take place immediately after her return home at the beginning of the month aforesaid.

She now corresponded regularly with Mr Heddegan. Her letters from him were seen, at least on the outside, and in part within, by Mrs Wace. Had she read more of their interiors than the occasional sentences shown her by Baptista she would have perceived that the scratchy, rusty handwriting of Miss Trewthen's betrothed conveyed little more matter than details of their future housekeeping, and his preparations for the same, with innumerable 'my dears' sprinkled in disconnectedly, to show the depth of his affection without the inconveniences of syntax.

II

It was the end of July – dry, too dry, even for the season, the delicate green herbs and vegetables that grew in this favoured end of the kingdom tasting rather of the watering-pot than of the pure fresh moisture from the skies. Baptista's boxes were packed, and one Saturday morning she departed by a waggonette to the station, and thence by train to Pen-zephyr, from which port she was, as usual, to cross the water immediately to her home, and become Mr Heddegan's wife on the Wednesday of the week following.

She might have returned a week sooner. But though the wedding day had loomed so near, and the banns were out, she delayed her departure till this last moment, saying it was not necessary for her to be at home long beforehand. As Mr Heddegan was older than herself, she said, she was to be married in her ordinary summer bonnet and grey silk frock, and there were no preparations to make that had not been amply made by her parents and intended husband.

In due time, after a hot and tedious journey, she reached Pen-zephyr. She here obtained some refreshment, and then went towards the pier, where she learnt to her surprise that the little steamboat plying between the town and the islands had left at eleven o'clock; the usual hour of departure in the afternoon having been forestalled in consequence of the fogs which had for a few days prevailed towards evening, making twilight navigation dangerous.

This being Saturday, there was now no other boat till Tuesday, and it became obvious that here she would have to remain for the three days, unless her friends should think fit to rig out one of the island sailing-boats and come to fetch here – a not very likely contingency, the sea distance being nearly forty miles.

Baptista, however, had been detained in Pen-zephyr on more than one occasion before, either on account of bad weather or some such reason as the present, and she was therefore not in any personal alarm. But, as she was to be married on the following Wednesday, the delay was certainly inconvenient to a more than ordinary degree, since it would leave less than a day's interval between her arrival and the wedding ceremony.

Apart from this awkwardness she did not much mind the accident. It was indeed curious to see how little she minded. Perhaps it would not be too much to say that, although she was going to do the critical deed of her life quite willingly, she experienced an indefinable relief at the postponement of her meeting with Heddegan. But her manner after making discovery of the hindrance was quiet and subdued, even to passivity itself; as was instanced by her having, at the moment of receiving information that the steamer had sailed, replied 'Oh,' so coolly to the porter with her luggage, that he was almost disappointed at her lack of disappointment.

The question now was, should she return again to Mrs Wace, in the village of Lower Wessex, or wait in the town at which she had arrived. She would have preferred to go back, but the distance was too great; moreover, having left the place for good, and somewhat dramatically, to become a bride, a return, even for so short a space, would have been a trifle humiliating.

Leaving, then, her boxes at the station, her next anxiety was to secure a respectable, or rather genteel, lodging in the popular seaside resort confronting her. To this end she looked about the town, in which, though she had passed through it half-a-dozen times, she was practically a stranger.

Baptista found a room to suit her over a fruiterer's shop; where she made herself at home, and set herself in order after her journey. An early cup of tea having revived her spirits, she walked out to reconnoitre.

Being a schoolmistress she avoided looking at the schools, and having a sort of trade connection with books, she avoided looking at the booksellers; but wearying of the other shops she inspected the churches; not that for her own part she cared much about ecclesiastical edifices; but tourists looked at them, and so would she – a proceeding for which no one would have credited her with any great originality, such, for instance, as that she subsequently showed herself to possess. The churches soon oppressed her, She tried the Museum, but came out because it seemed lonely and tedious.

Yet the town and the walks in this land of strawberries, these headquarters of early English flowers and fruit, were then, as always, attractive. From the more picturesque streets she went to the town gardens, and the Pier, and the Harbour, and looked at the men at work there, loading and unloading as in the time of the Phoenicians.

'Not Baptista? Yes, Baptista it is!'

The words were uttered behind her. Turning round she gave a start, and became confused, even agitated, for a moment. Then she said in her usual undemonstrative manner, 'O – is it really you, Charles?'

Without speaking again at once, and with a half-smile, the new-comer glanced her over. There was much criticism, and some resentment – even temper – in his eye.

'I am going home,' continued she. 'But I have missed the boat.'

He scarcely seemed to take in the meaning of this explanation, in the intensity of his critical survey. 'Teaching still? What a fine schoolmistress you make, Baptista, I warrant!' he said with a slight flavour of sarcasm, which was not lost upon her.

'I know I am nothing to brag of,' she replied. 'That's why I have given up.'

'O – given up? You astonish me.'

'I hate the profession.'

'Perhaps that's because I am in it.'

'O no, it isn't. But I am going to enter on another life altogether. I am going to be married next week to Mr David Heddegan.'

The young man – fortified as he was by a natural cynical pride and passionateness – winced at this unexpected reply, notwithstanding.

'Who is Mr David Heddegan?' he asked, as indifferently as lay in his power.

She informed him that the bearer of the name was a general merchant of Giant's Town, St Maria's Island – her father's nearest neighbour and oldest friend.

'Then we shan't see anything more of you on the mainland?' inquired the schoolmaster.

'O, I don't know about that,' said Miss Trewthen.

'Here endeth the career of the belle of the boarding school your father was foolish enough to send you to. A "general merchant's" wife in the Lyonesse Isles. Will you sell pounds of soap and pennyworths of tin tacks, or whole bars of saponaceous matter, and great tenpenny nails?'

'He's not in such a small way as that!' she almost pleaded. 'He owns ships, though they are rather little ones!'

'O, well, it is much the same. Come let us walk on; it is tedious to stand still. I thought you would be a failure in education,' he continued, when she obeyed him and strolled ahead. 'You never showed power that way. You remind me much of some of those women who think they are sure to be great actresses if they go on the stage, because they have a pretty face, and forget that what we require is acting. But you found your mistake, didn't you?'

Don't taunt me, Charles.' It was noticeable that the young schoolmaster's tone caused her no anger or retaliatory passion; far otherwise: there was a tear in her eye. 'How is it you are at Pen-zephyr?' she inquired.

'I don't taunt you. I speak the truth, purely in a friendly way, as I should to anyone I wished well. Though for that matter I might have some excuse even for taunting you. Such a terrible hurry as you've been in. I hate a woman who is in such a hurry.'

'How do you mean that?'

'Why – to be somebody's wife or other – anything's wife rather than nobody's. You couldn't wait for me, O, no. Well, thank God, I'm cured of all that!'

'How merciless you are!' she said bitterly. 'Wait for you? What does that mean, Charley? You never showed – anything to wait for – anything special towards me.'

'O come, Baptista dear; come!'

'What I mean is, nothing definite,' she expostulated. 'I suppose you liked me a little; but it seemed to me to be only a pastime on your part, and that you never meant to make an honourable engagement of it.'

'There, that's just it! You girls expect a man to mean business at the first look. No man when he first becomes interested in a woman has any definite scheme of engagement to marry her in his mind, unless he is meaning a vulgar mercenary marriage. However, I *did* at last mean an honourable engagement, as you call it, come to that.'

'But you never said so, and an indefinite courtship soon injures a woman's position and credit, sooner than you think.'

'Baptista, I solemnly declare that in six months I should have asked you to marry me.'

She walked on in silence, looking at the ground, and appearing very uncomfortable. Presently he said, 'Would you have waited for me if you had known?' To this she whispered in a sorrowful whisper, 'Yes!'

They went still farther in silence – passing along one of the beautiful walks on the outskirts of the town yet not observant of scene or situation. Her shoulder and his were close together, and he clasped his fingers round the small of her arm – quite lightly, and without any attempt at impetus; yet the act seemed to say, 'Now I hold you, and my will must be yours.'

Recurring to a previous question of hers he said, 'I have merely run down here for a day or two from school near Trufal, before going off to the north for the rest of my holiday. I have seen my relations at Redrutin quite lately, so I am not going there this time. How little I thought of meeting you! How very different the circumstances would have been if, instead of parting again as we must in half-an-hour or so, possibly for ever, you had been now just going off with me, as my wife, on our honeymoon trip. Ha-ha – well – so humorous is life!'

She stopped suddenly. 'I must go back now – this is altogether too painful, Charley! It is not at all a kind mood you are in to-day.'

'I don't want to pain you – you know I do not,' he said more gently. 'Only it just exasperates me – this you are going to do. I wish you would not.'

'What?'

'Marry him. There, now I have showed you my true sentiments.'

'I must do it now,' said she.

'Why?' he asked, dropping the off-hand masterful tone he had hitherto spoken in, and becoming earnest; still holding her arm, however, as if she were his chattel to be taken up or put down at will. 'It is never too late to break off a marriage that's distasteful to you. Now I'll say one thing; and it is truth: I wish you would marry me instead of him, even now, at the last moment, though you have served me so badly.'

'O, it is not possible to think of that!' she answered hastily, shaking her head. 'When I get home all will be prepared – it is ready even now – the things for the party, the furniture, Mr Heddegan's new suit, and everything. I should require the courage of a tropical lion to go home there and say I wouldn't carry out my promise!'

'Then go, in Heaven's name! But there would be no necessity for you to go home and face them in that way. If we were to marry, it would have to be at once, instantly; or not at all. I should think your affection not worth the having unless you agreed to come back with me to Trufal this evening, where we could be married by licence on Monday morning. And then no Mr David Heddegan or anybody else could get you away from me.'

'I must go home by the Tuesday boat,' she faltered. 'What would they think if I did not come?'

'You could go home by that boat just the same. All the difference would be that I should go with you. You could leave me on the quay, where I'd have a smoke, while you went and saw your father and mother privately; you could then tell them what you had done, and that I was waiting not far off; that I was a schoolmaster in a fairly good position, and a young man you had known when you were at the Training College. Then I would come boldly forward; and they would see that it could not be altered, and so you wouldn't suffer a lifelong misery by being the wife of a wretched old gaffer you don't like at all. Now, honestly; you do like me best, don't you, Baptista?'

'Yes.'

'Then we will do as I say.'

She did not pronounce a clear affirmative. But that she consented to the novel proposition at some moment or other of that walk was apparent by what occurred a little later.

III

An enterprise of such pith required, indeed, less talking than consideration. The first thing they did in carrying it out was to return to the railway station, where Baptista took from her luggage a small trunk of immediate necessaries which she would in any case have required after missing the boat. That same afternoon they travelled up the line to Trufal.

Charles Stow (as his name was), despite his disdainful indifference to things, was very careful of appearances, and made the journey independently of her though in the same train. He told her where she could get board and lodgings in the city; and with merely a distant nod to her of a provisional kind, went off to his own quarters, and to see about the licence.

On Sunday she saw him in the morning across the nave of the pro-cathedral. In the afternoon they walked together in the fields, where he told her that the licence would be ready next day, and would be available the day after, when the ceremony could be performed as early after eight o'clock as they should choose.

His courtship, thus renewed after an interval of two years, was as impetuous, violent even, as it was short. The next day came and passed, and the final arrangements were made. Their agreement was to get the ceremony over as soon as they possibly could the next morning, so as to go on to Pen-zephyr at once, and reach that place in time for the boat's departure the same day. It was in obedience to Baptista's earnest request that Stow consented thus to make the whole journey to Lyonesse by land and water at one heat, and not break it at Pen-zephyr; she seemed to be oppressed with a dread of lingering anywhere, this great first act of disobedience to her parents once accomplished, with the weight on her mind that her home had to be convulsed by the disclosure of it. To face her difficulties over the water immediately she had created them was, however, a course more desired by Baptista than by her lover; though for once he gave way.

The next morning was bright and warm as those which had preceded it. By six o'clock it seemed nearly noon, as is often the case in that part of England in the summer season. By nine they were husband and wife. They packed up and departed by the earliest train after the service; and on the way discussed at length what she should say on meeting her parents, Charley dictating the turn of each phrase. In her anxiety they had travelled so early that when they reached Pen-zephyr they found there were nearly two hours on their hands before the steamer's time of sailing.

Baptista was extremely reluctant to be seen promenading the streets of the watering-place with her husband till, as above stated, the household at Giant's Town should know the unexpected course of events from her own lips; and it was just possible, if not likely, that some Lyonessian might be prowling about there, or even have come across the sea to look for her. To meet anyone to whom she was known, and to have to reply to awkward questions about the strange young man at her side before her well-framed announcement had been delivered at proper time and place, was a thing she could not contemplate with equanimity. So, instead of looking at the shops and harbour, they went along the coast a little way.

The heat of the morning was by this time intense. They clambered up on some cliffs, and while sitting there, looking around at St Michael's Mount and other objects, Charles said to her that he thought he would run down to the beach at their feet, and take just one plunge into the sea.

Baptista did not much like the idea of being left alone; it was gloomy, she said. But he assured her he would not be gone more than a quarter of an hour at the outside, and she passively assented.

Down he went, disappeared, appeared again, and looked back. Then he again proceeded, and vanished, till, as a small waxen object, she saw him emerge from the nook that had screened him, cross the white fringe of foam, and walk into the undulating mass of blue. Once in the water he seemed less inclined to hurry than before; he remained a long time; and, unable either to appreciate his skill or criticize his want of it at that distance, she withdrew her eyes from the spot, and gazed at the still outline of St Michael's – now beautifully toned in grey.

Her anxiety for the hour of departure, and to cope at once with the approaching incidents that she would have to manipulate as best she could, sent her into a reverie. It was now Tuesday; she would reach home in the evening – a very late time they would say; but, as the delay was a pure accident, they would deem her marriage to Mr Heddegan to-morrow still practicable. Then Charles would have to be produced from the background. It was a terrible undertaking to think of, and she almost regretted her temerity in wedding so hastily that morning. The rage of her father would be so crushing; the reproaches of her mother so bitter; and perhaps Charles would answer hotly, and perhaps cause estrangement till death. There had obviously been no alarm about her at St Maria's, or somebody would have sailed across to inquire for her. She had, in a letter written at the beginning of the week, spoken of the hour at which she intended to leave her country schoolhouse; and from this her friends had probably perceived that by such timing she would run a risk of losing the Saturday boat. She had missed it, and as a consequence sat here on the shore as Mrs Charles Stow.

This brought her to the present, and she turned from the outline of St Michael's Mount to look about for her husband's form. He was, as far as she could discover, no longer in the sea. Then he was dressing. By moving a few steps she could see where his clothes lay. But Charles was not beside them.

Baptista looked back again at the water in bewilderment, as if her senses were the victim of some sleight of hand. Not a speck or spot resembling a man's head or face showed anywhere. By this time she was alarmed, and her alarm intensified when she perceived a little beyond the scene of her husband's bathing a small area of water, the quality of whose surface differed from that of the surrounding expanse as the coarse vegetation of some foul patch in a mead differs from the fine green of the remainder. Elsewhere it looked flexuous, here it looked vermiculated and lumpy, and her marine experiences suggested to her in a moment that two currents met and caused a turmoil at this place.

She descended as hastily as her trembling limbs would allow. The way down was terribly long, and before reaching the heap of clothes it occurred to her that, after all, it would be best to run first for help. Hastening along in a lateral direction she proceeded inland till she met a man, and soon afterwards two others. To them she exclaimed, 'I think a gentleman who was bathing is in some danger. I cannot see him as I could. Will you please run and help him, at once, if you will be so kind?'

She did not think of turning to show them the exact spot, indicating it vaguely by the direction of her hand, and still going on her way with the idea of gaining more assistance. When she deemed, in her faintness, that she had carried the alarm far enough, she faced about and dragged herself back again. Before reaching the now dreaded spot she met one of the men.

'We can see nothing at all, Miss,' he declared.

Having gained the beach, she found the tide in, and no sign of Charley's clothes. The other men whom she had besought to come had disappeared, it must have been in some other direction, for she had not met them going away. They, finding nothing, had probably thought her alarm a mere conjecture, and given up the quest.

Baptista sank down upon the stones near at hand. Where Charley had undressed was now sea. There could not be the least doubt that he was drowned, and his body sucked under by the current; while his clothes, lying within high-water mark, had probably been carried away by the rising tide.

She remained in a stupor for some minutes, till a strange sensation succeeded the aforesaid perceptions, mystifying her intelligence, and leaving her physically almost inert. With his personal disappearance, the last three days of her life with him seemed to be swallowed up, also his image, in her mind's eye, waned curiously, receded far away, grew stranger and stranger, less and less real. Their meeting and marriage had been so sudden, unpremeditated, adventurous, that she could hardly believe that she had played her part in such a reckless drama. Of all the few hours of her life with Charles, the portion that most insisted in coming back to memory was their fortuitous encounter on the previous Saturday, and those bitter reprimands with which he had begun the attack, as it might be called, which had piqued her to an unexpected consummation.

A sort of cruelty, an imperiousness, even in his warmth, had characterized Charles Stow. As a lover he had ever been a bit of a tyrant; and it might pretty truly have been said that he had stung her into marriage with him at last. Still more alien from her life did these reflections operate to make him; and then they would be chased away by an interval of passionate weeping and mad regret. Finally, there returned upon the confused mind of the young wife the recollection that she was on her way homeward, and that the packet would sail in three-quarters of an hour.

Except the parasol in her hand, all she possessed was at the station awaiting her onward journey.

She looked in that direction; and, entering one of those undemonstrative phases so common with her, walked quietly on.

At first she made straight for the railway; but suddenly turning she went to a shop and wrote an anonymous line announcing his death by drowning to the only person she had ever heard Charles mention as a relative. Posting this stealthily, and with a fearful look around her, she seemed to acquire a terror of the late events, pursuing her way to the station as if followed by a spectre.

When she got to the office she asked for the luggage that she had left there on the Saturday as well as the trunk left on the morning just lapsed. All were put in the boat, and she herself followed. Quickly as these things had been done, the whole proceeding, nevertheless, had been almost automatic on Baptista's part, ere she had come to any definite conclusion on her course.

Just before the bell rang she heard a conversation on the pier, which removed the last shade of doubt from her mind, if any had existed, that she was Charles Stow's widow. The sentences were but fragmentary, but she could easily piece them out.

'A man drowned – swam out too far – was a stranger to the place – people in boat – saw him go down – couldn't get there in time.'

The news was little more definite than this as yet; though it may as well be stated once for all that the statement was true. Charley, with the over-confidence of his nature, had ventured out too far for his strength, and succumbed in the absence of assistance, his lifeless body being at the moment suspended in the transparent mid-depths of the bay. His clothes, however, had merely been gently lifted by the rising tide, and floated into a nook hard by, where they lay out of sight of the passers-by till a day or two after.

IV

In ten minutes they were steaming out of the harbour for their voyage of four or five hours, at whose ending she would have to tell her strange story.

As Pen-zephyr and all its environing scenes disappeared behind Mousehole and St Clement's Isle, Baptista's ephemeral, meteor-like husband impressed her yet more as a fantasy. She was still in such a trance-like state that she had been an hour on the little packet-boat before she became aware of the agitating fact that Mr Heddegan was on board with her. Involuntarily she slipped from her left hand the symbol of her wife-hood.

'Hee–hee! Well, the truth is, I wouldn't interrupt 'ee. "I reckon she don't see me, or won't see me," I said, "and what's the hurry? She'll see enough o' me soon!" I hope ye be well, mee deer?'

He was a hale, well-conditioned man of about five and fifty, of the complexion common to those whose lives are passed on the bluffs and beaches of an ocean isle. He extended the four quarters of his face in a genial smile, and his hand for a grasp of the same magnitude. She gave her own in surprised docility, and he continued:

'I couldn't help coming across to meet 'ee. What an unfortunate thing you missing the boat and not coming Saturday! They meant to have warned 'ee that the time was changed, but forgot it at the last moment. The truth is that I should have informed 'ee myself, but I was that busy finishing up a job last week, so as to have this week free, that

I trusted to your father for attending to these little things. However, so plain and quiet as it is all to be, it really do not matter so much as it might otherwise have done, and I hope ye haven't been greatly put out. Now, if you'd sooner that I should not be seen talking to 'ee – if 'ee feel shy at all before strangers – just say. I'll leave 'ee to yourself till we get home.'

'Thank you much. I am indeed a little tired, Mr Heddegan.'

He nodded urbane acquiescence, strolled away immediately, and minutely inspected the surface of the funnel, till some female passengers of Giant's Town tittered at what they must have thought a rebuff – for the approaching wedding was known to many on St Maria's Island, though to nobody elsewhere. Baptista coloured at their satire, and called him back, and forced herself to commune with him in at least a mechanically friendly manner.

The opening event had been thus different from her expectation, and she had adumbrated no act to meet it. Taken aback she passively allowed circumstances to pilot her along; and so the voyage was made.

It was near dusk when they touched the pier of Giant's Town, where several friends and neighbours stood awaiting them. Her father had a lantern in his hand. Her mother, too, was there, reproachfully glad that the delay had at last ended so simply. Mrs Trewthen and her daughter went together along the Giant's Walk, or promenade, to the house, rather in advance of her husband and Mr Heddegan, who talked in loud tones which reached the women over their shoulders.

Some would have called Mrs Trewthen a good mother; but though well meaning she was maladroit, and her intentions missed their mark. This might have been partly attributable to the slight deafness from which she suffered. Now, as usual, the chief utterances came from her lips.

'Ah, yes, I'm so glad, my child, that you've got over safe. It is all ready, and everything so well arranged, that nothing but misfortune could hinder you settling as, with God's grace, becomes 'ee. Close to your mother's door a'most, 'twill be a great blessing, I'm sure; and I was very glad to find from your letters that you'd held your word sacred. That's right – make your word your bond always. Mrs Wace seems to be a sensible woman. I hope the Lord will do for her as he's doing for you no long time hence. And how did 'ee get over the terrible journey from Tor-upon-Sea to Pen-zephyr? Once you'd done with the railway, of course, you seemed quite at home. Well, Baptista, conduct yourself seemly, and all will be well.'

Thus admonished, Baptista entered the house, her father and Mr Heddegan immediately at her back. Her mother had been so didactic that she had felt herself absolutely unable to broach the subjects in the centre of her mind.

The familiar room, with the dark ceiling, the well-spread table, the old chairs, had never before spoken so eloquently of the times ere she knew or had heard of Charley Stow. She went upstairs to take off her things, her mother remaining below to complete the disposition of the supper, and attend to the preparation of tomorrow's meal, altogether composing such an array of pies, from pies of fish to pies of turnips, as was never heard of outside the Western Duchy. Baptista, once alone, sat down and did nothing; and was called before she had taken off her bonnet.

'I'm coming,' she cried, jumping up, and speedily disapparelling herself, brushed her hair with a few touches and went down.

Two or three of Mr Heddegan's and her father's friends had dropped in, and expressed their sympathy for the delay she had been subjected to. The meal was a most merry one except to Baptista. She had desired privacy, and there was none; and to break the news was already a greater difficulty than it had been at first. Everything around her, animate and inanimate, great and small, insisted that she had come home to be married; and she could not get a chance to say nay.

One or two people sang songs, as overtures to the melody of the morrow, till at length bedtime came, and they all withdrew, her mother having retired a little earlier. When Baptista found herself again alone in her bedroom the case stood as before: she had come home with much to say, and she had said nothing.

It was now growing clear even to herself that Charles being dead, she had not determination sufficient within her to break tidings which, had he been alive, would have imperatively announced themselves. And thus with the stroke of midnight came the turning of the scale; her story should remain untold. It was not that upon the whole she thought it best not to attempt to tell it; but that she could not undertake so explosive a matter. To stop the wedding now would cause a convulsion in Giant's Town little short of volcanic. Weakened, tired, and terrified as she had been by the day's adventures, she could not make herself the author of such a catastrophe. But how refuse Heddegan without telling? It really seemed to her as if her marriage with Mr Heddegan were about to take place as if nothing had intervened.

Morning came. The events of the previous days were cut off from her present existence by scene and sentiment more completely than ever. Charles Stow had grown to be a special being of whom, owing to his character, she entertained rather fearful than loving memory. Baptista could hear when she awoke that her parents were already moving about downstairs. But she did not rise till her mother's rather rough voice resounded up the staircase as it had done on the preceding evening.

'Baptista! Come, time to be stirring! The man will be here, by Heaven's blessing, in three-quarters of an hour. He has looked in already for a minute or two – and says he's going to the church to see if things be well forward.'

Baptista arose, looked out of the window, and took the easy course. When she emerged from the regions above she was arrayed in her new silk frock and best stockings, wearing a linen jacket over the former for breakfasting, and her common slippers over the latter, not to spoil the new ones on the rough precincts of the dwelling.

It is unnecessary to dwell at any great length on this part of the morning's proceedings. She revealed nothing; and married Heddegan, as she had given her word to do, on that appointed August day.

V

Mr Heddegan forgave the coldness of his bride's manner during and after the wedding ceremony, full well aware that there had been considerable reluctance on her part to acquiesce in this neighbourly arrangement, and, as a philosopher of long standing, holding that whatever Baptista's attitude now, the conditions would probably be much the same six months hence as those which ruled among other married couples.

An absolutely unexpected shock was given to Baptista's listless mind about an hour after the wedding service. They had nearly finished the midday dinner when the now husband said to her father, 'We think of starting about two. And the breeze being so fair we shall bring up inside Pen-zephyr new pier about six at least.'

'What – are we going to Pen-zephyr?' said Baptista. 'I don't know anything of it.'

'Didn't you tell her?' asked her father of Heddegan.

It transpired that, owing to the delay in her arrival, this proposal too, among other things, had in the hurry not been mentioned to her, except some time ago as a general suggestion that they would go somewhere. Heddegan had imagined that any trip would be pleasant, and one to the mainland the pleasantest of all.

She looked so distressed at the announcement that her husband willingly offered to give it up, though he had not had a holiday off the island for a whole year. Then she pondered on the inconvenience of staying at Giant's Town, where all the inhabitants were bonded, by the circumstances of their situation, into a sort of family party, which permitted and encouraged on such occasions as these oral criticism that was apt to dis-turb the equanimity of newly married girls, and would especially worry Baptista in her strange situation. Hence, unexpectedly, she agreed not to disorganize her husband's plans for the wedding jaunt, and it was settled that, as originally intended, they should proceed in a neighbour's sailing boat to the metropolis of the district.

In this way they arrived at Pen-zephyr without difficulty or mishap. Bidding adieu to Jenkin and his man, who had sailed them over, they strolled arm in arm off the pier, Baptista silent, cold, and obedient. Heddegan had arranged to take her as far as Plymouth before their return, but to go no further than where they had landed that day. Their first business was to find an inn; and in this they had unexpected difficulty, since for some reason or other – possibly the fine weather – many of the nearest at hand were full of tourists and commercial travellers. He led her on till he reached a tav-ern which, though comparatively unpretending, stood in as attractive a spot as any in the town; and this, somewhat to their surprise after their previous experience, they found apparently empty. The considerate old man, thinking that Baptista was educated to artistic notions, though he himself was deficient in them, had decided that it was most desirable to have, on such an occasion as the present, an apartment with 'a good view' (the expression being one he had often heard in use among tourists); and he therefore asked for a favourite room on the first floor, from which a bow-window pro-truded, for the express purpose of affording such an outlook.

The landlady, after some hesitation, said she was sorry that particular apartment was engaged; the next one, however, or any other in the house, was unoccupied.

'The gentleman who has the best one will give it up tomorrow, and then you can change into it,' she added, as Mr Heddegan hesitated about taking the adjoining and less commanding one.

'We shall be gone tomorrow, and shan't want it,' he said.

Wishing not to lose customers, the landlady earnestly continued that since he was bent on having the best room, perhaps the other gentleman would not object to move at once into the one they despised, since, though nothing could be seen from the window, the room was equally large.

'Well, if he doesn't care for a view,' said Mr Heddegan, with the air of a highly artistic man who did.

'O no – I am sure he doesn't,' she said. 'I can promise that you shall have the room you want. If you would not object to go for a walk for half an hour, I could have it ready, and your things in it, and a nice tea laid in the bow-window by the time you come back?'

This proposal was deemed satisfactory by the fussy old tradesman, and they went out. Baptista nervously conducted him in an opposite direction to her walk of the former day in other company, showing on her wan face, had he observed it, how much she was beginning to regret her sacrificial step for mending matters that morning.

She took advantage of a moment when her husband's back was turned to inquire casually in a shop if anything had been heard of the gentleman who was sucked down in the eddy while bathing.

The shopman said, 'Yes, his body has been washed ashore,' and had just handed Baptista a newspaper on which she discerned the heading, 'A Schoolmaster drowned while bathing', when her husband turned to join her. She might have pursued the subject without raising suspicion; but it was more than flesh and blood could do, and completing a small purchase almost ran out of the shop.

'What is your terrible hurry, mee deer?' said Heddegan, hastening after.

'I don't know – I don't want to stay in shops,' she gasped.

'And we won't,' he said. 'They are suffocating this weather. Let's go back and have some tay!'

They found the much desired apartment awaiting their entry. It was a sort of combination bed and sitting-room, and the table was prettily spread with high tea in the bow-window, a bunch of flowers in the midst, and a best-parlour chair on each side. Here they shared the meal by the ruddy light of the vanishing sun. But though the view had been engaged, regardless of expense, exclusively for Baptista's pleasure, she did not direct any keen attention out of the window. Her gaze as often fell on the floor and walls of the room as elsewhere, and on the table as much as on either, beholding nothing at all.

But there was a change. Opposite her seat was the door, upon which her eyes presently became riveted like those of a little bird upon a snake. For, on a peg at the back of the door, there hung a hat; such a hat – surely, from its peculiar make, the actual hat – that had been worn by Charles. Conviction grew to certainty when she saw a railway ticket sticking up from the band. Charles had put the ticket there – she had noticed the act.

Her teeth almost chattered; she murmured something incoherent. Her husband jumped up and said, 'You are not well! What is it? What shall I get 'ee?'

'Smelling salts!' she said, quickly and desperately; 'at the chemist's shop you were in just now.'

He jumped up like the anxious old man that he was, caught up his own hat from a back table, and without observing the other hastened out and downstairs.

Left alone she gazed and gazed at the back of the door, then spasmodically rang the bell. An honest-looking country maid-servant appeared in response.

'A hat!' murmured Baptista, pointing with her finger. 'It does not belong to us.'

'O yes, I'll take it away,' said the young woman with some hurry. 'It belongs to the other gentleman.'

She spoke with a certain awkwardness, and took the hat out of the room. Baptista had recovered her outward composure. 'The other gentleman?' she said. 'Where is the other gentleman?'

'He's in the next room, ma'am. He removed out of this to oblige 'ee.'

'How can you say so? I should hear him if he were there,' said Baptista, sufficiently recovered to argue down an apparent untruth.

'He's there,' said the girl, hardily.

'Then it is strange that he makes no noise,' said Mrs Heddegan, convicting the girl of falsity by a look.

'He makes no noise; but it is not strange,' said the servant.

All at once a dread took possession of the bride's heart, like a cold hand laid thereon; for it flashed upon her that there was a possibility of reconciling the girl's statement with her own knowledge of facts.

'Why does he make no noise?' she weakly said.

The waiting-maid was silent, and looked at her questioner. 'If I tell you, ma'am, you won't tell missis?' she whispered.

Baptista promised.

'Because he's a-lying dead!' said the girl. 'He's the schoolmaster that was drowned yesterday.'

'O!' said the bride, covering her eyes. 'Then he was in this room till just now?'

'Yes,' said the maid, thinking the young lady's agitation natural enough. 'And I told missis that I thought she oughtn't to have done it, because I don't hold it right to keep visitors so much in the dark where death's concerned; but she said the gentleman did-n't die of anything infectious; she was a poor, honest, innkeeper's wife, she says, who had to get her living by making hay while the sun sheened. And owing to the drownded gentleman being brought here, she said, it kept so many people away that we were empty, though all the other houses were full. So when your good man set his mind upon the room, and she would have lost good paying folk if he'd not had it, it wasn't to be supposed, she said, that she'd let anything stand in the way. Ye won't say that I've told ye, please, m'm? All the linen has been changed, and as the inquest won't be till tomorrow, after you are gone, she thought you wouldn't know a word of it, being strangers here.'

The returning footsteps of her husband broke off further narration. Baptista waved her hand, for she could not speak. The waiting-maid quickly withdrew, and Mr Heddegan entered with the smelling salts and other nostrums.

'Any better?' he questioned.

'I don't like the hotel,' she exclaimed, almost simultaneously. 'I can't bear it – it doesn't suit me!'

'Is that all that's the matter?' he returned pettishly (this being the first time of his showing such a mood). 'Upon my heart and life such trifling is trying to any man's temper, Baptista! Sending me about from here to yond, and then when I come back saying 'ee don't like the place that I have sunk so much money and words to get for 'ee. 'Od dang it all, 'tis enough to – But I won't say any more at present, mee deer, though it is just too much to expect to turn out of the house now. We shan't get another quiet place at this time of the evening – every other inn in the town is bustling with rackety folk of one sort and t'other, while here 'tis as quiet as the grave – the country, I would say. So bide still, d'ye hear, and tomorrow we shall be out of the town altogether – as early as you like.'

The obstinacy of age had, in short, overmastered its complaisance, and the young woman said no more. The simple course of telling him that in the adjoining room lay a corpse which had lately occupied their own might, it would have seemed, have been an effectual one without further disclosure, but to allude to that subject, however it was disguised, was more than Heddegan's young wife had strength for. Horror broke her down. In the contingency one thing only presented itself to her paralysed regard – that here she was doomed to abide, in a hideous contiguity to the dead husband and the living, and her conjecture did, in fact, bear itself out. That night she lay between the two men she had married – Heddegan on the one hand, and on the other through the partition against which the bed stood, Charles Stow.

VI

Kindly time had withdrawn the foregoing event three days from the present of Baptista Heddegan. It was ten o'clock in the morning; she had been ill, not in an ordinary or definite sense, but in a state of cold stupefaction, from which it was difficult to arouse her so much as to say a few sentences. When questioned she had replied that she was pretty well.

Their trip, as such, had been something of a failure. They had gone on as far as Falmouth, but here he had given way to her entreaties to return home. This they could not very well do without repassing through Pen-zephyr, at which place they had now again arrived.

In the train she had seen a weekly local paper, and read there a paragraph detailing the inquest on Charles. It was added that the funeral was to take place at his native town of Redrutin on Friday.

After reading this she had shown no reluctance to enter the fatal neighbourhood of the tragedy, only stipulating that they should take their rest at a different lodging from the first; and now comparatively braced up and calm – indeed a cooler creature altogether than when last in the town, she said to David that she wanted to walk out for a while, as they had plenty of time on their hands.

'To a shop as usual, I suppose, mee deer?'

'Partly for shopping,' she said. 'And it will be best for you, dear, to stay in after trotting about so much, and have a good rest while I am gone.'

He assented; and Baptista sallied forth. As she had stated, her first visit was made to a shop, a draper's. Without the exercise of much choice she purchased a black bonnet and veil, also a black stuff gown; a black mantle she already wore. These articles were made up into a parcel which, in spite of the saleswoman's offers, her customer said she would take with her. Bearing it on her arm she turned to the railway, and at the station got a ticket for Redrutin.

Thus it appeared that, on her recovery from the paralysed mood of the former day, while she had resolved not to blast utterly the happiness of her present husband by revealing the history of the departed one, she had also determined to indulge a certain odd, inconsequent, feminine sentiment of decency, to the small extent to which it could do no harm to any person. At Redrutin she emerged from the railway carriage in the black attire purchased at the shop, having during the transit made the change in the empty compartment she had chosen. The other clothes were now in the bandbox and parcel. Leaving these at the cloak-room she proceeded onward, and after a wary survey reached the side of a hill whence a view of the burial ground could be obtained.

It was now a little before two o'clock. While Baptista waited a funeral procession ascended the road. Baptista hastened across, and by the time the procession entered the cemetery gates she had unobtrusively joined it.

In addition to the schoolmaster's own relatives (not a few), the paragraph in the newspapers of his death by drowning had drawn together many neighbours, acquaintances, and onlookers. Among them she passed unnoticed, and with a quiet step pursued the winding path to the chapel, and afterwards thence to the grave. When all was over, and the relatives and idlers had withdrawn, she stepped to the edge of the chasm. From beneath her mantle she drew a little bunch of forget-me-nots, and dropped them in upon the coffin. In a few minutes she also turned and went away from the cemetery. By five o'clock she was again in Pen-zephyr.

'You have been a mortal long time!' said her husband, crossly. 'I allowed you an hour at most, mee deer.'

'It occupied me longer,' said she.

'Well – I reckon it is wasting words to complain. Hang it, ye look so tired and wisht that I can't find heart to say what I would!'

'I am – weary and wisht, David; I am. We can get home tomorrow for certain, I hope?'

'We can. And please God we will!' said Mr Heddegan heartily, as if he too were weary of his brief honeymoon. 'I must be into business again on Monday morning at latest.'

They left by the next morning steamer, and in the afternoon took up their residence in their own house at Giant's Town.

The hour that she reached the island it was as if a material weight had been removed from Baptista's shoulders. Her husband attributed the change to the influence of the local breezes after the hot-house atmosphere of the mainland. However that might be, settled here, a few doors from her mother's dwelling, she recovered in no very long time much of her customary bearing, which was never very demonstrative. She accepted her position calmly, and faintly smiled when her neighbours learned to call her Mrs Heddegan, and said she seemed likely to become the leader of fashion in Giant's Town.

Her husband was a man who had made considerably more money by trade than her father had done: and perhaps the greater profusion of surroundings at her command than she had heretofore been mistress of, was not without an effect upon her. One week, two weeks, three weeks passed; and, being pre-eminently a young woman who allowed things to drift, she did nothing whatever either to disclose or conceal traces of her first marriage; or to learn if there existed possibilities – which there undoubtedly did – by which that hasty contract might become revealed to those about her at any unexpected moment.

While yet within the first month of her marriage, and on an evening just before sunset, Baptista was standing within her garden adjoining the house, when she saw passing along the road a personage clad in a greasy black coat and battered tall hat, which, common enough in the slums of a city, had an odd appearance in St Maria's. The tramp, as he seemed to be, marked her at once – bonnetless and unwrapped as she was her features were plainly recognizable – and with an air of friendly surprise came and leant over the wall.

'What! don't you know me?' said he.

She had some dim recollection of his face, but said that she was not acquainted with him.

'Why, your witness to be sure, ma'am. Don't you mind the man that was mending the church-window when you and your intended husband walked up to be made one; and the clerk called me down from the ladder, and I came and did my part by writing my name and occupation?'

Baptista glanced quickly around; her husband was out of earshot. That would have been of less importance but for the fact that the wedding witnessed by this personage had not been the wedding with Mr Heddegan, but the one on the day previous.

'I've had a misfortune since then, that's pulled me under,' continued her friend. 'But don't let me damp yer wedded joy by naming the particulars. Yes, I've seen changes since; though 'tis but a short time ago – let me see, only a month next week, I think; for 'twere the first or second day in August.'

'Yes – that's when it was,' said another man, a sailor, who had come up with a pipe in his mouth, and felt it necessary to join in (Baptista having receded to escape further speech). 'For that was the first time I set foot in Giant's Town; and her husband took her to him the same day.'

A dialogue then proceeded between the two men outside the wall, which Baptista could not help hearing.

'Ay, I signed the book that made her one flesh,' repeated the decayed glazier. 'Where's her good-man?'

'About the premises somewhere; but you don't see 'em together much,' replied the sailor in an undertone. 'You see, he's older than she.'

'Older? I should never have thought it from my own observation,' said the glazier. 'He was a remarkably handsome man.'

'Handsome? Well, there he is – we can see for ourselves.'

David Heddegan had, indeed, just shown himself at the upper end of the garden; and the glazier, looking in bewilderment from the husband to the wife, saw the latter turn pale.

Now that decayed glazier was a far-seeing and cunning man – too far-seeing and cunning to allow himself to thrive by simple and straightforward means – and he held his peace, till he could read more plainly the meaning of this riddle, merely added carelessly, 'Well – marriage do alter a man, 'tis true. I should never ha' knowed him!'

He then stared oddly at the disconcerted Baptista, and moving on to where he could again address her, asked her to do him a good turn, since he once had done the same for her. Understanding that he meant money, she handed him some, at which he thanked her, and instantly went away.

VII

She had escaped exposure on this occasion; but the incident had been an awkward one, and should have suggested to Baptista that sooner or later the secret must leak out. As it was, she suspected that at any rate she had not heard the last of the glazier.

In a day or two, when her husband had gone to the old town on the other side of the island, there came a gentle tap at the door, and the worthy witness of her first marriage made his appearance a second time.

'It took me hours to get to the bottom of the mystery – hours!' he said with a gaze of deep confederacy which offended her pride very deeply. 'But thanks to a good intellect I've done it. Now, ma'am, I'm not a man to tell tales, even when a tale would be so good as this. But I'm going back to the mainland again, and a little assistance would be as rain on thirsty ground.'

'I helped you two days ago,' began Baptista.

'Yes – but what was that, my good lady? Not enough to pay my passage to Penzephyr. I came over on your account, for I thought there was a mystery somewhere. Now I must go back on my own. Mind this – 'twould be very awkward for you if your old man were to know. He's a queer temper, though he may be fond.'

She knew as well as her visitor how awkward it would be; and the hush-money she paid was heavy that day. She had, however, the satisfaction of watching the man to the steamer, and seeing him diminish out of sight. But Baptista perceived that the system into which she had been led of purchasing silence thus was one fatal to her peace of mind, particularly if it had to be continued.

Hearing no more from the glazier she hoped the difficulty was past. But another week only had gone by, when, as she was pacing the Giant's Walk (the name given to the promenade), she met the same personage in the company of a fat woman carrying a bundle.

'This is the lady, my dear,' he said to his companion. 'This, ma'am, is my wife. We've come to settle in the town for a time, if so be we can find room.'

'That you won't do,' said she. 'Nobody can live here who is not privileged.'

'I am privileged,' said the glazier, 'by my trade.'

Baptista went on, but in the afternoon she received a visit from the man's wife. This honest woman began to depict, in forcible colours, the necessity for keeping up the concealment.

'I will intercede with my husband, ma'am,' she said. 'He's a true man if rightly managed; and I'll beg him to consider your position. 'Tis a very nice house you've got here,' she added, glancing round, 'and well worth a little sacrifice to keep it.'

The unlucky Baptista staved off the danger on this third occasion as she had done on the previous two. But she formed a resolve that, if the attack were once more to be repeated she would face a revelation – worse though that must now be than before she had attempted to purchase silence by bribes. Her tormentors, never believing her capable of acting upon such an intention, came again; but she shut the door in their faces. They retreated, muttering something; but she went to the back of the house, where David Heddegan was.

She looked at him, unconscious of all. The case was serious; she knew that well; and all the more serious in that she liked him better now than she had done at first. Yet, as she herself began to see, the secret was one that was sure to disclose itself. Her name and Charles's stood indelibly written in the registers; and though a month only had passed as yet it was a wonder that his clandestine union with her had not already been discovered by his friends. Thus spurring herself to the inevitable, she spoke to Heddegan.

'David, come indoors. I have something to tell you.'

He hardly regarded her at first. She had discerned that during the last week or two he had seemed preoccupied, as if some private business harassed him. She repeated her request. He replied with a sigh, 'Yes, certainly, mee deer.'

When they had reached the sitting-room and shut the door she repeated, faintly, 'David, I have something to tell you – a sort of tragedy I have concealed. You will hate me for having so far deceived you; but perhaps my telling you voluntarily will make you think a little better of me than you would do otherwise.'

'Tragedy?' he said, awakening to interest. 'Much you can know about tragedies, mee deer, that have been in the world so short a time!'

She saw that he suspected nothing, and it made her task the harder. But on she went steadily. 'It is about something that happened before we were married,' she said.

'Indeed!'

'Not a very long time before – a short time. And it is about a lover,' she faltered.

'I don't much mind that,' he said mildly. 'In truth, I was in hopes 'twas more.'

'In hopes!'

'Well, yes.'

This screwed her up to the necessary effort. 'I met my old sweetheart. He scorned me, chid me, dared me, and I went and married him. We were coming straight here to tell you all what we had done; but he was drowned; and I thought I would say nothing about him: and I married you, David, for the sake of peace and quietness. I've tried to keep it from you, but have found I cannot. There – that's the substance of it, and you can never, never forgive me, I am sure!'

She spoke desperately. But the old man, instead of turning black or blue, or slaying her in his indignation, jumped up from his chair, and began to caper around the room in quite an ecstatic emotion.

'O, happy thing! How well it falls out!' he exclaimed, snapping his fingers over his head. 'Ha-ha – the knot is cut – I see a way out of my trouble – ha-ha!'

She looked at him without uttering a sound, till, as he still continued smiling joyfully, she said, 'O – what do you mean? Is it done to torment me?'

'No – no! O, mee deer, your story helps me out of the most heart-aching quandary a poor man ever found himself in! You see, it is this – *I've* got a tragedy, too; and unless you had had one to tell, I could never have seen my way to tell mine!'

'What is yours – what is it?' she asked, with altogether a new view of things.

'Well – it is a bouncer; mine is a bouncer!' said he, looking on the ground and wiping his eyes.

'Not worse than mine?'

'Well – that depends upon how you look at it. Yours had to do with the past alone; and I don't mind it. You see, we've been married a month, and it don't jar upon me as it would if we'd only been married a day or two. Now mine refers to past, present, and future; so that –'

'Past, present, and future!' she murmured. 'It never occurred to me that *you* had a tragedy too.'

'But I have!' he said, shaking his head. 'In fact, four.'

'Then tell 'em!' cried the young woman.

'I will – I will. But be considerate, I beg 'ee, mee deer. Well – I wasn't a bachelor when I married 'ee, any more than you were a spinster. Just as you was a widow-woman, I was a widow-man.'

'Ah!' said she, with some surprise. 'But is that all? – then we are nicely balanced,' she added, relieved.

'No – it is not all. There's the point. I am not only a widower.'

'O, David!'

'I am a widower with four tragedies – that is to say, four strapping girls – the eldest taller than you. Don't 'ee look so struck-dumb-like! It fell out in this way. I knew the poor woman, their mother, in Pen-zephyr for some years; and – to cut a long story short – I privately married her at last, just before she died. I kept the matter secret, but it is getting known among the people here by degrees. I've long felt for the children – that it is my duty to have them here, and do something for them. I have not had courage to break it to 'ee, but I've seen lately that it would soon come to your ears, and that hev worried me.'

'Are they educated?' said the ex-schoolmistress.

'No. I am sorry to say they have been much neglected; in truth, they can hardly read. And so I thought that by marrying a young schoolmistress I should get some one in the house who could teach 'em, and bring 'em into genteel condition, all for nothing. You see, they are growed up too tall to be sent to school.'

'O, mercy!' she almost moaned. 'Four great girls to teach the rudiments to, and have always in the house with me spelling over their books; and I hate teaching, it kills me. I am bitterly punished – I am, I am!'

'You'll get used to 'em, mee deer, and the balance of secrets – mine against yours – will comfort your heart with a sense of justice. I could send for 'em this week very well – and I will! In faith, I could send this very day. Baptista, you have relieved me of all my difficulty!'

Thus the interview ended, so far as this matter was concerned. Baptista was too stu-

pefied to say more, and when she went away to her room she wept from very mortifi-
cation at Mr Heddegan's duplicity. Education, the one thing she abhorred; the shame
of it to delude a young wife so!

The next meal came round. As they sat, Baptista would not suffer her eyes to turn
towards him. He did not attempt to intrude upon her reserve, but every now and then
looked under the table and chuckled with satisfaction at the aspect of affairs. 'How very
well matched we be!' he said, comfortably.

Next day, when the steamer came in, Baptista saw her husband rush down to meet
it; and soon after there appeared at her door four tall, hipless, shoulderless girls, dwin-
dling in height and size from the eldest to the youngest, like a row of Pan pipes; at the
head of them standing Heddegan. He smiled pleasantly through the grey fringe of his
whiskers and beard, and turning to the girls said, 'Now come forrard, and shake hands
properly with your stepmother.'

Thus she made their acquaintance, and he went out, leaving them together. On
examination the poor girls turned out to be not only plain-looking, which she could
have forgiven, but to have such a lamentably meagre intellectual equipment as to be
hopelessly inadequate as companions. Even the eldest, almost her own age, could only
read with difficulty words of two syllables; and taste in dress was beyond their comprehension. In the long vista of future years she saw nothing but dreary drudgery at her
detested old trade without prospect of reward.

She went about quite despairing during the next few days – an unpromising, unfortunate mood for a woman who had not been married six weeks. From her parents she
concealed everything. They had been amongst the few acquaintances of Heddegan
who knew nothing of his secret, and were indignant enough when they saw such a
ready-made household foisted upon their only child. But she would not support them
in their remonstrances.

'No, you don't yet know all,' she said.

Thus Baptista had sense enough to see the retributive fairness of this issue. For some
time, whenever conversation arose between her and Heddegan, which was not often,
she always said, 'I am miserable, and you know it. Yet I don't wish things to be otherwise.'

But one day when he asked, 'How do you like 'em now?' her answer was unexpected. 'Much better than I did,' she said, quietly. 'I may like them very much some
day.'

This was the beginning of a serener season for the chastened spirit of Baptista
Heddegan. She had, in truth, discovered, underneath the crust of uncouthness and
meagre articulation which was due to their Troglodytean existence, that her unwel-
comed daughters had natures that were unselfish almost to sublimity. The harsh disci-
pline accorded to their young lives before their mother's wrong had been righted, had
operated less to crush them than to lift them above all personal ambition. They considered the world and its contents in a purely objective way, and their own lot seemed
only to affect them as that of certain human beings among the rest, whose troubles they
knew rather than suffered.

This was such an entirely new way of regarding life to a woman of Baptista's nature, that her attention, from being first arrested by it, became deeply interested. By imperceptible pulses her heart expanded in sympathy with theirs. The sentences of her tragi-comedy, her life, confused till now, became clearer daily. That in humanity, as exemplified by these girls, there was nothing to dislike, but infinitely much to pity, she learnt with the lapse of each week in their company. She grew to like the girls of unpromising exterior, and from liking she got to love them; till they formed an unexpected point of junction between her own and her husband's interests, generating a sterling friendship at least, between a pair in whose existence there had threatened to be neither friendship nor love.

Mark Guy Pearse

The New Vicar and his Sister

It was mid-summer when the new parson came, and a crowded church assembled, full of curiosity and excitement. Only the squire's pew was empty, for he was abroad, on his way home from no one quite knew where, and Joan was away on the cliffs by herself.

To her the loss of the 'Daddy' was a grief for which she could hope for no consolation. He could have no successor. No one had caught more than a stray glimpse of the new vicar, and there was a stir and a buzz as he came into the church, for the whole parish had gathered to sit in criticism. He was a tall, lank, black-browed man, with a white face and red lips that worked perpetually. No one could call him handsome, but there was fire in his eye. His voice was soft in its undertones, then rose into harshness as his fervour increased. He read the early part of the service in a sort of cold hurry that did not commend him to his hearers, but the sermon was impassioned and even eloquent, and got hold of the quick, emotional Cornishman.

'Iss – powerful praicher, sure enough!' was the general verdict, and some went so far as to say that the 'old parson couldn't hold a candle to he, not in the pulpit!' The old parson had always read his sermons, which were as like one another as the daisies in a plot of grass, and had something of the same open-eyed simplicity about them. But he never drew a crowd to church, and was content without them, knowing that he had the hearts of all the parish in his keeping.

It was easy to see that this man was another man altogether. He was evidently prepared to stand or fall by his sermon, for, while the old parson had been used to hurry off his surplice in order to greet his congregation one by one with inquiries into their affairs, this one came out in a leisurely way by the side path across the little churchyard, and joined his sister, who, with down-dropped eyes and erect, graceful figure, pursued her way alone.

'London ways is very stand-offish!' said Moses Minedew to his wife, who in all her Sunday finery had naturally desired to create an impression, and looked disconsolately after the vanishing figures.

'Is he a widow-man or a bachelor?' she asked, her thoughts taking another direction, for they ran in a few well-beaten tracks.

'Bachelor, I 'spose,' said Moses.

'Time 'e was wed,' said Mrs Minedew meditatively. 'There's Miss Joan now – a brave fitty maid she be growin'.'

'Law, my dear life – an' her hair down her back, an' bare legs! 'Twouldn't do at all.'

'Moses, don't 'ee be so foolish!' said his wife. 'Squire's maid can look where she've a mind to for a sweetard! She's a beauty, an' so I tell 'ee, an' if the man's got eyes in his head he'd see it for 'isself! He must marry – likewise must she! 'Tis only natural!'

'Well, he can preach, anyhow!' said Moses Minedew, who counted himself an authority on this and other literary matters. ''Tis meat and drink, too, as the man said when he tumbled into the tan-pit.'

Other observant eyes were on the pair as they took their way to the little parsonage. Old Mrs Rosewarne on Zacchy's arm watched them go with a glance as keen as kindly.

'She've a-got a will of her own, for all she do look so meek,' she said, with decision.

Zacchy only stared at her smooth plaits of red-gold hair and her elegant sloping shoulders.

He had to describe the newcomers in what detail he could muster to Joan, whom he met on the cliffs in the afternoon, as they strolled down through the fields where the hedges were wreathed in wild roses.

'She's a well-favoured woman. The hair of her's red like copper, and her skin's so white as milk,' said Zacchy. 'She isn't a maid 'zactly, an' she isn't old neither. Mother do think she do look meek and artful.'

'I hate her,' cried Joan, her brown face flushing suddenly. 'I hate red hair and nasty, quiet, sneaking ways!'

'Aw, I never went for to say all that. If that isn't a maid all over!' said Zacchy, laughing, though secretly a little pleased. He was unconsciously dreading lest these newcomers should stand between himself and Joan. Since the old parson's death they had been more than ever together, and she was constantly out in his boat.

'She's just like a cat, I know,' went on Joan; 'a smooth, sleek thing that walks like velvet, and sits in the warmest corner sharpening its claws.'

Zacchy laughed aloud. But at the moment, as it happened, the parson's sister herself came in the fields towards the stile that Joan and Zacchy had just reached. Joan looked at her dainty shoes and graceful dress; then she laid her own brown hand on the top bar and cleared the stile at a bound. Zacchy followed, and they turned down by the hedge.

'What a handsome girl!' said the Vicar.

'Yes; rather bold-looking, I thought.'

'Such an air! She can never belong to these fisher people. She was quite Spanish.'

'A touch of Spanish is not uncommon in these parts, but *I* thought she looked quite a peasant.'

'*Never!*'

The rest of the reply was lost. Joan's cheeks were blazing. How dared they discuss her like that – and she within hearing! She would show them whether she was a peasant. A *peasant!* – the word rankled. She had never heard it used before, and was uncertain of the precise degree of indignity implied. It was the inflection of contempt in the quiet voice that really stabbed.

The high, sharp stroke of a distant bell cleft the sweet evening air, an insistent summons to hurry on the straight and narrow way.

'Going to chapel, are 'ee, Zacchy?' she asked, her voice shaking a little for all her effort at control.

'Iss; mother 'd be terrible put out if I didn't take her.'

'I'll go along with you,' said Joan briskly.

Although she had not been to church this morning, to go to chapel gratified for the moment, in some subtle way, her sense of antagonism. The parson and his sister were strolling in the other direction; it was obvious that they had no intention of going.

There was no evening service as yet at the church. That innovation was born of Methodism. Church hours still, according to the law, are from eleven to one, and from three to five – an ordinance which is observed to-day only by the public-houses. John Wesley, in his anxiety not to come into collision with the Establishment, commenced the evening service which others have adopted; but only, so far as I know, among the English-speaking people.

The next week the squire returned. A brief interview sufficed to secure for the vicar's sister the post of governess to Joan, at a salary which Miss Desmond meant most conscientiously to merit; for she was one of those people with whom the most trivial matters are carried into the exalted realm of conscience.

No more subtle or delicate bit of craft is there in the world than that of the spider. If one could but understand the spider's language, surely the speech and manners would be aristocratic and gracious beyond measure. Never was host so hospitable, never stranger welcomed with more courtesy. 'Ah, my dear sir,' we hear it say, or 'madam,' as the case may be, 'you have condescended to visit my little home. How delightful! You will not misunderstand me, I am sure, but will feel more perfectly at home, and comfortable, if I may throw over your shoulders this coverlet of silk.' And whilst the words are being spoken, swiftly the silken thread, so soft and seemingly so powerless, is being wrapped around the victim. 'I have spun it myself, my dear, and know it is of the best, though it is not for me to say so. What! Rather tight did you say? Dear, dear, I am so very sorry. And I tried to be so careful, too, but it will be all right when you get used to it. And this silk suits you so admirably, matches so well your complexion, so soft to lie upon, too; you will find it at once a palace and a couch.'

A palace and a couch, indeed! It proved to be a prison and a tomb. Miss Desmond, the new parson's sister, had amongst her many gifts, beyond all others, the power of the spider. Her tone, her smile, her manner, were all silk. Her very hair suggested it, light, fluffy, gossamer. A smile reigned perpetually upon her lips only; it knew its place and purpose, nor outwardly exceeded it. Her eyes were a light blue, and skilfully concealed to the sharpest-sighted the power to stab; but the stab was most deadly when she smiled most sweetly. It was difficult to think that anybody could be quite so innocent as Miss Desmond looked. She might have sat for the portrait of Tennyson's *Isabel*, such sweetness was there in her looks.

> 'Locks not wide dispread,
> Madonna-wise on either side her head,
> Sweet lips whereon perpetually did reign
> The summer calm.'

But there the likeness ended. Her power lay in apparent helplessness. She began her sentences appealingly, and then left them unfinished, as if her modesty failed to ask so much as she timidly ventured to suggest. Her soft, white hand, slowly and most tenderly laid upon Joan, carried with it a kind of hypnotism, but which was in no wise a sleep. Its compulsion maddened the girl all the more because she felt herself powerless to resist it.

We must set Joan before us as she was at this time, a girl of sixteen developed beyond her years; with all the fierce pride that she had inherited both from her father and her mother, but especially from her mother. The long black hair lay about her shoulders as unrestrained as her own life had been, and to her it was the emblem of her own freedom, and she loved to feel it blown about in the winds that swept from the sea, as she climbed the cliffs or pulled an oar, with Zacchy behind her, over the tumbling waves, for she had learned to manage a boat as well as the fishermen themselves. Her black eyes flashed with a passionate excitement that could be instantly softened and subdued to a passionate love.

The long aquiline nose and firm rounded chin added to her look of pride and resoluteness. Her full-blooded lips could be tightly set with rigid defiance, or could be loosened with wild laughter, that displayed her teeth of ivory.

Miss Desmond, herself tall and stately, was yet by an inch or two shorter than Joan. The first glance of her pupil told her of the difficulty that lay before her, if she was to subdue the girl to her own will.

Up to this time Joan had mostly gone without shoes, and had governed the fishermen as a queen amongst them whose will was law. Her every wish was not only gladly accepted, but even anticipated and lovingly indulged.

Miss Desmond sat in the library of the squire's house with a terrific pile of books before her, such as she considered needful for a pupil so advanced in years, for she could not condescend readily to those branches of education which are called elementary.

Reluctantly Joan came into the room, evidently in her most defiant mood, and flung herself down at the table. Miss Desmond rose, and came to her side. 'Forgive me, my dear,' she began, laying the soft white hand almost imperceptibly upon Joan's hair; 'of course, if you would rather not –' and the words abruptly gave place to a gentle little laugh. 'Just as an experiment, you know. I hope you will like it. One has to consider what is becoming.'

There were pauses between the sentences, in which the soft white hands had drawn the long hair tightly back.

'Such beautiful hair,' she purred, 'so very beautiful. It is a pity that custom should require –.'

It was tightly knotted behind Joan's head.

Joan was furious. Her lips were bitten white with rage; she pressed her feet hard on the floor, whilst her eyes flashed their fiercest fires. And yet she was powerless to resist the silken thread, so soft, it held her as an iron band.

'I think that is charming,' said Miss Desmond in her softest voice; 'but of course, dear, if you would rather not –' And again the sentence ended, and the sweetest of little laughs.

Poor Joan! She felt her doom; her liberty was ended. And the despair was made complete as Miss Desmond began to initiate her into the mysteries of Euclid and Algebra.

A day or two afterwards came another proposal. 'I am going into Penzance, my dear.' The soft white hand was laid on Joan's shoulder, and then slipped down until the arm encircled the girl's waist. 'I am a stranger here, you know; of course, one is so ignorant and so helpless. Will you come with me? Of course, if you would rather not –'

Joan said nothing. Now there was no help for it.

Before that day was done, she felt herself no longer Joan. Miss Desmond could do with her what she would; and so, a few days after, she stood a prim young lady in long dress, the bare arms covered.

The fishermen saw her no more, and even old Mrs Rosewarne felt as if a great gap had opened between herself and her foster-child. But, none the less, beneath the silken thread there burned and fumed the fiery soul.

Joseph Henry Pearce

Joel

To the west of the village, ever confronting and dominating it, rose the long, irregular line of hill-tops of which Castle-an-Dinas is the culminating point.

To Joel Tregurtha, standing smoking at his cottage door of an evening, the huge, peaked hill, with the mouldering ruin on its crest, was a perpetual provocation and challenge to thought. At midsummer the sun set directly behind it, lighting up its shoulders with his enormous rays, and filling the heavens behind it with the largess of his gold: while in winter 'the owld haythen', as Joel irreverently termed the sun, setting further towards the south, glorified certain of the lower hill-tops, leaving the slopes of Castle-an-Dinas weighted with gloom.

To Joel the hill seemed to have a sentient individuality. He could imaging it rejoicing in its glowing crown at midsummer, and grieving inarticulately when it was lashed and sodden with the rains and the sun bestowed his favours on the rivals at its side.

As a lad, when he had to rise shivering in the mornings, that he might be in time to start work at the mine at seven o'clock, Joel used to glance up at the long dun slopes, which stretched far above the chimneys and buildings of the mine, and occasionally he would mutter, as he ran along the road, 'Darn it all! I wish I was thee, thee gayte duffer! Nawthin' to do all day set there in the sun.'

As he grew older, however, he was less jealous of the hill. He had now a bonny little sweetheart to stare at and wonder over, and no mere lump of granite, though a very god for idleness, could ever taste a pleasure such as sweethearting could supply.

But sweethearting seemed likely to be a rather long affair. One could not get married on ten shillings a week, especially when one had a widowed mother to consider: and in many ways life seemed to become a rather confused tangle. One must wait upon Providence, evidently, and hope for the best.

Through it all, however, the great hill stood there patiently, apparently as stable as the solid earth itself. The gulls winged their way across it and the skylarks mounted above it singing, and the ferns and heather clothed it with their thick green tangles, and it sheltered the fox and the rabbit and the lizard and the snake; but whether it rejoiced at these things or merely endured them passively, was as much a mystery as the unvoiced secrets of the heart.

And just as sluggishly Joel Tregurtha lived in his groove. Almost as powerless to unclasp the iron hands of Circumstance as was the great green giant that he watched so wistfully, Joel endured his existence patiently and made no complaint.

By-and-by his sweetheart grew weary of waiting for him. She was in the heyday of her life, with her wishes all unrealized, and her day-dreams began to haunt her, moving as shadows among her thoughts.

Joel was by this time a man; but heavily burdened. His sister, who was always ailing, still lived at home unmarried; and his mother, though she was now an aged woman, was hale and hearty yet and, he hoped, would live for years. He was as weighted with expense as if he were a married man, though the pleasure of possessing a wife was denied to him.

He represented to his sweetheart the position of affairs and begged her to wait for him – something might possibly turn up: though what the 'something' was likely to be he neither defined to her nor to himself.

'Why not go to America like the awthers?' asked Lizzie.

Joel looked up at Castle-an-Dinas, now black against the golden after-glow, and a queer feeling of forlornness seemed to clutch him at the heart.

'Iss … I cud do that,' he muttered, hoarsely.

'If thee'll go to America, I doan't mind waitin' for 'ee,' said Lizzie.

'I'll think it over,' said Joel; and went home greatly perturbed.

All that night Joel tossed sleeplessly on his bed: his love for Lizzie, and his even deeper love for his cradle-land, filled his mind with a turmoil of wishes and regrets that tired him more than a hard day's work.

'Wha's wrong weth 'ee, Joel?' his mother called to him from her bedroom; hearing the sounds of his restless tossings. 'Anything the matter weth 'ee? Shall I git up an' maake a cup o' tay? Oppen the winda, ef thee find it too close.'

'All right, mawther; 'tes the het, b'leeve,' said Joel. 'I'll oppen the winda a bit an' go to slaip.'

'Iss, do,' said Biddy; 'else thee'll be fine an' tired tomorra.'

So Joel rattled the window noisily, and Biddy went to sleep.

But there was no sleep for Joel for hours yet. Not that he was thinking very clearly or connectedly: he was rather suffering from a sense of unusual bewilderment; a feeling as if he were oppressed by a suffocating weight.

He fell asleep at last through sheer weariness, and did not wake till he heard his mother calling to him from her bedroom: 'Jo-el! Jo-el! 'tes time to git up!'

He managed to see Lizzie on the following evening and informed her that he would go to America, as she had suggested.

'When 'ull 'ee start?' she asked, eagerly

'In the spring,' said Joel.

'O-h!' said Lizzie. 'Tha's anawther sex months.'

'It'll taake all that time to get ready,' he replied.

'Well,' said Lizzie, dubiously, 's'pose we must wait.'

All that winter Joel was full of unrest. It was as if some misfortune were stealing on him stealthily and he could faintly hear the approach of his enemy, though unaware of the form in which it would appear. He could stand for an hour at a time smoking at his door, contemplating the long, irregular line of hills with the windy sky stretching greyly behind them and on either hand the steel-blue glint of the sea. For here, on the sloping heights above Goldsithney, one could see across the narrow neck of the peninsula, and from Joel's little cottage the two channels were visible, with the superb panorama of the rugged hills to boot. And the man's heart yearned towards the familiar landscapes, as the heart of a mother towards the faces that have surrounded her table, and out of whose traits the net of memory has been spun. The wide expanse of scenery fronting him daily, if not an inspiration was, at least, a steadying influence. The love and mercy of God were more believable to him here than they would be if he were shut up in some eye-restricted valley, or, worst of all, were prisoned helplessly among the buildings of a town. How could he leave the hills of his own dear Cornwall? The distant glimpses of Penzance, St Michael's Mount, Castle-an-Dinas – it would merely break his heart if he had to give up these! And vague and inarticulate though the sorrow within him was, its effect grew still more noticeable every day.

'Thee doan't seem happy,' said Lizzie, suspiciously.

'No, nor I arn't,' said Joel, lifelessly.

And the pleasures of sweethearting 'dragged' in sympathy with the mood.

'Arn't 'ee 'most ready for startin'?' asked Lizzie, when the winds of March began to wail across the peninsula and the long brown hill-slopes were beginning to be splashed with green.

'To tell 'ee the truth,' said Joel, hesitatingly, 'mawther ben beggin' me not to layve her. She's owld; an' she's afeered she'll never see me no more. I think, b'leeve, I'll ha' to stay home, after all.'

'Then it must be all ovver between us,' said Lizzie, firmly. 'I'm losin' all the fun o' life, hangin' on like this.' And he was aware of the angry discontent in her eyes.

He would have pleaded with her, but words always came to him contentedly: and, in a case like this, the difficulties of expression were insurmountable. He had his feelings – if she would only interpret them as easily as she seemed to interpret his affection if he merely put his lips to hers! But language he knew well he could not manipulate. If he had to explain his feelings in words, then there was no hope for him.

'O' coorse, ef thee put thy mawther before *me* … ' and Lizzie waited to hear a possible disclaimer. 'I must look after meself as thee waan't, simminly: it had better be off between us,' she added, presently.

'Ef it must be, s'pose it must,' said Joel, helplessly.

And with this they parted dumbly in a suddenly-darkened world.

If Joel grieved for the loss of his sweetheart, his grief was inarticulate. He ate his meals as usual, and went to mine as regularly as of old. More than this one could only have affirmed of him by a stretch of imagination, for he made no attempt to discuss the matter, remaining as stolidly incommunicative as a cormorant on a rock.

Lizzie, being a rather attractive young woman, though no longer in the first bloom of girlhood, presently found another sweetheart in the village; and, about twelve months after her parting from Joel, she had the pleasure of standing before the parson as a bride.

Joel made no attempt to find a second sweetheart: he devoted himself instead, to making his mother comfortable and to living as inoffensively and quietly as his surroundings would permit.

Often, as he stood at the cottage door of an evening, he would fall to musing over the perplexing puzzle of life, and a flavour of something like hopelessness would become perceptible in his thoughts. But, before he had been long solacing himself with his pipe, his eyes would seek, and rest contentedly on, their familiar landmark, and, therewith, his sour dissatisfaction would vanish as rapidly as the flush of a winter sunset, and an almost bovine quiet would settle on his thoughts. The great solemn hill, with its sure foothold in the world and its simple, primitive wants and pleasures, affected him as if it were a human companion: only a companion cleansed from human passions and infirmities; strong, unselfish, perennially calm.

When Lizzie became a mother, Joel looked at the infant wistfully, and with a vague twitch of pain in the recesses of his heart. But as Lizzie herself remained good-temperedly stolid, without a sign of unusualness either in her eyes or at her lips, he ultimately settled down to the acceptance of her maternity and was as kind as a godfather to her chubby little boy.

About ten years after Lizzie's marriage, when she was a stout and pleasant matron with a troop of sturdy children, Joel's mother passed away peacefully and almost painlessly, and he was left alone with his sister – now a soured old maid.

Joel still lived in the same thatched cottage in which he had been born forty years before, and the rugged granite hill-tops were still the companions of his musings as he stood smoking of an evening between the posts of the door. Through all the changes and crowding disappointments of his life he had never wavered in his affection for the great dun hill, whose crest his eyes sought instinctively morning and night: and its power to soothe him and to attemper his thoughts to patience, seemed, if anything, to have grown with the advancing years. He was as quiet under impositions, and as unresentful of wrongs, as the placid hill that carried its burden of cottages and mine-stacks, as cheerfully as it carried its airy tuft of ferns.

One day Joel's sister took to her bed. According to the doctor, she was suffering from some grave internal ailment and there was little likelihood that she would ever be better while she lived.

This, of course, meant an additional burden for Joel; but he bore it uncomplainingly and with small expenditure of words.

During the long drudgery of his life he had always been careful, and he had managed to save about thirteen pounds. But now this treasure hoard had constantly to be drawn upon, and he saw it gradually melting away before his eyes.

Joel tried to wean himself from his beloved pipe: but this bit of heroism he was unable to accomplish. He, however, reduced his allowance of tobacco from an ounce to less than half an ounce a week, and contented himself, when he was short of the 'weed', by merely keeping the empty pipe nursed between his lips.

His sister lingered long enough to practically exhaust his savings, leaving him, at her death, with barely a pound in hand.

He could not make up his mind to have her buried by the parish, so the remainder of his savings he expended on her funeral, and, at forty-five, started the world afresh with nothing but his wages of three pounds a month.

After the death of his sister, Joel lived alone: getting a woman to drop in occasionally to do the chores, but otherwise attending to everything himself.

He felt poor and depressed and very lonely, and, for the first time in his life, thoroughly disheartened with everything. His world seemed empty: and even his pipe had lost its flavour like everything else.

But when he went to the door of his cottage and turned his eyes to the hills, the feeble ticking of self in a great empty world seemed to die away completely: and the mysterious tranquillity of the hills fell in him – the deep, grave calm of the wise and ancient hills.

He stood for hours gazing at the long, green barrier, with the villages at its feet and the sky above its head, and a peculiar exaltation took possession of him. He was glad of the beauty of the world, and he rejoiced, with awe, at its many mysteries. Surely, after all, life was not an empty riddle, though its meaning might wisely be hidden from us here. He watched the sunset almost reverently: the hills were patient, and he could wait.

About eighteen months after Joel's sister died, his old sweetheart, Lizzie, became a widow; her husband having succumbed to an attack of typhoid fever.

Though he was now nearly fifty, Joel had some thoughts of by-and-by asking Lizzie to marry him: and Lizzie, on her part, seemed to be expecting some such offer, if one might judge by the increased friendliness of her attitude towards him.

While matters were in this unsettled state – Joel eyeing Lizzie wistfully, and Lizzie meeting him more than half-way – Joel still continued to mine as regularly as of old, never missing a 'coor' on any pretence.

One summer evening, when he was what is called 'night coor', Joel, in passing Lizzie's cottage, saw her standing at the door, and they exchanged a few words of halting gossip.

'Thee must find it lonely comin' home of a mornin',' said Lizzie, 'not a bit o' fire in the house, an' nowan to give 'ee a cup o' tay. I'll give 'ee a kittle of hot water when thee'rt passin' tomorra, ef thee like.'

'Thank 'ee,' said Joel, awkwardly. 'I shall be glad to have un, you.'

'Tap to the door in passin', an' I'll have un ready for 'ee.'

'Thank 'ee, I will: an' much obliged to 'ee,' said Joel.

And they parted with a nod and a friendly 'goodnight'.

The next morning Lizzie was up before five – though she knew Joel could not call for the water till nearly seven – and by six o'clock she had the kettle ready on the hob and was warming a huge pasty in the oven as an additional peace-offering for her old sweetheart.

Suddenly a lad, with a white scared face, came clattering up the empty roadway.

'Heerd the news?' he called out, as she came to the door on hearing the footsteps.

'No! what news? Anything happened down to mine?'

'Bra' bad accident in shuttin' wan o' the hawls! Wan man killed, an' two or three hurt!'

'Do 'ee knaw their names?' asked Lizzie, suddenly paling with apprehension.

'Joel Tregurtha es killed, an' Dicky Fire have lost 'es haand, an' owld Bob Hurry's skat blind!' said the lad.

Lizzie went indoors and seated herself heavily on a chair.

She sat there for quite a considerable time; her hands on her lap, and her eyes wandering vaguely around the homely little room.

Presently she was aware of the smell of something burning. It was the pasty beginning to blacken in the oven.

She jumped up hastily. 'It'll do for the children,' she ejaculated.

And just then there was the sound of trampling feet in the roadway.

She placed the pasty on a plate and rushed to the door.

Past the little chapel came a group of miners with a litter, over which two of them had considerately placed their coats.

'Who es 'a?' she asked, staring at the litter on their shoulders.

'Joel Tregurtha, poor fella!' said one of the bearers. 'He was killed in shuttin' a hawl laast night.'

'Poor fella!' said Lizzie. And again: 'Poor fella!'

'Good job 'a got nowan to layve behind un,' said the bearer.

'Poor fella!' said Lizzie: and went indoors.

J. Henry Harris

SOULS FOR GOLD

Old Hecka, the fish jowster, brought the news when he passed through the village with his donkey and cart in the early morning.

'Now, my dears, you'll give me a suvran each for my pilchers when I tell 'ee th' good news,' said the old man with a keen eye to business.

'You'm sly, Hecka, I knaw tha tricks of old,' said a woman, picking out five fat pilchards from the flasket which she intended to have for her penny.

'An' you'm an ould kill-joy,' said Hecka, grieved to see five fat pilchards disappear at the price.

'Whatever es th' news, Hecka? do 'ee tell us, like a good man,' chorused a group of women around the cart with cracked saucers, old dishes, and pieces of broken earthenware in their hands.

'Have th' pilchers clunked th' say?' asked a black-haired woman with shawl thrown over her head, and a mocking look in her hazel eyes.

'Nothing for naught, my dears; but ef you buy my fat pilchers, three a penny, I'll tell 'ee what'll make yer hair to curl better than tay drinkin', I fath et will.'

The women bargained for five and then for four, but Hecka was firm. "Gee up, Sammy!" cried he to his donkey, "lev us get on to where th' wimmen'll lev a pore man an' es dunkey live.

"Ef I had as much money as I cud tell,
  D'st tha think I'd car' pilchers to sell?" '

'Fresh pilchers, three a penny,' he shouted, and as the donkey moved on the women relented, and paid the price grumblingly.

'You'm a hecky-owla, an' ef you ate up the Mount you'd get no fatter,' said a fair customer who delighted in giving Hecka a bit of her tongue whenever she had the worst of a bargain.

'Razers bean't ov much account where you do live, my dear, and you'll be a fortin' to a man weth a beard, ess fy you will,' said he, pocketing the coppers.

'But what's th' good news?' asked the crowd of women impatiently, for they were well used to these 'tungin' matches' between Hecka and all-comers.

'Run away home and tell the men there's gold in South Africy, dags ov et, mountains ov et, and running down like sand in rivers.'

'B'ee tellin' true?'

'As true as "Amen" es in th' Bible. Cap'n 'Siah Coose, to St Agnes, es mazed to travel to wance, for they do say the fust to come'll get th' nuggets. All the young men to St Agnes weth sprawl en 'em be singin' "O be joyful!" like Tom cats to a weddin'.'

'My man es out there,' said a young woman with a child in her arms. 'You are not making game, are 'ee?' One hand she laid tremblingly upon Hecka's arm, her face was pale and her eyes glistened.

'No, my dear, tes true. Yer man'll send 'ee money, tummels ov money!'

'My man went away when things were black 'bout here, an' th' ould people an' me hav' fought against want; and now there's another mouth to feed, and I'm run dry!'

'Tes livin' gospel, I tell 'ee. Ef I was young I'd sell Sammy and go to wance. Gee up! Three a penny pilchers.'

The old man spread the news, and a thrill of joy passed over the moors, so that faces shone again like charlock in the sun.

The reports from the Rand, splendid as they were, became flat and colourless after passing through the excited brains of the young miners out of work, but panting to handle the pick, the shovel, and the drill. There was nothing with which they could compare the riches of the land but the new Jerusalem from the glowing pencil of St John. They had lived so long in misery, hoping on hoping ever, and singing when hungered to keep hope alive. Old or young the miner is a child of hope – 'to-morrow we shall cut the lode; to-morrow the price will rise'; faith in to-morrow keeps alive hungry souls to-day.

So through the villages and all over the downs the news spread like fire among bracken. The budding manhood, full of sap and hope, panted to get to South Africa. The old people should live at home in clover if every bal in the county were shut down, they said. The old people caught the fever of unrest, and sighed that they could not go also, for they remembered 'rushes' in the old times when men went to Australia and California, and came back 'rich beyond the dreams of avarice'. Grand old days! and now a new generation was going to exploit a new land, wherein the mountains were of gold, and the rivers washed it like sand in tin streams. A new light suffused homes of misery, a new song reached the lips; the old praised God that He had heard their prayers, the young married in joyous abandonment, and started for the Land of Gold.

It took time to get to the Rand in the days when Johannesburg was represented by straggling shanties on the veldt, but pegged out and throbbing with an inward consciousness of life that must be born. The slow movements of oxen trekking from farm to farm chafed the eager souls from beyond the seas fearing, at times, that all might be a delusion and a snare of the Evil One. And the veldt, red and arid, powdered under the deadly heat! They could not believe that this land, whereon stunted karroo bushes fell to dust at the touch, was ever green and studded with flowers. Now it was as a desert, dry and waterless and dazzling in an atmosphere which baked, and under a sun which scorched. How they welcomed a line of hills, or kopjes, breaking the awful monotony of the burning desert without horizon – limitless and silent. If they could have but a glimpse of the deep-blue sea shoaling into green and breaking into foam upon the Cornish cliffs, the sight would be as refreshing to inflamed eyes as a cupful of water from the cool depths of the wells at home to parched tongues.

At times they saw natives, black and naked, looking on them with pitying wonder as scarecrows that had lost their way; and the weary immigrants sometimes asked one another whether it could be true that these fine men, the possessors of the land, could have been such fools as to have allowed mountains of gold, for which the world went mad, to remain unworked; or whether they were so far above the white races that they treated with scorn the one object of the world's lust? It seemed hardly possible that the natives would not know if the gold were there, or pass it by in scorn if they knew.

Doubt arose and maddened them at times when they thought of 'home'. Many of the immigrants had mortgaged their futures to the usurers in the towns to buy outfits and pay their passage money. The market was active; the money-lenders hard. Two hundred, five hundred per cent was asked and obtained from men eager to be off, and reckless of their promises to pay if only they could get to the land of gold. The young men left their almost virgin wives as moral security to the money-lenders for the carrying out of their obligations. The usurers had better security than they fancied, for Cousin Jacky's affections centre at home, and when he is smitten there he withers.

When they reached the friendly shelters at Johannesburg their first illusion vanished. Capital had been before them, and they must work for wages with the pick, the shovel, and the drill. But the wages were good, and there was room for them and as many more as would come.

The African mail brought the news to those at home yearning with heart-hunger for their sons and husbands – often husbands only of a week. The wages dazzled those who remained behind, and there was such an exodus of youth that the valleys ceased to echo to the hymns, set to marching tunes, which the young men were wont to sing when going to and from the mines. A good rousing marching tune helped them greatly. The trains and steamers which drained the land of its young blood, returned with a stream of gold, putting new life in the veins of the old, and making life worth living for 'One and All'. Not of so much consequence was it now that the mines had stopped and the music of the stamps entirely ceased in whole districts, for there was a land of shafts and pumps, a new Cornwall beyond the sea, with open arms for Cousin Jacky, where the pick and the drill and the stamps ruled. The new Cornwall sent a flow of rich arterial gold into the decaying veins of the old land, in exchange for knowledge and lusty manhood; and there were those who saw in South Africa the future home of the ancient Cornish race, and the dream was only interrupted by the thunders of war.

* * * * *

Four young men sat around a table in the Café Chantant, commonly known as the 'Nuggie'; three were old-timers, and the fourth a new chum, known as Bill Carkeek, whose knowledge of the world had, at home, been limited to occasional visits to Redruth. The new chum looked curiously about him, and then buttoned up his pockets. Johannesburg had grown up as by magic since the advent of the early settlers, and there were in full swing, drinking saloons, music and dancing halls, cheap and gaudy and smelling vilely of paint and varnish. Men of all nationalities were sitting around tables or lounging about, smoking, drinking, and cursing the Kaffir boys who served them with some show of propriety. Shuffling between the tables were hook-nosed birds of prey from Peru, who carried on an illicit trade in vile spirits amongst the natives, and a soul-destroying traffic amongst the whites. The natives, who were cursed, moved as gentlemen amongst a lower race.

The entertainment this night was a 'Variety' – songs in German, French, and English, legerdemain, and dance. Mlle Lilith was the attraction of the hour. Her dance this night represented the ingathering of the harvest. The story was told with rare skill, with no other orchestration than a piano. As she danced, the scenes shifted from the cutting and binding to the carrying of the corn and the joyous advent of the gleaners. Then the harvest dance, with its abandonments and love passes; and as the dance proceeded, the girl threw off her light garments and floated in a cloud of tulle, until that, too, was cast off, and there was Aphrodite panting and radiant. The allegory was told with grace and truth. The men were breathless, forgetting even to smoke, and when they cheered, the sounds had the confusion of Babel.

The new chum was fascinated. He had never known that life possessed expressions such as these. During the dance he had conjured up the cornfields at home, reaped with the scythe, shocked, and carried with no more abandonment of joy than might be conveyed in the words 'fine weather for harvest, sure, an' all well saved'; or in the harvest thanksgivings, when the chapel was decorated with the fruits of the earth, tea and cake for all who could pay, and sly squeezes of the hands between the boys and maidens. He never dreamed that a young girl could be like this, or that life – the commonplace ingathering of the harvest – could have such exquisite expressions. He stood gazing like one entranced after the girl had left the stage, and whilst the black boys were busy collecting the gold pieces which the men showered upon the boards in a frenzy of admiration.

'What be thinkin' 'bout, Bill Carkeek?' asked one of the old-timers, pulling him by his jacket.

'I'm thinkin' ov home.'

The old-timers laughed: 'Tedn't a prayer-meetin', say you?'

'Shall I ever be able to look my Grace Ann in the face again, arter seein' a maid like that? An' my mother, 'twould take her breath away! Why ded 'ee bring me here, John? Shall I ever pray again with that maid flashing before my eyes?'

'We all felt like that wance, and then, well, we know better,' replied John, and the other old-timers nodded assent.

'Who do 'ee think the dancing maiden es?'

'A daughter of Sodom, I should say, for she'll kill souls.'

'No, she ednt; she's the daughter of John Jose to Marazion.'

'What! a Cornish maid?'

'Cornish to heel, and as good a maid as ever clunked a figgy-hobben. Her father es a poor turn-out, an' was scat in Mexico, where th' maid larnt dancing among the Spaniards. They do say he's going to take her round the world. Say you, comrades, ef he was to take her to the old county?'

'They'd sclow her,' said one old-timer.

'They'd duck her,' said the other.

'They'd pray over her,' said the new chum.

The vision of the dancing-girl haunted Bill Carkeek, so whenever he was able he went to the Café Chantant and shouted with the rest, and threw his piece of gold upon the stage. He found out when she went away in her rickshaw, and ran around to the door to see her leave, so that she noticed a black-haired young man, with a look of intense longing on his face, jealously watching over her. One night she smiled at him as at an acquaintance, and then from adoration he passed to worship. He followed her from music hall to music hall, and when she appeared as the 'snake charmer', and, with hands and feet alone, conjured up a scene in which she met and charmed and made her slave a gigantic python threatening annihilation, a thrill went through the house and Lilith was the goddess for the night.

Bill Carkeek was amongst those who shouted loudest in the throng around the private door, and then ran after her rickshaw. A little French engineer who gallantly raised his hat to Lilith and then *sacréd* her in Bill Carkeek's hearing, measured his full length on the floor for the honour of the old county. There was a riot in the building, the nations making common cause without knowing why, and the Cousin Jackys fighting shoulder to shoulder for the love of battle and good comradeship. The Kaffir boys looked on serenely, and amidst this throng of shouting, cursing, fighting humanity seemed to belong to a higher scale of being.

Bill Carkeek and his comrades marched over the veldt that night with exultation: they had got away without much damage. Before them rose from the 'sloots' and earth cracks in the veldt, black forms like great wingless bats which ran and disappeared. Sometimes a pistol-shot was sent after them by way of warning, for these were natives lying in wait to rob and murder, and then sell their plunder to the hook-nosed birds of prey from Peru who supplied them with raw spirits.

'Shall I ever pray again?' said Bill Carkeek to his friends.

'I wud ef I cud,' said an old-timer, 'and that quickly, for ef you run after John Jose's dancin'-maid, and fight in th' music shanties for her good name, you won't have many chances. I'd leave John Jose to look after his own maid. He gets her earnings and gambles them away, so she's valuable to him.'

'I know you mean well, but the gal's my life now.'

'Take my tip,' said the other old chum, 'and work in another mine until the maid is gone. Her father'll want to make more money out of her, or the maid'll get a bit stale here and they'll shift. Then you can come back.'

But the young man would go his own way; and he followed the girl, making himself her champion, until one day he was missing, and the Dutch police could find no trace.

The news came home that Bill Carkeek had gone mazed over a dancing-maid, who had bewitched him and slocked him away to destruction; and there was bitter grief in the little cottage wherein his old father and mother dwelt.

'My son, my son, whyever did I send 'ee away, or let tha go? I have been eating thy flesh and drinking thy blood these months past, and now thy precious soul is gone. Why dedn't us clem, an' clem, an' clem, an' keep th' boy weth us? We could only die, and now es precious soul –'

The old man had no words of comfort on his tongue, for he had encouraged the boy to go. Could he foresee?

The aged mother burst out again:

'A new Cornwall, es et? South Africy a new home? A purty home which has been baptised in the blood of our children. Doan't 'ee tell me, father, et es so – we've sold our children's souls for gold to lengthen out our span of years. Oh, my son, would to God that I had died for thee!'

And she would not be comforted.

Arthur Quiller-Couch

These-an'-That's Wife

In the matter of These-an'-That himself, public opinion in Troy is divided. To the great majority he appears scandalously careless of his honour; while there are just six or seven who fight with a suspicion that there dwells something divine in the man.

To reach the town from my cottage I have to cross the Passage Ferry, either in the smaller boat which Eli pulls single-handed, or (if a market-cart or donkey, or drove of cattle be waiting on the slip) I must hang about till Eli summons his boy to help him with the horse-boat. Then the gangway is lowered, the beasts are driven on board, the passengers follow at a convenient distance, and the long sweeps take us slowly across the tide. It was on such a voyage, a few weeks after I settled in the neighbourhood, that I first met These-an'-That.

I was leaning back against the chain, with my cap tilted forward to keep off the dazzle of the June sunshine on the water, and lazily watching Eli as he pushed his sweep. Suddenly I grew aware that by frequent winks and jerks of the head he wished to direct my attention to a passenger on my right – a short, round man in black, with a basket of eggs on his arm.

There was quite a remarkable dearth of feature on this passenger's face, which was large, soft, and unhealthy in colour: but what surprised me was to see, as he blinked in the sunlight, a couple of big tears trickle down his cheeks and splash among the eggs in his basket.

'There's trouble agen, up at Kit's,' remarked Eli, finishing his stroke with a jerk, and speaking for the general benefit, though the words were particularly addressed to a drover opposite.

'Ho?' said the drover: 'that woman agen?'

The passengers, one and all, bent their eyes on the man in black, who smeared his face with his cuff, and began weeping afresh, silently.

'Beat en blue las' night, an' turned en to doors – the dirty trollop.'

'Eli, don't 'ee –' put in the poor man, in a low, deprecating voice.

'Iss, an' no need to tell what for,' exclaimed a red-faced woman who stood by the drover, with two baskets of poultry at her feet. 'She's a low lot; a low trapesin' baggage. If These-an'-That, there, wasn' but a poor, ha'f-baked shammick, he'd ha' killed that wife o' his afore this.'

'Naybours, I'd as lief you didn't mention it,' appealed These-an'-That, huskily.

'I'm afeard you'm o' no account, These-an'-That: but sam-sodden, if I may say so,' the drover observed.

'Put in wi' the bread, an' took out wi' the cakes,' suggested Eli.

'Wife! – a pretty loitch, she an' the whole kit, up there!' went on the market-woman. 'If you durstn't lay finger 'pon your wedded wife, These-an'-That, but let her an' that long-legged gamekeeper turn'ee to doors, you must be no better'n a worm, – that's all I say.'

I saw the man's face twitch as she spoke of the gamekeeper. But he only answered in the same dull way.

'I'd as lief you didn' mention it, friends – if 'tis all the same.'

His real name was Tom Warne, as I learnt from Eli afterwards; and he lived at St Kit's, a small fruit-growing hamlet two miles up the river, where his misery was the scandal of the place. The very children knew it, and would follow him in a crowd sometimes, pelting him with horrible taunts as he slouched along the road to the kitchen-garden out of which he made his living. He never struck one; never even answered; but avoided the school-house as he would a plague; and if he saw the Parson coming would turn a mile out of his road.

The Parson had called at the cottage a score of times at least: for the business was quite intolerable. Two evenings out of the six, the long-legged gamekeeper, who was just a big, drunken bully, would swagger easily into These-an'-That's kitchen and sit himself down without so much as 'by your leave'. 'Good evenin', gamekeeper,' the husband would say in his dull, nerveless voice. Mostly he only got a jeer in reply. The fellow would sit drinking These-an'-That's cider and laughing with These-an'-That's wife, until the pair, very likely, took too much, and the woman without any cause broke into a passion, flew at the little man, and drove him out of doors, with broomstick or talons, while the gamekeeper hammered on the table and roared at the sport. His employer was an absentee who hated the Parson, so the Parson groaned in vain over the scandal.

Well, one Fair-day I crossed in Eli's boat with the pair. The woman – a dark gipsy creature – was tricked out in violet and yellow, with a sham gold watch-chain and great aluminium earrings: and the gamekeeper had driven her down in his spring-cart. As Eli pushed off, I saw a small boat coming down the river across our course. It was These-an'-That, pulling down with vegetables for the Fair. I cannot say if the two saw him: but he glanced up for a moment at the sound of their laughter, then bent his head and rowed past us a trifle more quickly. The distance was too great to let me see his face.

I was the last to step ashore. As I waited for Eli to change my sixpence, he nodded after the couple, who by this time had reached the top of the landing-stage, arm in arm.

'A bad day's work for *her*, I reckon.'

It struck me at the moment as a moral reflection of Eli's, and no more. Late in the afternoon, however, I was enlightened.

In the midst of the Fair, about four o'clock, a din of horns, beaten kettles, and hideous yelling broke out in Troy. I met the crowd in the main street, and for a moment felt afraid of it. They had seized the woman in the taproom of the 'Man-o'-War' – where the gamekeeper was lying in a drunken sleep – and were hauling her along in a Ramriding. There is nothing so cruel as a crowd, and I have seen nothing in my life like the face of These-an'-That's wife. It was bleeding; it was framed in tangles of black, dishevelled hair; it was livid; but, above all, it was possessed with an awful fear – a horror it turned a man white to look on. Now and then she bit and fought like a cat: but the men around held her tight, and mostly had to drag her, her feet trailing, and the horns and kettles dinning in her wake.

There lay a rusty old ducking-cage among the lumber up at the town-hall; and some fellows had fetched this down, with the poles and chain, and planted it on the edge of the Town Quay, between the American Shooting Gallery and the World-Renowned Swing Boats. To this they dragged her, and strapped her fast.

There is no heed to describe what followed. Even the virtuous woman who stood and applauded would like to forget it, perhaps. At the third souse, the rusty pivot of the ducking-pole broke, and the cage, with the woman in it, plunged under water.

They dragged her ashore at the end of the pole in something less than a minute. They unstrapped and laid her gently down, and began to feel over her heart, to learn if it were still beating. And then the crowd parted, and These-an'-That came through it. His face wore no more expression than usual, but his lips were working in a queer way.

He went up to his wife, took off his hat, and producing an old red handkerchief from the crown, wiped away some froth and green weed that hung about her mouth. Then he lifted her limp hand, and patting the back of it gently, turned on the crowd. His lips were still working. It was evident he was trying to say something.

'Naybours,' the words came at last, in the old dull tone; 'I'd as lief you hadn' thought o' this.'

He paused for a moment, gulped down something in his throat, and went on –

'I wudn' say you didn' mean it for the best, an' thankin' you kindly. But you didn' know her. Roughness, if I may say, was never no good wi' her. It must ha' been very hard for her to die like this, axin your parden, for she wasn' one to bear pain.'

Another long pause.

'No, she cudn' bear pain. P'raps *he* might ha' stood it better – though o' course you acted for the best, an' thankin' you kindly. I'd as lief take her home now, naybours, if 'tis all the same.'

He lifted the body in his arms, and carried it pretty steadily down the quay steps to his market-boat, that was moored below. Two minutes later he had pushed off and was rowing it quietly homewards.

There is no more to say, except that the woman recovered. She had fainted, I suppose, as they pulled her out. Anyhow, These-an'-That restored her to life – and she ran away the very next week with the gamekeeper.

John Baragwanath King

THE LAUGHING CORNISHMAN

John Menadhu was a well-to-do man, but only in recent years had affluence become his permanent guest. For thirty years he had trudged through Cornwall for a commercial firm when, one day, after a week of hard work, he computed what he had spent in hotel bills in all that time. His calculations showed that hotel keeping was profitable. Within a month he had bought a tumbledown house and had transformed it into an hotel. The situation was good: the view along the coast line to Trevose unequalled. Within two years his takings had repaid him and he had added what was known to his more select guests as 'Menadhu's Parlour'; and it was in this parlour that he now sat and laughed heartily.

His guests who sat in after-dinner comfort included Major Blake, a Worcestershire man about fifty years old. A compatriot, one Captain Severn, a man of similar age, sat next to him; occupying a high-backed chair was the Reverend Frederick K. Kingston, rector of Namby, Malvern.

'Menadhu!' called the Major.

'At your service, sir,' replied the host, appearing.

'Are you a Worcestershire man?'

'Why do you ask?'

'No one but a fellow countryman of mine could laugh like you.'

The rector shook his head. 'What a curious belief,' he remarked.

'Other than Worcestershire men can laugh,' added the Captain.

'But not like our men, Severn,' said the Major.

'Captain Severn is against you, Major,' again put in the rector.

'What is your opinion, sir?' asked Manadhu of the rector.

'I am old enough to be guarded in my opinion.'

'Well, sir, I am not a Worcestershire man.'

'Then you have missed much,' said the Major. 'You have missed the honour of belonging to the finest county in England.'

'I thought Yorkshiremen made that claim,' replied Menadhu.

'No,' replied the Major. 'Yorkshire may be big, but half of it is moorland and wild. It's no better than parts of this county with its mine dumps and a shore cursed with sand.'

'Not all of Cornwall, surely?' cried Manadhu, reproachfully.

'A large part of it, I think. You recollect remarking on the waste when we motored to Lelant, Severn?'

The Captain nodded.

'Miles of it,' continued the Major, 'mine dumps covered in places with that yellow stuff – what is it?'

'Gorse,' answered the rector, 'and a beautiful thing it is.'

'It certainly serves a good purpose in hiding the scars made by the old mining maniacs,' retorted the Major.

'Ah, Major,' said the rector, 'you haven't seen the best of Cornwall.'

'I've seen as much as I want to.'

'But your knowledge of it is very limited?'

The Major shrugged his shoulders. 'I admit we haven't been here long nor motored far; but what we have seen has been unflattering. Apart from the mine dumps, the shore is cursed with blown sand. At St Enodoc we saw it; at Lelant it was worse.'

'But my dear sir,' expostulated the Rector, 'those sand hills – or towans, as they are called – are the joy of all good golfers.'

'They may be all right for golf,' said the Major; 'I'm thinking of value. Carry your mind from this waste to Worcestershire. There we have hundreds of square miles of fruitful soil. There are watered vales with trees laden to the ground; beautiful hills and wooded knolls. In our rare county a man may boast that whatever he eats and drinks – in fact, all that he uses – can be found in it.'

'Can Worcestershire provide a good dinner?' asked Menadhu.

'A good dinner, Menadhu!' cried the Major. 'Why man, my county feeds half the country. I will wager anything that something of what we have eaten here today came from Worcestershire. You may laugh, Menadhu, but I can assure you that the county which can turn out a Prime Minister, can turn out anything. Worcestershire can provide not only its own dinner but its breakfast and its supper as well. Even after doing that, Worcestershire will have enough left over to supply Cornwall.'

'Major, Major!' cried the rector warningly, 'in your patriotic zeal you forget other shires equally favoured. Somerset, Gloucester and Devon are all agriculturally famous. Surely it is over-bold to assert that Worcestershire supplies half England?'

At this point Menadhu moved towards the door.

'Surely you are not off,' said the Major. 'Stay a little longer.'

'I must go, Major.'

'Are you going to find what Worcestershire sends to Cornwall?'

Manadhu laughed. 'No,' he said, 'I'm going to find what Cornwall sends to Worcestershire; and, while I think of it, I am preparing a little dinner for you tomorrow evening. A special dinner.'

'Special, eh?' asked the Major.

'Yes, sir, special. And if I may say so, a special dinner deserves a special appetite.'

Having agreed that their host's final remark had reason in it, the three men from Worcestershire next day engaged in a thirty-six hole match on the Newquay links. Eight miles of golf, surely, are warranted to give even a dyspeptic the hunger of a hunter.

Before dinner-time the jolly host devoted particular attention to the dining room. The usual mahogany board was replaced by one of oak. Quaint candlesticks of brass gleamed on the mantel. Copper trays shone on the sideboard; and burnished fireirons glorified the hearth. An old grandfather's clock ticked away the seconds; and on each side of the clock high-backed oak chairs added to the old world air of the room. Pictures on glass and woven samplers adorned the walls. A copper warming pan hung near the old clock. Menadhu put tufts of pink and white heather in serpentine vases, arranged the silver, and produced pewter tankards. Finally he looked at one of three menu cards and laughed.

Coad, Menadhu's trusted waiter, was in his place when the three guests took their places. Manadhu officiated at a side table, and a smart maid brought the dishes from the kitchen.

'An aperitif, sir?' asked Coad, of the rector.

'No thanks, Coad. But look, my friends: look at the menu. Is this your composition, Manadhu?'

'The French is a proof, sir.'

The Major read:

HORS D'OEUVRES   POTAGE
Sardines à l'huile   Consommé à Duché
Oeufs de Hareng

POISSON
Huitres à la Helford
Turbot à la Saint Ia
Saumon Mayonnaise

ENTREES
Bécassins à la Goss Moor

Oyster Patties   Asparagus

RÔTI
Perdrix à la St Columb
Pommes de terre
Laitue de Gulval

ENTREMETS DESSERT
Crême, Gâteau de Miel, Pommes, Raisins,
Fromage de Restormel

Tabac   Tre-pol-pen

The glasses clinked, the plates clattered and made a merry accompaniment to the talk of the gay diners. The soup gave way to the oysters.

'You have fine oysters in Worcestershire, sir?' asked John Menadhu of the Major.

'I won't say that; but these Whitstable natives are delicious.'

With the arrival of the turbot the host put a similar inquiry.

'No, no, Menadhu,' said the Major, who was eating the fish with gusto, 'we don't boast everything in Worcestershire. This is splendid.'

'It was alive this morning,' said the host quietly.

'Alive this morning? Come, come; you know you bought it at Billingsgate.'

'Cider, sir?' said Coad.

'Fill up, Coad,' replied the Major. 'Menadhu, I have you now. This is Worcestershire cider. Evesham apples made it.'

'Note that, Menadhu,' said the rector, smiling.

'And while you are about it, put on record my belief that this salmon came from the Severn,' said the major as the mayonnaise was served.

The snipe on toast aroused no particular comment, but with the patties Major Blake extolled the merits of Whitstable oysters. He claimed to be a judge, for he had lived in Whitstable for many years. With the partridges, new potatoes, and salad, the diners vowed that the meal was fit for a king. 'You have excelled yourself, Menadhu,' said the rector. 'Better partridges I never ate. Do you claim that they came from Worcestershire, Major?'

'Well, no.'

'But you have the cider and the salmon.'

'I have; and also this fine "grass",' said the Major as the asparagus was helped.

'You'll never find asparagus like this outside my county.'

Laughing to himself, Menadhu assisted Coad to serve the tart. It was blackberry, and with the clotted cream was declared delicious.

'Cream like this is the most excellent luxury devised by the wit of man,' observed the rector.

'Yes,' agreed the Major. 'In this, Manadhu, I confess you beat us. We cannot touch you here.'

'Try this next, Major,' said Menadhu, producing a small cheese.

'That's St Ivel,' remarked Captain Severn, positively.

'Never, Severn,' said the Major. 'Take it from me. This is Cheddar.'

'Menadhu is laughing again,' said the rector. 'I believe you have both missed the mark.'

'It is splendid,' said the Major, 'but I feel sure it is Cheddar.'

With the dessert the Major's eyes gleamed.

'Here's old Worcestershire again, friends. This apple grows in one parish only at home. I've forgotten the name. Did the seller tell it you, Menadhu?'

'I didn't buy them, Major. I grew them.'

'You grew them?'

'I grew them on my little farm a few miles from here. These grapes were ripened under glass there as well. Try these filberts, gentlemen.'

'The wine is better,' said Captain Severn.

'It is certainly very good,' agreed the rector.

'Capital indeed,' said the Major. 'It is dry, with quite a heady finish to it.'

'And none the worse for its bite,' added the rector, holding his glass of ruby drink to the light.

The Major smacked his lips with the air of a connoisseur. 'You are right, rector. That bite is the making of a good wine. But after a good wine there should be a good cigar.'

'Pardon me, sir,' said Menadhu, producing a copper box filled with tobacco. 'Try this Tre-pol-pen mixture with a churchwarden pipe.'

Coad cleared away. Menadhu replaced the pewter tankards and when all was in order, at the invitation of his guests, he seated himself with them.

'Now, Menadhu, we drink to you. A better dinner never was served. You must have scoured the country for it.'

Menadhu, responding, said: 'A few days ago I said that Cornwall was not dependent upon Worcestershire. Listen to me and say whether I was right. This grandfather's clock was made in Helston. The brass candlesticks were cast and finished at Hayle in 1840. The pewter tankards were made in Camborne seventy years ago. The firedogs were cast by a Cornishman. The table of Boconnoc oak was made in Truro when Wesley was in Cornwall. The flower vases were quarried and turned at the Lizard and the heather in them was plucked on the Goonhilly Downs. Those late sweet peas were grown by me and the roses on the sideboard by my neighbour. My copper trays and boxes were beaten in Cornwall. The fender was designed and made at Newlyn. That silver which you saw on the board was mined in Wheal Rose, and the pewter was of metals dug in the mining Division. That statuette of Davy was cast from an ingot of native copper from Caradon Mine. The clay of these churchwardens was dug in St Dennys.'

Sipping his wine, Menadhu paused a moment. Then he continued: 'I have spoken of the things outside the dinner. Now for the menu. Pilchards from Newlyn and herrings from St Ives gave me the *hors d'oeuvres*. I got the ingredients for the soup from my garden and establishment. The oysters came from Helford fisheries –'

'What, not from Whitstable?' cried the Major.

'No, sir. They were Helford oysters. The turbot I bought in St Ives and the salmon came from the Dunmeer Pool near Bodmin.'

'What about your Severn salmon now?' asked the rector with his eyes a-twinkle.

Menadhu went on: 'The snipe were shot on the Goss Moor and the partridges in the Parish of St Columb. The new potatoes – you liked them, gentlemen?'

'We did!' came the chorus.

'They came from Gulval, as also did the lettuce. The asparagus was found in the neighbouring parish. As for the tart, I need scarcely say that the fruit was grown on Cornish hedgerows and that the pastry was made from flour made from wheat of Cornish growing. The cheese –'

'St Ivel, I'll be bound,' interrupted Captain Severn.

'No; Cheddar, surely,' said the Major.

'Sorry, Major; sorry, Captain; but the cheese was made from milk of Cornish cows at Restormel, near Lostwithiel. The nuts grew at St Columb and the chestnuts at St Germans. As for the drinks, the stout which washed down the Helford oysters was brewed at Redruth, and the fine ale at St Austell. The wine which we are now drinking is from Cornish berries with a little cognac – overproof – to give it a sherry vinosity. The cider was pressed at Kea. Even the tobacco was Cornish grown. And now I have done: I said I would prove that Cornwall was not dependent upon –'

'Stop, stop!' said Major Blake. 'I'll withdraw all that I said about Cornwall. More, I'll wager that no other county can beat this little one.'

'One thing I had nearly forgotten,' said Menadhu. 'This old bed warmer was made in Penzance in 1802, and has been with my people for generations. I believe it has brought me luck; and, as a Cornishman, I am too superstitious to part with it.'

'May luck be your permanent guest, Menadhu,' said the rector.

'Hear, hear to that,' said the Major.

'Thank you, gentlemen,' said Menadhu. 'Now let me tell you a little secret: private hotel keeping has paid me so well here that I have bought a fully licensed inn in a neighbouring town. It is on the main road through Cornwall, and I hope for a good return from the motorists who will use it. The only thing that worries me is a suitable sign.'

The rector rose and put his churchwarden on a shelf. 'I have the very thing in my mind,' he said. 'Tell me, Menadhu, shall you personally manage this inn?'

'At first I shall give my whole time to it until it becomes fairly established.'

'Here, then, is your sign,' said the rector scribbling on a piece of paper. 'On this swinging sign you must have a jolly fellow painted underneath and these words:

"THE LAUGHING CORNISHMAN".'

'Well done, rector,' said the Major.

'Most appropriate,' added Captain Severn. 'I take it that the portrait will be that of Menadhu?'

'Certainly,' replied the rector.

'I don't know about the portrait,' said Menadhu, laughing,' but the words shall certainly be "The Laughing Cornishman". And now, gentlemen, I bid you good night.'

* * * * *

Trevose lights flashed over the dark-blue waters of the North Cornwall shore as, from his bedroom window, the rector looked out. The pure air of the Atlantic entered the room to the accompaniment of the sound of the surf rolling in on the Watergate and Porth sands. From somewhere in the house came the sound of the laughter of its merry host.

'He is laughing again,' thought the rector. 'God bless him. Surely, when he laughs somebody is the better for it. Laugh on, John Menadhu, you Laughing Cornishman.'

C. A. Dawson Scott

A Cry in the Night

'If Mick were to home, he would soon have potato patch weeded and th' grass cut,' Micho Dugga told herself. She stood at the door of her cottage, looking across the neglected garden. Wanted a man to teal it, so it did, but her son was in South Afriky and would not be back before the turn of the year, if then. She herself, what with the sewing and the tending on the village women when they had their babies, she had enough to do.

The tall, dun stems of seeded grass shook, as if the wind had got at their roots. Her sharp, country eyes detected a sinuous movement, a gleam of warm brown. Day-fall had brought out the stoats. 'Thirsty as a bullock, they be,' she said, 'but they bain't thirsty for water.'

Micho was more interested in the stoats – eight of them – running fiercely, like angry thoughts, than in the red of the evening sky. Flames in the west, and fainter flames in the east, a canopy of colour over her tiny remote cottage, one room down and one up. The cottage stood on a hill. 'Forty-'leven' miles away she saw the sun rise over the round of the world. At the bottom of a long descent she saw it drop into the fireshot grey of the sea. Top of the earth, like a hat on a man's head!

'A terrible great view!' Whoever wanted to see that far? Not she. The grey stone house and the bit of flat garden, it was plain in the sight of all – like a wart. Not a thing she did but the village down in the hollow knew. It had mattered once, but of course, now that she was old –

On her table lay breadths of material. She was making a gown for Mrs Rosevear's Rowena. Maid was having of her first baby at Christmas, and thought to wear it soon as she was about again, but Micho Dugga knew better. She did not tell what she knew – at least not often. People had to beg and beg before she would.

Not a matter of money with her. She made more than she needed. The stocking in the old chest was crammed as full as it would hold, and every week there was more to go in. She liked work, she did, and she wouldn't tell things – unless she had a mind to.

Rowena was asking for the dress, and if Micho were to finish it that week she must make the most of the light. She did not care to work after she had put a match to the lamp, drawn down the dark-blue blinds, drawn across it the red curtains. That was her hour, the hour to which she looked forward throughout the day. Her tablecloth was dark, and when she lighted the hanging lamp, brightness fell from under its shade, making a pool.

She stood for a moment to watch the trailing stoats, then turned into the cottage.

Through the window the glow of the west fell on to the table, on to the purple of the fine woollen gown. The woman seated herself on the beach and the red light fell over her shoulder as she set the stitches, turning the fray under her thumb and thinking.

She was not working as swiftly as she belonged to. Her mind sprang about and she paused, went on again. Restless, she was, as a girl expecting her sweetheart.

A long while since she had done aught but turn from one bit of work to another. Dreams were for young people, so they were, and she had hers – and much good they had done her!

Would have liked a husband so well as other women; a man to dig in the garden, summer-time, and set by the fire o' winter evenings. Someone to go up around with, and talk to – but, well, she couldn't put another in Ben's place. He had not treated her right, but there it was.

Queer fit that she should be dreaming again after all this time. She could have said that she was listening for a certain step. Dusk and his step on the hard country of the road! He had not come that way for a-pretty-many years.

She looked up, hearing the click of the gate. Last night she had 'seen' his face in the pool of lamp-light. She felt no surprise, therefore, that the man hesitating on the drexel should be Farmer Williams of West Vose.

Last time he had come to Noon Vears he had been a young man – both of them young – now he was middle-aged and had grown so fat the jelly of him shook. Some hill to come up, so it was, and he was panting like a wind-broken snail.

He stood, looking in, looking across at Micho Dugga. Physically distressed his expression was also deprecating. Though he was a strong farmer, had lately bought the land he tealed, he would not venture to cross this threshold unless given leave.

The woman was in no hurry to ask him in. She put her work aside and went to the door. 'You?' she said.

He stood before her like a child whose misdoings have been brought home to it, and who wants to be taken back into favour. 'I never done you no 'arm,' he said anxiously.

'You can come in,' and he followed her like a whipped dog. 'There – I don't bear you no ill-will, Ben; nor,' she hesitated – 'nor the boy don't neither.'

'He knaw then?'

'Village don't like for anyone to grow up iggorant.'

Williams crossed the flagged blue floor, took the chair at the end of the table. He was tired and under his eyes the patches of loose skin were creasy full. Micho Dugga began to fold away the breadths of purple. ''Tes a braäve walk for you from Vose – nowadays.'

'Seemed natural to walk, somehow,' the man told her. 'And, anyway, the mare didn't 'pear to be right at all.'

In the days of their mutual youth he had not had a horse. His walking to-day told her that he was come by way of the past.

'What be you wanting of me, Ben?'

He hesitated, leaning on the table and looking anxiously across at the woman whom, to please his father, he had left. She understood – all the things he didn't and, if she didn't hold the past against him, why, she might tell him what to do. 'You – you always had the sight.'

The bitterness she had felt when she saw him at the door had given place to pity. Poor chap. Poor old chap. 'That's of it,' she agreed. 'I can "see", but I can't do nothing.'

'You can tell I what to do, and 'tis all I do want.' His fat reddish face crinkled in an annoyed self-pity. 'There's someone who is ill-wishing of me, and I got to know who 'tis. Things is all turning bad. Last week old sow ate her farrow, and now mare's acting as if she'm bewitched. Sure, I don't want to lose she.'

The crimsons were dying off the great arch from Brown Willhay to the sea, and it was dark in the room. Micho lit the lamp and drew the red curtains across the blue blind. 'You got to "see" for yourself,' she said. 'Abide there while I get the glass.'

She ran – a girl again – up the boarded-off stairs, but, once in the upper room, put a hand to her breast and sank down on the side of the bed. To see him once more, to have him sitting there below.

As the years between were such a many, she belonged to have forgotten, yet her heart was beating like on that first day …

She must pull herself together, for poor dear needed her help, yes fye, and she would do what she could. Once before he had come to her in distress – his father had wanted him to marry Annie Nichols because she had been left money, and he had come to her, Micho Dugga.

She had not been able to prevent him doing of it, neither. A man travels his own road. Now again …

She wiped her tears, tried to still the trembling of her body. She must keep steady, but oh, 'twas troubling, so it was. A man digged a grave with his tongue and fulled it in and you thought that was the end, but the ghostes crep out. You could not lay them. Heave their heads up they did, spite of the years and that.

She took the mirror from the wall and went downstairs. She did not need to look in the glass; could 'see' in the pool of light; and even when she shut her eyes. It grew on you – 'seeing'. But it was different with Ben.

'Stand there, your back to the light. There, so that it fall on the glass. Now, look in steady while I say the words.' She muttered the ancient formula which, after all, was prayer – of a sort. He could not hear what she said. It was not right that he should. He only knew that the incantation was repeated three times and that – gradually – the polished surface of the mirror was growing dark – like water when it is near the boil.

She hushed and waited. If he 'saw', she knew who it would be. The woman had not kept her mouth shut, and it was common talk that Williams had cheated her.

'There's a cloud,' he said, his voice thick.

Micho stood at his elbow. 'And in the cloud?'

'Something –' he blinked to clear his sight, 'something black. She've her back turned, but I know who 'tis.'

'Ah!'

''Tis Sandra Treffry.'

'Why should she ill-wish you?'

We fallied out over Gorm Medder. I told she not to bid for 't at the sale, that if she didn't I'd see she wasn't the loser. You do know the farm was sold in one lot and so she couldn't have bid. Yet she think she've a right to that field. But 'tis my farm and I am not going to give she the pick o' the land.'

Certain of his righteousness he was, but Mrs Treffry told a different tale. She had been offered the field before ever the farm was put up to auction and he had asked her not to take it but to come in with him and buy the whole. She had agreed to that. Then he had gone privily to the owner and made an offer, which the man had accepted.

Micho did not challenge his story. It was nothing to her. 'But Sandra Treffry have a dark power,' she said.

He gave the glass to her and she turned it face down on the table.

'Don't I know it?' he cried. 'Isn't that why I'm here to-night?'

The woman shook as if caught in a sudden breath of arctic air. Yes, fye, Ben asked, and people – people like herself – gave.

'Bible can tell 'ee what's best to do,' was all she said.

'Yes, sure.' This was an oracle he had often consulted. He had done so in this very cottage, and he went to the shelf.

Micho's heart contracted. Ah, then, so he, too, he had not forgotten? The book was old, with time-browned pages and a number of scratchy entries – births and deaths – on the inside of the cover. Williams gave it to her and fetched the door-key.

''Twill tell us right,' he said, cheerfully expectant.

She set the book between them on the table, then, taking Ben's hand – oh, the touch of him – held it while she uttered the prescribed formula, and opened the book. Shutting his eyes, he laid the key blindly on the page. They bent greying heads to read: –

'Agree with thine adversary quickly.'

The man stood back. 'What do it mean?'

'It mean that if Sandra Treffry think she've a right to Gorm Medder,' she said reluctantly, 'you've got to let she have it.'

The red of his face darkened, his lips turned bluish, but he looked set as Vose Head. 'I can't, my dear; I can't.' Gorm was worth more to him than a farrow of pigs, more even than his mare. 'Set you down a minute and I'll tell 'ee for why.'

She obeyed and, leaning on the table, stared into the darkly bright pool below the lamp. A dark surround of cloth and the splash of light.

''Tis this way. I've got Peter coming back from Canada to help me with the farm. 'Tain't to be supposed he'd hold with my giving a bite out of it. You know how Gorm lie, side on to the sea. That bit of coast has its vally ...'

He spoke from the shadow beyond the lamp and she could hardly hear what he said. She was listening to the cries of drowning men. Driven out of her course by a succession of Atlantic gales, the ship had struck a rock. She knew Peter, Ben's only son, by sight, and she was 'seeing' him in the pool.

A drowned, pallid face – Peter would not come home to help his father teal West Vose.

'Then I got to put by for Jennifer's marriage penny.'

Jennifer? Micho was not 'seeing' now, but she knew. Luke Hellier was some handsome, and the maid was snaking out to meet him unbeknownst. She met him in the fields by day and, after dark, in the deep lanes – and Luke was a married man. No need of marriage pennies for the like of Jennifer.

'Your grandchildren,' said Micho quietly, 'will be like my son – bastards.'

He looked up, more than startled. 'What be saying, you?'

Her face – wide and with eyes slightly aslant – was that of a sleep-walker. 'At long last,' she told him in a stilly way that was empty of personal emotion, 'things do be evened up. You'd be wise if you gave Sandra the medder.'

He proffered a last excuse. 'I got to think of me old age.'

'Yours?' She was beholding the heart at which the knives of Mrs Treffry's ill-will were jabbing – that diseased, fat heart.

'Year or two after Peter come home I want to goo out of the farm and live "independent"! Got to save all I can for that.'

She put a hand between her eyes and the pool of light. She had seen, and she did not want to see. The knowledge that she had was too heavy – it was the end. No, for even now … if he would take heed. A following fate was at his heel, crowding upon him. It might be delayed – oh, surely – turned aside.

'Ben, my dear life,' she said, and her voice trembled with the urgency of her unchanging heart. 'Sandra Treffry's cottage is between this and the farm. You pass it going home. Ben – stop and settle up with she. 'Tis most urgent that you should.'

'I'd rather risk –'

'You dunno what 'tis you risk.'

'But you'll help me all you can?'

Her voice rose. 'Ah, my dear, I haven't no dark power. Don't 'ee delay, Ben. Agree with her …'

He stared, a little shaken. 'I – I dunno.'

'She'm stronger'n you.'

'Stronger'n me?' Aw, now –' He felt uncomfortable. Was there real danger? He doubted, could not quite believe. 'Do you mean that if Sandra Treffry think she have a grievance against me, I'm to give in about it and let her have her way?'

Micho nodded eagerly. 'I do that.'

'Tedn't jonic, then.' It wasn't fair, indeed it was not, and if it had been other than Micho who urged this on him he would have laughed. But Micho – he could not go against her. Yet, give up Gorm! If it had been Cunegar, or Pigs' Park, but Gorm –

What was Micho saying in that queer voice? 'In a matter of life and death – land is dirt.'

'Death?' he repeated, thinking of the mare. Lose she, would he? And all for an old woman's spite. He would like to let out her black blood, so he would. He had come on a fool's errand, for here was no aid but only advice he did not want to take. Not if he could anyway help it, no. Well, well, nothing to do but clop over home again.

He got up gloomily and found Micho between him and the door. It seemed as she could not let him go. She talked, and every word she said made him feel more uneasy. Them tales of hers, true they were and he knew it. Might be a good thing to do as she was telling. Might be – well, he didn't know, he would think it over.

'Agree with thine adversary *quickly*.' Micho wouldn't hear of his thinking it over.

'"This very night",' said she, and her words struck through his unwillingness. Something outside Micho, outside his mind, was 'requiring' this of him. Well, then, he'd – he'd do it. See Sandra that very night. On his way back –

'Haven't got a drop of something, I suppose?'

'Don't keep nothing in the house.'

Poor dear looked tired, done. 'But if you'll wait I could make 'ee a cup o' tea. 'Twould hearten 'ee for a walk back – and no trouble, no trouble at all.'

'No, no; I must be getting on. 'Tis a long way across they commons.'

She could remember when it had been too short for her reputation, and her smile was thin. Not that she had ever borne him ill-will. As she saw the matter, it had been her fault that she had gotten a hurt at his hands. A woman should not trust a man; if she did, she must take the consequences – and every mother's daughter belong to know that.

Moreover, to-night, the past was remote and unimportant. Between herself and Ben was the tie – the tie that links a man to his woman – and he had proved it by coming to her. At the bottom and at the back of things was his reliance on her and her inevitable response. 'Tisn't the living alone that makes a body feel lonely.

Micho went with her man to the door – to the gate – then stood in the lane to watch him take the field path which led across the unfenced lots to the commons. The last time she would be watching him from her cottage.

A light was burning in Sandra Treffry's window, and with a shudder, Micho thought of the widow's thoughts running, dark and fierce, running like stoats on a trail. She went in and shut the door between herself and them. Although she had not 'the power' she could pray.

The night was moonless but, above the sea, light lingered. Williams crossed the field of ripening barley, the field of lucerne, the freshly-ploughed land. The soil was light and sandy, yet for a tired man this last was heavy going. The excitement of his talk with Micho was passing and he realized that he was weary. The plod, plod of one foot after another was as much as he could manage, and it was fulish of Micho, so it was, to have asked him to see Mrs Treffry that night. Later on.

Perhaps

After all, wrongdoing was a matter of law and, as Mrs Treffry had no writing to show, his conscience was clear. Besides, how did he know Micho Dugga wasn't in league with the woman? Once on a time he had promised to marry Micho and it hadn't been convenient. Maybe she was still holding of it against him.

He couldn't be sure …

A piece of unfenced road took him past the gate of Mrs Treffry's cottage. Although the red blind was drawn, he knew that she was behind it. He thought of his wife. If she ever heard tell of what he had been doing that evening she'd give him no peace. Say he had been 'fried for a fool', she would.

More especially if he gave way about Gorm Meddow. No – best sleep on it. Perhaps he would ride over the morrow's morn and come to some arrangement. He would not give Sandra Treffry the meadow, but he might let her rent it. He would do it because she was a poor widow and he had a good heart. Witching him? He wasn't afraid of that.

Fulish of Micho to think he could stop on his way home, and he so tired; stop and go in and settle the matter. Woman would think he was maäzed. No, to-morrow ...

* * * * *

In the hush of her cottage Micho sat with her back to the lamp. The grey walls ringed her from the black of the night, and about them the whips of feathered tamarisk were stirless in the still air. She was muttering to herself, saying the same words over and over. But although she prayed, she also listened, waiting.

From somewhere in her neglected garden a thin scream of anguish cut the dark. The prayer was hushed on her lips. 'They stoats have made their killing,' she thought, shivering.

They would no longer be thirsty.

* * * * *

In the valley bottom some labouring men, on their way to work the following morning, found Farmer Williams with his face towards the farm he had lately bought, and with his hands clutching the earth.

His death, the doctors said at the inquest, had been due to fatty degeneration of the heart.

H. D. Lowry

ON FRIDAY NIGHT

'Love and Duty were at odds;
Duty seemed to win the day:
But when Love made feint to flee,
Duty flung his arms away.'

I

Every Friday evening the volunteers assemble at the barracks for drill, and afterwards march down into the town to the music of their band. It is not yet decided which of the volunteer bands of the neighbourhood is actually the best: the question, in truth, is continually under discussion in the correspondence columns of the *Western Argus*. But we may at least assert with confidence that ours is a very good band when not called upon for tunes beyond its knowledge; and since one can't live, even in Tallywarn, with a pulse perpetually at sixty, we are ever glad of the advent of Friday evening.

The barracks, a rusty square-built erection, stands in a great walled yard, where the recruits learn to form fours and to hold a rifle courageously. In this yard the drill takes place on Fridays, and from here when drill is over the volunteers march forth into the town. Their way lies always through Tallywarn Street, a thoroughfare demanding the minutest possible description.

A long time ago, I think, a few miners built themselves cottages beside the highroad at a spot conveniently near to the mines at which they worked, and gradually a little village grew up thereabouts. They called it Tallywarn, and as the village grew into a town – a 'church-town' – the parent street still kept its original name. Even I remember when, except for certain shops at the end nearest the town, it was but a double line of two-story cottages.

They were tiny dwellings, built of rough-hewn blocks of granite, and rusty, shapeless stones brought hither from the 'burrows' which have been thrown up in the sinking of mine-shafts. The outlines of each stone, where the mortar showed, were touched out with whitewash, and he was a lazy man, or in the very grip of poverty, who did not see to it this tracery was frequently renewed. The doors, painted dark-green by preference, were usually open; and there the women stood in hours of leisure for purposes of social intercourse, and to watch the current of life in the long street. Through the doorway one saw in passing the mantel with its array of shiny chinaware, its 'clomen' image of a blood-stained white 'Bethgelert', and the pitted concrete floor strewn carefully with sand. From the rough slate roof, daubed here and there with plaster to keep out the wet, the rain dripped overwhelmingly upon the pavements, for 'launders' in those days were things as yet beyond the horizon of our dreams. Therefore on rainy nights one chose the middle of the road, fearing the collected downpour of the roofs. On finer days – let it suffice that the pavements were of the kind known as 'cobble'. The name has been supposed to hint at a suspicion that they were the invention of a cobbler gifted with a keen eye for the interest of his trade. At any rate, it was neither pleasant nor prudent to choose the pavements in the old days of Tallywarn Street.

But all this is rapidly changing. The pavements are of granite now, or of concrete; and in the houses there is vast improvement. He that would build a house in Tallywarn can lease land only upon the curious 'three lives system'; and nowadays each cottage as the lives fall in is straightway demolished to make room for a building of much greater pretensions. In the old days there were displayed in the front window of almost every cottage a few oranges, a card of pen-holders, or half a dozen bottles wherein the gaudy sweets had melted to a Liberty-hued mass of stickiness. In most of them, also, you could buy such 'marinated' pilchards as made a feast of the miner's tea. But all this is altered nowadays, for there are fine shops all along Tallywarn Street, and on the spot where old Tom Penberthy's cottage used to stand there is a big establishment, which has already had one fire and a narrow escape. I have reason to remember the spot, for it was Penberthy that first taught me to smoke, on the afternoons when I took him an allowance of tobacco I had secured for him. It soothed his pride, I fancy, to have me share the shag, especially as the pipe I used was his. But conceive the delicacy which kept him from confessing that pigtail – a thing I could not have touched – was in reality far more to his taste than the milder brand we shared. Some day, then, Tallywarn Street will be a handsome one. At present, inasmuch as many of the cottages remain, the architecture is a little mixed.

At about seven o'clock on Friday nights the people begin to gather in twos and threes on the pavement in Tallywarn Street. The miners come to their doors in shirt-sleeves and smoke. A feeling of quiet expectation is in the air, and presently there is a general stir when the sound of martial music comes from afar off. You can tell the Tallywarn band by the tunes they play; and immediately all the people look up the long street to where it takes a sudden turn and the Bryanite chapel seems to block the way. At last a black mass, gleaming here and there with brass and steel, is visible against the chapel, and the volunteers come marching down the street. The crowd that accompanies and envelopes the band is so large as to fill the whole breadth of the street: going the other way you must take shelter in shop or doorway until it has passed. 'Tis a smaller concourse, but still considerable, that marches alongside of the volunteers themselves. And, indeed, there is something fine in this brief hebdomadal grandeur of quite ordinary and approachable men. We who are not of the corps cannot but admire the far-away splendour which our friends of other days put on for this one hour of Fridays. So the crowd grows larger, the music louder, until a sharp, stern voice, strained a little, and unnatural, as if the tones were but assumed for this one splendid moment, cries 'Right Wheel!' and the band, the volunteers, and the attendant crowd, pour into the Square. They halt, and the band ceases to play. Then that same sharp voice commands the volunteers to do one or two of the things that volunteers are in the habit of doing. A bugle sounds, and the men fall out.

The Literary Institution stands within the Square, and from beneath its portico of granite some half a dozen of its *habitués* watch the scene. It is generally understood that the one night in all the week when you can be sure of getting a look at the *Times* is Friday. Every night at half-past six, old Cap'n Tregurtha (the oldest member) walks up to meet Smith's boy, and secures the paper, and you are lucky if he has laid it aside at nine o'clock. But on Friday nights there is a struggle within him as soon as the band becomes audible, between his love of information and what I may call the Tallywarn in him. Always the inborn craving for excitement conquers eventually. He lays aside the paper with an obvious regret, and with a meaning look, as of one that would fain put the company upon their honour. But it is still possible, if you are moderately inured to pathos, to ignore the fact that he has not yet read all that interests him.

In the Square itself the crowd is thick. Shrill whistles tell that friends are seeking one another, and on the pavement, in the Square, or a little way up the street that runs out of it, you may see many a girl waiting more or less obviously for the coming of her lover. A few of the volunteers stroll for the rest of the evening through the streets of the town. I have known young couples from the country to spend their brief honeymoon of a single day in wandering through the streets of Tallywarn Church-town; but that was when the shops were open and the fountain was playing with its gilded ball, pre-eminent among the wonders of a certain curio-crowded, small garden. Some, it is said, are content to go home and put off uniform at quite an early hour in the evening. But they are the exception: many have learned to make Mars the avenger of wounds wrought by Cupid. In Tallywarn a sweetheart is a 'shiner', and down in Shiners' Lane, on Fridays, the Queen's uniform is quite commonly visible. It is currently reported amongst the young men of the town that certain swains, being unhappy in their love, have 'listed before now as a last resource, and found their ladies grew kind beyond all expectation at sight of a chin-strap and rifle.

And these things I have set forth at considerable length, and with all necessary detail, in order that I might impress upon you the great importance of this one event of the week, enabling you to realize the depth of disgrace into which 'Siah Pascoe fell, publicly, and by his own act.

II

'Siah was a miner, and went to work every day at Wheal Fraternity Mine. He was altogether a commonplace young man, not very tall or very handsome, but strongly-built and moderately active. He made no pretensions to good looks, and certainly was by no means clever; but he had a large amount of straightforward common-sense. His world was perhaps a limited one, but he was happily unconscious of restriction, and the things that fell within his horizon were one and all distinctly visible to him. At the time of this narration, for example, he saw very clearly that he loved Tamsin Chegwidden. He met her in the first place at a Sunday-school treat, on Whit-Monday; or, at least, that was the day upon which the story seemed always afterwards to have begun, though he had known her more or less all his life. On this occasion he played at 'kissing-ring', 'twos-and-threes', and 'dig-in-the back' with her, and after a while he began to find these games quite unamusing. He would have delighted in playing at 'dig-in-the-back' with Tamsin in a ring where all the rest were girls. His constant choice of her under those circumstances might have revealed to her the depth of his devotion, otherwise beyond the power of expression. But now there were at least a score of males in the ring, and each of them was eager, so far as he was free from supervision of a recognised sweetheart, to render Tamsin the delicate attentions for which these Whitsun games afford so many opportunities.

And the worst of it was that Tamsin clearly liked their courtesies: was as pleased when she had to chase young Tom Trevail round the ring as when it was 'Siah himself that fled from her. Tamsin's father was a miner, earning about a pound a week, and the girl herself was apprenticed to a draper of the town; but she had enjoyed a board-school education, and the gentler sex – albeit none may deny their capacity of extravagance – have power to make a very little material cover great spaces if ever economy is hopelessly necessary. So Tamsin was much more highly veneered than 'Siah.

She was a pretty little thing. For myself, I have ever found it hard to lay aside a kaleidoscope, taken up in an idle moment, even when there were brought to bear upon me the attractions of an occupation far more seriously interesting. One never knows what pretty arrangement of colours may appear at the next turn of the screw. Tamsin was a sort of kaleidoscope in her effect upon the opposite sex. The bits of glass were few in number, perhaps, nor were they capable of falling into a design of great complexity; but the effect was always pleasing, and young men said all sorts of foolish things to her, just to see what prettiness was to come next. If she had been a lady, and they her peers, they would have whispered pretty sayings to her – for she was of the sort that inspire such blossomings of the fancy – and made love laughingly. As it was, they were a little rough sometimes: they shook their kaleidoscope, so to speak.

But in 'Siah's love-making there was no element of light laughter. He was in deadliest earnest before evening came, and it may well be that Tamsin had observed the fact, for it was with him she elected to walk home when the treat was over. They wandered arm-in-arm through the quiet lanes, 'Siah labouring with great thoughts he could not utter, and oppressed by a conflict waged within him between the desire he had to kiss her and a certain stupid something that told him this would be a piece of impossible audacity. For Tamsin rather awed him, now that he was alone with her, and his newborn love. So they walked on almost in silence, and presently came back into the town, and down the quiet street where Tamsin lived. They stopped as they neared the cottage.

'Good-night,' said Tamsin. 'You'll remember Sunday?' For she had told him that on Sundays she attended the evening service 'up to Bryanites'.

'I'll be there,' said 'Siah shortly.

Tamsin waited for a moment, with her hand in his; then she drew it away a little roughly.

'Good-night,' she said again.

'Siah stood and heard the door shut and bolted, and a tired voice greeted her from within the house. And when the shadows of the geraniums had vanished from the white blind of the kitchen, and all was still in the house, he cursed his folly that he had not kissed her. So did Tamsin, mildly, I fancy, or perhaps she only wondered.

III

After this fashion did the love-story of 'Siah Pascoe begin, and for several months it went on pleasantly enough, though not without sundry passages wherein was revealed to him the humanity of his goddess. 'Siah had become economical. He had bought, and now cherished fondly in his home, a really handsome looking-glass. For he thought it manifestly unfair that Tamsin, when he married her, should be the one person in all the world to whom was not permitted the pleasure which arose upon contemplation of her beauty. He even hoped that the money thus expended would bear heavy interest, by arousing in her that love of home, which is the brightest jewel in the crown of the virtuous wife. Also, of the man that sold 'clome' in the Market Square on Saturdays, he had bought several sets of jugs, basins, and so on. And thus his hope of having some day a home of his own seemed assured of speedy realization, when suddenly a genuine catastrophe befell him.

They were walking down Shiners' Lane, and Tamsin had been preternaturally kind. For 'Siah had given her that evening a brooch with big red stones in it – never were rubies redder, rarely half so large – which had cost more than many sets of jugs. And it really was by way of being specially kind that Tamsin told him of the entertainment which was to be given in the Bryanite schoolroom on the next Friday. They are great at entertainments in Tallywarn, and on some nights in winter there must be one, at least, for every hundred of the adult inhabitants. Thus do we keep the pulse from dying away to nothing per minute from sheer lack of excitement. This was a Band of Hope affair of which Tamsin spoke, and there was to be a magic-lantern show, with 'The Life and Death of Livingstone', and the famous comic slides at which everyone in Tallywarn has laughed habitually from childhood. Tamsin told her lover of this entertainment, which was to be given 'admission free, a collection at the close to defray expenses'. Then she awaited his reply; but 'Siah made no proposal.

'Shall us go, 'Siah?' she asked presently.

It is curious how often Love and Duty find themselves ranged upon opposite sides. And then, the other person never will understand that the claims of Duty are paramount. 'Siah, poor fellow! realized this.

'I should like to go,' he said hesitatingly; 'but 'tis drill-night, Friday.'

He paused for an answer not vouchsafed.

'I mus' go t' drill,' he said desperately; ''tis inspection in a fortnight, an' I haven' made myself efficient yet. I shan' have no chance to, neither, not if I don't go Friday. There's sure to be entertainments up to Bryanites' again, an' I don't care 'bout entertainments myself, not in the summer. You come down to Square like you'd belong to, an' we'll gone fer bit walk after drill is done.'

Tamsin said nothing, only his arm seemed to feel the waist falling away from it, and she made a curious little noise in her throat. It sounded unpleasantly.

'Aren't vexed, are 'ee?' said 'Siah, stopping and facing her.

'Well,' she said rapidly, 'I mus' say, 'Siah Pascoe, you'm enough to vex any person. I can't see how you're fo'ced t' go t' drill 't all, an' I don't believe you are, neither. I s'pose you're fine an' proud, walkin' down Tallywarn Street with a gun, an' a great helmet, an' a band playin'. Of course you'd know what you'd like best, an' I can go t' Bryanites' by myself – or get some person else to take me.'

They had emerged from Shiners' Lane, and stood now in the centre of the town, in sight of the tall clock. It was but nine o'clock, and Tamsin might well have stayed with him a little longer; but not even her last threat of unfaithfulness could shake his resolution.

Tamsin gave herself a little angry shake, and said curtly: 'Good-night, then.'

'Siah saw her moving down the street alone, and felt impelled for a moment to follow and at all costs submit himself to her caprice; but meanwhile another girl had joined her, and so the lover went off disconsolate in the opposite direction.

During a long solitary walk he looked at the position of affairs from all possible points of view, and the conclusion forced upon him was that he could not in its hour of need desert the corps he had been so proud to join. He would have defied and outraged all the great ones of the earth to gratify his sweetheart's smallest caprice; but a man's public duty is no light matter. Moreover, there is a sweetness in the first quarrel of true lovers – a melancholy joy in the reflection that one is certainly the most unhappy of earth's prisoners.

As for Tamsin, she felt that she had only shown a proper respect for her own dignity. She had yielded in too many things already to this lover of hers, whose position in life was certainly not all she might have demanded. She would surely go to the entertainment; she would go with some other male, and she would be careful to let 'Siah know what he had lost through his devotion to the pomp and circumstance of being a volunteer. Tom Trevail would jump at the opportunity of taking her, if once he had a hint of her willingness to go with him.

The hint was given. Tom Trevail liked Tamsin, naturally, and he loved adventure. He concealed his astonishment, therefore, and was told to be waiting outside of Tresidder's shop on Friday evening. The shop is situated in Tallywarn Street, towards the centre of the town, and Tamsin had told Tom that she would be able to get away rather early.

It was curious, then, that she did not make her appearance until the Tallywarn band was clearly audible in the distance.

Tom was wont to pride himself upon his fluency and self-possession, but he found it strangely hard to make conversation that night. Tamsin had never looked prettier, but she was silent and ill at ease. She had the air of one having embarked rashly upon an enterprise whose dangers were terrific, once they had been grasped. Her nervousness grew more marked as the volunteers appeared at the top of the street and marched towards them. Even Tom began to realize that 'Siah would very probably have something to say concerning his deeds of that evening.

Poor 'Siah! It was not merely the military ardour of the moment that pursed his lips and gave his eyes their sternness. He had passed a miserable week, and when the town-clock struck eight, as they went down Tallywarn Street, he had a sudden vision of

Tamsin taking her seat in the Bryanite schoolroom – with someone else?

He held his head up well, and looked resolutely straight in front of him. But he could not fail to recognise the familiar scarlet of a ribbon he had given his sweetheart long, long ago, in the days when they were happy together. And then, of course, he needs must steal a look at Tamsin herself. He had thought she would return his glance with scorn and defiance. He could not understand why it was she seemed ashamed of herself, of what she was afraid.

Then he saw Tom Trevail and understood.

It was a summer evening, remember, and the whole of this little drama was clearly visible to all the world. 'Siah did not stop to think. He left his place upon the instant, and walked straight across the road, under the very feet of the other three privates who were in his rank. They stopped, involuntarily, bringing the whole of the rear ranks to halt in wild confusion. Then the crowd stood still to see what catastrophe had befallen, and some of the other volunteers lingered and looked back, wondering that their comrades did not follow. Even the band forgot to keep good time. There was a shouting and much laughter. Through the mingled noises of the mob the torrent of Lieutenant Cock's vituperation cut as the hiss of a rocket is heard through the hum of a gala-night.

But 'Siah heeded none of these things. He walked straight across the road to Tamsin, who turned very pale, and seemed almost to cower against the wall. Tom Trevail turned to meet his enemy, but there was no scene whatever.

'That thee, is it, Tom?' said 'Siah cheerfully. 'Well, I reck'n thee's better go 'long home, m' son. There edn' no call for 'ee t' stop here.'

Tom might have objected, had it been worthwhile; but Tamsin was obviously of 'Siah's opinion, and so he took the proffered advice, vowing inwardly to have no more dealings with women. The volunteers had got themselves into some sort of order by this time, and were marching down the street.

Then 'Siah turned to Tamsin.

'Shall us gone for a walk somewhere, Tamsin?'

And when the volunteer authorities were informed as to the causes which had led to 'Siah's tremendous eccentricity, they agreed that these were a sufficient excuse for an offence which had seemed at first unpardonable.

'For,' as Corporal Tregaskis put it in summing up, 'there edn' no tellin' what a man'll do for a maid.'

Charles Lee

Mr Sampson

On a moorland by-road two cottages stood under one roof. One had four rooms, the other only two – a kitchen below and a bedroom above. It was a lonely spot; the nearest house was a mile away, the nearest village twice as far. Catherine and Caroline Stevens occupied the larger dwelling; the other had been vacant for many years. The sisters owned both houses, and had a modest little income besides, which they supplemented by the sale of the produce of their poultry-yard. Catherine was fifty-five, Caroline fifty-three, and they had dwelt in this solitary place all their lives. Seniority, and a shade of difference in their temperaments, gave Catherine the rule. She was the more active of the two, and had what she humbly called a temper. Speaking in parables, she drank weak tea, while milk and water sufficed for the gentle Caroline. Catherine was the business woman. Eight o'clock on every Thursday morning saw her trudging down the road on her way to a neighbouring market town, with a basket on her arm containing eggs and perhaps a chicken or two, while Caroline, who seldom stirred abroad, stood at the gate and watched her out of sight. Caroline was on the watch again at five in the evening, to greet her on her return with the week's supply of groceries and gossip.

One Thursday she was back a full half-hour before her time. She panted as she sat down, and her eyes were bright with excitement. Caroline's pulse began to flutter.

'Sister,' she said faintly, 'what is 'a'?

Catherine pointed to the fireplace.

'There's somebody want to take it,' she said.

'The house? Never!'

'Ess, the house. A man.'

'Sister! A single man!'

'Ess. A stranger from up the country.'

'Aw, Cath'rine! You didn' –'

'Ess, I did. Why not? Trust me. I know better from worse. A staid man, and his name's Isaac Sampson, and that's a good respectable name – took out of Scripture, both ends of it. And he's to work 'pon the roads, breaking stones, and there an't no solider trade than that, I should think. And he'll pay a shilling a week, and I've took the arnest-money for the first week, and him and the furniture's coming up to-morrow. There!'

Caroline gasped.

'Cath'rine! A single man, and a foreigner! And us all alone!'

'You'm talking foolish, sister. A staid, respectable man, I tell 'e, and sixty if he's a day.

You've seed en too, and spoke to en. He passed o' Tuesday and give us the time o' day.'

'There was two people passed o' Tuesday.'

'This one passed in the morning.'

Caroline reflected.

'Grey whiskers all round, soft black hat up to 'm, stooped a bit, and said "Marnen," broad-like?'

'That's the chap. I reco'nized him to once when 'a spoke to me. A civiller-spoken man I never look to meet. Recommended by the butcher, too. Ess, I asked Mr Pearse about him, and 'a said 'a was honest enough for all he knowed – and that's a deal for a man to say that kill his own meat. I'll tell 'e how 'twas'.

With all its ramifications of detail and comment, the telling of the five minutes' interview in the market-place took half an hour at least. By that time the idea which at first had so terrified Caroline had grown familiar and accepted.

'P'raps if we ask him,' said she, 'he'll kill the chickens for us. I shan't never get over wringing the poor dear mortals' necks, not if I live to be a hundred.'

It was late next evening when Mr Sampson arrived with his possessions in a farm-cart. The sisters watched, peeping from behind the geraniums into the rainy April twilight, while the furniture was being unloaded. Evidently Mr Sampson was no Sybarite. When a chair, a table, a bed, a box, and a miscellaneous bundle had been carried in, the empty cart drove off, and the new tenant went in and shut the door.

'My life! did 'e see?' exclaimed Catherine. 'No carpet, no mats, no ornyments, not so much as a li'll picksher! A rough sort, I seem. I do 'most wish I hadn' took his shilling.'

'Poor soul!' murmured Caroline. 'At his age, and nobody to look after him! I'm glad we laid the fire. He'll be looking for a bit o' comfort in a strange house, and there an't no better comp'ny than a good fire, nor no worse than a black grate this wisht malincholy weather. I hope he'll light the fire.'

'He'll be biling the water for his tay, I reckon,' said Catherine, 'so he's bound to light en.'

'Catherine! I didn' see no kettle carr'd in!'

'Nor I nuther, come to think. P'raps 'twas in his box.'

'With his Sunday clo'es! A dirty black kettle! Aw, Cath'rine!'

'Well, must be somewheres. The man must have his tay. 'Tidn' in nature for a mortal to go without tay.'

'Well, I do hope he've lighted the fire. That kitchen's like a bird-cage for draughts ... Aw, my dear life! what was that?'

They were sitting by the fire, and out of the back of the grate came a sudden sound, a sharp double tap, twice repeated. They looked at each other in some alarm, for it seemed to be in the room with them. Then Catherine's face cleared.

'I know,' she said confidently. 'He's knocking his pipe agin the bars of the grate. He's a-setting there, close up to we, smoking away 'front of the fire.'

'Like father used,' said Caroline. 'Nice and comfor'ble, with his boots off, I shouldn' wonder. There! now he's raking the fire. 'Tis 'most as if 'a was in the same room with us.'

They kept silence for a while, trying to realize their new neighbour's proximity through the party wall, straining their eyes after the shadow of his company. Presently Catherine had an idea.

'How if we should rattle the fire-showl a bit?' she suggested. ''Twill seem more sociable, like.'

Caroline stretched out her hand, and drew it back, reddening.

'I don't like to, somehow. It seem so – so forward, like-a-thing.'

'Aw, nonsense! How's going to know we done it a-purpose? And the grate wants righting up, anyhow. Here, give it me.'

She scraped up the ashes with defiant vigour, and let the shovel fall clattering.

'There! Now call your sister all the bold 'uzzies you can think for!'

Caroline smiled faintly, holding up her finger. But even if Mr Sampson heard the signal, he was not imaginative enough to interpret its kindly meaning, and respond. It was ten minutes before they heard another sound – the double tap again.

'One more pipe, and then to bed,' commented Catherine. 'That was father's way.'

They remained over the fire, talking a little in discreet tones, their ears ready to seize the slightest sound through the wall, their imaginations busy with the man who sat unconscious within a few feet of them. Once he coughed, and they speculated on the sound. Was it an ordinary clearing of the throat, as Catherine maintained, or was Caroline right in detecting a hollow ring, and arguing a weakness of the chest? Once he whistled a few slow notes; they recognised a fragment of a revival hymn, and drew faourable deductions. If it had been a low pothouse song –! At last they heard once more the tap-tap of the pipe-bowl, followed immediately by the scraping of chair-legs on the bare floor.

'Just like I said!' exclaimed Catherine. 'He's going to bed now. La me! 'tis nine o'clock! How quick the time have gone, to be sure!'

'I'm glad we took him in, good man,' said Caroline. 'It make a bit o' comp'ny, don't 'a?'

Sleep was long in coming to them after the social excitements of the evening. They awoke later than usual next morning, and were only down in time to see Mr Sampson go past on his way to work. They hurried to the gate.

'He don't stoopy so much as I thought,' said Caroline. 'A clever man for his age, I seem. Idn' his left-hand coat pocket plummed out, like?'

'So 'tis. Got his dinner inside, I reckon. Wonder what 'a is.'

'Cath'rine! How's going to manage for his meals?'

'Dunnaw. Cook 'em himself, s'pose, same as we. And a wisht poor job 'a 'll make of it, I seem.'

'Poor chap! We – we couldn' offer to cooky for 'm, s'pose?'

'Wouldn' be fitty – not till we do know him better. Pretty and foolish we'd look if 'a was to say "No, thank 'e." '

'P'raps he'll ask us to,' said Caroline as they turned to go in. 'Aw, Catherine! If 'a haven' gone and left the door all abroad!'

'So 'a have, the careless chap! I've a mind –'

She turned about, looked warily down the road, and then marched resolutely out of the one gate and in at the other.

'What be doing, sister? Cath'rine, what be about?'

Catherine's face was set. 'I'm going to geek in,' she said, and went straight up to the door. A fearful fascination drew Caroline after her. Together they peeped into the room.

'There's his mug and tay-pot on the table,' whispered Catherine. 'I don't see no plate.'

'Nor no kettle,' murmured Caroline. 'I'd a jealous thought 'a hadn' got no kettle. Look, he've a-bilet the water for his tay in that dinky saucepan.'

'I'm going inside,' Catherine announced, and stepped boldly forward. Caroline cast a nervous glance behind her, and followed.

'Here's a frying-pan, all cagged with gress; haven' been claned, not since 'twas bought, by the looks of it. He've had bacon for his brukfas'.'

'Here's the piece in the cupboard – half a pound of streaky; and nothing else but the heel of a loaf.'

'I claned up the floor yes'day, and now look to en! Such a muck you never behold.'

'Cath'rine! We can't leave en go on this-a-way! It go to my heart to see en so.'

'No more we won't We'll come in after brukfas' and do up the place.'

'But he'll know. He might be vexed.'

'Don't care,' said Catherine recklessly. 'If he's vexed, he can take himself off. This room have got to be clane and fitty agin Sunday, and clane and fitty we'm going to make it.'

One thing led to another. On his return Mr Sampson found the house swept and garnished. The grate was polished, the fire laid; a strip of old carpet was spread before the hearth, another strip guarded the entry. A piece of muslin had been nailed across the window, and on the window-shelf stood two geranium plants, gay with scarlet blossom. The table was set for a meal, with knife, fork, mug, and plate, and on the plate was an inviting brown pasty. He went upstairs, and found his bed neatly made, and a bright-coloured text pinned on the wall where it would meet his waking eyes. Mr Sampson pondered on these things while he ate the pasty to the last crumb. Presently he went out and knocked at his neighbours' door. Catherine opened it; the other conspirator trembled in the background.

'Thank 'e marm,' said Mr Sampson shortly.

'You'm welcome, Mr Sampson. Anything we can do to make 'e comfor'ble –'

Mr Sampson shifted his feet, spat respectfully behind his hand, and said nothing. Catherine gained courage.

'Won't 'e step inside?' she asked, and immediately bobbed backwards, uttering an odd little squeak, as her skirt was tugged from behind by the alarmed Caroline. Mr Sampson stared at her in mild astonishment.

'No, thank 'e – do very well here,' he said. 'Pasty was capital,' he added after a pause.

'Sister made it. She's gen'rally reckoned a good hand.'

'Thank 'e marm', said Mr Sampson, raising his voice and addressing the obscure interior over Catherine's shoulder. The vague figure within responded with a flutter and an inarticulate twitter. 'If you'll leave me know what's to pay –'

'We won't say nothing 'bout that, Mr Sampson. But I was going to say – sister and me have been talking things over – and I was going to ask 'e –'

With many hesitations Catherine expounded a plan of mutual accommodation, by which she and Caroline were to cook his food and keep his rooms tidy in return for the heavier outdoor work – digging the garden, gathering fuel from the moor, and the like. A special clause stipulated for the wringing of the chickens' necks. Mr Sampson agreed readily, and grew spasmodically confidential. Lived with a widowed sister till last year. Sister married again, and gone to live in the shires. Doing for himself ever since, and making a terrible poor job of it. Knew no more about cooking than a cow did about handling a musket. Could make shift to fry a rasher, and that was about all. Reckoned he'd do very well now, and was properly grateful to the ladies for their proposal.

'Aw, you'm kindly welcome, Mr Sampson!' It was Caroline who spoke, close up to her sister's elbow.

'Thank 'e marm,' he replied, and Caroline shrank back into the shadows.

The arrangement worked capitally. Every evening on returning from work, Mr Sampson found his house in order, his table laid, and something savoury warming at the fire – a broth of leeks and turnips, maybe, or maybe a potato pie. The pasty for to-morrow's 'crowst' was ready in the cupboard. Having supped and digested, he would go forth and work in the garden till dusk, when he would come round to the door for a few goodnight words with the sisters. Bit by bit, Caroline's maidenly tremors sub-sided. She gathered confidence before this mild, slow-spoken old man, and when at the end of the second week he came to pay his rent, and was invited once more by Catherine to step inside, and was politely demurring, it was the younger sister's soft: 'Do 'e now, Mr Sampson,' that decided him to enter.

When he had gone, they agreed that his company manners were unexceptionable. Thrice he had to be pressed to light his pipe before he would consent, and then – what touched them most – every few minutes he bestirred his stiff joints, went to the door, and put his head outside like a real gentleman, instead of making a spittoon of their spotless fireplace. They felt safe in repeating the invitation. Soon no invitation was needed. He dropped in as a matter of course every evening at the accustomed hour, sat for the accustomed period in his accustomed chair, and bore his part in the accustomed talk. It was a wonder to Caroline that she had ever been afraid of him, now that he had come to be as much a part of the natural scheme of things as the grandfather clock that ticked in the corner by the staircase. Indeed, with his round moon-face, his slow and weighty speech, and his undeviating regularity of habits, he bore no small resemblance to that venerable timepiece. The comparison does him great honour; for Grand'fer, as the sisters affectionately called it, held a deservedly high place in their esteem. Those who dwell in crowded marts may regard their clocks and watches as mere mechanical contrivances; but to two lone women in a solitary place, the household clock, especially if it be such a clock as Grand'fer, with his imposing seven foot of stature and his solemn visage of shining brass, is something more than a mere nest of cogs and pulleys. Such a clock is the real master of the house; he orders the comings and goings, the down-sit-tings and uprisings of his votaries; his ponderous ticking pervades every room; when he huskily clears his throat, voices are hushed and respectful silence is kept till he has delivered his hourly message to transient mortality; the operation of winding him up is an affair of solemn ritual. It was not long before Mr Sampson heard the history of the two outstanding events in Grand'fer's otherwise untroubled existence – the vain and impious attempt of a misguided stranger to carry him off in exchange for a paltry twenty pounds in gold, and that other episode of his frenzy, when, in the dead of night, he had a false alarm of Eternity, and struck a hundred and seventeen on end, while the sisters, called from their beds by the dread summons, hovered about him, white-robed and tearful.

The four made a comfortable and well-balanced *partie carrée*. Catherine led the talk; Mr Sampson seconded her bravely; Caroline was the best of listeners; while Grandf'er filled the gaps, when gaps occurred, with his well-conned discourse, sooth-ing to hear with a clear conscience at the end of a well-spent day. There was no more harmonious and happy a fireside company in all the countryside.

Then came the catastrophe. One evening – it was a Thursday, about three months after Mr Sampson's arrival – he knocked at the door as usual. It remained shut. He tried the latch. It would not open. He called out, and Catherine's voice made answer:

'Grieved to say it, Mr Sampson, but you can't come in.'

'How? What's up with 'e?'

'I can't tell 'e, but you mustn' come in. Will 'e plaise to go away, Mr Sampson?'

He thought it over slowly. 'No,' he said at last. 'Not till I do know what's the mat-ter.'

'Aw dear!' There were tears in her voice. 'I beg of 'e, go!'

'Not till I hear what's up,' he repeated.

A murmur of agitated talk came to his ears.

'If you'll open door,' he said, 'you can tell me comfor'ble. I won't come in if you don't wish, but I'm bound to know what's up.'

More whispering. Then a bolt was withdrawn and the door opened an inch or two.

'Come,' he said, and pushed gently. The door resisted.

'I can't look 'e in the face. If I must tell 'e, I must, but I die of shame if I look 'e in the face.'

'So bad as that?'

'Worse. Worse 'n anything you could think for. Aw dear! How be I to tell 'e?'

The door threatened to close again. Mr Sampson said nothing, but quietly set his foot in the gap between door and door-post. It was a substantial foot, substantially shod. The mere toe of it, which alone was visible within, was eloquent of masculine determination. Catherine made a desperate plunge.

'Mr Sampson, they'm a-talking about us.'

'How *us*?'

'You and we. 'Tis all over the country – scand'lous talk. Aw, that I should live to see the day!'

'If you'll kindly give me the p'tic'lars, marm,' he said patiently, after a pause.

'We never thought no harm,' she sobbed. ''Twas only neighbourly to offer to do for 'e, and you all alone and so helpless. I'm sure the notion never come into our heads.

'Tis a sin and shame to say such things.'

'Say *what* things?'

'Say – we – we'm a-trying to catch 'e!'

The terrible word was out. The pair within awaited the result with trembling expectation. It came – first a long low whistle; then – could they believe their ears? – an unmistakable chuckle. Catherine shrank back as from the hiss of an adder. The door swung open and Mr Sampson confronted them, his eyes a-twinkle with sober enjoyment.

'That's a stale old yarn,' he said. 'Heard en weeks ago. Only 'twas told *me* 'tother way about. Don't mind telling 'e I mightn' have thought of it else.'

'Thought of what, Mr Sampson?'

'Why, courting of 'e, to be sure,' said the gentleman placidly.

The ladies gasped in unison.

'You don't mane to say you – you'm –' stammered Catherine at last.

'Ess, I be, though. This fortnit, come Sunday. If you'll kindly take it so, and no offence.'

'But – but we never noticed nothing.'

'No, s'pose. 'Tis like the cooking, you see – I'm a terrible poor hand at it. Now 'tis out. Ben't vexed, I hope.'

'Aw, no! But –'

'There!' he hurried on. 'Think it over, will 'e? There's the saving to consider of, you see, money and trouble both. And I've put by a pound or two. Not so young as I was, but we an't none of us that. And not so dreadful old, nuther. Wouldn' think of parting of 'e; reckon we could be pretty comfor'ble together, the three of us, though I can't marry but one of 'e, 'course. So talk it over, will 'e? I'll be round agin to-morrow evening. Good night.'

He had reached the gate before Catherine found voice to recall him.

'Mr Sampson! Plaise, Mr Sampson!'

Well, marm?' he said, slowly returning.

'Ascuse my asking, but – would 'e mind telling – telling *whichy* one you was thinking of – of courting?'

Mr Sampson's fingers went to the back of his head.

'Now you'll be laughing upon me,' he said. 'Whichy one? Well, I don't know whichy one, and that's the truth. But it don't make no odds,' he added cheerfully. 'Settle it between yourselves. I ben't noways p'tic'lar.'

'La, Mr Sampson! Who ever heard tell of such a thing? cried Catherine, giggling in spite of herself.

'That's right!' he chuckled. 'Laugh so much as you've a mind to. Sister laughing too?'

Caroline's nervous titter passed muster.

'Now we'm comfor'ble,' he remarked. 'Reckon I can step inside now, and no scandal.'

In he walked, none hindering, took his usual chair, spread his hands on his knees, and beamed on the sisters.

'Ess,' he continued. 'I'm like the old cat in the bonfire – don't know which course to steer. Never was such a case, s'pose. I've turned it over this way, and I've rolled it over that way, and I can't come to no conclusion. Always seeing you together, you see, I can't part 'e nohow, no more than milk from water. But don't matter, as I said before. If only you'll be so kind as to settle it between yourselfs –'

'We couldn' do that,' said Catherine emphatically.

'Couldn' 'e, now?' He turned inquiringly to Caroline. Caroline shook her head.

'Wouldn' be fitty,' she murmured.

'Well, you do know best,' said Mr Sampson, a little dashed, and pondered, his eyes on the ground, while the sisters shot sidelong glances at him and avoided each other's looks. He lifted his head and caught Caroline's eye.

'Cath'rine's the best to manage things,' said Caroline, in a hurry.

He looked hopefully at Catherine.

'Caroline's the best cook by far,' she hastened to say.

Mr Sampson thumped his knee.

'That's where 'tis!' he exclaimed. 'The pair of 'e rolled up together 'ud make a complete masterpiece. A man couldn' look for a better wife than the two of 'e 'ud make. That's where 'tis, nor I don't see no way out of it – not in a Christian country. Ah!' he added meditatively. 'These heathen Turks – they know a thing or two after all, don't they?'

'Mr Sampson, I wonder at 'e!' cried Catherine, shocked at this libertine sentiment.

''Tidn' to be thought of, I know that,' he apologized. 'But I can't think of no other way. Without' – he brightened – 'without we should spin up a ha'penny and bide by the fall of en.'

'Never in this house!' exclaimed Catherine, more shocked than ever.

'Don't see how we shouldn',' he maintained stoutly. ''Tis just the same as casting lots, and that's a good Scripture observance. The reg'lar way with these old patriarchs, so I'm given to onderstand; only 'twas shekels with them, I reckon. But shekels or ha'pennies, 'tis all one.'

'If you'm sure 'tis Scriptural,' said Catherine, impressed and half convinced.

'Sound Bible doctrine, my word for 'n. An't that so, marm?' he added, appealing to Caroline.

'I mind a text in Proverbs,' said Caroline shyly, 'which say, "The lot causeth contentions to cease." '

'See!' ejaculated Mr Samson. 'That's of it. "The lot causeth contentions to cease." 'Tis aimed straight at our case. Out o' Proverbs, too! Old Solomon's the chap for we. See how 'a settled that argyment 'bout the baby. And there was two ladies in *that*. Well, then?'

Catherine shook her head doubtfully, but offered no further objection. Mr Sampson produced a handful of coins, chose one with fitting deliberation, and held it up for inspection.

'Now,' he announced. 'If 'a should turn up the old queen, then 'tis Cath'rine. If 'tis the young person with the prong, then Caroline's the one. And up she goes.'

It was not the spin of an expert, and he failed to catch the flying coin. It fell to the ground in the dark corner by Grandf'er. Mr Sampson went down on his hands and knees, while the sisters held their breaths.

'Well, I'm darned!'

The ladies jumped. Mr Sampson rose slowly to his feet, holding the halfpenny at arm's length and smiling foolishly upon it.

'If it had been a lime-ash floor, now,' he said.

'What's wrong?' Catherine found breath to ask.

'Fell in a crack o' the planching, my dear. Found en sticking there edge up, and no head to en, nor yet no tail. Old Solomon himself couldn' make nothing by en. But how come you to have a timbern floor to your kitchen, when mine's lime-ash?'

"Twas father's doing when the house was built,' said Caroline. 'He always liked to take off his boots of a' evening, and lime-ash is that cold-natured, 'tis apt to give 'e chilblains through your stockings.'

'Well, to see how things do turn out!' meditated Mr Sampson.

"Twas ordained, I seem,' said Caroline solemnly.

'A token, sure enough,' agreed Catherine. 'And father's eyes upon us this very minute, I shouldn' wonder. Mr Sampson – I doubt 'tis all foolishness, and we'd best say no more about it.'

'Don't see that,' said he. 'If your father didn' choose to wear slippers, that an't no lawful reason why I shouldn' get married if I want to. Must try some other way, that's all.'

Again he pondered, till Caroline broke the silence with a timid suggestion.

'If,' she hesitated, colouring, 'if we should wait a bit, Mr Sampson keeping away from us meanwhile, p'raps his heart 'ud speak.'

'So 'a might,' said the gentleman dubiously; 'and then agin 'a mightn'. A mazy old organ, b'lieve.'

'Absence make the heart grow fonder, so they say,' remarked Catherine.

'That's very well,' he replied. 'Don't doubt but what 'a do. But how if 'a should make en grow fonder of both of 'e? Where'd us be then? But we'll try if you do wish, though I doubt 'tidn' much use.'

Taking his leave, he paused at the door.

'All the same,' he said, 'I can't help wishing I'd been born a heathen Turk.'

Left alone, the sisters had plenty of food for thought. They sat without speaking, and the longer they sat the harder it became to break silence. For the first time in their lives a veil of reserve was drawn between them, and every moment it thickened and darkened. At last, with a few constrained words for decency's sake, they lit their candles and went to bed. Next morning two heavy-eyed women confronted each other with mistrustful looks over the breakfast-table. The day dragged through on a minimum of conversation, in which no word of their neighbour found a place. Through the morning of the next day they held no communication at all, and the air was heavy with suppressed thunder. In the afternoon Caroline set about her preparations for the usual Saturday baking. The materials were ready on the table, when Catherine came in from the garden. Her searching glance on the table hardened into a fixed glare.

'I thought as much,' she said, in a tense whisper. 'You've been taking those Wyandotte eggs!'

Caroline turned pale.

'S'posing I have!' she made answer at last.

Catherine raised her voice.

'You knowed very well I was going to set Toppy on those eggs to-day.'

Caroline trembled and clutched the edge of the table.

'S'posing I did!' she whispered.

'Then how come you to take those eggs?'

'I – I shall take what eggs I've a mind to – so there!'

'A mean trick, so 'tis. To take my eggs, what I've been saving up for Toppy, and she as cluck as cluck can be, as you very well know, and in her box this very minute, wearing her heart out over the chaney nest-egg, poor fond little worm! Of all the mean tricks, to take my eggs –'

'Aw, you and your bistly old eggs!'

Even for a maiden attempt at scornful sarcasm it was a wretchedly poor one, and its effect was further discounted when the perpetrator instantly burst into a flood of penitential tears. The next moment they were in each other's arms.

'To think of it!' exclaimed Catherine, as their sobs subsided. 'All these years with never a cross word, and now – Aw, drat the man!'

'Sister!'

'Drat the man!' she repeated, revelling in her own profanity. 'Wish we'd never set eyes 'pon him. Sarve him right if we sent him 'bout his business!'

'Sister! When we'm both so good as promised to 'n! Beside, 'a wouldn' go. He's terrible obstinate, for all his quiet ways.'

'A week's notice'll settle en,' said Catherine viciously.

'Cath'rine, we couldn'! Good man – to be slighted by two in one day, and turned out of house and home overplush – we couldn'!'

'It do seem hard,' admitted Catherine. 'But we can't go on like this, that's plain.'

'P'raps he've made his ch'ice by now.'

'If 'a have, 'a can't choose but one of us. And then, where'll the other be? Tell me that!'

'Sister,' said Caroline, and paused, and drew a long breath. 'Sister dear; I – I ben't in no p'tic'lar vi'lence to get married.'

'Caroline Stevens, there's the Bible 'pon the shelf. Lay your hand to 'n and say those words agin, if you can.'

Caroline hid her face in her hands. 'I can't,' she faltered.

'Nor I nuther. And here we be, the two of us, geeking round the corner after one man! At our age, too! 'Tis shameful! I'm black-red all over at the thought of it. Two silly old women – that's what we be.'

'Aw, *don't*, sister!' shuddered Caroline.

'Two silly old women,' repeated the merciless self-abaser. 'But it shan't be so. Thanks be, I got some sense left in my brain, though my heart's a caudle of foolishness. It shan't be so. The longer he stay, the worse 'twill be, and go he shall. How couldn' 'a make up his mind 'fore speak? 'Twouldn' have happened so then.'

''Twas fo'ced upon him to speak.'

'So 'a was. I mustn' be hard 'pon him. 'Tis Doom, I reckon; and better-fit Doom should tend to his battles and murders and sudden deaths, 'stead of coming and plagu-ing quiet, dacent folk. Well, and Doom shan't have it all his own way, nuther. There shan't be no jalous wife nor no sinful-thoughted sister-in-law, not in this locality.'

'Sister, such dreadful talk!'

''Tis my duty to speak plain. There's bound to be suffering come out of it; but any-ways we can choose to suffer respectable. Go he shall.'

The garden gate clicked.

'Cath'rine! Here 'a do come! And aw! if I do live, he's got his best clo'es up!'

'Then 'a *have* made up his mind after all, and he's come to tell us so. But 'tis too late now, and 'a shan't name no names, not if I can help. 'Twill be harder if we do know. Now, Caroline, you'm too soft for this job. You leave en to me, and don't say a word, and, whatever you do, don't start snooling – d'st hear? We got to be hard, or we'll never get rids of him.'

The door was tapped and opened, and Mr Sampson appeared. His hard-pressed holiday suit encased him in its rigid folds, like the stone garments of a statue; his face was one consistent solid smile; a substantial cabbage-rose adorned the lapel of his coat; and his hands – O wonder! – were mailed in enormous black kid gloves. Altogether he made a noble, if stiffish, figure, worthy of any woman's affection. Catherine felt her res-olution tottering. She advanced one desperate step and shot her bolt.

'Mr Sampson, you'll kindly take your week's notice from to-day.'

The wide expanse of smile slowly crumbled, and as slowly heaped itself up into a round O of ineffable astonishment. Caroline began to whimper. Catherine stealthily shook her by the arm, while Mr Sampson's eyes roved to the ceiling, the walls, and the floor, in search of symptoms of universal disintegraton.

'I'm a dazy old bufflehead, I know,' he began at last, 'and I don't azackly seem to get to the rights o' this.'

'There an't no rights to en!' cried Catherine wildly. '(*Will*'e stop snooling, sister!) 'Tis all so wrong as can be, and time to put an end to it. Nor you mustn' ask why, for we can never tell 'e. We'm grieved to put 'e out in any way, and we'm grieved to part with 'e; but go you must, and no questions asked.'

Mr Sampson's scattered wits obeyed his summons. 'If I ben't mistook,' he said, not without dignity, 'there was words passed between us consarning matrimony.'

'Foolish words!' interjected Catherine. 'Foolisher words were never spoke. They've got to be took back.'

'If I ben't mistook,' he continued stolidly, 'I was told to go away and make up my mind – or my heart, as you may say – if so be I could.'

''Tis too late. We'll be thankful if you won't say no more about it.'

'If I ben't mistook,' he went on, with a corroborative glance at his festal attire, 'I come here just now to say I'd come to a conformable conclusion at last. I come here to say – with doo respect to the other lady, who's good enough for anybody, – I come to say I'd pitched my ch'ice on the lady I should wish to commit matrimony with. And the name of that lady –'

'Don't say the word!' cried Catherine. ''Tis hard enough already; don't 'e go to make it harder. Whichever 'tis, her answer have got to be "No." An't that so, Car'line?'

Caroline speechlessly assented.

'With best thanks all the same,' continued Catherine in softer tones, 'and hoping you won't think too hardly of us, and never shall we think other than kindly o' you, and proud we'd ha' been, ayther one of us, if it hadn' been ordained otherwise, as you'll mind I said to once when the ha'penny stood on edge, and – Aw, *will*'e go, and not stand glazing there like a stuck pig!'

Mr Sampson stiffened his back. 'Very well, marm' he replied, and began peeling off a glove. 'I ben't one to fo'ce myself 'pon nobody.' He attacked the other glove. 'Nor I ben't going to state no grievance, nor ask no questions, nor mention no names.' He rolled the gloves into a forlorn and crumpled ball.

'You'll spile 'em,' said Catherine, sniffing audibly. 'Give 'em here.'

She took them, smoothed them out, laid them together, turned one neatly inside out over the other, and gave them back.

'Thank 'e', he said. 'Bought 'em for a funeral I didn' go to; never put 'em on till to-day. Queer how things do turn out. Well, if I got to go, then the sooner the better.' He took the flower from his buttonhole and laid it on the table. '(Meant for the lady of my ch'ice, not to mention no names.) So I reckon I'll go to once.' He fumbled in his pocket. 'I can get a bed over to Churchtown – very good beds at the inn, so I'm told – and I'll send along for my things later on.' He counted some silver out on the table. 'And there's the money owing; two shilling rent for this week and next.'

'Mr Sampson –' Catherine protested through her tears. He raised an implacable hand.

'If you plaise, marm. According to the law of the land, and not wishing to be beholden to nobody. And that's about all, b'lieve. Good-bye.'

'You'll shake hands 'fore go,' pled Catherine.

'No, I don't think,' said the unforgiving old man. ''Tis the Christian thing to do, I know; but there an't no mistake about it, I ought to have been born a heathen Turk.'

Without another word he turned and went. His bent figure passed the window and disappeared.

'He'll scorn us all his life!' wailed Caroline.

'We've done what's right,' said Catherine, 'so don't matter what he think of us. *I* don't care, for one.'

The rose caught her eye. She took it up and lifted it to her face.

'Give it to me,' said Caroline, dry-eyed of a sudden. 'I'll take care of it.'

Catherine whipped it behind her back.

'Meant for the lady of his ch'ice,' she said. 'Maybe you think –'

'I've so much right as you to think –'

They held each other's eyes, and gentle Caroline's look was as hard as her sister's. But the crisis passed as quickly as it had come – with Caroline in a fresh flood, with Catherine in a resolute stamp of the foot.

'It shan't be so!' she declared. Going to the fire, she opened the top of the grate and dropped the flower within. It shrivelled and vanished.

'And there's an end to en,' she said. 'Dust and ashes. And now, sister, snooling won't help us, but work will, or so they say else. Time to pitch baking; come, bustle.'

Phyllis Bottome

An Awkward Turn

She had made the great surrender; she had given up – it was probably only for a short time; still, she had given up – all that she had been trained to think a woman must have. Her husband was fishing in Norway, and she was in Cornwall with the man she loved.

No one knew that she was there; she could go back if she grew tired of it, but at present she wasn't in the least tired of it. She became surer each day that she had been meant for the real things of life: simplicity, love, ideal companionship, the spiritual value of ideas.

Edward Lockett was full of ideas. His tiny bungalow on the headland of the cliff, with the rocks and the sea in the garden, was one of them. A long time ago the farm in which his wife lived, a mile away, was another. He had not been able to unite the two. His wife was one of those capable women, without sympathy, who fall by accident into marriages with literary men.

She made him comfortable, but it is a great mistake to suppose that comfort is all that a man of Edward Lockett's type needs. He needed a woman to make him uncomfortable as well.

Rosamund fulfilled this further need. When she first met him in London she was tired of everything – of yachting, of motoring, of the Russian dancers, even of her dressmaker; for several years she had been extremely tired of her husband. She thought her life was very unreal, and she assured Edward Lockett that there was nothing she found so unbearable as unreality. Edward Lockett believed her, though there were moments when he had his doubts.

The worst of these came after he had inadvertently kissed her and she wrote that they must part. 'Petrarch and Laura had done it,' Rosamund wrote, 'and they must do it, too.' Edward Lockett whistled when he read about Petrarch and Laura; however, they didn't part.

There were inconveniences attached to their situation, and the question was simply whether the inconveniences would grow greater than the situation, or the situation become so absorbing as to overcome the inconveniences.

In the first place, there was always Petrarch and Laura to fall back upon, and in the second, Edward told her of his bungalow by the sea. His wife never came near it, and his daily attendant had never spoken since the day she saw her husband and two sons drowned before her eyes.

It was an intensely romantic idea. Rosamund hesitated, because she was eight and twenty and she had never yet been romantic. It was like eating a new kind of fruit and not being quite sure if it wouldn't poison you. Edward, however, assured her that it wouldn't. He had experienced romances before, and he knew that they were extremely nourishing; he always did his best work after them. He did not tell her this because the great thing about romance is that it shouldn't be in the plural. Still, perhaps she guessed it.

They said it would be for ever; it had already lasted a week. The weather was wonderful for June; the air was full of the scent of the short wild thyme.

All night long they heard at the foot of the lawn the summer music of the sea; all day the heavy bees blundered in and out of the tiny garden. The narrow, empty glen, with its soft-blue summit of sky was as much their own as if they had made it, untenanted, serene, and brimful of their love.

Rosamund was amazed at the immensity of her own feelings. Of course she had always said that love was the strongest force in the world; but still it was a little surprising that, with nothing going on, she wasn't in the least bored. It seemed to her as if she and the earth and Lockett had all been made for this one perfect consummation.

Lockett was clever with her despite their solitude; she did not see too much of him. He wrote for three hours every morning, and when he joined her she had to use all her skill to win him back from his imaginary world. She said to him before she came there:

'Sha'n't I interfere with your work?' And he answered:

'The woman one loves always interferes.'

But he had taken every precaution to prevent her interference. When he had finished writing he came out to her on the rocks. This morning he seemed longer than usual. The sea's soft, pearly blue turned hard and flat; deep shadows fell on the gray rocks; the air grew heavy and drowsy with the summer noon. Rosamund slept; she woke with a start at the sound of sea-gulls laughing overhead. They shook the silence out of the glen; but after they had passed it came back again oppressively, as if it were the herald of something uneasy and sinister. She looked at her watch and sprang to her feet. It was one o'clock. Edward had never been so late before. It was Sunday, and the woman who looked after the house had cleaned up early and left them for the day; she must have passed close by Rosamund while she slept.

The first change in a definite habit is terrible to lovers. Rosamund felt as if her perfect world had suddenly been guilty of a flaw; but she was not a young girl to cry out at the signal for retreat. Perhaps his work was harder than usual, or perhaps, like herself, the drowsy summer stillness had sent him to sleep.

She crept noiselessly toward the window of the room where he wrote. At first she still thought he was asleep. He was sitting huddled up in an arm-chair by the window, with his head fallen forward. It was a very uncomfortable position in which to go to sleep. Then he raised his eyes, and she saw that he was in pain. He looked like a creature caught in a trap: his mouth was open; there were blue lines round it; and his chest shook as if something had got hold of it and was dragging it to and fro. But it was his eyes that were most terrible, they were like nothing Rosamund had ever seen. They were like the eyes of some one who is drowning, and cannot drown. They were fighting, but they did not want to fight; the struggle was compulsory and hopeless.

She ran forward into the room and bent over him. He moved then; a strange voice croaked at her:

'Don't! Air!'

She stepped back half offended and half terrified. His eyes seemed weighing her; there was nothing in them but a kind of violent prayer, neither recognition nor acceptance of the presence that had stirred him to passionate delight. In the same strange tortured voice he said: 'Go – Ellen – quick!'

Her brain registered the words, but it was some time before she understood what he meant. She had never had anything to do with ill people before. In her world there were always trained nurses, eau de Cologne, and darkened rooms. If people were in too much pain, you did not see them.

The merciless summer sunshine poured through the little bungalow, and the man before her, dressed in his usual clothes, helpless and expecting something from her, was presumably dying – dying in this unsuitable, exacting way on her hands!

He had nothing whatever to do with Edward Lockett. His face had changed in a few hours; he looked like some old, shivering wretch outside a public house on a winter's morning, come to the end of his tether; only there was no ambulance to drive up and take him away.

Ellen was his wife. It was manifestly impossible that Rosamund could go up to the farm and reveal herself to Mrs Lockett; that was the one person she must not meet.

Rosamund did not feel so aware of fear now as she did of being aggravated, on edge, utterly uncomfortable and at a loss. She wanted to put a cushion behind Edward's head, but she was afraid to touch him, he was shaken so; she was afraid that if she touched him he might break. Why hadn't he told her that he had attacks like these? Surely there was something he could take? Wasn't there always something that people could take?

She asked him; she spoke very calmly and plainly. She felt vaguely that she ought to speak in a whisper in a sick-room, but this hardly resembled a sick-room. Besides, his breathing was so loud that he couldn't have heard her if she had whispered. His breathing was a most peculiar sound; it reminded her of the night-jar they had listened to the evening before in the pines.

He moved his hand out towards the window in the direction of the farm. There was a long silence except for the quick, soft rattle of his breath. Lockett did not look at Rosamund again; he seemed taken up with staring at one of his hands that pulled unceasingly at the chair-cover. A peculiar dark shadow came over his face, like the deep noon shadows Rosamund had just been watching on the rocks outside.

She became suddenly terrified; what she was afraid of was that he would go on like this for hours without dying; she would have given anything in the world to see him die.

She turned and ran out of the room into the open sunshine. The little glen lay there, serene and empty, like a lovely golden trap. The silence pressed down upon her, and she realized that she couldn't get rid of it. She couldn't get rid of anything; she must act. She had never been in a position before where one has to act, when one can't ring a bell or send for a servant or go into another room. The nearest house was the farm, a mile away.

There was nothing for it; she must sacrifice her reputation, she must meet his wife. She felt an intense relief at this decision, and as she set off by the white ribbon of road her mind became exalted with a rush of ideas. She saw all that she must say to this hard woman to melt her and save the man she loved (the moment she was out of sight of Lockett he was still the man she loved). Words came to her with an ease and clarity which was almost miraculous. She would begin: 'We are two women –' Far away across the cliffs the church bells were ringing; the sound of them reminded her of her childhood. She used to think angels rang them. Rosamund had always had beautiful thoughts.

A woman stood at the gate in front of her leading to the farm.

'This is private ground,' the young woman said briefly. 'What do you want?'

They looked at each other, and it occurred to Rosamund that this was Lockett's wife. Nothing else occurred to her; it was as if speech had ceased to exist. The woman before her had evidently just returned from church; she was dressed in black and had a prayer-book in her hand. She was good-looking and had very thick hair.

'What is it?' she repeated, frowning impatiently. 'I suppose you want something?'

Then Rosamund heard her own voice; it sounded strangely flat and weak.

'There is a man down there at the bungalow taken very ill,' she gasped. 'I want help.'

'Go back and boil the big kettle,' said Mrs Lockett. 'I'll be with you in a few minutes.' She put the prayer-book down on top of the gate, gathered up her black skirts, and ran up the hillside toward the farm. Rosamund called after her, but the woman did not stop or even turn her head. The world was just as empty as it had been before. It did not seem possible to Rosamund to go back to the bungalow. Why hadn't she gone to Norway with her husband? Then this would never have happened. Nothing ever did happen in Norway (that was why she had not gone there, but she did not remember that now). And certainly she would not have been told to go back and boil a big kettle.

Nevertheless, there was a feeling in her that she must go back. Perhaps Lockett would be better or perhaps he would be dead.

He was neither; he was just the same. She heard as she approached the house the same steady rattle of his breathing; she did not dare go into the room, but through the open window she saw the gray shadow of his face. She hurried into the kitchen and hunted for the big kettle; the old woman had left them a good fire. It took an interminable, terrifying time to find the kettle, and she was still looking for the tap to fill it from when she heard the swift approaching steps of Mrs Lockett. Mrs Lockett knew where everything was. She went at once to her husband, but she called out in a businesslike way where Rosamund would find the tap.

She hardly gave her time to fill the kettle before she called her again. Rosamund would have given any great, unreasonable thing to have been spared going into the room of the man she loved, but the woman's voice took her coming profoundly for granted. Rosamund had meant to plead with her to forgive Edward, but she found herself fully occupied in helping Mrs Lockett move him to the sofa. Mrs Lockett was apparently not afraid that he would break, but before she moved him she had slit up his sleeve and given him an injection. The strange sound of his breathing altered a little. There were great drops of perspiration on his face, and his wife wiped them methodically away. Once she said, 'There, then,' very quietly, as if she were speaking to a child.

He did not push her away or tell her that he wanted air. He did not speak to her at all, but his eyes looked less hopelessly urgent.

'As soon as the water boils, fill all those bottles you'll find under the dresser and bring them in,' said Mrs Lockett. 'There's some oxygen in the scullery, too; I always keep some handy. Pour some of that water before it gets too hot into the cylinder; here it is in the cupboard.' Rosamund obeyed her. It occurred to her now that Edward wasn't, after all, so very ill. A moment later she heard the bubbling sound of the oxygen.

The water took a long while to boil; she sat on the edge of the kitchen table, and felt very sorry for herself. Edward ought to have warned her. She remembered that he had once said that he had something the matter with his heart, and she had said, 'What an awful nuisance!' And he had said, 'Yes, it is rather a nuisance,' but he hadn't gone on with the subject. He hadn't at all explained how awful it might be for her.

She took the bottles in one by one. Mrs Lockett did not say that he was better; she did not say anything at all. She seemed always doing something, very quietly, and without the slightest sign of hurry; and Edward was not breathing nearly so loudly. He was lying much lower on the cushions, but his face had a strange, sunken look, and all his features stood out with a curious sharpness. His eyes were shut. Rosamund wondered if he were asleep. She looked at her watch, and found it was only three o'clock. It seemed to her that time had literally stood quite still.

Then she heard Mrs Lockett's voice; she was not talking to Edward, she was speaking to her.

'Have you had anything to eat?' asked Mrs Lockett. Then she added, 'There ought to be something in the larder.'

Rosamund went into the larder. It seemed to her as if the food would choke her, but it did not choke her. After she had eaten as well as she could, she filled up a plate and took it out to Mrs Lockett. She hardly knew which of them was the hostess, and she was afraid Mrs Lockett might be angry; but Mrs Lockett merely looked up and said, 'I'll eat later.' Time again stood still for half an hour. Then Mrs Lockett said through the open door:

'It's no use; the injections won't act.'

Rosamund stared at her, she had been so sure Edward was getting better; she could hardly hear his breathing at all now. Mrs Lockett looked at her curiously, then she said:

'Wouldn't you like to come in and sit the other side of him? He might know you presently.'

Rosamund hung her head; she did not want to go in. Mrs Lockett still looked at her; then she said gently: 'It's all right now, you know; he's not suffering.'

Rosamund came in and sat down on the other side of the sofa. The flowers on the table shook in the light air; through the windows she could hear the soft lap-lapping of the little summer waves. This time yesterday he had been writing her a poem about their love. Their love? This great possession seemed now like the forgotten hum of yesterday's gnat.

'You see, he might or he might not come round again,' said Mrs Lockett. 'Anyway, we can't do any more. I sent for the doctor up along, but he must be out. Still, there's nothing he could do if he was here. When was he taken bad?'

'I don't know,' stammered Rosamund. 'He was writing; he didn't come out, and I came back and – and found him.'

'Poor thing!' said Mrs Lockett, but she did not say to which of the two she was referring.

Edward stirred a little; the fait jerking of his chest stopped. 'Now!' said Mrs Lockett, quickly. The two women leaned forward. He raised his wide blue eyes and stared straight in front of him.

'Clara,' he said distinctly; then he fell back, and his eyes wavered as if something that was in them was going away.

'He's gone,' said Mrs Lockett; then she added conscientiously, 'My name is not Clara.'

Rosamund covered her face with her hands. She tried to faint; but she could not faint.

'You'd better leave him with me,' said Mrs Lockett, kindly, 'unless you'd like to help me lay him out.'

Rosamund sprang to her feet and ran to her room. She stood aghast and trembling at the open doorway. It was her room and his; but it seemed all his now. Then she forced herself into action; she drove her will power like an unwilling horse.

It was terrible to pack her things in that room, full of memory; but it was more terrible to stay there listening to Mrs Lockett's footsteps in the next room, and doing nothing. It was strange how the consciousness kept being forced back on her that there is sometimes no alternative to terrible things.

The doctor came, and she held her breath with a new fear. Surely Mrs Lockett would give her away! Force her forward into some new position of shame and exposure? Didn't the injured wife always take her revenge? And yet even while Rosamund stood there trembling, she couldn't see Mrs Lockett playing the injured wife.

The doctor pushed back his chair and went to the door.

'Just such another attack as usual, I suppose?' she heard him say, and Mrs Lockett's quiet: 'Yes; more severe, but the same kind.'

'It was a mercy you happened to be here with him.'

'Yes,' said Mrs Lockett; 'I'm glad I came.'

'Well, well,' said the doctor, getting into his trap, 'I'm sorry for you.'

Mrs Lockett said nothing.

When Rosamund rejoined her, Mrs Lockett had finished all that she had to do. She was sitting opposite the body; there was a curious unseeing look in her eyes.

Rosamund was afraid to speak; it was as if she was not sure which of them was dead. It was the first time that she had seriously acknowledged the existence of Edward's wife. The woman who sat by him now was his wife; there was a bond between them deeper than a casual affinity. They had not suited each other, but they had gone deep into the law of possession, and as Rosamund looked at them, living and dead, it seemed to her as if they were one being, and as if she had no place with them at all.

Mrs Lockett turned her head and saw Rosamund.

'I've sent for a cart for you,' she said quietly. 'It will carry you to the junction in time for the London train.' As she spoke she drew a sheet forward and covered up Edward's face.

Rosamund heard the approaching wheels from the farm; her heart beat with joy at the sound of her escape into freedom. Life had taken her measure, and she knew that reality was not for her. This was the end of romance.

Mrs Lockett came forward and helped the carter lift Rosamund's trunk into the trap.

'You've got such little hands,' she said to Rosamund in explanation.

Then she stepped back quickly. It did not seem to Rosamund as if Mrs Lockett wanted to touch her hand.

She got into the trap, and while the driver seated himself, Mrs Lockett moved toward her again.

She spoke in a low tone and flushed a little, like an anxious hostess who is afraid a visit has not been a success. For the first time that day she appeared a little embarrassed and confused.

'I'm sure I'm very sorry,' she said, 'things happened the way they did. Edward would have been sorry, too. It was an awkward turn.'

D. H. Lawrence

SAMSON AND DELILAH

A man got down from the motor-omnibus that runs from Penzance to St Just-in-Penwith, and turned northwards, uphill towards the Polestar. It was only half-past six, but already the stars were out, a cold little wind was blowing from the sea, and the crystalline, three-pulse flash of the lighthouse below the cliffs beat rhythmically in the first darkness.

The man was alone. He went his way unhesitating, but looked from side to side with cautious curiosity. Tall, ruined power-houses of tin-mines loomed in the darkness from time to time, like remnants of some by-gone civilization. The lights of many miners' cottages scattered on the hilly darkness twinkled desolate in their disorder, yet twinkled with the lonely homeliness of the Celtic night.

He tramped steadily on, always watchful with curiosity. He was a tall, well-built man, apparently in the prime of life. His shoulders were square and rather stiff, he leaned forwards a little as he went, from the hips, like a man who must stoop to lower his height. But he did not stoop his shoulders: he bent his straight back from the hips.

Now and again short, stump, thick-legged figures of Cornish miners passed him, and he invariably gave them good-night, as if to insist that he was on his own ground. He spoke with the west-Cornish intonation. And as he went along the dreary road, looking now at the lights of the dwellings on land, now at the lights away to sea, vessels veering round in sight of the Longships Lighthouse, the whole of the Atlantic Ocean in darkness and space between him and America, he seemed a little excited and pleased with himself, watchful, thrilled, veering along in a sense of mastery and of power in conflict.

The houses began to close on the road, he was entering the straggling, formless desolate mining village, that he knew of old. On the left was a little space set back from the road, and cosy lights of an inn. There it was. He peered up at the sign: 'The Tinners' Rest'. But he could not make out the name of the proprietor. He listened. There was excited talking and laughing, a woman's voice laughing shrilly among the men's.

Stooping a little, he entered the warmly-lit bar. The lamp was burning, a buxom woman rose from the white-scrubbed deal table where the black and white and red cards were scattered, and several men, miners, lifted their faces from the game.

The stranger went to the counter, averting his face. His cap was pulled down over his brow.

'Good evening!' said the landlady, in her rather ingratiating voice.

'Good evening. A glass of ale.'

'A glass of ale,' repeated the landlady suavely. 'Cold night – but bright.'

'Yes,' the man assented, laconically. Then he added, when nobody expected him to say any more: 'Seasonable weather.'

'Quite seasonable, quite,' said the landlady. 'Thank you.'

The man lifted his glass straight to his lips, and emptied it. He put it down again on the zinc counter with a click.

'Let's have another,' he said.

The woman drew the beer, and the man went away with his glass to the second table, near the fire. The woman, after a moment's hesitation, took her seat again at the table with the card-players. She noticed the man: a big fine fellow, well dressed, a stranger.

But he spoke with that Cornish-Yankee accent she accepted as the natural twang among the miners.

The stranger put his foot on the fender and looked into the fire. He was handsome, well coloured, with well-drawn Cornish eyebrows, and the usual dark, bright, mindless Cornish eyes. He seemed abstracted in thought. Then he watched the card-party.

The woman was buxom and healthy, with dark hair, and small, quick brown eyes. She was bursting with life and vigour, the energy she threw into the game of cards excited all of the men, they shouted, and laughed, and the woman held her breast, shrieking with laughter.

'Oh my, it'll be the death o' me,' she panted. 'Now, come on, Mr Trevorrow, play fair. Play fair, I say, or I s'll put the cards down.'

'Play fair! Why who's played unfair?' ejaculated Mr Trevorrow. 'Do you mean t'accuse me, as I haven't played fair, Mrs Nankervis?'

'I do. I say it, and I mean it. Haven't you got the queen of spades? Now, come on, no dodging round me. *I* know you've got that queen, as well as I know my name's Alice.'

'Well – if your name's Alice, you'll have to have it –'

'Ay, now – what did I say? Did you ever see such a man? My word, but your missus must be easy took in, by the looks of things.'

And off she went into peals of laughter. She was interrupted by the entrance of four men in khaki, a short, stumpy sergeant of middle age, a young corporal, and two young privates. The woman leaned back in her chair.

'Oh, my!' she cried. 'If there isn't the boys back: looking perished, I believe –'

'Perished, Ma!' exclaimed the sergeant. 'Not yet.'

'Near enough,' said a young private, uncouthly.

The woman got up.

'I'm sure you are, my dears. You'll be wanting your suppers, I'll be bound.'

'We could do with 'em.'

'Let's have a wet first,' said the sergeant.

The woman bustled about getting the drinks. The soldiers moved to the fire, spreading out their hands.

'Have your suppers in here, will you?' she said. 'Or in the kitchen?'

'Let's have it here,' said the sergeant. 'More cosier – *if* you don't mind.'

'You shall have it where you like, boys, where you like.'

She disappeared. In a minute a girl of about sixteen came in. She was tall and fresh, with dark, young, expressionless eyes, and well-drawn brows, and the immature softness and mindlessness of the sensuous Celtic type.

'Ho, Maryann! Evenin', Maryann! How's Maryann, now?' came the multiple greeting.

She replied to everybody in a soft voice, a strange, soft *aplomb* that was very attractive. And she moved round with rather mechanical, attractive movements, as if her thoughts were elsewhere. But she had always this dim far-awayness in her bearing: a sort of modesty. The strange man by the fire watched her curiously. There was an alert, inquisitive, mindless curiosity on his well-coloured face.

'I'll have a bit of supper with you, if I might,' he said.

She looked at him, with her clear, unreasoning eyes, just like the eyes of some non-human creature.

'I'll ask mother,' she said. Her voice was soft-breathing, gently singsong.

When she came in again:

'Yes,' she said, almost whispering. 'What will you have?'

'What have you got?' he said, looking up into her face.

'There's cold meat –'

'That's for me, then.'

The stranger sat at the end of the table, and ate with the tired, quiet soldiers. Now, the landlady was interested in him. Her brow was knit rather tense, there was a look of panic in her large, healthy face, but her small brown eyes were fixed most dangerously. She was a big woman, but her eyes were small and tense. She drew near the stranger. She wore a rather loud-patterned flannelette blouse, and a dark skirt.

'What will you have to drink with your supper?' she asked, and there was a new, dangerous note in her voice.

He moved uneasily.

'Oh, I'll go on with ale.'

She drew him another glass. Then she sat down on the bench at the table with him and the soldiers, and fixed him with her attention.

'You've come from St Just, have you?' she said.

He looked at her with those clear, dark, inscrutable Cornish eyes, and answered at length:

'No, from Penzance.'

'Penzance! – but you're not thinking of going back there tonight?'

'No – no.'

He still looked at her with those wide, clear eyes that seemed like very bright agate. Her anger began to rise. It was seen on her brow. Yet her voice was still suave and deprecating.

'I *thought* not – but you're not living in these parts, are you?'

'No – no, I'm not living here.' He was always slow in answering, as if something intervened between him and any outside question.

'Oh, I see,' she said. 'You've got relations down here.'

Again he looked straight into her eyes, as if looking her into silence.

'Yes,' he said.

He did not say any more. She rose with a flounce. The anger was tight on her brow. There was no more laughing and card-playing that evening, though she kept up her motherly, suave, good-humoured way with the men. But they knew her, they were all afraid of her.

The supper was finished, the table cleared, the stranger did not go. Two of the young soldiers went off to bed, with their cheery:

'Good-night, Ma. Good-night, Maryann.'

The stranger talked a little to the sergeant about the war, which was in its first year, about the new army, a fragment of which was quartered in this district, about America.

The landlady darted looks at him from her small eyes, minute by minute the electric storm welled in her bosom, as still he did not go. She was quivering with suppressed, violent passion, something frightening and abnormal. She could not sit still for a moment. Her heavy form seemed to flash with sudden, involuntary movements as the minutes passed by, and still he sat there, and the tension on her heart grew unbearable. She watched the hands of the clock move on. Three of the soldiers had gone to bed, only the crop-headed, terrier-like old sergeant remained.

The landlady sat behind the bar fidgeting spasmodically with the newspaper. She looked again at the clock. At last it was five minutes to ten.

'Gentlemen – the enemy!' she said, in her diminished, furious voice. 'Time, please. Time, my dears. And good-night, all!'

The men began to drop out, with a brief good-night. It was a minute to ten. The landlady rose.

'Come,' she said. 'I'm shutting the door.'

The last of the miners passed out. She stood, stout and menacing, holding the door. Still the stranger sat on by the fire, his black overcoat opened, smoking.

'We're closed now, sir,' came the perilous, narrowed voice of the landlady.

The little, dog-like, hard-headed sergeant touched the arm of the stranger.

'Closing time,' he said.

The stranger turned round in his seat, and his quick-moving, dark, jewel-like eyes went from the sergeant to the landlady.

'I'm stopping here to-night,' he said, in his laconic Cornish-Yankee accent.

The landlady seemed to tower. Her eyes lifted strangely, frightening.

'Oh! indeed!' she cried. 'Oh, indeed! And whose orders are those, may I ask?'

He looked at her again.

'My orders,' he said.

Involuntarily she shut the door, and advanced like a great, dangerous bird. Her voice rose, there was a touch of hoarseness in it.

'And what might *your* orders be, if you please?' she cried. 'Who might *you* be, to give orders, in the house?'

He sat still, watching her.

'You know who I am,' he said. 'At least, I know who you are.'

'Oh, do you? Oh, do you? And who am *I* then, if you'll be so good as to tell me?'

He stared at her with his bright, dark eyes.

'You're my Missis, you are,' he said. 'And you know it, as well as I do.'

She started as if something had exploded in her.

Her eyes lifted and flared madly.

'*Do* I know it indeed!' she cried. 'I know no such thing! I know no such thing! Do you think a man's going to walk into this bar, and tell me off-hand I'm his Missis, and I'm going to believe him? – I say to you, whoever you may be, you're mistaken. I know myself for no Missis of yours, and I'll thank you to go out of this house, this minute, before I get those that will put you out.'

The man rose to his feet, stretching his head towards her a little. He was a handsomely built Cornishman in the prime of life.

'What you say, eh? You don't know me?' he said, in his sing-song voice, emotionless, but rather smothered and pressing: it reminded one of the girl's. 'I should know you anywhere, you see. I should! I shouldn't have to look twice to know you, you see. You see, now, don't you?'

The woman was baffled.

'So you may say,' she replied, staccato. 'So you may say. That's easy enough. My name's known, and respected, by most people for ten miles round. But I don't know *you.*'

Her voice ran to sarcasm. 'I can't say I know *you.* You're a *perfect* stranger to me, and I don't believe I've ever set eyes on you before to-night.'

Her voice was very flexible and sarcastic.

'Yes, you have,' replied the man, in his reasonable way. 'Yes, you have. Your name's my name, and that girl Maryann is my girl; she's my daughter. You're my Missis right enough. As sure as I'm Willie Nankervis.'

He spoke as if it were an accepted fact. His face was handsome, with a strange, watchful alertness and a fundamental fixity of intention that maddened her.

'You villain!' she cried. 'You villain, to come to this house and dare to speak to me. You villain, you down-right rascal!'

He looked at her.

'Ay,' he said, unmoved. 'All that.' He was uneasy before her. Only he was not afraid of her. There was something impenetrable about him, like his eyes, which were as bright as agate.

She towered, and drew near to him menacingly.

'You're going out of this house, aren't you?' – She stamped her foot in sudden madness. '*This minute!*'

He watched her. He knew she wanted to strike him.

'No,' he said, with suppressed emphasis. 'I've told you, I'm stopping here.'

He was afraid of her personality, but it did not alter him. She wavered. Her small, tawny-brown eyes concentrated in a point of vivid, sightless fury, like a tiger's. The man was wincing, but he stood his ground. Then she bethought herself. She would gather her forces.

'We'll see whether you're stopping here,' she said. And she turned, with a curious, frightening lifting of her eyes, and surged out of the room. The man, listening, heard her go upstairs, heard her tapping at a bedroom door, heard her saying: 'Do you mind coming down a minute, boys? I want you. I'm in trouble.'

The man in the bar took off his cap and his black overcoat, and threw them on the seat behind him. His black hair was short and touched with grey at the temples. He wore a well-cut, well-fitting suit of dark grey, American in style, and a turn-down collar. He looked well-to-do, a fine, solid figure of a man. The rather rigid look of the shoulders came from his having had his collar-bone twice broken in the mines.

The little terrier of a sergeant, in dirty khaki, looked at him furtively.

'She's your Missis?' he asked, jerking his head in the direction of the departed woman.

'Yes, she is,' barked the man. 'She's that, sure enough.'

'Not seen her for a long time, haven't ye?'

'Sixteen years come March month.'

'Hm!'

And the sergeant laconically resumed his smoking.

The landlady was coming back, followed by the three young soldiers, who entered rather sheepishly, in trousers and shirt and stocking-feet. The woman stood histrionically at the end of the bar, and exclaimed:

'That man refuses to leave the house, claims he's stopping the night here. You know very well I have no bed, don't you? And this house doesn't accommodate travellers. Yet he's going to stop in spite of all! But not while I've a drop of blood in my body, that I declare with my dying breath. And not if you men are worth the name of men, and will help a woman as has no one to help her.'

Her eyes sparkled, her face was flushed pink. She was drawn up like an Amazon.

The young soldiers did not quite know what to do. They looked at the man, they looked at the sergeant, one of them looked down and fastened his braces on the second button.

'What say, sergeant?' asked one whose face twinkled for a little devilment.

'Man says he's husband to Mrs Nankervis,' said the sergeant.

'He's no husband of mine. I declare I never set eyes on him before this night. It's a dirty trick, nothing else, it's a dirty trick.'

'Why, you're a liar, saying you never set eyes on me before,' barked the man near the hearth. 'You're married to me, and that girl Maryann you had by me – well enough you know it.'

The young soldier looked on in delight, the sergeant smoked imperturbed.

'Yes,' sang the landlady, slowly shaking her head in supreme sarcasm, 'it sounds very pretty, doesn't it? But you see we don't believe a word of it, and *how* are you going to prove it?' She smiled nastily.

The man watched in silence for a moment, then he said:

'It wants no proof.'

'Oh, yes, but it does! Oh, yes, but it does, sir, it wants a lot of proving!' sang the lady's sarcasm. 'We're not such gulls as all that, to swallow your words whole.'

But he stood unmoved near the fire. She stood with one hand resting on the zinc-covered bar, the sergeant sat with legs crossed, smoking, on the seat halfway between them, the three young soldiers in their shirts and braces stood wavering in the gloom behind the bar. There was silence.

'Do you know anything of the whereabouts of your husband, Mrs Nankervis? Is he still living?' asked the sergeant, in his judicious fashion.

Suddenly the landlady began to cry, great scalding tears, that left the young men aghast.

'I know nothing of him,' she sobbed, feeling for her pocket handkerchief. 'He left me when Maryann was a baby, went mining to America, and after about six months never wrote a line nor sent me a penny bit. I can't say whether he's alive or dead, the villain. All I've heard of him's to the bad – and I've heard nothing for years an' all, now.' She sobbed violently.

The golden-skinned, handsome man near the fire watched her as she wept. He was frightened, he was troubled, he was bewildered, but none of his emotions altered him underneath.

There was no sound in the room but the violent sobbing of the landlady. The men, one and all, were overcome.

'Don't you think as you'd better go, for to-night?' said the sergeant to the man, with sweet reasonableness. 'You'd better leave it a bit, and arrange something between you. You can't have much claim on a woman, I should imagine, if it's how she says. And you've come down on her a bit too sudden-like.'

The landlady sobbed heart-brokenly. The man watched her large breasts shaken. They seemed to cast a spell over his mind.

'How I've treated her, that's no matter,' he replied. 'I've come back, and I'm going to stop in my own home – for a bit, anyhow. There you've got it.'

'A dirty action,' said the sergeant, his face flushing dark. 'A dirty action, to come, after deserting a woman for that number of years, and want to force yourself on her! A dirty action – as isn't allowed by the law.'

The landlady wiped her eyes.

'Never you mind about law nor nothing,' cried the man, in a strange, strong voice. 'I'm not for moving out of this public to-night.'

The woman turned to the soldiers behind her, and said in a wheedling, sarcastic tone:

'Are we going to stand it, boys? – Are we going to be done like this, Sergeant Thomas, by a scoundrel and a bully as has led a life beyond *mention*, in those American mining-camps, and then wants to come back and make havoc of a poor woman's life and savings, after having left her with a baby in arms to struggle as best she might? It's a crying shame if nobody will stand up for me – a crying shame –!'

The soldiers and the little sergeant were bristling. The woman stooped and rummaged under the counter for a minute. Then, unseen to the man away near the fire, she threw out a plaited grass rope, such as is used for binding bales, and left it lying near the feet of the young soldiers, in the gloom at the back of the bar.

Then she rose and fronted the situation.

'Come now,' she said to the man, in a reasonable, coldly-coaxing tone, 'put your coat on and leave us alone. Be a man, and not worse than a brute of a German. You can get a bed easy enough in St Just, and if you've nothing to pay for it sergeant would lend you a couple of shillings, I'm sure he would.'

All eyes were fixed on the man. He was looking down at the woman like a creature spell-bound or possessed by some devil's own intention.

'I've got money of my own,' he said. 'Don't you be frightened for your money, I've plenty of that, for the time.'

'Well, then,' she coaxed, in a cold, almost sneering propitiation, 'put your coat on and go where you're wanted – be a *man*, not a brute of a German.'

She had drawn quite near to him, in her challenging coaxing intentness. He looked down at her with his bewitched face.

'No, I shan't,' he said. 'I shan't do no such thing. *You'll* put me up for to-night.'

'Shall I?' she cried. And suddenly she flung her arms round him, hung on to him with all her powerful weight, calling to the soldiers: 'Get the rope, boys, and fasten him up. Alfred – John, quick now –'

The man reared, looked round with maddened eyes, and heaved his powerful body. But the woman was powerful also, and very heavy, and was clenched with the determination of death. Her face, with its exulting, horribly vindictive look, was turned up to him from his own breast; he reached back his head frantically, to get away from it. Meanwhile the young soldiers, after having watched this frightful Laocoon swaying for a moment, stirred, and the malicious one darted swiftly with the rope. It was tangled a little.

'Give me the end here,' cried the sergeant.

Meanwhile the big man heaved and struggled, swung the woman round against the seat and the table, in his convulsive effort to get free. But she pinned down his arms like a cuttlefish wreathed heavily upon him. And he heaved and swayed, and they crashed about the room, the soldiers hopping, the furniture bumping.

The young soldier had got the rope once round, the brisk sergeant helping him. The woman sank heavily lower, they got the rope round several times. In the struggle the victim fell over against the table. The ropes tightened till they cut his arms. The woman clung to his knees. Another soldier ran in a flash of genius, and fastened the strange man's feet with the pair of braces. Seats had crashed over, the table was thrown against the wall, but the man was bound, his arms pinned against his sides, his feet tied. He lay half fallen, sunk against the table, still for a moment.

The woman rose, and sank, faint, on to the seat against the wall. Her breast heaved, she could not speak, she thought she was going to die. The bound man lay against the overturned table, his coat all twisted and pulled up beneath the ropes, leaving the loins exposed. The soldiers stood around, a little dazed, but excited with the row.

The man began to struggle again, heaving instinctively against the ropes, taking great, deep breaths. His face, with its golden skin, flushed dark and surcharged, he heaved again. The great veins in his neck stood out. But it was no good, he went relaxed. Then again, suddenly, he jerked his feet.

'Another pair of braces, William,' cried the excited soldier. He threw himself on the legs of the bound man, and managed to fasten the knees. Then again there was stillness. They could hear the clock tick.

The woman looked at the prostrate figure, the strong, straight limbs, the strong back bound in subjection, the wide-eyed face that reminded her of a calf tied in a sack in a cart, only its head stretched dumbly backwards. And she triumphed.

The bound-up body began to struggle again. She watched fascinated the muscles working, the shoulders, the hips, the large, clean thighs. Even now he might break the ropes. She was afraid. But the lively young soldier sat on the shoulders of the bound man, and after a few perilous moments, there was stillness again.

'Now,' said the judicious sergeant to the bound man, 'if we untie you, will you promise to go off and make no more trouble.'

'You'll not untie him in here,' cried the woman. 'I wouldn't trust him as far as I could blow him.'

There was silence.

'We might carry him outside, and undo him there,' said the soldier. 'Then we could get the policeman, if he made any more bother.'

'Yes,' said the sergeant. 'We could do that.' Then again, in an altered, almost severe tone, to the prisoner. 'If we undo you outside, will you take your coat and go without creating any more disturbance?'

But the prisoner would not answer, he only lay with wide, dark, bright, eyes, like a bound animal. There was a space of perplexed silence.

'Well, then, do as you say,' said the woman irritably. 'Carry him out amongst you, and let us shut up the house.'

They did so. Picking up the bound man, the four soldiers staggered clumsily into the silent square in front of the inn, the woman following with the cap and overcoat. The young soldiers quickly unfastened the braces from the prisoner's legs, and they hopped indoors. They were in their stocking-feet, and outside the stars flashed cold. They stood in the doorway watching. The man lay quite still on the cold ground.

'Now,' said the sergeant, in a subdued voice, 'I'll loosen the knot, and he can work himself free, if you go in, Missis.'

She gave a last look at the dishevelled, bound man, as he sat on the ground. Then she went indoors, followed quickly by the sergeant. Then they were heard locking and barring the door.

The man seated on the ground outside worked and strained at the rope. But it was not so easy to undo himself even now. So, with hands bound, making an effort, he got on his feet, and went and worked the cord against the rough edge of an old wall. The rope, being of a kind of plaited grass, soon frayed and broke, and he freed himself. He has various contusions. His arms were hurt and bruised from the bonds. He rubbed them slowly. Then he pulled his clothes straight, stooped, put on his cap, struggled into his overcoat, and walked away.

The stars were very brilliant. Clear as crystal, the beam from the lighthouse under the cliffs struck rhythmically on the night. Dazed, the man walked along the road past the church-yard. Then he stood leaning up against a wall, for a long time.

He was roused because his feet were so cold. So he pulled himself together, and turned again in the silent night, back towards the inn.

The bar was in darkness. But there was a light in the kitchen. He hesitated. Then very quietly he tried the door.

He was surprised to find it open. He entered, and quietly closed it behind him.

Then he went down the step past the bar-counter, and through to the lighted doorway of the kitchen. There sat his wife, planted in front of the range, where a furze fire was burning. She sat in a chair full in front of the range, her knees wide apart on the fender. She looked over her shoulder at him as he entered, but she did not speak. Then she stared in the fire again.

It was a small, narrow kitchen. He dropped his cap on the table that was covered with yellowish American cloth, and took a seat with his back to the wall, near the oven. His wife still sat with her knees apart, her feet on the steel fender and stared into the fire, motionless. Her skin was smooth and rosy in the firelight. Everything in the house was very clean and bright. The man sat silent, too, his head dropped. And thus they remained.

It was a question who would speak first. The woman leaned forward and poked the ends of the sticks in between the bars of the range. He lifted his head and looked at her.

'Others gone to bed, have they?' he asked.

But she remained closed in silence.

''S a cold night, out,' he said, as if to himself.

And he laid his large, yet well-shapen workman's hand on the top of the stove, that was polished black and smooth as velvet. She would not look at him, yet she glanced out of the corners of her eyes.

His eyes were fixed brightly on her, the pupils large and electric like those of a cat.

'I should have picked you out among thousands,' he said. 'Though you're bigger than I'd have believed. Fine flesh you've made.'

She was silent for some time. Then she turned in her chair upon him.

'What do you think of yourself,' she said, 'coming back on me like this after over fifteen years? You don't think I've not heard of you, neither, in Butte City and elsewhere?'

He was watching her with his clear, translucent, unchallenged eyes.

'Yes,' he said. 'Chaps comes an' goes – I've heard tell of you from time to time.'

She drew herself up.

'And what lies have you heard about *me*?' she demanded superbly.

'I dunno as I've heard any lies at all – 'cept as you was getting on very well, like.'

His voice ran warily and detached. Her anger stirred again in her violently. But she subdued it, because of the danger there was in him, and more, perhaps, because of the beauty of his head and his level drawn-brows, which she could not bear to forfeit.

'That's more than I can say of *you*,' she said. 'I've heard more harm than good about *you*.'

'Ay, I dessay,' he said, looking in the fire. It was a long time since he had seen the furze burning, he said to himself. There was a silence, during which she watched his face.

'Do you call yourself a *man*?' she said, more in contemptuous reproach than in anger. 'Leave a woman as you've left me, you don't care to what! – and then to turn up in *this* fashion, without a word to say for yourself.'

He stirred in his chair, planted his feet apart, and resting his arms on his knees, looked steadily into the fire, without answering. So near to her was his head, and the close black hair, she could scarcely refrain from starting away, as if it would bite her.

'Do you call that the action of a *man*?' she repeated.

'No,' he said, reaching and poking the bits of wood into the fire with his fingers. 'I didn't call it anything, as I know of. It's no good calling things by any names whatsoever, as I know of.'

She watched him in his actions. There was a longer and longer pause between each speech, though neither knew it.

'I *wonder* what you think of yourself!' she exclaimed, with vexed emphasis. 'I *wonder* what sort of a fellow you take yourself to be!' She was really perplexed as well as angry.

'Well,' he said, lifting his head to look at her, 'I guess I'll answer for my own faults, if everybody else'll answer for theirs.'

Her heart beat fiery hot as he lifted his face to her. She breathed heavily, averting her face, almost losing her self-control.

'And what do you take *me* to be?' she cried, in real helplessness.

His face was lifted watching her, watching her soft, averted face, and the softly heaving mass of her breasts.

'I take you,' he said, with that laconic truthfulness which exercised such power over her, 'to be the deuce of a fine woman – darn me if you're not as fine a built woman as I've seen, handsome with it as well. I shouldn't have expected you to put on such handsome flesh: 'struth I shouldn't.'

Her heart beat fiery hot, as he watched her with those bright agate eyes, fixedly.

'Been very handsome to *you*, for fifteen years, my sakes!' she replied.

He made no answer to this, but sat with his bright, quick eyes upon her.

Then he rose. She started involuntarily. But he only said, in his laconic, measured way:

'It's warm in here now.'

And he pulled off his overcoat, throwing it on the table. She sat as if slightly cowed, whilst he did so.

'Them ropes has given my arms something, by Ga-ard,' he drawled, feeling his arms with his hands.

Still she sat in her chair before him, slightly cowed.

'You was sharp, wasn't you, to catch me like that, eh?' he smiled slowly. 'By Ga-ard, you had me fixed proper, proper you had. Darn me, you fixed me up proper – proper, you did,'

He leaned forwards in his chair toward her.

'I don't think no worse of you for it, no, darned if I do. Fine pluck in a woman's what I admire. That I do, indeed.'

She only gazed into the fire.

'We fet from the start, we did. And, my word, you begin again quick the minute you see me, you did. Darn me, you was too sharp for me. A darn fine woman, puts up a darn good fight. Darn me if I could find a woman in all the darn States as could get me down like that. Wonderful fine woman you be, truth to say, at this minute.'

She only sat glowering into the fire.

'As grand a pluck as a man could wish to find in a woman, true as I'm here,' he said, reaching forward his hand and tentatively touched her between her full, warm breasts, quietly.

She started, and seemed to shudder. But his hand insinuated itself between her breasts, as she continued to gaze in the fire.

'And don't you think I've come back here a-begging,' he said. 'I've more than *one* thousand pounds to my name, I have. And a bit of a fight for a how-de-do pleases me, that it do. But that doesn't mean as you're going to deny as you're my Missis ...'

Anne Treneer

TAKE STARS FOR MONEY

I

They called him the Falmouth man, and the Laughing man, and Take-stars-for-money, a name which the children shortened to Mr Takestars. He had come from Falmouth way, but no one knew where he had dwelt before that. He had come from Falmouth way, with a black man called Dom Pockett. First he had stayed at the Inn, at the Pendragon Arms whose granite walls rose flush with the village street. Then he had gone to look at a little tumbledown cottage in the lane leading to the Towans. And there, without waiting for anything to be done in the way of repairs, it was summer time and if the roof leaked the wet soon dried up, he set up house, he and old Dom Pockett. The Devil never needed much shelter, was the remark Nyas Trevarthen made; the Devil, he said, carried his warmth in his own vitals.

Sometimes Mt Takestars and Dom disappeared for days at a time, but always they came back looking as shabby as ever. Indeed, Dom was considered a disgrace to the parish by everyone but the children. To them he told stories. To the older ones he told stories of cat burglaries and breathless escapes; to the little ones he told stories of old man Caterpillar and his Gang. When it was sunny he told his stories under the apple-tree by the cabbage patch. Seated on a stump, and listening to the apple-bees and the birds, he played with old man Caterpillar. He never wearied of playing with old man Caterpillar. He would take a green striped one, and set it on a leaf, and watch it crawl to the edge, and then rear itself up, with its horns out over the empty space.

'Old man Caterpillar, he fall over one day,' he would remark. But always he put the leaf gently down and the caterpillar would go on its way. 'Old man Caterpillar he over-reach hisself one day,' he would say again to the children, as an elegant green and gold caterpillar reached the end of the leaf and tried the empty space this way and that. Or a furry brown and orange caterpillar reached the end of a stick. 'He very rich,' Dom would say; 'he have fur jacket; but he over-reach hisself one day too.' St Gwendron children annoyed their mothers by watching caterpillars and grasshoppers and lady-birds with Dom Pockett. Sometimes Mr Takestars came out and watched too.

The two did nothing to tidy up Diamond Panes and make a nice cottage of it with a flower garden. Any flowers grew that liked. Dandelions drank the fire of the sun, Mr Takestars said. Damn weeds, Sol Tyack said, damn weeds with damn seeds flying over his hedge. But when Sol had a gathering on his thumb, and Takestars cured it with

Virgin Mary, Sol wasn't so sure about weeds. Even dandelions had their virtue, according to Takestars. He talked about the virtue of flowers and gems, 'elemental flowering lights' he called these latter. He said they moved the mind with admirable beauties, that they were a cordial, and of an influence religious. Three books were all he had. One was Doughty's *Travels in Arabia Deserta*; the second was Gerard's *Herbal*, a great old book in black letter. Doughty ought to be printed that way, too, he said. His third book was the *Poems* of George Herbert. He had a Bible, too, and a Prayer Book; for he and Dom went to church every Sunday evening. What they did on Sunday mornings nobody knew. They hid themselves on Sunday mornings. But Sunday evenings they went to church, and Dom could be heard singing, 'My Soul doth magnify de Lord.'

Mr Takestars composed many a quarrel in St Gwendron, and soothed many an irate woman or man of St Gwendron congregation. Church is liable to make a man or woman hot-headed, perhaps through too much kneeling. And musicians are often touchy. Hannibal Dredgett was very touch indeed, though not so voluble as Mrs Dredgett. There was a fine to-do when the new parson had the harmonium moved to the gallery, without so much as a word to either of the Churchwardens. Hannibal came into the church and looked blankly around. 'Where's me organ to?' he said. When it was pointed out to him how much better it was for him in the gallery he could only say, 'I do feel lonely up there.' And Mrs Dredgett said, 'I can't see Hannie,' she said, 'I can't see un up there; and if I can't see Hannie I'm going chapel.' And the new parson's wife said Mrs Dredgett could go to chapel for all anybody cared. The church wouldn't fall down for that, she said. And so it went on till Mr Takestars smoothed it all over. He said the harmonium sounded exactly like a pipe organ, a proper pipe organ up in the gallery. And why couldn't Bessie Dredgett sit up in the gallery too? Then Hannibal wouldn't be lonely, and Bessie would be able to rejoice her eyes with the sight of her man as well as ever. So it was all arranged.

And it was all arranged about Mr Pook's will, too. It wasn't so much about a will as because there wasn't any will at all. So every man, woman and child by the name of Pook tried to get something out of what old Billy Pook had left. The only certain sure thing anybody knew as to what Billy meant to do with his possessions was that Dinah Parnell should stay in her cottage as long as she lived, because she'd spent most of her life looking after Billy. But all the Pooks wanted to turn her out and sell the cottage, and add that little bit to the hundreds of pounds to be divided up. But somehow Mr Takestars dissuaded them. He quoted to them out of the poems of Herbert his favourite lines that he'd quoted so often:

> What skills it, if a bag of stones or gold
> About thy neck do drown thee? Raise thy head;
> Take stars for money, – stars not to be told
> By any art, yet to be purchased,
>   None is so wasteful as the scraping dame;
>   She loseth three for one – her soul, rest, fame.

He had a wonderful voice and way of speaking, and somehow the Pooks were turned from their greed. And Dinah lived in her cottage till she died. And every Saturday she made Mr Takestars a beef-and-taty pasty. The labourer was worthy of his hire, she said. But she never made a pasty for Dom Pockett. She had to draw the line somewhere. Black was black and white was white, she said; though, no doubt, Dom had to have his little keg filled like everybody else; but it wasn't for her to fill Dom Pockett's keg.

Miss Hussey made no such distinction. She cooked a dish of under-roast every Wednesday, the day butcher Trelawney brought the meat, a dish big enough for both Dom and Takestars. For Mr Takestars had cured her of incipient baldness. Caroline Hussey had been in a taking, to be sure, about her hair. She washed it and washed it, and tried all manner of things advertised in the papers; but still it came out and came out. She had the combings made up, but what was the use of that when everybody was having their hair bobbed? Not that Caroline ever did. She didn't hold with it. Mary Magdalene had wiped his feet with her hair, and that just showed. But to be bald! The thought of that cast Caroline Hussey utterly down. She lay awake to think of it, or she fell asleep to dream of it. Then one day, when she had called at Diamond Panes with some shirts she'd made for Mr Takestars, he saw that she had been crying.

'And why have you been crying, Caroline?' he said.

'Oh, Mr Takestars, my hair is just coming out, and coming out, and coming out.' And she began to cry again then and there.

'Let's have a look at Gerard!' said Takestars. 'Dom, fetch the book.'

So Dom fetched the book and Mr Takestars read out, 'The juice (of onions), anointed upon a pild or bald head in the sun, bringeth the haire againe very speedily.'

Whether it was onion, or whether it was tansy, or whether it was another decoction Takestars made up for her, or whether it was just faith, who can say? But Caroline stopped dreaming of baldness, and her hair grew as well as anybody else's. She never had it bobbed. She wound it round her head in plaits. And whenever she plaited her hair she thought of Takestars, and put an extra little bit of beef with parsley stuffing for a change – into his Wednesday's dish of under-roast.

On Fridays Mr Takestars and Dom always had a little fish. Other people might be only hoping for a pilchard, but at Diamond Panes it would be on the gridiron. And for why? Mr Takestars had cured little Stella Tresidder of the spine trouble. She'd been in a jacket, and she'd worn calipers. For the spine is the tree of the body, as Mrs Tresidder said, and anything wrong with the spine will send the whole body awry. And Mr Takestars said to Annie Tresidder, 'Will you trust me with the child, Annie?' And Annie said she would. And he did something to little Stella with his hands; it frightened Annie, I'll tell you. But the child was trustful, and did exactly what Mr Takestars said, and did not cry. And she told her mother it was like as if a gate had been off his hinges, and Mr Takestars had clicked it to proper again. Stella was soon as right as any other little girl of twelve in St Gwendron. And the Tresidders always sent Mr Takestars a bit of fish on Fridays, if Amos Tresidder had had any luck at all with his nets; or a crab or a lobster, if he was in any abundance with his pots. He'd rather have Stella running about, laughing and happy, than catch Leviathan, he said; though no doubt a fish that size ... but there! What is Leviathan? Even the parson can't tell ee. What's the good of talking about it?

Only old Nyas Trevarthen cherished, as the years went by, a dislike of Takestars and Dom Pockett. Ananias was Nyas's proper name. His mother had had him christened that, because she was in a temper at his being born at all. Nyas was grave-digger at St Gwendron and proper graves he made, too. He used to tell people he was a skilful fellow because he'd never been to school. 'I went wan day,' he used to tell people, 'and if I'd been another they'd have made a proper fool of me.' He dug the graves and pared the hedges, and cracked the stones, and trapped rabbits. In the evenings, when his work was done, he had his proper place in the settle at the Pendragon Arms. The people he hated were the 'totlers, as he called the teetotalers. With them he associated Takestars. He classed the medicinal brews of the Falmouth man with yarbie (herbie) beer. He loved to 'put down' Mr Takestars. There was the celebrated tale of how he told Mr Takestars of what became of the 'trash' when he'd pared the hedges. Bramble, furze, thorn, oak and hazel; stinging nettle and dock; devils' buttons, toad-flax, honeysuckle, hedge roses – there it all was, cut down one day and gone the next.

'It's been soon carted away this year, Trevarthen,' observed Mr Takestars.

'Never no trouble to get rids of the trash,' says Nyas.

'How is that?' says Takestars. 'There's no value in it?'

'Aw, iss! They do take it for yarbie beer,' says Nyas. This tale invariably drew a great laugh at the Pendragon Arms. So did Nyas's other tale of how he had got drunk on lamb's wool – egg and milk beaten up together.

''Tidn' the strength of it, my sonnies; 'tes the quantity!' Nyas used to say.

'How do ee make that out, Nyas?'

'I went up Higher Perkellis Farm once,' Nyas, thus invited, would relate, 'I went up Higher Perkellis, and they gived me lamb's wool to drink. Went down suant, it did. So I clunkied, and clunkied, and clunkied. And when I got out I was blind to the world. Had to be 'sisted home. That'll tell ee what these here 'totlers' drinks 'll do to ee. Too much for mortal flesh, too much for mortal flesh!'

Even when Mr Takestars cured the Beast of the rheumatism, Nyas could not get over his prejudice; and the Beast himself kicked Mr Takestars for his pains – a procedure which proved that the healer was more devil than angel. For the Beast was as knowledgeable as Balaam's ass, and a sight better looking – from the pictures. 'The Beast,' said Nyas, 'do KNAW.' There never was in the world such a little dunk for knowledgeableness as the Beast. 'Take the time,' Nyas often said, 'when Lady Menheniot's bicycle shied at un, and her ladyship fell off. Did the Beast kick her? Not he. He stood looking down upon her as gentle as a lambkin. I said to her, I said, "I've never knowed that make of bicycle shy at the Beast before," I said. And she laughed so much she forgot to remember that me and the dunk and the wheels was right across the road. She went clean over the handle-bars when she clapt on her brakes hard. Pitched on her head she did, and I expect that addled her a bit. What with that and me little joke …'

The Beast knew a lady when he saw one it was clear; likewise he knew a gentleman, according to Nyas, and he knew the Devil too. And the Devil was Takestars. Who but the Devil would make such a fuss about trapping rabbits? Nyas had always trapped rabbits. He belonged to Trap rabbits. And so did Sol Tyack. But Takestars threw Sol out on his ear when Sol set some traps in the wild garden of Diamond Panes while Takestars and Dom were away on one of their secret jaunts. They turned up and landed in a ship's boat at Fisherman's Cove one moonlight night. They walked up to Diamond Panes, found Sol in the garden, had some words with him, and threw him out.

'Kill un!' said Nyas to Sol when told of this treatment. 'Kill un! I'll go halves with ee in the 'spense. He'll make it soon that the women and children wean't eat rabbit at all in St Gwendron, leave alone trapped ones. Cruel! Rabbits is used to it. They belong to be trapped. And what do he and Dom Pockett do when they'm away to Plymouth, or London or Amsterdam – that a Christian place should have such a name! Something worse than trapping rabbits, I'll be bound'

'He'll be drowned some fine night, anyway,' said Sol. 'Fisherman's Cove is no place for landing a boat in all weathers.'

'You can't drown the Devil, but you can choke un,' said Nyas.

'The place is a lot happier since he's been here, that's all I know,' said Caroline Hussey, who, on her way to Diamond Panes with her offering of savoury meat, had stopped to chat with Sol and Nyas. 'If you were to look at the stars a bit, Nyas Trevarthen, instead of always trying to make money trapping rabbits, it might be the better for you.'

'And while I was star-gazing the rabbits would increase and multiply and eat up every green blade in St Gwendron parish,' said Nyas. '"Take stars for money" is a good text I allow. But the stars won't feed a body. They don't feed the Laughing Man. You're taking to un meat you do need yourself.'

'If I do 'tis because I like to do it,' says Caroline.

'Then tidn' virtue, tha's all I can tell ee. Pleasing yourself idn' virtue. Though no doubt if it do make your heart glow 'tis a good thing. 'Tis good to have your heart made to glow, whether by beer or kindness.'

Usually when Takestars and Dom left St Gwendron's for any length of time it was spring, or summer, or, at most, early autumn. Winter they spent in Diamond Panes, which had become very snug and sound as time went on. After Takestars cured Carpenter Charlie Ventry's old mother, when her pipes were so crazed that Dr Prance had given her up, Charlie would do anything for him. And so would Bill Trounce, the mason, after Takestars had cured him of sty in the eye. Bill plastered the walls of Diamond Panes and Charlie mended the wood-work; and put a new garden gate for pure loving kindness. It seemed as though there was nothing St Gwendron folk would-n't do for Takestars and Dom. It didn't cost the two of them twopence a week to live. No wonder they had time to gaze at the stars. And they did seem to pass a good deal of time in gazing.

'What's hanging on that little chain he do wear round his neck?' said Nyas. 'That's what I should like to know.'

'How do you know he do wear anything round his neck, Nyas?'

'I see'd un one day, bathing mother-naked in Fisherman's Cove – mother-naked except for something hanging round his neck.'

'I expect 'tis the portrait of the beautiful young woman that jilted un, in a locket,' said Caroline Hussey.

'How do you know he's been jilted?'

'It stands to reason, a handsome man like that. How else wouldn't he have got married?'

'There's other things that do occupy a man besides females,' said Nyas, 'there's money, and there's mischief.'

'He doesn't care about money, and he doesn't care about mischief,' said Caroline.

'When the Devil away he gets, abroad he rogues,' said Nyas; 'that's what my old mother used to say.'

'You and your talk of the Devil!' scoffed Caroline.

''Tisn't only me, 'tis the Beast,' said Nyas; 'and the Beast do knaw.'

And so the talk veered, this way and that, this way and that; and then, one mild day in February, just as the primroses were beginning to bloom in low places, when the Towans were veiled in mist, and a black fog was reported in London, Takestars and Dom disappeared and stayed away for a longer time than ever before.

II

The gale that blew on March the fifteenth, following the disappearance of Mr Takestars and Dom Pockett, was of a fierceness never before remembered by the inhabitants of St Gwendron, inured as they were to storms. The roar of the waves could be heard far inland. The spume flew yellow and thick. Below the cliffs by Fisherman's Cove the world was turned to a chaos of raging wind and contending sea. It seemed a miracle, when signals made it known that a ship was in distress, that by means of the rocket apparatus communication should be established and the crew, using the breeches buoy, be brought to land. It was when the last of the rescued sailors was nearing safety that two other men, hitherto unperceived, were seen to be on board, and signalling for help. They must, said the Captain, have stowed themselves away when the ship was in a London dock. Almost simultaneously Nyas Trevarthen, who had been looking at the ship through a telescope, recognised the two as Takestars and Dom. He had hardly announced his discovery than a wave, more gigantic than its predecessors, washed Takestars into the flood; and Dom was seen to jump in after him.

Nyas Trevarthen was a powerful swimmer.

'Tie a rope round me, my sonnies; I'm going in,' said Nyas.

'You'm mazed, Nyas; you'll be drowned.'

'Can't be drowned more'n wance, a b'lieve.'

How he succeeded in bringing the two to the shore no one ever quite knew. But both were found to be dead; choked, not drowned the doctor thought. The little bags which both wore round their necks on silver chains had caused their deaths. The bags contained jewels, people learnt, stolen jewels.

Never before had there been such a to-do at St Gwendron: police, photographs, interviews; more detectives; more photographs, more interviews. Mr Takestars and Dom had gazed frequently on other stars than those which bespangled the heavens. What seemed strange was that they appeared never to have attempted to turn their booty into money. The elemental flowering lights had glittered unseen, except to the eyes of those who stole them, and who had contrived to hoard them in Diamond Panes.

Many who had, in St Gwendron, been loud in praise of Mr Takestars and Dom Pockett, now were malignant in speech against them. Only Nyas was silent and thoughtful; then he delivered his word. 'The man,' he said, 'may have been a rogue; but he had a good text. And he made hearts glow here in St Gwendron. I tell ee, my son-nies, everything is mixed here below; and 'tis beyond the wit of we poor toads to fathom ut. But I for wan are going to Takestars' funeral, and I think we ought to sing, "Now the labourer's task is o'er." We don't get the chance of singing un very often, and Sol Tyack can do the bass of he proper.' And then he added after a long pause, 'But the little dunk, he wadn' deceived; the Beast,' he said, 'do KNAW.'

A. L. Rowse

The Stone that Liked Company

It was the Christmas vacation: and those few Fellows who were still up – happy to see the backs of their undergraduates and to be quit of the dreary routine of lectures and tutorials for a blessed five weeks – had fore-gathered that evening, after a quiet common-room dinner, in the rooms of the Dean. The Dean, in spite of his name, was a secular person; his inclinations were hospitable, indeed he was rather overmuch given to entertaining. Though he had the cold, wary eyes of an intelligent fish, he was in fact a jovial person, not happy unless he had one or two of his friends in after dinner to sip his admirable port.

Tonight they were five: four of them drinking port and one – the wisest of them – with his glass of burgundy. This last was just raising his glass to his lips, when suddenly the lights went out. In itself no remarkable, nor that winter infrequent, circumstance; for it had happened several times of late that there had been a breakdown at the electric light works from which the college current came. The winter was a severe one; floods had broken out by the river and the works flooded. There was no knowing how long before the light would come on again.

Patient men, sitting heavy after a substantial meal, they sat there for a moment, their faces lit up momentarily by the gleams from the oak-log burning in the grate. Then the Dean rose, fetched out of the corner cupboard two pleasant little candlesticks, lit them and placed them on the mantelpiece: their flame, when it caught up, revealed their pretty Regency pattern, a single column with a wreath of foliage running round the stem.

'Hadn't somebody better tell a story?' said the Economics don: a hearty man with rubicund face and white sweater to match. He had a knack of saying what everybody thought.

'Yes, let's tell sad stories of the death of kings,' said the English don, a young man who had only recently joined the college.

'Well, who's got a story to tell?' said the Dean.

The general opinion was that he had; indeed he was well known for his stories. As host he couldn't very well have declined, even if he had wanted to. It was a situation he loved, for his inclination was all in favour of a story – his own story, and himself telling it.

'Well, since you will have it –' he began, settling himself well into the back of his chair, his head between the two side flaps in deep shadow, looking more than ever like some queer extinct animal with large flapping ears, while from the depths gleamed those intelligent eyes behind the spectacles. 'There's a house in Cornwall that I know –' he went on.

'Oh! come, Mr Dean', said the Economics don, who knew well the Dean's penchant for old houses in Cornwall haunted by ghosts.

'Well, as a matter of fact, it's not that kind of house at all,' said the Dean, quite unperturbed. 'It's a modern house, built after the last war. In fact, it's a bungalow, or what I believe is called a semi-bungalow. Some friends of mine took it for a bit some years ago, perhaps as much as fifteen years ago – how time flies! *Pereunt et imputantur.* They took it for a bit. They didn't stay there long.' He paused, dug further into the back of his chair, hugging himself, then resumed.

'I said "friend of mine": but really it was the widow of a friend of mine and her son, a delicate lad, liable to asthma and bronchitis, and that sort of thing. He was very highly strung, I gather, but intelligent and extremely sensitive – at any rate, he was as a child, the only time that I saw him. The mother took this house in Cornwall for the benefit of his health because of the climate. The climate agreed with him; it wasn't the climate that –'

'What was it?' said the eager young English lecturer, not used to the Dean's round-about way of telling a story.

'Just you wait, young man,' said he, not at all put out. 'The house was ideal from their point of view: not too large, very convenient, and could be run with one servant and a man in occasionally to look after the garden. My friend, Mrs Wilford, took a great deal of interest in it. Not so the boy: perhaps it would have been better for him if he had.

'His hobby was antiquities. He was just about the age when boys are mad about archaeology, would go chasing off on his bicycle to take rubbings of brasses in Cornish churches and all that sort of thing. Probably did him no good: he was a restless, inquiring sort of lad who could never take things easily. There was always an element of over-strain about him. I suppose he must have been eighteen or nineteen: he would have been up here if it hadn't been for his health. I'm not sure that he wasn't a good deal spoiled by his mother: her only child, and he being rather an invalid. He was good-looking, too, like his father: I saw a photograph of him after – well, after what happened. He had that striking combination of jet-black hair with deep-blue eyes which you sometimes come across in Scots people. He was tall and rather overgrown. There was a curious fanatic look in his eyes. He had another passion, too, besides archaeology – music. He would sit for hours listening to concerts on the wireless – in those early days of wireless. He was beginning to compose, too: not very professional, perhaps, but he certainly had a streak of something, more than talent.

'It so happened that a couple of fields away from the house there was a longstone: one of those megaliths which you get in Cornwall and Ireland – this was a particularly fine specimen. The Devil's Walking-stick, the local people called it: they have some story about how it came to be there – you know the kind of thing. It is there no longer. After what happened –'

There was a movement of impatience on the part of the eager young man. The Dean poured himself out a second glass of burgundy in leisurely fashion.

'Well – some on the young miners thereabouts got together one night and blew it up.'

'What?' said the Classics don in a tone of horror: he was himself interested in archaeology in a mild way. 'An interesting megalithic monument like that, destroyed by these vandals only a few years ago? I've never heard of such a thing. How did it come to happen? Of course, we all know that in previous centuries when people didn't value these things, didn't know what they were, they sometimes broke them up and used them for gate-posts on their farms, or for road-stone.'

'How do you know that they didn't know what they were doing?' said the Dean, with an odd tone in his voice. His eyes had a curious intense look in them. 'That they meant to break it up, and did it deliberately? They might have been *afraid* – he underlined the word significantly with his smooth voice – 'and even though they were afraid, they nevertheless went through with it. I call that courage of a sort.

'You wouldn't have heard of it,' he resumed in his ordinary speaking voice, with no suggestion in it. 'Nothing was said about it in public. All the local people were in it: they knew who had done it all right. But they never would say; for they all wanted it done. And I think,' he said, fixing the Classics don with his eyes, 'after you have heard what I am going to tell you, you will agree that they were not without reason.

'Of course it was an enormous attraction to the house in young Christopher's eyes when he first discovered the stone. He took it as if he were its first discoverer – "silent upon a peak in Darien" and that sort of thing – would he had been, poor lad!

'As a matter of fact, he could get nothing out of the local inhabitants about the stone or its history. They knew nothing about it – or said they knew nothing about it. In itself sufficiently curious when you come to think of it, for it was an exceedingly fine one. Young Christopher himself took its measurements. He found that it was over nine feet above ground: that meant that there must have been at least four or five feet more buried in its socket underground. At its broadest it was about two feet nine inches; it had a curious shape, for beneath the head the stone was, of course, unhewn; it had not, so far as one could tell, been shaped by human hands – all the same it gave the impression, a very strong one, of having a head slender and pointed. But beneath the head it broadened out noticeably on one side like a huge misshapen shoulder, rather threatening in appearance.

'Christopher was wildly anxious to dig round it, expose the socket if possible, and see what he could find. He never mentioned it to anyone – nobody seemed to be interested. It never occurred to him to ask permission of anyone – least of all of the stone,' the Dean added quietly.

'One autumn afternoon – there was nobody about much on that part of the coast – he started operations upon the socket. It was all very enthusiastic and unwise: if he had been successful and got on far enough with it he might have loosened the stone sufficiently for it to have toppled over – perhaps on to him. But he didn't get so far as that. He had no experience of digging or of professional archaeology: he was just the enthusiastic amateur. You will agree, my dear Done,' he said, addressing the historian among them, who had so far not spoken, was in fact struck by the story, which touched a chord in his experience – 'you will agree that there is no more dangerous person – even though the danger is more to himself than to others.' The Dean leaned forward, took up his glass from the little mahogany wine-bracket by the fireside, sipped two mouthfuls of burgundy, and went on.

'Young Christopher didn't as a matter of fact get very far with his digging operations. It was a pleasant enough day when he set out across the intervening fields, with their magnificent view of the bay spread out beneath in a kind of shelving curve; for the stone stands – or rather stood – in a splendid natural situation overlooking the bay. In primitive days before the coppices and plantations thereabouts had been laid out, and when all the fields were open downs, an uncultivated moor, it must have been a dominating object on the skyline from the coast below: a long forefinger pointing heavenwards, perhaps a propitiatory object, no doubt the centre of the religious cult of the primitive people round about, almost certainly the scene of human sacrifice with its attendant rites.

'The boy had not been long at work, heaving up the earth feverishly, in a frantic state of excitement – very bad for him – when there came on, as happens in Cornwall at that time of year, a sudden change in the weather. The sky was quickly filled with lowering grey cloud, which cast a cold uncomfortable atmosphere upon the scene – you know that sinister grey half-light than which there is nothing more cheerless in the world, or more sinking to the spirits. You might have felt a sensation of well-being and contentment a moment before, and then this dark cloud comes down upon you like a weight of lead. From being a warm afternoon it became suddenly cold; and very soon there followed a stiff shower of hail, for shelter from which Christopher ran to the heavy stone hedge, such as you have in the West Country. While sheltering there he was struck by the changed appearance of the stone. Whether it was that he was cowering down for shelter from the blast, it seemed to him that the stone had grown enormously larger. He noticed how it looked exactly to the west and the setting sun, and the thought of primitive sacrifice came into his mind. He almost fancied that he could see the blood running into the groove that he had exposed, hear the demented shrieks of the gibbering throng in that

Home of the silent vanished races,

like the innumerable mammering of bats' voices in the air. There was something horrible in the threatening headlessness of the stone, the shapelessness that was yet suggestive of power, of a ruthless natural force imprisoned in it incapable of expressing itself, or of any release. Suddenly, terrified, he could bear it no longer. But he was a lad of courage and he was too proud to take to his heels. He withdrew in good order, even going so far as to retrieve his pick and shovel, but having the feeling that he was fighting a rear-guard action all the way out of the field and over the hedge. It was the end of his digging operations. He had had a scare – even if it had been possible to resume, which it was not; for the hail shower was the prelude to a blizzard, which very unwontedly snowed them up for a week or two. It was the stone that resumed operations, in its own way, in its own time.'

There was a pause. A coal fell from the fire into the grate. The Dean leaned forward and put another log on, which burned up brightly, lighting up the intent faces of his colleagues. He sank back into the shadows. You could hear the soft ticking of his tiny clock in its Chippendale case, with the little lion's head handles, on the mantelpiece.

'The scare that he had had did not put the boy off. It might have been better if it had. I repeat that he was a lad of courage, like his father; though very excitable and nervous, he had spirit. The scare only increased his fascination for the stone: he longed to know more about it, to get to the bottom of it. He was determined to go on – you know the way such boys have of never letting sleeping dogs lie, they won't let a thing alone when it's better it should be – even if that stone had been a sleeping dog and prepared to be left alone.

'During those weeks of snow and sleet and slush' –

(Fire and fleet and candle-lighte
And Christe receive thy saule

– the words ran through the mind of the young English don) – 'very exceptional for Cornwall,' commented the prosaic mind of the Dean, 'Christopher got to work to read everything he could lay hand on that might give him some information. He began naturally with Carew's *Survey of Cornwall* – his father had had a copy of the very pleasant 1769 edition. He drew a blank: nothing whatever about the stone. He went on to all the other old histories of Cornwall, Polwhele, Borlase, Davies Gilbert. Borlase's *Natural Antiquities of Cornwall* did mention the stone and its position, but gave no further particulars.

'However, his reading was not without some effect, for he gathered two bits of information which enabled him to piece together a picture of the district in primitive times in his mind. Less than a mile away, towards the other end of the bay, was a farm called Castle Dennis. There was a stile-field just above the farm, with a path leading across it which cut off a roundabout corner going by the road. After you left the field by the second stile, you found yourself deep in a little lane leading to the third. It was a favourite walk of his. For some reason the field had got the name "the Field of the Dead" in his mind. It always had a curious intimate feeling for him: "Campo dei Morti" he would say over to himself crossing it, and one day he wrote a poem about it in which occurred the line –

So many dead men have made this their home.

But it had never occurred to him, what now he learned from these old authorities, that that field actually was the inside of a primitive camp, that the little lane into which you descended was the deep ditch or foss outside the rampart: that the name Castle Dennis was a corruption of the old Celtic *dinas*, meaning fortress. He learned, too, that at the other end of the bay, not far from the longstone, there had been a series of barrows which had been broken into in the eighteenth century and robbed of their funeral urns with their contents of charred human bones.

'The whole picture of the district as it was in primitive times came clear in his mind. There at the other end of the bay had been their encampment, their town, for centuries: there was even a little cliff castle down upon the headland for refuge in time of danger, in those dangerous days when life was so precarious. At the opposite end of the bay was the town of the dead, the cemetery with its barrows where they buried the burned bones of their chieftains. Near the latter was the longstone, the centre of their worship with its fearful barbarous rites.

'In a fever of excitement he read on and on in those weeks. From works on Cornwall he turned to books on stone-age Britain, on the megalithic period, on megalithic religion, on Avebury and Stonehenge. It made a strong, an unforgettable impression when he read that when the altar-stone at Stonehenge was excavated they had found the cleft skull of an infant, evidently a dedicatory sacrifice. He could not forget it. Still his mind raced on and on, forgetting everything else, putting on one side his music, poetry – neglecting everything for the sake of this passion, this morbid fascination.

'At the same time his reading had made him very knowledgeable about the history of the locality. When some local female society – I think it was a Women's Institute – kept badgering his mother to go and lecture to them, his mother, who was a very shy and timid woman, let him go and take her place. He promised he would give them a lecture on the history of their parish – very bold of him, but he had the temperament for it, and what with his enthusiasm and good looks it was a great success. Of course, it was all, or mainly, about the longstone and the portrait of the district in primitive times that he had constructed in his mind. He told them that here was one of the finest megalithic monuments in the county – by far the oldest historical monument in the district – and nobody seemed the least proud of its possession or even interested in it. One had never even heard of its existence. Oughtn't it to be put on the map, etc.? He ended by asking them for any information they had about it, any stories connected with it. The audience did not seem to take the subject up with any enthusiasm; they were more interested in him. He was too young to note that in fact they rather sheered off it, and quite deftly – though in the manner of Cornish people purely instinctively – they succeeded in deflecting him from it.

'But a day or two later when walking in the vicinity he ran into a woman who stopped him and talked to him about the subject. She was an odd sort of woman, rather masculine in type with a way of swinging to and fro on her hips as if she were a sailor. She was, as a matter of fact, the wife of a captain of a vessel, and prided herself on the fact: so perhaps she got the habit from him. She came close up to the young man, putting her face into his – he stepped down off the pavement unobtrusively into the gutter to give her room.

'"By the way, Mr Wilford," she said, "you won't know me. My name is Mrs Chynoweth. But I was very interested by the lecture you gave to our institute the other day. You spoke of the old longstone over there in the field. Well, I remember Mr Coombe who used to live in the farm just below, and his family before him for a hundred years back; and he used to say that there was a tradition that somebody had been executed there – oh, hundreds of years ago. I don't mean executed just like that, you know –"

'"You mean – human sacrifice?" said Christopher; somehow there flashed across his mind what he had read of somewhere, the picture of some poor creature left out on a last outpost of rock facing the setting sun, with a loaf of bread and a pitcher, the tide around those islands rising higher and higher.

"'Yes, that's it," she said, rolling her fine dark eyes at him and revealing her powerful dentures in a broad smile. "And I remember," she went on, "when we were children in the village we never used to play in that field. Nobody ever did, or went into it if they could help it." She moved nearer to him, like an old man of the sea whom he couldn't shake off even if he would; though he was in fact fascinated. "Have you ever noticed how threatening it looks with that great heavy shoulder, crouching like somebody ready to lurch out at you?" She made the motion expressively with her heavy body. Christopher moved a shade further away. "Just as if they were waiting to attack you," she said.

'Christopher did not encourage these suppositions; they made all the greater impression upon him.

' "Are you interested in spiritualism?" she said, and without waiting for an answer continued, "Well, I am. And once in London when I went to a spiritualist church and they asked for questions, I thought I'd ask about this old longstone and whether it had any influence upon people's lives round about. The answer came that I was psychic, and should keep away from such things: they are liable to exert a sinister influence on you."

'Deviating into egoism, released and unashamed, she ceased to be interesting. Christopher found some halting excuse, took his leave, and went on his way.

'His way took him back along the coast by the path that skirted the field where the stone was. From the shelter of the hedge he could observe the figure, as it were without being observed. There was no doubt it bore an extraordinary resemblance to the figure of a hooded and shrouded woman. The great bulging shoulder might be a child it was carrying, that it had taken in its arms for some purpose, draped and veiled. But it was the very formlessness of it, the shaped shapelessness, the fact that headless it seemed to have a head, shoulderless and armless it seemed to have shoulders and arms, or at least on this side shoulder and arm; the blankness of it, standing there through the centuries looking to the west with unseeing eyes, a blind face to the setting sun, that made it at once so terrible and so pathetic. For tonight he could see its pathos, its loneliness, the embodiment of grey despair, deserted for centuries by its votaries, living its own terrible secret life, the embodiment of imprisoned force.

'Greatly affected by the spectacle and his own teeming imaginings, he hurried by. Yet when he crossed the gap of the gate, from which he could be observed, he could not but feel a distinct tremor run through his nerves. Greatly daring, he turned back for a last look. The stone looked quite different: a bar of angry light from the west rested upon its upper face: it looked blank, impersonal, menacing.

'Christopher had been pestering his mother for days to come and visit the stone with him, wanted to have the name of the house changed to Longstone House, so great was his mania on the subject. At last, not in the least interested, she went along with him to pacify him. That same evening he quarrelled bitterly with her. It was their first (and last) quarrel: they had never so much as bickered before. But that night Christopher, led on by what impulse, uttered things to his mother – about his father, for example, whom he scarcely remembered – such as had never even entered his head before. It was as if a preternaturally old experience of life had suddenly been injected into his veins.

'From that moment everything began to go wrong. As if he had some presentiment of this and of how things would end, he began to keep secretly a journal of the terrible experience that he was to undergo. Later, his mother sent it to me, and after her death it remained in my possession.

'Rarely can a lad of his years have endured such hallucinations – if hallucinations they were that led to such an indubitable result.

'From the eastern window of the house, where Christopher's bedroom was on the ground floor, the longstone was visible, as I have said, across a couple of intervening fields. It seems that the lad got the sense that he was being ceaselessly watched. One night as he was going to bed late, as his habit was, his nerves on edge, he drew back the curtains to peer out. What he saw there in the moonlight, very lovely and unearthly upon the snow, made him draw back in terror. There was no sleep for him that night; he fancied he had seen the stone – which, as you know, was a couple of fields away – as large as life, as if it were on watch outside his window.

'Of course, it was just the disordered fancy of a child. He said not a word of what he suffered, but wrote down what he at any rate was convinced of in the journal he kept. But he never slept in that room again. It was shut up. He moved upstairs to a little attic room under the roof, with a dormer window that looked to the west.

'Nothing happened any more for a few days. He fancied he was safe. He took his mind off the obsession and turned to his music. He began to forget the scare he had had. It is dangerous to forget.

'One night he went to have a bath before going up to bed. The bathroom was at the back of the house and looked to the north. There was just enough light for him to see, and he was lying full length humming some theme that had occurred to him that evening, trying it out various ways in his head, when he looked up casually to see a long gaunt finger of shadow resting upon the window from outside. He turned cold with horror. Grabbing his dressing-gown he fled upstairs to the safety of his room.

'But now he knew that he was no longer safe wherever he was. The bathroom looked to the north; the longstone stood in the fields to the east of the house. He could no longer console himself with the thought that it was an hallucination. He longed to leave the house; he hated the thought of the shadow that lay upon it and about it, that laid siege to it on every side. But he was afraid – afraid to confess that he was afraid, and so held on.

'The very next day he ran into Mrs Chynoweth out walking again.

' "You don't seem to look very well," she said in her breezy, familiar way. She was dressed as usual in dark tweed with a man's soft felt hat worn slightly on one side. She carried a walking-stick with which she executed little cuts in the air; she was jauntier than ever. "Cornwall not agreeing with you, perhaps? I shouldn't wonder, not in that house of yours with the name it's got with people here."

' "What name?" said Christopher, surprised into indiscretion. So far as he was aware it was simply known as "The Bungalow."

' "Oh, people here call it 'Longstone House'. Didn't you know what happened there a year or two ago with the last tenants who had the house? They didn't tell you when you took it? No, of course not. People are so secretive about things; I can never understand why. Now I'm different; I'm open; I believe in being candid."

'She certainly did. She didn't need Christopher's apprehensive invitation to tell him what had happened before plunging into her story.

' "Well, it was very nasty for the time," she said, "and that was why the house stood empty until you came. There was a very nice couple that built the house just after the war. They came down here from London with their little girl. She was about ten or eleven – yes, eleven, the same age as my little girl. One evening just as it was getting dark she went down the drive to the gate – you know, where the path leads out into the road that comes from the longstone. She was found there a little later. They missed her from the house, and when they went down the drive there she was lying just outside her own gate. It was supposed that she had been knocked down by a passing lorry. But nobody had seen one. Nobody here believed that it was a lorry that was responsible. When they picked the poor little thing up, her right shoulder was shattered and there was a fracture of the right temple: just as if she had been lurched into by something very heavy. And believe me, it wasn't a car that did it.

' "Now, I don't know if you are interested in spiritualism, Mr Wilford –"

'Christopher did not need her assurance, and the thought of her philosophising on the subject after what he had been through himself was more than he could bear. He took to his heels and unashamedly fled back to the house.

'That night alone he sat up late to listen in to a concert he particularly wanted to hear, for it included the Fourth Symphony of Sibelius, the most monolithic of them all. He shut himself in the dining-room of the house, a room with heavy brocade curtains across the big window that looked due south. He had his journal out before him, into which he poured his soul: all his fears, agonies, all the things he felt he could share with no one: all written in pell-mell as if he had no time to spare – nor had he, poor lad ! – mixed up with musical themes jotted down, which he was trying out for some work that he wanted to compose – there was the title: "Campo dei Morti".

'As he listened, everything seemed to become unnaturally clear to him; there was the inevitability of fate in the great marching strides of the basses in the first movement, very low, menacing steps coming nearer and nearer, which nothing could stop. In all this stony waste of sound, no tenderness, no sweetness, until at the moment of sacrifice the flutes sounded clear like human voices, wringing a certain sweetness out of the very stone, the heart of stone. Then there came the shrill insistent lament of violins, that pathetic motif of protest against the menacing rhythm of those monolithic steps. As he listened and wrote, his nerves on edge, a sixth sense rather than any reason told him that the moment had come, that the long striding steps of the basses in the music led in the world of space out through the window, that beyond the curtains there was that waiting for him to which all his brief life had been a pilgrimage. In short, if he tore open the curtains there would be the stone waiting for him.

'He could bear the suspense no longer, but flung back the curtains, threw open the window – at least that's the way it seems he must have gone – rushed down the drive to the gate, the way the little girl had gone before him, and along the path to where the stone awaited him. It would seem that that stone had a hunger for what was young and innocent.

'It was not until the early hours of the morning that they found him, lying like a sacrificial offering at the foot of the socket he had ventured to uncover. His right shoulder was crushed and the whole right side of his face was bruised and grazed as in some embrace that had been too strong for him. They found him in the grey light of a morning moon: an old moon, a rind of a moon upon its back in the west, which turned the whole landscape into death's kingdom and lit his face with a strange glimmer there where it lay at the stone's foot.'

The Dean's story had come to an end. His eyes shone with an unusual intensity, as if he were more concerned by it than he cared to admit. Just before the end the electric light had come on again, with something of a shock; so that the end of the story had been told in the hard glitter of unaccustomed light in their eyes, while the candles wavered their rather ghostly light on the mantelpiece. Nobody said anything for a moment. Then the young English don recited half aloud, half to himself:

> This ae nighte, this ae nighte,
> – Every nighte and alle,
> Fire and fleet and candle-lighte,
>   And Christe receive thy saule.

Shortly afterwards, with a few brief words and Christmas greetings, they dispersed severally to their beds.

Mary Williams

No Ticket

The mist was quickly thickening into fog, and I wondered why I hadn't had the sense to stop at the last village and put up for the night. But before starting off on my Cornish walking trip, the doctor had said, 'Whatever you do get out into the fresh air and walk. Walk yourself so tired your body will fall to sleep the moment you get to bed. It's the only way, Rogers. Breakdowns are funny things. Drugs can help at the beginning, but in the end it's only nature and commonsense will do the trick. You're a fit enough man physically. So give the brain a bit of a rest, and you'll soon find the nightmares will go.'

Naturally I'd taken his advice, and for the first week things had gone better for me than I'd expected. It was autumn, with the moors washed bronze and gold under the pale sun, and the mingled smell of fallen leaves, blackberries and distant tang of woodsmoke hovering rich in the air with the faint drift of sea-blown brine. Heady, nostalgic weather, stirring the lost emotion of youth to life again. Not difficult then to push the rat-race of London journalism behind me, forgetting even … except in sudden rare stabs of renewed pain … my break with Claire.

Each day I'd walked a little further, and when I came to some attractive looking old inn catering for visitors had stopped for the night, setting off again after a hearty breakfast for further exercise and adventure.

Yes, there was adventure in the experience; mostly, I suppose because of the terrain … Cornwall. Changeless in the sense of atmosphere and 'place' magic, yet at almost every corner providing a vista of alternating scene. At one moment lush and verdant between high hedges and clumps of woodland, the next opening to stretches of barren countryside dotted with the stark relics of ruined mine works huddled granite hamlets perched above windblown cliffs. As I trod the winding lanes and moorland roads of West Penwith this sense of agelessness and primitive challenge had deepened and drawn me on, almost as though into another dimension.

I should have stopped at The Tramping Woman of course, an ancient hostelry on the outskirts of Wikka; but ignored it and continued along the high road between coast and rocky hills, although the sun was already dying, leaving a film of pale gold beneath the greenish sky.

I'd walked almost a mile to the west when the mist started to rise; thinly at first, like a gauze veil over the fading landscape, then thickening into furry uncertainty so the boulders and windblown trees assumed gradually the menacing quality of ancient gigantic beasts and legendary creatures risen to torment and mislead. When I came at last to a crossroads with a decrepit sign-post pointing in three directions like a gibbet, I paused searching for my torch to try and locate any names given. It was impossible. The archaic lettering further distorted by the wreathing fog made no sense at all. In fact as I went close up, clinging to the post, the cloying atmosphere completely shrouded it into negation, warning me that far from improving, the light and weather were steadily getting worse.

A sickening sense of claustrophobia filled me, choking at my throat, filling my lungs with a hysterical feeling of being unable to breathe. The torch suddenly flickered and went out. I was alone, and lost, and if I hadn't forced myself to move quickly I knew I'd be there until morning, by which time, for me, it might be too late.

So I struck ahead taking what I thought ... or hoped ... was the main road.

How long I continued in this way, moving by instinct rather than any coherent sense of direction I don't know. Occasionally I lurched against a bush or humped tree ... maybe something more sinister ... that flapped me with the clammy slap of a dead hand. Once I fell against a looming slab of stone that emitted to my distorted fancy malicious elemental glee as I pulled myself away with my heart pumping furiously. I could imagine the ancient cromlechs and standing stones on the moors above leering down on my puny shape as I struggled blindly on, with my coat gripped close over my chest, head thrust forward in a futile attempt to get a clear glimpse of the ground.

Except for the dripping of the fog, the stillness was oppressive ... an entity in itself. Watchfulness encompassed me. From the furry grey walls on every side it seemed to me that eyes were peering. Secret haunted eyes of elemental evil and atavistic greed. Unconsciously I put out an arm to defend myself, knowing that I couldn't continue for much longer. My thighs already felt deadened, the breath in my body absorbed by the sucking lips and tongue of hungry fog.

And then, suddenly, I heard it; the distant thrum of an engine ... tangible evidence of reality in an unreal world. A car or bus surely? 'Thank God,' I thought, swerving to the side of the road.

A minute later, headlights appeared dimly emerging as two immense wan eyes through the curdling fitful grey. The road temporarily came into blurred focus ... snaking like some ghostly ribbon towards me until the cumbrous dark shape dimmed it again into darkness. The vehicle seemed to sway slightly and slow down as it passed; sufficiently for me to pull myself by the rail over the step inside.

I paused briefly, gasping for breath, then staggered on flinging myself into the first vacant seat. Only one dim light shone from the front, showing the dark shoulders of the driver at the wheel and above, in the vicinity of the windscreen, the glow of a printed name, ABMUT, which was a new one on me. I'd never heard of the place, and never been in such an antiquated omnibus before. It was a real 'boneshaker', and as we jogged on, with the dripping fog flapping the windscreen, streaming in rivulets down the dreary windows, I could almost hear my own jaws and knees creaking in unison with the macabre tempo of the ancient engine.

There were about a dozen passengers inside, no more, and they were a silent crowd, sitting speechless and hunched into their grey clothes, faces pale discs of misery, eyes mere shadowed pools of emptiness in the queer half light. My presence seemed to evoke no interest whatever; the entrance of a stranger generally does on a country journey.

Thinking back now, I can't recall a single individual face except those of an aged bearded man with a kind of muffler round his head, a lantern-jawed woman wearing a grey hooded cape, and a young boy who seemed more alert than the rest, although his forehead was bandaged, and I guessed he'd been in an accident. He looked round once at me, and I saw in his eyes such supplication and pleading I hoisted myself up and went to sit beside him. No one seemed to notice. There was no comment, no flicker of surprise or movement from the crouched chill forms. Even the child himself didn't speak; but I could feel him shivering, and when my hand touched his it was icily cold. But I felt he was grateful to have me there.

How long that dreary journey to Abmut took, I've no idea. Time seemed to have died. The silence, except for the monotonous chug-chugging of the engine, was oppressive and somehow unearthly. There were only brief intervals when the landscape took form, showing momentary glimpse of a looming hill-side or humped boulder at a corner of the lane. Still, I thought. Abmut must be our destination, and where there was a village or town, presumably there would be an inn, however primitive. I had a compulsive almost irrational desire at one point to get up and jump out. But as I made the first instinctive movement, several heads turned to look at me, and their dumb, pale, almost hostile faces filled me with such aversion I remained rooted to the spot, my hand automatically tightening on the boy's.

If there'd been a conductor I'd have forced information from him, but the vehicle was obviously a one-man affair as some still are in remote places; therefore all I could do was to hope for the best, and somehow battle against the sickening fear which was intensifying in me every moment that passed.

At last through the window I saw thankfully the first glimmer of lifting light in a fold of the moors below the road. As the bus took a sharp turn down a steep track between dripping walls of hedges, the blurred outline of a huddled hamlet took shape, dimly at first … a mere outline of grey squat buildings that gradually clarified, assuming a quivering brilliance against that desolate landscape of grim uniformity. It was as though nature, in a quixotic moment had designed a macabre backcloth purely as a setting for this one benighted village.

And then the singing began … from a church presumably … although the soughing and sighing and rising and falling of the mournful yet unwelcoming chorus held, for my ears, more of the wind's moan and the sea's lonely call than the quality of human voices. At the same time I was aware of movement, a shuffling and stirring around me as one form after another moved cumbrously from each seat and waited, heads hunched forward, for the bus to stop.

It came to a halt at the top of a track about a hundred yards from the hamlet which appeared by then to emerge from a sea of vaporized grey, roof tops and church spire tipped with silver. I waited until the last of the throng, the boy, had clambered out. The driver had dismounted and was waiting to give a nod before each joined the mournful procession downwards. Then I swung myself wearily by the rail to the ground.

'Ticket?' I heard him murmur above the weird cacophony of sighs that rose and fell intermittently on a drift of rising wind. His voice was hushed yet grating, like the branch of a very ancient tree about to snap, the dark holed eyes watchful from the bearded face. Drifts of grey hair blew fitfully in the clammy air, brushing my face softly with the choking touch of a cobwebbed shroud.

Revolted, I drew away.

'I've no ticket,' I told him.

'No ticket?' He shook his head as the mist curdled and cleared again briefly, revealing a mournful dropped jaw and skeleton-like visage moving incredulously on a thin neck.

'That's right,' I said, 'I got on further back, where you slowed down? I can pay now, and the rest necessary to take me on. Or … are you returning to Wikka?' As I spoke the wild hope stirred in me this might be so. I had a growing irrational desire to be away from Abmut as soon as possible. In spite of the gathering radiance there and the muted singing which was gradually dying into a subdued murmur, there was something odd and greedy about the place … something sensed rather than seen that appalled me.

Then he spoke in a wheezing voice that was more of a harsh whisper, holding condemnation in it as well as a threat.

'There's no return from here. No one leaves once they've come. *No* one …'

A crawling shuddering fear pricked my spine. I could feel my nails digging into my palms. 'What do you mean no one leaves? What the hell *is* this place … this *Abmut*?

Before the mist clouded his face into a mere blurred disc I saw the lips stretch in an obscene grin from ear to ear. 'Not Abmut,' he muttered in the same sibilant undertone. 'Tumba. That's the name. Tumba.' And the laughter rose from his ancient throat more harsh than the sound of dried bones cracking on stone, colder and more deadly than death itself.

Forcing myself to mobility I rushed, half staggering, to the front of the bus. It was just as he said … TUMBA printed at the top of front window in stygian green lettering that for a moment caught all the reflected light from the hamlet below. What I'd seen from the inside had been the wrong way round.

TUMBA.

It took some moments for the truth to register, and when at last the meaning of the word penetrated my cold brain, I rushed as though in some nightmare of doom over the rim of the slope. From there, against the quivering uncertain vista of fog mingled with luminous quivering light, the sad, limping, column of shuffling figures was visible; grey humped forms moving rhythmically and with an inevitability of purpose that I knew no human hand could allay.

Shuddering, I watched helplessly, as for a brief space of time the fog lifted, under a green sky, revealing a gaunt landscape of tumbled rock and giant standing-stones where the hamlet had formerly been. All sound except the screaming and moaning of the strengthening wind had died. There was no singing any more, no murmur of voices or whispered comment from the macabre driver, and when I turned there was no sign of him at all. Nothing but dripping negation … an emptiness and desolation so intense it seemed that no human foot had ever stepped there.

I looked again, towards the column of creeping shuffling beings, and as I stood watching, impelled by some dark power impossible to combat, the pale stones toppled and the earth opened with a shriek. Greedy grey arms clawed upwards through the brown earth, with skeleton fingers reaching for their own. Skulls leered and lolled among the stones, jaws bared in unholy welcome, the whole scene becoming a seething struggling vortex of death and decay ... a lustful avaricious breeding ground for the terrifying 'earth-bound' and the damned.

Sickened I had to wait while the crowd of erstwhile passengers suddenly lunged forward and were taken to their own corruption. The ground closed over them like an immense elemental mouth devouring, with a shudder, its own.

All but the boy.

When the heaving and roaring of the earth had subsided, I saw him lying there by a shining white stone. The mist had dispersed considerably, and nothing moved over that lonely terrain but a bird's sudden flight and squawking from the undergrowth. I looked behind me; the moorland road above the slope was almost clear; pale and empty under an eerie moonlit sky. No sign of any vehicle or indication there had ever been one.

Slowly I turned and made my way to where the recumbent young form lay stretched on his back in the heather. There was no fear on his face, for the innocent have no need of it; only a tremendous loneliness and sadness for the days he should have had.

Automatically I crossed his hands over his chest and touched his cold forehead once, where the bandage had been torn away. The scar was vivid still from the impact that had taken his life. In that moment his delicate features were impressed indelibly and forever into my mind.

Just then I had neither the wish nor strength to rationalise my haunting and macabre experience. It was all I could do to get to my feet, somehow making my way to the main moorland road.

Once there all initiative and sense of purpose faded into dark overwhelming negation. There was a roaring in my ears, a sound as though the universe was crumbling around me, and then I fell.

When I recovered consciousness I was aware only of greyness at first; a furry grey that slowly lifted to clean calm white. There was a face above me, a woman's face in a nurse's cap, and very gradually it dawned on me I was in hospital. My head was aching abominably, yet memory still registered with dreadful disconcerting clarity.

I think I said something about 'Tumba'. She merely smiled, took my wrist between finger and thumb, a thermometer in the other hand, and after a minute said quietly, 'You're doing fine, Mr Rogers. Rest now. The doctor will be in presently.'

'Who found me?' I asked. 'How could anyone know I was there, by that awful place?'

'The driver, of course,' she replied. 'There was an accident. You swerved in the fog ...'

'No, no,' I told her, as my heart started to pump rapidly against my ribs, 'there was no accident. I got on to a bus, a pretty nasty vehicle. And when it stopped we were at Tumba. It was ... *foul* ...'

'Shsh ...' she said, 'you mustn't excite yourself. Concussion plays strange tricks with the memory. In time everything will become normal again ...'

But it never did; not quite. Eventually I had to accept that I had been involved in some sort of a crash on that benighted moorland road. The driver of a perfectly ordinary car verified this in his statement to the police, and his word was accepted. Perhaps I might even have persuaded myself in the end there was nothing more to it, if something rather odd hadn't happened a few days later.

By then, having mostly recovered from physical cuts and shock, I was able to sit up in bed and glance at a local weekly newspaper.

At the middle page I got a start. There, facing me, was the smiling photograph of a boy. A face I well knew, of the youngster who'd ridden beside me on that ghastly bus bound for Tumba, and whose cold forehead I'd touched with my hand before making for the road again.

Beneath the heading of 'TRAFFIC ACCIDENT' I read:

> Anthony Treneer, aged twelve, died yesterday when a car skidded in the fog across the moorland road above Wikka. He had been out walking with a friend, and was returning to Verrys Farm, his home, when the tragedy occurred. Death was instantaneous. He was the younger son of Mr and Mrs Robert Treneer, both well known and respected members of the farming community.

I was still staring at the paragraph when my nurse entered.

'That's the boy,' I said, pointing to the photograph.

'You knew him?'

'He was on the bus with me,' I told her unthinkingly, 'the bus to Tumba.'

'Tumba?' she said half pityingly. 'You must forget all about that. It was just an illusion, a nightmare.'

Her obtuseness suddenly irritated me.

'That's what you always say I suppose when you come up against something that can't be rationally explained. The fact remains, nurse, I'm not out of my mind, and although the whole thing may appear moonshine to you, the boy was *with* me …'

Her voice was clipped when she said, 'He can't have been. Your accident took place at least three miles from the spot where he was hit. Another thing … there's no such place as Tumba, and there never has been. Now you really must try and put such morbid fancies behind you, Mr Rogers. Thinking that way won't help your complete recovery at all.'

Realising there was no point in further argument, I let the matter drop. Whether she realised the significance of the name 'Tumba' was doubtful. But in an ancient dictionary of mine it is alluded to as a *tomb*.

Incidentally, the evening of the boy's death was the same as that of my haunted 'bus' journey. The only difference being, I suppose, he had a ticket out of this life, whereas I had none.

Daphne du Maurier

The Old Man

Did I hear you asking about the Old Man? I thought so. You're a newcomer to the district, here on holiday. We get plenty these days, during the summer months. Somehow they always find their way eventually over the cliffs down to this beach, and then they pause and look from the sea back to the lake. Just as you did.

It's a lovely spot, isn't it? Quiet and remote. You can't wonder at the old man choosing to live here.

I don't remember when he first came. Nobody can. Many years ago, it must have been. He was here when I arrived, long before the war. Perhaps he came to escape from civilization, much as I did myself. Or maybe, where he lived before, the folks around made things too hot for him. It's hard to say. I had the feeling, from the very first, that he had done something, or something had been done to him, that gave him a grudge against the world. I remember the first time I set eyes on him I said to myself, 'I bet that old fellow is one hell of a character.'

Yes, he was living here beside the lake, along of his missus. Funny sort of lash-up they had, exposed to all the weather, but they didn't seem to mind.

I had been warned about him by one of the fellows from the farm, who advised me, with a grin, to give the old man who lived down by the lake a wide berth – he didn't care for strangers. So I went warily, and I didn't stay to pass the time of day. Nor would it have been any use if I had, not knowing a word of his lingo. The first time I saw him he was standing by the edge of the lake, looking out to sea, and from tact I avoided the piece of planking over the stream, which meant passing close to him, and crossed to the other side of the lake by the beach instead. Then, with an awkward feeling that I was trespassing and had no business to be there, I bobbed down behind a clump of gorse, took out my spy-glass, and had a peep at him.

He was a big fellow, broad and strong – he's aged, of course, lately; I'm speaking of several years back – but even now you can see what he must have been once. Such power and drive behind him, and that fine head, which he carried like a king. There's an idea in that, too. No, I'm not joking. Who knows what royal blood he carries inside him, harking back to some remote ancestor? And now and again, surging in him – not through his own fault – it gets the better of him and drives him fighting mad. I didn't think about that at the time. I just looked at him, and ducked behind the gorse when I saw him turn, and I wondered to myself what went on in his mind, whether he knew I was there, watching him.

If he should decide to come up the lake after me I should look pretty foolish. He must have thought better of it, though, or perhaps he did not care. He went on staring out to sea, watching the gulls and the incoming tide, and presently he ambled off his side of the lake, heading for the missus and home and maybe supper.

I didn't catch a glimpse of her that first day. She just wasn't around. Living as they do, close in by the left bank of the lake, with no proper track to the place, I hardly had the nerve to venture close and come upon her face to face. When I did see her, though, I was disappointed. She wasn't much to look at after all. What I mean is, she hadn't got anything like his character. A placid, mild-tempered creature, I judged her.

They had both come back from fishing when I saw them, and were making their way up from the beach to the lake. He was in front, of course. She tagged along behind. Neither of them took the slightest notice of me, and I was glad, because the old man might have paused, and waited, and told her to get on back home, and then come down towards the rocks where I was sitting. You ask what I would have said, had he done so? I'm damned if I know. Maybe I would have got up, whistling and seeming unconcerned, and then, with a nod and a smile – useless, really, but instinctive, if you know what I mean – said good day and pottered off. I don't think he would have done anything. He'd just have stared after me, with those strange narrow eyes of his, and let me go.

After that, winter and summer, I was always down on the beach or the rocks, and they went on living their curious, remote existence, sometimes fishing in the lake, sometimes at sea. Occasionally I'd come across them in the harbour on the estuary, taking a look at the yachts anchored there, and the shipping. I used to wonder which of them made the suggestion. Perhaps suddenly he would be lured by the thought of the bustle and life of the harbour, and all the things he had either wantonly given up or never known, and he would say to her, 'Today we are going into town.' And she, happy to do whatever pleased him best, followed along.

You see, one thing that stood out – and you couldn't help noticing it – was that the pair of them were devoted to one another. I've seen her greet him when he came back from a day's fishing and had left her back home, and towards evening she'd come down the lake and on to the beach and down to the sea to wait for him. She'd see him coming from a long way off, and I would see him too, rounding the corner of the bay. He'd come straight in to the beach, and she would go to meet him, and they would embrace each other, not caring a damn who saw them. It was touching, if you know what I mean. You felt there was something loveable about the old man, if that's how things were between them. He might be a devil to outsiders, but he was all the world to her. It gave me a warm feeling for him, when I saw them together like that.

You asked if they had any family? I was coming to that. It's about the family I really wanted to tell you. Because there was a tragedy, you see. And nobody knows anything about it except me. I suppose I could have told someone, but if I had, I don't know … They might have taken the old man away, and she'd have broken her heart without him, and anyway, when all's said and done, it wasn't my business. I know the evidence against the old man was strong, but I hadn't positive proof, it might have been some sort of accident, and anyway, nobody made any inquiries at the time the boy disappeared, so who was I to turn busybody and informer?

I'll try and explain what happened. But you must understand that all this took place over quite a time, and sometimes I was away from home or busy, and didn't go near the lake. Nobody seemed to take any interest in the couple living there but myself, so that it was only what I observed with my own eyes that makes this story, nothing that I heard from anybody else, no scraps of gossip, or tales told about them behind their backs.

Yes, they weren't always alone, as they are now. They had four kids. Three girls and a boy. They brought up the four of them in that ramshackle old place by the lake, and it was always a wonder to me how they did it. God, I've known days when the rain lashed the lake into little waves that burst and broke on the muddy shore near by their place, and turned the marsh into a swamp, and the wind driving straight in. You'd have thought anyone with a grain of sense would have taken his missus and his kids out of it and gone off somewhere where they could get some creature comforts at least. Not the old man. If he could stick it, I guess he decided she could too, and the kids as well. Maybe he wanted to bring them up the hard way.

Mark you, they were attractive youngsters. Especially the youngest girl. I never knew her name, but I called her Tiny, she had so much go to her. Chip off the old block, in spite of her size. I can see her now, as a little thing, the first to venture paddling in the lake, on a fine morning, way ahead of her sisters and the brother.

The brother I nicknamed Boy. He was the eldest, and between you and me a bit of a fool. He hadn't the looks of his sisters and was a clumsy sort of fellow. The girls would play around on their own, and go fishing, and he'd hang about in the background, not knowing what to do with himself. If he possibly could he'd stay around home, near his mother. Proper mother's boy. That's why I gave him the name. Not that she seemed to fuss over him any more than she did the others. She treated the four alike, as far as I could tell. Her thoughts were always for the old man rather than for them. But Boy was just a great baby, and I have an idea he was simple.

Like the parents, the youngsters kept themselves to themselves. Been dinned into them, I dare say, by the old man. They never came down to the beach on their own and played; and it must have been a temptation, I thought, in full summer, when people came walking over the cliffs down to the beach to bathe and picnic. I suppose, for those strange reasons best known to himself, the old man had warned them to have no truck with strangers.

They were used to me pottering, day in, day out, fetching driftwood and that. And often I would pause and watch the kids playing by the lake. I didn't talk to them, though. They might have gone back and told the old man. They used to look up when I passed by, then glance away again, sort of shy. All but Tiny. Tiny would toss her head and do a somersault, just to show off.

I sometimes watched them go off, the six of them – the old man, the missus, Boy, and the three girls, for a day's fishing out to sea. The old man, of course, in charge; Tiny eager to help, close to her dad; the missus looking about her to see if the weather was going to keep fine; the two other girls alongside; and Boy, poor simple Boy, always the last to leave home. I never knew what sport they had. They used to stay out late, and I'd have left the beach by the time they came back again. But I guess they did well.

They must have lived almost entirely on what they caught. Well, fish is said to be full of vitamins, isn't it? Perhaps the old man was a food faddist in his way.

Time passed, and the youngsters began to grow up. Tiny lost something of her individuality then, it seemed to me. She grew more like her sisters. They were a nice-looking trio, all the same. Quiet, you know, well-behaved.

As for Boy, he was enormous. Almost as big as the old man, but with what a difference! He had none of his father's looks, or strength, or personality; he was nothing but a great clumsy lout. And the trouble was, I believe the old man was ashamed of him. He didn't pull his weight in the home, I'm certain of that. And out fishing he was perfectly useless. The girls would work away like beetles, with Boy, always in the background, making a mess of things. If his mother was there he just stayed by her side.

I could see it rattled the old man to have such an oaf of a son. Irritated him, too, because Boy was so big. It probably didn't make sense to his intolerant mind. Strength and stupidity didn't go together. In any normal family, of course, Boy would have left home by now and gone out to work. I used to wonder if they argued about it back in the evenings, the missus and the old man, or if it was something never admitted between them but tacitly understood – Boy was no good.

Well, they did leave home at last. At least, the girls did.

I'll tell you how it happened.

It was a day in late autumn, and I happened to be over doing some shopping in the little town overlooking the harbour, three miles from this place, and suddenly I saw the old man, the missus, the three girls and Boy all making their way up to Pont – that's at the head of a creek going eastward from the harbour. There are a few cottages at Pont, and a farm and a church up behind. The family looked washed and spruced up, and so did the old man and the missus, and I wondered if they were going visiting. If they were, it was an unusual thing for them to do. But it's possible they had friends or acquaintances up there, of whom I knew nothing. Anyway, that was the last I saw of them, on the fine Saturday afternoon, making for Pont.

It blew hard over the weekend, a proper easterly gale. I kept indoors and didn't go out at all. I knew the seas would be breaking good and hard on the beach. I wondered if the old man and the family had been able to get back. They would have been wise to stay with their friends up Pont, if they had friends there.

It was Tuesday before the wind dropped and I went down to the beach again. Seaweed, driftwood, tar and oil all over the place. It's always the same after an easterly blow. I looked up the lake, towards the old man's shack, and I saw him there, with the missus, just by the edge of the lake. But there was no sign of the youngsters.

I thought it a bit funny, and waited around in case they should appear. They never did. I walked right round the lake, and from the opposite bank I had a good view of their place, and even took out my old spy-glass to have a closer look. They just weren't there. The old man was pottering about as he often did when he wasn't fishing, and the missus had settled herself down to bask in the sun. There was only one explanation. They had left the family with friends in Pont. They had sent the family for a holiday.

I can't help admitting I was relieved, because for one frightful moment I thought maybe they had started off back home on the Saturday night and got struck by the gale;

and, well – that the old man and his missus had got back safely, but not the kids. It couldn't be that, though. I should have heard. Someone would have said something. The old man wouldn't be pottering there in his usual unconcerned fashion and the missus basking in the sun. No, that must have been it. They had left the family with friends. Or maybe the girls and Boy had gone up country, gone to find themselves jobs at last.

Somehow it left a gap. I felt sad. So long now I had been used to seeing them all around, Tiny and the others. I had a strange sort of feeling that they had gone for good. Silly, wasn't it? To mind, I mean. There was the old man, and his missus, and the four youngsters, and I'd more or less watched them grow up, and now for no reason they had gone.

I wished then I knew even a word or two of his language, so that I could have called out to him, neighbour-like, and said, 'I see you and the missus are on your own. Nothing wrong, I hope?'

But there, it wasn't any use. He'd have looked at me with his strange eyes and told me to go to hell.

I never saw the girls again. No, never. They just didn't come back. Once I thought I saw Tiny, somewhere up the estuary, with a group of friends, but I couldn't be sure. If it was, she'd grown, she looked different. I tell you what I think. I think the old man and the missus took them with a definite end in view, that last weekend, and either settled them with friends they knew or told them to shift for themselves.

I know it sounds hard, not what you'd do for your own son and daughters, but you have to remember the old man was a tough customer, a law unto himself. No doubt he thought it would be for the best, and so it probably was, and if only I could know for certain what happened to the girls, especially Tiny, I wouldn't worry.

But I do worry sometimes, because of what happened to Boy.

You see, Boy was fool enough to come back. He came back about three weeks after that final weekend. I had walked down through the woods – not my usual way, but down to the lake by the stream that feeds it from a higher level. I rounded the lake by the marshes to the north, some distance from the old man's place, and the first thing I saw was Boy.

He wasn't doing anything. He was just standing by the marsh. He looked dazed. He was too far off for me to hail him; besides, I didn't have the nerve. But I watched him, as he stood there in his clumsy loutish way, and I saw him staring at the far end of the lake. He was staring in the direction of the old man.

The old man, and the missus with him, took not the slightest notice of Boy. They were close to the beach, by the plank bridge, and were either just going out to fish or coming back. And here was Boy, with his dazed stupid face, but not only stupid – frightened.

I wanted to say, 'Is anything the matter?' but I didn't know how to say it. I stood there, like Boy, staring at the old man.

Then what we both must have feared would happen, happened.

The old man lifted his head, and saw Boy.

He must have said a word to his missus, because she didn't move, she stayed where she was, by the bridge, but the old man turned like a flash of lightning and came down the other side of the lake towards the marshes, towards Boy. He looked terrible. I shall never forget his appearance. That magnificent head I had always admired now angry, evil; and he was cursing Boy as he came. I tell you, I heard him.

Boy, bewildered, scared, looked hopelessly about him for cover. There was none. Only the thin reeds that grew beside the marsh. But the poor fellow was so dumb he went in there, and crouched, and believed himself safe – it was a horrible sight.

I was just getting my own courage up to interfere when the old man stopped suddenly in his tracks, pulled up short as it were, and then, still cursing, muttering, turned back again and returned to the bridge. Boy watched him, from his cover of reeds, then, poor clot that he was, came out on to the marsh again, with some idea, I suppose, of striking for home.

I looked about me. There was no one to call. No one to give any help. And if I went and tried to get someone from the farm they would tell me not to interfere, that the old man was best left alone when he got in one of his rages, and anyway that Boy was old enough to take care of himself. He was as big as the old man. He could give as good as he got. I knew different. Boy was no fighter. He didn't know how.

I waited quite a time beside the lake but nothing happened. It began to grow dark. It was no use my waiting there. The old man and the missus left the bridge and went on home. Boy was still standing there on the marsh, by the lake's edge.

I called to him, softly. 'It's no use. He won't let you in. Go back to Pont, or wherever it is you've been. Go to some place, anywhere, but get out of here.'

He looked up, that same queer expression on his face, and I could tell he hadn't understood a word I said.

I felt powerless to do any more. I went home myself. But I thought about Boy all evening, and in the morning I went down to the lake again, and I took a great stick with me to give me courage. Not that it would have been much good. Not against the old man.

Well ... I suppose they had come to some sort of agreement, during the night. There was Boy, by his mother's side, and the old man pottering on his own.

I must say, it was a great relief. Because, after all, what could I have said or done? If the old man didn't want Boy home, it was really his affair. And if Boy was too stupid to go, that was Boy's affair.

But I blamed the mother a good deal. After all, it was up to her to tell Boy he was in the way, and the old man was in one of his moods, and Boy had best get out while the going was good. But I never did think she had great intelligence. She did not seem to show much spirit at any time.

However, what arrangement they had come to worked for a time. Boy stuck close to his mother – I suppose he helped her at home, I don't know – and the old man left them alone and was more and more by himself.

He took to sitting down by the bridge, humped, staring out to sea, with a queer brooding look on him. He seemed strange, and lonely. I didn't like it. I don't know what his thoughts were, but I'm sure they were evil. It suddenly seemed a very long time since he and the missus and the whole family had gone fishing, a happy, contented party. Now everything had changed for him. He was thrust out in the cold, and the missus and Boy stayed together.

I felt sorry for him, but I felt frightened too. Because I felt it could not go on like this indefinitely; something would happen.

One day I went down to the beach for driftwood – it had been blowing in the night – and when I glanced towards the lake I saw that Boy wasn't with his mother. He was back where I had seen him that first day, on the edge of the marsh. He was as big as his father. If he'd known how to use his strength he'd have been a match for him any day, but he hadn't the brains. There he was, back on the marsh, a great big frightened foolish fellow, and there was the old man, outside his home, staring down towards his son with murder in his eyes.

I said to myself, 'He's going to kill him.' But I didn't know how or when or where, whether by night, when they were sleeping, or by day, when they were fishing. The mother was useless, she would not prevent it. It was no use appealing to the mother. If only Boy would use one little grain of sense, and go …

I watched and waited until nightfall. Nothing happened.

It rained in the night. It was grey, and cold, and dim. December was everywhere, trees all bare and bleak. I couldn't get down to the lake until late afternoon, and then the skies had cleared and the sun was shining in that watery way it does in winter, a burst of it, just before setting below the sea.

I saw the old man, and the missus too. They were close together, by the old shack, and they saw me coming for they looked towards me. Boy wasn't there. He wasn't on the marsh, either. Nor by the side of the lake.

I crossed the bridge and went along the right bank of the lake, and I had my spyglass with me, but I couldn't see Boy. Yet all the time I was aware of the old man watching me.

Then I saw him. I scrambled down the bank, and crossed the marsh, and went to the thing I saw lying there, behind the reeds.

He was dead. There was a great gash on his body. Dried blood on his back. But he had lain there all night. His body was sodden with the rain.

Maybe you'll think I'm a fool, but I began to cry, like an idiot, and I shouted across to the old man, 'You murderer, you bloody God-damned murderer.' He did not answer. He did not move. He stood there, outside his shack with the missus, watching me.

You'll want to know what I did. I went back and got a spade, and I dug a grave for Boy, in the reeds behind the marsh, and I said one of my own prayers for him, being uncertain of his religion. When I had finished I looked across the lake to the old man.

And do you know what I saw?

I saw him lower his great head, and bend towards her and embrace her. And she lifted her head to him and embraced him too. It was both a requiem and a benediction. An atonement, and a giving of praise. In their strange way they knew they had done evil, but it was over, because I had buried Boy and he was gone. They were free to be together again, and there was no longer a third to divide them.

They came out into the middle of the lake, and suddenly I saw the old man stretch his neck and beat his wings, and he took off from the water, full of power, and she followed him. I watched the two swans fly out to sea right into the face of the setting sun, and I tell you it was one of the most beautiful sights I ever saw in my life: the two swans flying there, alone, in winter.

J.C. Trewin

Window in the Attic

Over on the southern horizon, where Cornish sky met Cornish sea, the lighthouse was flashing. It had begun an hour or so earlier, for this was deep now in an October evening, its grey and umber lost in the all-embracing dark.

As the car approached St Rumon, its driver saw with a pang of memory a long beam that fanned across the peninsular coast and the half-mile of bare down behind. Transiently the beam rested on an isolated building that stood a few hundred yards off the Meriol road. Then it fanned back across rocks and sea, its own lime-washed tower, and the distant curve of the eastern cliffs.

It was a cold, dampish night in the early nineteen-sixties. There was no one on the plateau-road from Meriol; at this time of year there seldom was. As he stopped his car at the head of a muddy, brambled track, the man asked again – and a shade petulantly – why he had come. By now it must be getting on for seven o'clock; half an hour ago he had been sitting with the local paper in the lounge of Meriol's single hotel, wondering how to waste the remainder of a drab evening. Then this inexplicable wish possessed him; he must get back to St Rumon, and at once.

At the moment it had appeared to him less of a wish than a summons, almost a peremptory call. Nonsense, of course: he realised that. But he yielded, arguing with himself that there were worse things than a quick run, ten, eleven miles down the southern road.

All these years away from it, he had had comfortably romantic ideas about the place where his ancestors were bred. Until that morning he had not seen it since he was a young child, and in the drizzle it had hardly excited him: the upper barrens, the church-town cottages bunched in their cup beside a granite tower, the lighthouse white on the cliff-edge. It was not a friendly hamlet; it had never powerfully wanted visitors, and it did not try to help them. The summer cars from Meriol soon turned back.

He could turn back himself once he had had a look at the old place in the darkness. Here, anyway, he was; and here again was the house he had owned since his brother's death a month ago. Frank, a wealthy, amiable bachelor, had not troubled about it in a quarter of a century. There had been some hit-or-miss caretaking, but the man had died, and (so Hocking, the solicitor, had said that afternoon) no one seemed eager to take on the job. They had other things to do at St Rumon.

A thankless job, Edward Paynter thought, as he loitered now in the mouth of the lane. The wheeling light had hesitated upon the façade of Tree, and upon a broken, jagged window on the attic storey, the window (he supposed) that Hocking had talked about. An odd tale, but it was an odd enough house. In the alternation of darkness and phantasmal light it looked dangerously insubstantial; a thin steel engraving; a stage-set with nothing behind it. Even the name, Tree House, was false. Few trees survived on the upland. In the cleft of the church-town valley, yes; but the house was square to every gale that attacked the flat, shorn downs. Behind it were a pair of stunted Cornish elms, wind-bent. Someone had endowed the place with the usual monkey-puzzle, a 'bristly' to St Rumon children, and through the years an embarrassed stranger.

Nothing else rose from the jungled lawns; the last caretaker had had to scythe a path through to the front door. Beyond the loose stone wall, the swishing tamarisk feathers, the rank grasses, Tree stood roughly as it had done since the ebb of the eighteenth century. Its period meant nothing whatever. There were unimaginative builders then, as now; and Tree had little to grace it. Its front door was pleasantly canopied; otherwise it was a plain stone structure, ridiculously large. Above the ground floor were three tiers of shuttered windows; over these the low sprawl of the attic floor, unshuttered, and with that one hole, a jagged gash, through which the winter winds would drive. Useless to repair it, Hocking had said; no sooner was it re-glazed than it splintered into fragments.

By this time it scarcely mattered; not much did. There had never been any pilgrimage to Tree. Not a guide-book named it; no one had hurried to the village to say that it must be preserved at any cost, its plaster scrolls, the carved cedar screen in its dining-room. It had neither screen nor plaster: nothing but its range of empty rooms and the attics where the 'girls' had lived, the maids, the Lidgeys, who had staffed the place, generation by generation, for over a century. Since the coastguards had left it after the second world war, it had simply waited for the end. Occasionally a District Councillor was inquisitive; but that was all. St Rumon kept its affairs to itself.

Edward stepped carefully towards a gap in the boundary wall where the stones had toppled. He must not be late, he repeated to himself. Late? For what? Why this silliness? He shook himself and paused in the middle of the jungle path as the fanning beam returned. He noticed how still the evening was; so still that he feared to disturb with any footfall a world that was poised and listening.

Well, the old house must go. Obviously it would be simpler to clear the site. To build again? To sell the land? As yet he was unsure; he would have to consider. Who would want a house the size of Tree, and on the edge of the beyond? It had been reasonable in his grandfather's Edwardian time. Size was not worrying then, and the Lidgey girls had 'belonged', an endless supply of daughters, nieces, cousins, from the fishermen's, labourers' families that lived in St Rumon church-town. Emma, Mildred, Jenny; Eva and Margaret, Mary and Lucy and Alice; the house had been their natural work: Paynters at Tree, Lidgeys from the village. One or two, older and unmarried, had been in service for most of their lives. Laura, the last and dominant parlourmaid, was over seventy: she had been in control when Edward stayed, as a child, with his grandparents, and she was in a sheaf of pictures in the family album – wherever that was now; one day he must search for it.

The good years were far back. The Lidgey girls had gone; today the only pair of that name from St Rumon were teaching up-country, towards Plymouth or farther. The feudal system was just a village legend, though there might be someone in the pub at night to revive an old tale.

Way back – it would be before the first world war – Alice, an eighteen-year-old Lidgey, had fallen sheer from her window. What business, they asked in the village, had young William Paynter to be in the attics on an October midnight? He told the Coroner that he had heard a scream and run up to find the room empty and the window smashed. They called it accidental death, but presently the young man left Tree and few Lidgey girls went there again. That was the beginning of the end; the closing of parts of the house, the family's dispersal, the old people left with only Laura to watch them. All were dead: since then (after that brief period of a second war) simply solitude and decay.

A glum affair, Edward reflected. William Paynter had been his father: not, he would have said, given to any kind of melodrama. Still, after all, this was Edwardian, a primeval period when practically anything could have happened, and did. During the early nineteen-twenties his parents had sent him, with Frank to stay at Tree, but they never came themselves and the house was not left to them: significantly it missed a generation.

Pacing down the muddy path, Edward had a blurred memory of the place as it used to be, the grandfather clock in the hall, Old Testament oil-paintings in the dining-room, upstairs a range of closed doors, in the kitchen Laura and another starched and silent maid, her younger sister Milly, who married the St Rumon carpenter. Not much to do or to see; for a child (and he had to admit it) those days had dragged.

From a distance tonight he could hear, very faintly, the flat wash of the tide: not a flutter in the grass and heather, not a quiver in the monkey-puzzle branches. He heard his own too anxious breathing. Why in the world had he come?

It was then that, with a sudden whirring, a clearing of its throat, a grandfather clock struck seven.

Startled, Edward halted in mid-strike, mechanically counting the beats until the last stroke faded. It could have come only from the house, but the house was bare and dead.

The clock had been gone for twenty-five years. Frank had sold it with the other things at Lutton's before the war: the clock, the huge gong of Benares brass, the inlaid mahogany dining-table, the paintings (which brought next to nothing, even the descent from Sinai), the deep sitting-room carpet, the billiards-table, a dozen beds: he recalled the auctioneer's slightly ghoulish catalogue. For himself he had bought one of the stray lots, half-a-dozen shell candlesticks, and an oil-lamp on a veined serpentine base that used to shimmer in its dull red and a mottled green.

Edward was shivering a little; for no reason (he insisted) his hands were clenched. Seven o'clock: then he was late. Someone in this house was waiting for him, but need he go in? Relief overwhelmed him. Even if he wanted to, he could not; that afternoon he had left the key at Hocking's office and the house was safely locked. He would do no more than drive back to Meriol; dinner at the hotel, what sleep he could get, a word with Hocking in the morning, a final decision. He twisted on his heel; and, as she did so, the light flickered across the doorway.

Beneath its curved canopy the door stood wide open.

He was late. He knew without question that he had to keep his word, and he hurried forward up the three steps and into a square hall where once the grandfather clock had filled its alcove.

Darkness was profound until the lighthouse ray slipped across the dusty spaces, a few lank trails of cobweb, a floor where uneven boards squeaked to his tread.

Vaguely now he imagined that he heard a rustle of starched skirts, saw a pallid glimmer, even felt a hand on his arm. But nothing stirred and the swinging ray did not return. Someone had shut the door.

He moved instinctively to his left, groping along the wall until the china knob he wanted turned smoothly in his grasp and he was in what had been the western sitting-room. It was his grandparents' room; long ago the family would have gathered there before dinner. Shutters blocked both windows, but the fanning light still flickered eerily through any crack. Remembering a torch in his overcoat pocket, he felt for it vainly. He was not wearing an overcoat, yet he had been when he entered the house. For a moment he stood irresolute. Then the recurring gleam showed to him, beside the dark hearth, the tasselled, knotted length of a dull crimson bell-rope. Edward reached across and pulled at it: a long hard tug.

Out in the recesses of the house a bell jangled.

Half a minute passed as Edward waited. There came a tap on the door, a discreet two-fingered tapping, and the door creaked open along a furrow in the dust. Striding to the window, Edward tore at its shutter-bolt and pushed the panel aside. Briefly the next beam revealed a motionless figure: a woman who wore with a dignity of her own the starched, heavy apron of an Edwardian parlourmaid. Beneath the cap her face, with its sunken eyes, was pale and prim. He recognised her from many album pictures. She was younger than when he had known her, but he could not mistake Laura Lidgey who had been in St Rumon churchyard for nearly thirty years.

Now she bobbed ritually and held back the door while the house seemed to shake to the thudding of a brass dinner-gong.

Edward had tried to speak, but the words did not come, and what was there to say? He found himself walking diagonally across that mustily forsaken hall to a long room at the back; the former dining-room where in the cold light of midday he had seen only a battered Windsor chair.

There was some dim illumination now, though where it came from he had no idea. He seemed to be suffering from double vision, for the room as it had been that morning was overlaid by the room as it used to be: on flaking, damp-blotched walls the pictures (Moses after Sinai, and the rest) in shadowy gilt frames; on the mahogany table – only one place was set – glass and silver that showed no sparkle in the light; round the table a ceaseless coming-and-going, a soft crackle of skirts, a quick murmur; no word he could distinguish and no person he could see but Laura Lidgey as she passed by him or stood, with her sunken brown eyes on his, a silver dish in her hand.

He could not tell how long he sat there or what he did, but certainly he heard the chimes of nine o'clock and knew he must rise from the table. The door had opened before he could touch it, and he was in the hall, wondering why he had not seen the gong, with its padded stick upon the tray; the grandfather clock by Rowe of Falmouth; the wall mirror, which reflected precisely nothing; the bookcase with its calf folios behind the glass; and a great Hungarian rug on the polished floor.

Somewhere he could hear what sounded like the repeated click of billiard-balls. No time to speculate; he was back in the western sitting-room, treading on the pile of a carpet, florally Victorian, that he remembered in the sale at Lutton's. The hearth was alive with the bluish flame of driftwood, though whenever light flickered through the unboarded window the room was derelict and the hearth was dead.

Edward was aware of a younger maidservant, clearly one of the Lidgeys, a girl with a carriage as upright as Laura's, the same curiously sunken brown eyes, and a drift of brown hair beneath the absurd and repressive cap. Putting down what she carried, she lingered there, gazing at him boldly; and he realised what he must do. It was not yet time. Twice he heard the clock strike the hour. At eleven the girl entered again to place a candlestick beside him. He could have cried aloud, for that painted, hollowed rod, springing from the shell at its food, was one of those above his bed in the London flat a world away. Once more the girl paused to watch him. Then the door closed and Edward knew that the night was deadly cold. The room he stood in was in dark decay: no fire, no carpet, merely an ancient milking-stool, the floor's dirty planking, and the walls peeling and cracked.

Yet there by the hearth was his candlestick, filmed with dust. It held no candle, but he reached down for it. Time to go upstairs.

Pulling the door towards him, he walked cautiously into the blackness of a hall empty of furniture, emptied of any sound. He fumbled his way across to the dining-room, a frigid vault; within it he tripped over the shafts of a broken Windsor chair. He was conscious suddenly of a light over his shoulder, the faintest sheen; as he retreated into the hall he saw Laura Lidgey's face gazing down at him from the bend of the staircase and whiter than ever in the glow of the oil-lamp she carried on a mottled serpentine base. She vanished round the curve; and, dropping his candlestick with a clatter, he followed her up the uncarpeted treads that creaked and sighed beneath his weight.

Her light had gone. On the bleak landing he passed room by room, some fast-locked, other shuttered and dustily unused. He climbed to the next floor. Here there seemed to be a scurrying, a mutter, a bustle sensed rather than heard. He thought that there was laughter; and, with the thought, the young maid looked questioningly at him across the trembling wick of a candle. He leapt forward; the candle went out; every sound had fallen away.

Somehow he got up to the next floor, a copy of the others. The landing window was only half-shuttered: from it he could see the plateau blanched by a risen moon that dimmed the swinging beam. Thin in the distance, just visible over the cup of the church-town, were the spiked pinnacles of St Rumon tower. A wind, blowing harshly in from the sea, fretted about the eaves above him; he heard from below the noise of a clock collecting its strength before breaking into the twelve midnight chimes.

Halfway down that corridor a spiral ladder rose to the attic rooms of Tree. By it, holding her lamp, waited Laura Lidgey. For a last time he saw her, her face whiter than her apron. Then she had gone; and desperately, in the fading strokes of midnight, he clambered to the cramped passage below the roof where every door was shut but one.

This he pushed open. Within, the younger Lidgey girl rose to face him in a haze of moonlight, her back to the uncurtained window. She wore a nightgown; her hair was free; she stretched her arms in greeting. But, as he advanced, she slipped aside in the narrow space. Again, without speech or sound, she eluded him; and yet again. Then, so he imagined, and strangely, she began to fade: he cried out, bending urgently towards her, and in that moment a cold hand pressed his back and thrust him steadily to the low, unguarded window.

He could not check himself. Hurled against the starred and shattering glass, he lost his balance and dived headlong, a sheer drop into the night. Overhead, the wind was driving through the gap into a forlorn, dusty room; and on the southern horizon, where sky met sea, the lighthouse flashed.

*

They discovered Edward's body next morning. A hedger, who saw the car by the top of the lane, had walked down to Tree to find its owner. Dr Lanyon, hurrying from the church-town, shook his head.

'Who was he? Why was he here?'

He stared up at a broken attic window and turned to the man with him.

'Too late, Lidgey, but you had better ring for the ambulance. Meriol four-five'.

Winston Graham

Jacka's Fight

My grandfather was called Jacka Fawle. He used to tell this story, often he would tell this story, and often-times you could not stop him; but it did not matter so much because it was true. He lived into old age, and we children would know if any stranger came by that he would take the first opportunity of telling this story, you could rest assured, so that, hearing it so often, we knew it all by heart and would chime in if he left out a detail. But it was all true.

My grandfather, he was born in Helston in Cornwall in 1853 and went down a mine before he was twelve. At eighteen he married Essie Penrose and in the next twelve years they had eight children, my mother youngest of them all. In 1883, the mining slump came to its worst, and Wheal Marble, where he was working, closed down. So like many of his friends, he thought he would go to America to make his way. There was work there and opportunities there, money to be made. It was a long way and a hard journey, but men wrote home that they were doing well out there. Some even sent home money so that their wives could go out and join them.

Well, it was a hard parting from Jacka and Essie, but there was little chance of her going with him with all the little children crying around her feet. Not that she showed much sign of wishing to go, for, like many women born within the sight of the sea, she really feared it and trembled to set foot upon it. So she moved with her young brood of chicks into her father's tiny cottage and bade a tearful farewell to Jacka as he left home. With a Bible in his pocket and a bundle on his shoulder he set off one wet day in March, and they all stood in the doorway in the rain watching while his short sturdy figure grew smaller and smaller trudging down the lane. He walked west on the old coaching road, to Truro, to Mitchell, and thence to Padstow, where he took ship for San Francisco.

It was a terrible voyage – four months it took them around Cape Horn in villainous seas and then all the way up the western seaboard of the New World. Scurvy and sea-sickness and dysentery and bad food. Seven months passed near to the day when my grandmother opened her first letter from him. It was full of good cheer and good heart and he never mentioned the hardships for he still hoped she would join him in a year or two. But in fact he had been little enough time in California, casting around as you might say, before he changed his trade. Mines there might be, but much of it was more like prospecting than what he belonged to do. Chance of riches and chance of nothing at all. While building opportunies were everywhere. Houses, churches, factories, all were going up like mushrooms on a damp evening. And bricklayers were in short supply.

So he became a bricklayer, my grandfather became a bricklayer, and his wages were good and steady.

He too was good and steady because he had been reared in the Primitive Methodist connexion; and many times, he said, in those early years he was thankful for his careful upbringing. San Francisco was a wild and wicked place, where any man could go to hell for the price of a few weeks' wages. Indeed all California was the same: a lost continent where lust and strong drink and greed and vice were raging. So he made few friends and those were strictly of his own kind. There were other Cornishmen in the city and he tended to be drawn to them because of memories of home. And he attended chapel every Sunday.

Each month, on the first of the month, he wrote a letter home, and each month, regular as a clock, he sent home a small sum of money to help support his family. Each letter ended: 'Hopeing that soon dear wife you will be able joyne me your ever loving Husband.'

But the months turned into years and she did not join him. The children were all well and all growing, she wrote, but so slow. And Essie *could not* face the sea ...

If there had been any work at home Jacka would have returned, given up his regular well-paid work and gone home, for he was a family man, and it fretted him that all his children would be strangers to him. Sometimes too he could not help but cast his eye upon another woman; yet by grace he saw this as a lure of Satan and hurriedly dismissed carnal thoughts from his mind. Even his memories of Essie were fading. She wrote him: oh yes, she wrote him, telling him homely details of life in Helston; but she was no handy one with the pen, far worse than he; and the cost of the post was so high that often she missed a month.

All this time he was saving, was Jacka. He lived quiet and lived frugal and some he sent home and some he saved. But it was tedious work. First it was $500, then it was $800, then $1,000. By the time he was thirty-seven, he had saved $3,000 and had not seen his wife and family for seven years. Seven long years. It seemed a lifetime. But in all things he was canny, and he kept his money deposited in different banks to lessen the risk. He came to know northern California well, for all his work was not in San Francisco. He worked with Irishmen, Poles, Portugese, Swedes, Italians, and second generation Americans. But all the time he stayed true to himself and unchangingly Cornish. He would meet with five or six other Cornishmen every Sunday and they'd talk of Pasties and Leekie Pie and Pilchards and the damp beautiful landscapes of home.

One day in the early nineties one of these Cornishmen, called by the name of Sil Polglaze, he came to Jacka and told him that there was this middleweight boxer come to town just fresh come from New Zealand but a true Cornishman as ever was; and he was fighting a man called Abe Congle in the Park next Saturday afternoon and how about them going along? Jacka hesitated about this, wondering if there might be sin in it, but it did not seem so, so he said all right, he'd go. Thus he took his first look at Bob Fitzsimmons.

It was a motley crowd that day, no mistake, and nearly all of them shouting for Congle; but Fitzsimmons stunned Congle unconscious in the second round. So it was that all the patriotism in Jacka, lying underneath and scarce acknowledged, came bubbling out like an adit from a mine, and afterwards he pushed his way sore throated through the crowd and spoke to the Cornish boxer and his wife.

Now Fitzsimmons at this time was twenty-eight, and no figure of a boxer at all. You could laugh, and many did, for already he had a bald patch and had long arms and legs like thin poles quite out of proportion to his great chest and stomach. He weighed scarcely more than 150 lbs, and he had a round red face and his teeth were large and bright like wet tombstones and had stood all the unkindness of the ring. He would have done proud as a comic turn in a circus but it would be foolishness to take him seriously as a boxer. Only Congle did that. Only Congle, still being doused with water like a babe at a christening.

Soon Fitzsimmons was telling Jacka that he too had been born in Helston – in Helston of all places! – and asking all manner of questions about it and whether old so-and-so was still alive, and if the Hal-an-Tow was still danced. I reckon Jacka became his slave for life at that first meeting, and sure enough he was there at the seond fight when Fitzsimmons laid low a hard tough Negro called Black Pearl. This time it took him two more rounds, but the outcome was just the same. He went in soaking up the punishment which would have stopped any ordinary man, and then let fly with his long incredible fists and presently there was a black heap on the ground, and Fitzsimmons was standing there, Jacka said, with his long arms dangling and his white teeth glinting like a bone in his raw red face.

Afterwards, after Fitz left San Francisco, Jacka tried to keep track of him by reading the newspapers, but it wasn't that easy. Fitz went all over the States, but his news value was not high and sometimes the San Francisco papers did not bother to mention when he had been in a fight. Only the big ones were reported, and every now and then through the years that followed Jacka would find an item saying that Fitzsimmons had beaten Peter Maker, or Joe Godfrey or Millard Zenda.

Now although Jacka was a rare one for all things Cornish, he'd made no boast about it living in such a mixed community, and he was content to be called a Limey when talk of nationalities came up. But Fitz's appearance on the scene had fired his local loyalties with a hot new fire, and, while he was not the sort of man to make a show of himself in front of others, he was never above a mention of the wonderful prowess of his friend and fellow townsman Bob Fitzsimmons, and to let it be known what great fighting men Cousin Jacks were when their blood was up. So he became much more vocally Cornish, so to say, and so he found himself sometimes at odds with the Americans and the Swedes and the Irish. Just because he had so much to say for Fitzsimmons they derided Fitzsimmons the more. And so hard words and hard thoughts grew up, half jesting, half serious, and they centred around the name and the figure and the prestige of the scrawny, ungainly, ageing boxer.

When someone brought in the word that Fitzsimmons had put in his challenge for the heavyweight championship of the world everyone except Jacka fairly died with laughter. The great James J. Corbett, Gentleman Jim, six feet one inch in height and 190 lbs in weight, with not an ounce of spare flesh upon him, the best boxer of his age and the idol of the United States, was too superior in every way to be matched with this shambling creature. The challenge was of course refused, and all Jacka's mates told him that this refusal had saved Fitz's life. Quick to defend his idol, out on a limb on his behalf, Jacka shouted that Corbett was afraid and that Ruby Bob was being cheated of the title.

How they laughed! How they lay about and laughed till the tears ran into the bricks and mortar. From then on it was the recognized thing to have Jacka on about it. Any time anyone craved for a quick laugh they had only to mention this challenge and Jacka would be upon his feet and arguing for his friend. I think my grandfather was a good tempered sort of Christian most of his life, but he oftentimes lost his temper over this. It changed him a little, made him morose. He never fought anyone because fighting wasn't his way; but he came near to it more than once.

So more years passed. Jacka was growing grey at the temples and heavier in the girth of neck and stomach. His eldest son was twenty-five, his youngest daughter fourteen, and he was a grandfather four times over. He had not saved so much money in the last seven years as in the first seven, for he had come to live a little cosier himself, to value a good meal and a glass of beer and a pipe of tobacco at the day's end. But he had saved all the same. In another ten years he reckoned he would have enough to go home, to buy a smallholding somewhere around Helford River and live out the rest of his life in quietness and peace. By then all his children would have flown; but some of them with luck would not have flown so far, and he and Essie would be able to play with the grandchildren. It was an ambition as yet too far away to look forward to, but there it stood as a reward for a long life of toil. And patient Essie would be there waiting for him still.

Fitzsimmons too had gone on his way, putting all manner of boxers down and out, growing older too and scrawnier, but still not quite finished. He was too hard for the young ones – yet. They just had to bide their time, while age and hard knocks crept up on him. So one day the distinguished Corbett found he could no longer ignore this middleweight that no other middleweight could endure the course with. A match was made, arranged, actually fixed for 17 March next, the contest to be for the heavyweight championship of the world, in Carson City, Nevada, the winner to receive a purse of twelve thousand dollars.

And everyone knew for certain who that would be. In vain Jacka defended his idol. They jeered at Jacka, and the good nature had gone out of it on both sides. One big Irish bricklayer caled O'Brien was stronger even than most for Corbett – who was half Irish – and offered five to one in any amount and currency Jacka cared to name – if he dared to back his fancy. Jacka refused. In the years in California he had attended chapel whenever he could, and, although his sternest convictions had worn a little away, he still knew gambling to be sinful and he had never indulged in it.

In the weeks before the fight, however, O'Brien continued to goad him; and at last, hemmed into a corner where refusal spelt cowardice, he bet O'Brien fifty dollars at seven to one that Ruby Robert would win. The money was paid over to the foreman, a big Swede called Lindquist, who was known to be a straight and honest man.

Carson City is only just in the state of Nevada on the other side of Lake Tahoe, and so little more than 160 miles from San Francisco. It was only just off the main railway east, and it was told that the Virginia and Truckee Railroad were laying special tracks so that rich spectators could go all the way on special sleeping coaches, travel overnight and be ready fresh for the contest in the morning. The poorer folk by leaving before it was light could arrive in another special train just the same. Tickets for the fight were $5, and early Jacka bought one. Some of his mates would not pay the money but said they would be able to get in cheaper on the day.

Sitting over his pipe in the evening talking to Sil Polglaze and others of his cronies, Jacka thought much, he said, of the money he had wagered. He stood to lose fifty dollars – but to gain three hundred and fifty. The odds were not excessive, for eight and nine to one were being offered in some quarters. Jacka had the courage of his convictions and so trusted Fitz to win. So *he* stood to win. So he stood to win a considerable sum. It was a sin to gamble; but was this exactly gambling, properly to be so described? He did not feel sinful now he had risked the money. He did not think he would feel sinful if he even added to the money at risk.

He would never have done it but for the burning conviction within him that a good Cornishman was better than a good Irish-American. The patriotic resentment he felt towards his mates was as passionate as if he had been called to declare his Faith. And his passion, equally, was not based on judgement or on knowledge. He had not seen Fitzsimmons for six years. He had never seen Corbett in his life. But he was called upon to testify. And the only way he could testify was by risking his money. His hard-earned, laboriously hoarded money. Some of it. Not much, but some. Altogether in the world, if he counted every silver and gold coin he owned and every bank chit, he could muster about $5,600. It was some tidy little nest-egg. How much of it could he put at risk? $300 perhaps? He stood the chance of converting it into $2,000. Such a small investment – less six months' saving – to gain so much.

Where most of the bets were laid was in the pool rooms, and these were places which for long years Jacka had avoided as haunts of the devil. But this last four years he had taken to going into Scherz's Rooms with Silvester Polglaze for a quiet game of pool and a glass of beer. No wagers, mind. Just the play. They played for the pleasure and the relaxation. But this was where the wagers for the fight were placed, and the odds were put up on a blackboard, and Jacka licked his lips and saw them shortening, then lengthening again after Corbett gave an interview, then shortening as the time of the fight drew near. Scherz was a Swiss, a tough, hard, cold man but he'd never cheat you. A lot of working men left their money with him because they trusted him before the banks. So this was the place to risk your money if you wanted to risk your money, where it would be safe if you won. Jacka put on $200 on eight to one, $100 at six to one, another $100 at four to one; then when the odds stretched out again, he put on a further $300 at seven to one.

It was strange, Jacka said, that after he had put the money on, handed over the counter in gold dollars, he felt first a terrible hard nasty sinking sensation of depression, and then after an hour or so a sudden upsurge of hope. No twinges of conscience, that was strange, no feeling that he shouldn't have done it, only an urge to do more. It was like a drug; but it wasn't like the ordinary gambler's drug, when the wins and the losses, the sudden ups and downs of fortune carry a man fluctuating till he loses his stability altogether. There were no losses in this – nor as yet any wins: there was nothing to elate Jacka and nothing to depress him, only a burning conviction that somehow his ungainly hero would come through. A week before the fight he went with two Swedes into the California Athletic Club and, encouraged by them, put on another $500 at twenty to three. Then at work he took a bet with a man called Sullivan for $200. On the Wednesday before the fight, Jacka went like a thief to one of his banks – the one he trusted least – and withdrew $800. From there, with no one to accompany him and no one to egg him on, he went out and laid his bets.

The last days were an age in passing. Jacka lived in a daze, feverishly thumbing through the papers, talking scarcely to no one, refusing even the dangling bait of argument; only stopping in at one bank and then another to draw more money out. Before the fight more than half his total savings had been placed upon Fitzsimmons to win.

On the day all those who were going to the fight had to be up at four a.m. to catch the early morning train. All those leaving off work for the day lost a day's wages and a good conduct mark, but the absenteeism was so great that a whole mass of workers could not be penalized.

It was a long train drawing out of Oakland Station, and a slow one as it wound its way puffing up through the foothills of the Nevadas. Jacka sat with Sil Polglaze and a man called Mark Lothar; Jacka sat in a corner of the hard wooden carriage and spoke to no one. Only his eyes gleamed like one who has seen the light. The train was crowded, and men standing in the compartments shuffled and swayed against each other for four hours until at last it came to rest in the specially built sidings in Carson City.

Here everyone fell out in a swarm: it was as if the train could not have held so many men: they poured from every door and flooded off into the town. The sun was just rising on a brilliant day.

Carson City, the capital city of the State of Nevada, lies in a bowl of the Sierra Nevada at an altitude, so I am told, of nearly 5,000 feet, and is surrounded by mountains. It was then a flourishing township, Jacka said, with a population of about 2,000 people and had several handsome buildings, including the capitol, a mint and an orphans' home, and a good sprinkling of pool rooms. This morning the mountains were glimmering with snow, and an icy breeze loitered through the town. Dust whorls rose in the streets, and the wooden sidewalks were packed five abreast with men strolling through or looking for food or drifting slowly toward the arena to be sure of gaining good seats. In the gutter mendicants and others stood begging alms or selling favours and crying out for attention. Pretty many of the men who had come to see the fight already wore four-leafed clovers in honour of St Patrick's Day and to show they supported Corbett. Some of the badges were six inches across, and some men wore green shirts and green hats and green ribbons on their sleeves. Women were very absent from the scene.

Food was a big problem, for the eating-houses and tents were soon full, and long jostling angry queues formed outside them; but Jacka and his friends had brought meat and potato pasties that Jacka had cooked the night before, and so after a brief walk around the town they tramped off to the arena and got seats. Jacka was much concerned as to which corner the boxers were occupying; Corbett, they found, had been given the south-east corner, so they took seats as near to the north-west corner as they could get. It was a great amphitheatre of a place with the white peaks of the snow-covered mountains all around. You could see the ring from almost anywhere; but although the fight was supposed to start at ten it was scarce dotted with people when they arrived, and they squatted on the grass to break their fasts. After they had eaten they went off in turn, and Jacka, passing a betting booth which had the guarantee of the local bank to support it, could not refrain from slipping in and putting another $200 as a final token – though here he found the odds had shortened to five to two.

By ten the arena was almost half full, but no sign of the boxers and only one or two officials fussing round the ring. Old pugilists of one sort or another strolled all about, followed by their admirers. Sharkey was there, the only one who had beaten Fitzsimmons – though this, it was generally admitted, was with a foul blow. John L. Sullivan, grey-haired now but as big as ever. And Goddard, and Billy Madden and others. Not far from where Jacka was sitting was a strange contraption on wooden legs which he was told was a kinetoscope. This, they said, would take moving pictures of the fight – or rather many pictures which shown quickly one after the other would give the appearance of movement. It was said that this was the first time such an invention had ever been used at a boxing-match.

At ten-thirty the arena was three-quarters full, and the sun beat down and the wind had fallen away. This might be March and high in the Nevadas, but it was more like San Francisco in the summer. Everyone had come wrapped up for a cold day and everyone was now sweating. Coats, jerseys, mufflers, waistcoats came off. They lay in piles on the grass and cluttered up the aisles.

Now the famous boxers each made an appearance in the ring and made speeches, most of them challenging the winner of this fight: and they were greeted with applause or derision according to the wayward fancy of the crowd. Then there was a big cheer as Mrs Fitzsimmons came upon the scene. She looked some pale – though normally she was as rosy-faced as her husband – and went down the east aisle to sit in a box beside Governor Sadler and Senator Ingalls. A man behind Jacka who was a Carson City man and had a stake in the local newspaper said out loud that Fitzsimmons had told him that win or lose, this was his last fight. He would soon be thirty-five, and not many boxers stayed in the game above the age of thirty, except as human punch-balls. And Mrs Fitz was tired of travelling and longed for a quiet home life.

'Thirty-five, damme,' muttered Sil Polglaze, who had put fifty dollars on Fitz. ''Tis old, Jacka. 'Tis a bare five year youngerer than me, and I could no more fight than ride an ass backwards. It makes you think, Jacka.'

'*You*,' said Jacka, contemptuous, 'You could no more fight not when you was twenty. Fitz is differenter. Fitz'll not let us down.' But for the first time for days the veil of self-hypnosis that was upon him was shaken. This ageing man who talked of retiring – was he the man on whom you risked all your own hopes of retirement?

Muldoon, the timekeeper, was up there now, with Dan Stuart the promoter, Physician Guinan, Manager Brady, Billy Jordan the Master of Ceremonies, Referee Silver, and other big pots. The local man behind Jacka was useful, for he knew the names of them all and pointed them out in a loud voice.

Then suddenly there was a great roar from the crowd, which by now was barely short of 12,000 strong. Bob Fitzsimmons was coming down along the side seats. Martin Julian led the way, then came Fitz, and he was followed by his seconds and half a dozen of other men. Fitz was in a bright pink and mauve dressing-gown and looked just the same bald red-faced thin-legged man Jacka had met six years gone. All the fights he had been in since, all the punishment he'd given and accepted, hadn't altered his face except the skin round his eyes was puffier and he walked a little more with his neck thrust forward as if he was wearing a discomfortable collar. As he passed the box where his wife was sitting he stopped and kissed her, then went on to the ring.

Then before ever he had climbed in the great James J. Corbett had appeared from the other side, with his brother Joe at his side and six other men in attendance. The man behind Jacka was giving names to them all, but Jacka paid little attention. His heart was suddenly wanting to fall into his stomach as he saw the difference in physique betwixt the two fighters.

At the roars which went on and on, several thousand more folk outside the ground who had been waiting for a reduction in the price of the tickets concluded that after all they must pay the proper charge and came pushing and thrusting in, filling up the empty spaces. Few women were to be seen, and those few had peroxide hair and you could hazard a lively guess at their business. To all this Jacka was now blind, as he saw the preparations going forward in the ring. Near beside him the man working the kinetoscope came out to take sightings. One after another, men were making speeches in the ring. The time wanted twenty-five minutes of noon. Then Billy Jordan introduced these two fighters and everyone went mad again. When this was done, the fighters went back to their corners and a silence fell like the day before the Day of Judgement. Overhead was not a cloud, not a wisp, only the brilliant hot sun that made many men drape kerchiefs upon their heads. Fitzsimmons' bald patch shone like a polished saucer. The timekeeper took up his place beside the gong, and behind him stood a guard with a club to strike down anyone who tried to interfere. The referee was in the middle looking at Muldoon. Muldoon nodded, the two boxers stripped off their gowns and came into the centre of the ring, Fitz thin and gangling with his great chest, looking like a hairless ape, Corbett, far taller and heavier, handsome built, in the peak of condition, proudly ready for the fight. The gong sounded and they were off.

Jacka watched the beginning but says he could remember precious little of the first few seconds. Suddenly the veil was cleft altogether from before his self-opinionated eyes and he saw not two men struggling for a crown but his own wicked wanton recklessness in risking three-quarters of his fourteen years' savings on the outcome of a fight. He felt sick, his bowels rumbled, hammers beat in his head, the blows raining on Fitzsimmons might have been raining upon his own body.

And certainly blows were landing upon Fitzsimmons everywhere. He was lighter than Corbett, shorter than Corbett and *slower* than Corbett. He looked smaller even than his eleven stone four pounds. Everyone knew he had a punch like a mule, but he never was given a chance to use it. The crowd were in raptures of pleasure. Nine in every ten backed Corbett; he was from San Francisco, he was Irish-American, he was good-looking, he was quite the gentleman. Fitz was going to receive what was coming to him.

And Fitz does. After the third round it looks like a massacre. Corbett is boxing like a champion, powerful and fast, landing blow upon blow. Some Fitz partly parries, some he takes full strength on his face and his body, yet he scarcely ever seems to wince or cringe away. Every now and then he will snake out that terrible left of his, but it never finds its mark. His face is red, his mouth bleeding, one eye partly closed – already. It is a strange expression he has upon his face, Jacka says; there is sentiment and tragedy in it, and a sort of fixed grin that bears it all while he still keeps closing in, waiting for an opening, his eyes watchful. There is no temper in those eyes, Jacka says, no resentment, just watchfulness and utter determination that he must not be beat.

In the fourth round there is a lot of in-fighting, with Corbett landing three punches to Fitzsimmons' one. 'Good old Jim!' the crowd screams. 'Good old boy, good old Jim!' while Jacka sits there too paralysed even to shout for his man. Unmarked, Corbett steps away from Fitz, thumping in half arm blows the while, to the face, to the nose, to the ribs, to the jaw. Sometimes Fitz looks like a turtle, his head, red and damaged, half sunk between his great shoulders for protection from the storm.

In the fifth round it appears as if Fitz is done. His lips are swollen, the eye half closed, his nose bleeding, his body crimson all over, part with the blows it had received, part from the blood on Corbett's gloves. He begins to lie on Corbett's shoulder, trying to get a breather, trying to smother Corbett's blows to his ribs. 'Knock his head off, Jim!' they shout. 'Punch his 'ead!' 'Lay 'im out, boy!' It seems endless, that round. At the bell Corbett walks smiling to his corner. Fitz turns and plods slowly back to his. They are betting again around Jacka, or offering bets: no one is taking them. Eight to one it is again now. Back to the first odds. Now ten to one. Ten to one, a loud-mouthed check-shirted miner is shouting. Jacka gets up, near sick, fumbles in his pocket, takes out his purse and from it a hundred dollars in gold, offers it to Check-shirt. Everyone stares – there is a wild cackle of laughter. Check-shirt thumps Jacka on the back. 'Right, pard, right, it's a deal: settle after the fight.'

In the sixth round it is all Corbett, and he lands a tremendous smash in the second minute that forces Fitzsimmons to his knees and sends more blood spurting from his nose. Fitz climbs slowly up, patient, his great teeth still showing white in a face that no one any longer can recognize. Corbett's body is smeared with blood now, but it is not his own. The seventh round is much the same, Fitz crouching to avoid the worst punishment, and every now and then darting out his terrible blows that still have not lost all their strength.

In the eighth round Corbett has clearly decided to finish it off. Dropping his own skill, he steps in and lands almost as he likes, blows to the neck and the chest and the ribs and the heart. Men round Jacka shout: 'Why don't Fitz give up? Why don't he quit?' In the ninth Fitzsimmons is down again after a right upper-cut that would have put an ordinary man out for ten minutes. He is up on the count of nine, leaning on Corbett, hitting back, weakly but enough to prevent another knock-down before the bell. Corbett is smiling again as he walks back to his corner. So far as you can tell he in unmarked. The check-shirted miner offers Jacka another hundred dollars at fifteen to one. Jacka just stares and shakes his head.

The minute rest has given the seconds a chance again to sponge the blood off Fitz's face, and he comes up looking no different from what he looked six rounds ago. Corbett will need an axe to finish the job, nothing less will do. They fight toe to toe through the first half, and Fitzsimmons seems no weaker for all his terrible punishment. Now he suddenly lands hard and high and often on Corbett, and though Corbett is not hurt, it is blow for blow for the first time in all of the contest, and a significant change. He goes back to his corner with a more thoughtful look on his handsome face, and you even hear one or two men in the crowd shout: 'Game boy, Fitz!' The eleventh round is much the same, and much whispering after it in Corbett's corner. Divided counsels. There is no doubt Corbett can outbox this indestructible land crab but can he outlive him? Can he by boxing ever tire him out? It is a fight to a finish, and somehow Fitzsimmons must be put down for a count of ten. In the twelfth round Corbett is getting tired and he takes a breather. He boxes comfortably, leading Ruby Robert about the bloodstained ring, landing when he wants but avoiding a fight, while Fitzsimmons patiently pursues him. Suddenly at the end of the round, Fitz manoeuvres Corbett into a corner and lands some violent vicious punches to the body.

The bell goes and Corbett's face has changed. You can now see no expression on Fitz's at all; it is too badly cut and battered. So to the thirteenth and Corbett comes out with a last intent to finish it. Incredibly it is the fastest hardest round of all the bout. Now Fitzsimmons is giving as good as he gets, and the crowd stand up and shriek and bawl its head off. Toe to toe they fight, and Corbett again gets the best of it. A great blow to Fitz's ribs causes him to drop his hands and for a moment it looks all over. Corbett swings to the jaw, and by a split second Fitz takes the step back that saves him. Then they are at it hammer and tongs again to the last moment of the round.

So to the fourteenth and Jacka is standing up through it, jaw slack, eyes staring, like a revivalist who has seen the light. For Fitzsimmons is growing confident, those long thin terrible arms after all his punishment are shooting out like pistons, driving Corbett before them. The crowd are mad with the noise and the excitement. Fitz's blows knock aside the champion's defence, a half dozen take their toll, and then a withering deadly left just below the ribs and Corbett sags. Fitz's right comes up to the point of the jaw and Gentleman Jim Corbett topples and slides and kneels and falls, and is down and out.

Then all hell breaks loose. Within moments the ring is invaded, officials swept away. Men shout and scream, seconds fight to protect their man. In the middle of it Corbett comes round, dazed and shaken, and thinks the fight is still in progress – he lays out a newspaper man cold with one swing and rushes across to Fitzsimmons and gives him a tremendous punch in the face, which Fitz shakes bloodily off like all the rest. The men pull Corbett away and minutes pass in a maelstrom of fighting and shouting. Somewhere amidst it Referee Siler holds Fitzsimmons' shaking glove aloft, and somewhere amidst it Corbett, still protesting, accepts defeat.

Jacka is trembling from head to foot and his shirt is like it has been dropped in the river. He fights his way towards the ring and near him is Mrs Fitzsimmons fighting her own way, and he catches up with he and kisses her hand, mumbling meaningless expressions of joy. Others are fighting and falling over the chairs, and it is an age before anything like order and sanity is restored. Then the biggest surprise of all for Jacka is that he finds big-mouth Check-shirt waiting beside him shaking his shoulder and wanting to pay him a thousand dollars.

So my grandfather, as a result of a single fight for the heavyweight championship of the world, because of his reckless pig-headed belief in a fellow countryman and a fellow townsman (who was no more than a middleweight, and an ageing middleweight at that) and the insane risk he took in backing that belief – made $24,000. So with this and the little extra he had not put at risk, he came overland to New York and thence by sea to Falmouth, and from there by coach to Helston. And there he arrived in triumph and was met by Essie, grown grey and portly, and his five sons, all taller than he, and his three daughters, of whom my mother was the youngest, and his four daughters-in-law and his one son-in-law and his five grand-children, all waiting for him, all nineteen of them, who with Essie's mother made a round score, and they partook of a splendid tea together at the Angel in Helston and then went out their several ways all over the country, and all twenty of them never met together at the same time ever again.

But Grandfather Jacka, a rich man by the standards of the county and the time, bought a handsome little farm with land running down to the Helford River, and there I was born, and there he lived out a pleasant, useful, quiet and agreeable life for another thirty-six years. And never a stranger would pass the door but what Jacka must tell of how he came to be there and how he had risked so much over a fight in Carson City, Nevada, at the turn of the century.

And when it came to my turn, from that fight, thirty-six years later, I inherited three hundred pounds.

Jack Clemo

MARIA AND THE MILKMAN

Sammy Chegwidden had traipsed around Pengooth village four times that evening afore he catched sight o' Maria Blake; and he wad'n much better off when he did see her.

'Twas out beginning the lane that they mit, where the village ended, and nobody could'n see 'em. Maria'd bin pickin' smutties and was carrying a gurt pile in her arms, wearing a ole sack over her dress to catch the dirt.

Sammy listened to her taale without saying a word, but soon's she finished he shawed that he wad'n pleased 'bout it.

'You'm a purty maid, you be,' says he, scoffing. 'Makin' outs you love me an' yet willin' fer another chap …'

'I bean't willin', as I've told 'ee,' says Maria, glaazen hard to a telegraph pole on the hedge. 'But wot can I do? I've told Ginger Neale times and times that I woan't 'ave un, but he doan't take no notice. He's allis pesterin' me and I caan't git rids of un.'

'I doan't bleeve you want to, in the bottom,' says Sammy, all s'picious. 'If you maade it plain to un …'

'I 'ave,' says Maria, beginning to pant. 'So plain as daylight, Sammy. But he woan't see it. Whenever I go out he's waitin' around – everybody in the village knaw it an' think I'm goin' 'ave un.'

'Well, if you come walking with me he woan't be able to butt in, will a?'

'No, but – people'd say I was flirtin', knawing like they do how Ginger belong hang-in' round me.'

'Never mind wot people said!' snaps Sammy. 'If you do love me …'

'Well, if ever you see me go past your plaace be meself, you can come out. That's outside the village, and we need'n go far. Ther' might be a chance, but nobody mus'n knaw till …' A thought come to her and she hugged up her bundle o' smutties like if 'twas a baaby. 'Look, Sammy, if you can find some way to maake Ginger stop pesterin' me, I'll go weth 'ee, sure 'nuff. While he's on like this I'm tied hand an' foot. There's me poor mawther to think of – she suffer bad weth her heart and could'n stick the shock of it if it got out that I was flirtin'.'

Sammy glaazed up to the sky for a minute – coming rain 'twas, clouds lowering; the wind gitting up, too, nipping cold. Then he says, purty excited:

'I knaw, Maria! Neale's the milkman, edd'n a?'

'Course he is, but that aan't got nort …'

'You jist wait a day or two,' says Sammy, all mysterious. 'You'll be minse yet, Maria darlint, an' afore many weeks is past there'll be wedding bells ringin' in the future!'

Sammy went off home some proud, and all that evening he was thinking out his plan. If he could knack Neale's custom the fella'd go smash, and then he would'n have nort to offer Maria and would leave her quiet. But how could he knack Neale without risking his own neck? Make people believe Neale was charging of 'em too much for the traade they bought of un; or better still, make 'em think his stuff wad'n no cop at all – suggest as how he watered his milk, for instance! Once the idea come to un to try and take away Neale's custom by going in for the farm business hisself, seeing as he were out o'work; but he soon seed that that was out o' the question. No, he must go around quiet, drop a hint here and there, casual-like, so as not to rouse no s'picions – and see what happened.

The folleyin' day he put his resolve in action, making a start in his own house. Taytime 'twas, when he was setting fore to table with his mother and young brother, Freddie. Same as usual, the woman had cut a slice o' bread'n-butter and put it 'pon his plate. Sammy glaazed at it a minute, then took it up between his thumb and li'l finger. He bite off a bit, then put the slice back on his plate and made a face.

Mrs Chegwidden seed to once that something was wrong. 'Wot's matter?' ax she, leaning fore across the table.

'The butter,' groans Sammy, wrinkling up his nose. 'Awful strong or some'ing, edd'n it? Ted'n taastin' right somehow.'

'Git along!' says the woman, picking up the traade and smiling to it. 'Ther' edd'n nort wrong weth the butter. Tes yer stomach sour, Sammy, or yer temper. Wot'll ee 'ave nex?'

'Piece o' crame an' sugar,' answers Sammy, and he said it in sich a funny sort o' voice that both his mother and brother glazed hard at un for over a minute. Then without saying a word the woman spread his cream and flinked sugar over it.

Soon's 'twas put on his plate Sammy took it up, turning it over and over, and sniffing. At last he ventured to dig his teeth in one li'l corner o' the crest – and next minute he'd scat the chair flying and was tearing fore to the stove and leaning in over the ashbox like if he was goin' be sick.

'Wotever –!' gasp the woman. She was fitty scared, and Freddie'd half rised from his chair and made ready to scoot, 'fraid that Sammy was goin' git ramping.

'That crame! That crame!' spluttered Sammy, his head going from side to side. 'Tes gone poor I tell ee! Ugh!' And he made outs to urge.

Mrs Chegwidden was gitting a bit vexed by now. 'You'm making a fool o' yerself over nothin',' snaps she. 'That there crame is so sweet as I be – I 'ad a piece meself not ten minutes ago. You'm on 'pon some mischief, Sammy.'

'No sich thing!' screech Sammy, rocking to and fro over the ash-box and holding his head. 'I've tho't fer weeks there bin some'ing wrong weth the deery trade we been having. I aan't said nort, I sticked it so long as I could, but now tes got that I caan't hold in no longer!'

The woman turned to Freddie. 'You aan't taste nort wrong with it, 'ave ee? You'd be sure to spake if twad'n tasting fitty.'

Freddie was glazing to his brother, a bit frightened. He feeled twad'n safe to deny what Sammy was saying, though o'course he had'n found nort wrong with the stuff. 'I

– I dunnaw 'bout the crame,' says he, some flustered, 'but I bleeve I ded think the beef in me pasty yes'day was gone bit pindy.'

Sammy swinged around and clout un 'cross the nuddik. 'You thickhead!' he shouted. 'We bean't talkin' 'bout the *butcher*, tes Neale the milkman, and mawther got to finish wid'n to-morra.'

'I bean't goin' to, then!' snaps his mother, firing up. 'The fault's weth yer appetite, me sen.'

'Es it?' says Sammy, vicious, and he haaled the chair for to table again and squabbed down. 'Hand here a slab o' saffern caake an' you'll see whe'er I got a appetite or no.' And bless ee if he did'n git rids o' that chunk o' cake in less'n a minute!'

'Twas fair mystifying and the woman could'n make it up. Sammy was grizzling away to hisself all secret: she knawed he had some plan or other working away at, but could'n tell what twas.

'Be that as may,' she says when he'd finished the cake, 'you doan't catch me changin' milkmen jist to plaze one o' yer fads. You'm so pernickety 'bout what you do ate ...'

'You lost yer taasters, that's wot tes,' ansers Sammy, glowing at her. 'You'd ate half-a pound o' vinnid cheese an' not knaw ther' was ort wrong with et.'

'Wot 'bout Freddie?'

'He's 'fraid to awn up, cause he knaw you'd give un a lacing, but I've maade up me awn mind ...'

'Tes aunly the crame and butter, anyhow,' says Mrs Chegwidden. 'The milk ...'

But fore she could finish there come a splutter and Sammy's tay cup shoot 'cross the table. He'd took a zoop at the tay and there twas dribbling all over his chin – he could'n clunk it down.

'Sammy!' his mother burst out, desperate.

'Mawther!' gasp Sammy, wriggling in his chair and try-to-hold his mouth abroad. 'You got to finish weth Ginger Neale – 'morra morning. This milk – I never taaste nort like it. However you can clunk that ...'

'You'm dotty,' says his mother, withering; she glazed down in his tay-cup what he'd shuv'd up agin her elbaw. Freddie got up and renned from the room, 'fraid what was goin' happen next. 'Must be yer clunkers – unless you'm putting it all on. You bean't thusty I doan't bleeve.'

'Empt' out the milk from that tay an' I'll toss it off in one clunk,' Sammy ansers, feverish. 'The milk is curdled, gone so sour as ...'

He was looking to the tay proper taisy. His mother happened to glance out the winda. She glimpsed somebody's yella hat over the garden wall, and rised up quick to see who was passing. She wanted to turn the talk off to other matters – she'd had 'nuff o' Sammy's antics.

'Maid jist gone by outside,' says she. 'Maria Blake I bleeve.'

'Hey?' Sammy scared her wuss'n ever by what he done next. He jumped up and reshed across to the door and down to gate like a mazed man. Mrs Chegwidden seed un sticked up outside, his hair flying in the wind, glaazen fust one way and then t'other.

Arter a spur he come back in some flurrik. ''Tes no sich thing – she edd'n out there,' he holla'd out. 'Wot ded ee want to 'ave me on like that for!'

'Aw' says the woman, all quiet, glaazen at the bread'n-butter, the crame-and-sugar and the tay: she seed a bit o' daylight in 'em now. 'So that's of it, is it? Tho't you bin all quiet lately. Tes a maid – Maria Blake.'

Sammy coloured up, looking ratty. He ded'n said nothing, but he come fore to the chair and was making to sit down again, trembling like a jelly. But his mother says:

'I never maade it up 'toal. She *is* jist gone along outside – up around the corner spoase, aunly you'm so silly you ded'n think o' looking that way.'

The seat o' Sammy's trousers had titched the cushion, but 'pon that he bobbed up again like lightning and way-to-go. He jaaced fore past the garden wall to the corner and dashed around un, kipping in close agin the hedge to save time. But as it happened it hold un up instead. He stepped on something and next thing he knawed two raws o' teeth was hanging on to his leg. Sammy yowled out, glaazen down to see what twas. A dog – black-and-white terrier. Sammy screeched and danced around in the road but twas several minutes for the cretture left go. Then he glanced up the road – and his eyes fair start out o' their sockets. Up li'l way, standing still and glaazen back at 'n, was Maria and Ginger Neale!

Sammy seed red for a minute. His leg was hurting of 'n a bit, but he stanked up the road, hobbling on at some rate. 'Fore he got to 'em he started letting off steam.

'That's your dog, edd'n et?'

'Tes my dog,' ansers Ginger, frowning.

'Well, I'm goin' report un to the p'lice,' says Sammy. 'E's dangerous. See 'ow 'e grabbed hold o' me leg.' Twad'n till then that he dared to look at the maid – and he had a fright. She was looking vexed 'nuff to scat un down; and when she spoke 'twas a proper snap.

'Serve ee right!' she said to un. 'Taaren round the corner like that. You was like a maaze man – no wonder he bite ee; I'd 'ave done the same if I'd bin he.'

Something must be up! S'poase she was vexed cause he'd catched her with Ginger. But if twas that, she must have told un a pack o'lies. And Sammy says, all stiff:

'Aw. Who do ee think you'm talkin' to?'

'That's right,' says the maid, mocking. 'Maake outs you doan't knaw me – say you ded'n want me to go courtin' … Here! wot be ee doing of?'

Sammy, feeling waik all of a sudden, had cluckied down in the road and rolled up his trousers leg: he was beginning to pull down his socks. Maria glaazed for a croom, then flared up indignant.

'You'm acting insultin', shawing yer legs there in middle the road fer everybody to see. I'll report *you* to the p'lice if you doan't git up and go in to once.'

Sammy got down on one knee and waved his fist up at her. 'Tes the dog,' says he. 'I bleeve me leg's bliddin'.' His voice was all choky, partly with rage and partly – well, Sammy was a bit upset, as you might expect.

'I hope ee is,' the maid rapped out. 'Twill teach ee a lesson. I knaw wot you was on upon. You'd seed me go along and was coming arter me, you imperent old toad!'

Ginger was glaazen at her all the time she was speaking, proper flabbergasted. He'd never heard Maria carr' on like this afore, and he felt uncomfor'ble, I can tell ee. At last he says, all 'oarse:

'No need to git rampin' about it, Maria.'

'Aw, edd'n ther'?' says the maid, whizzing around 'pon un. 'That's all you knaw about it. If you knawed as I do 'ow he've pestered me ...'

'So you doan't want neither one of us?' says Ginger, sharp-like.

'Never mind wot I do want fer the minute; 'tis best to settle this business so far's *he's* concerned.' She stamped her feet, coming close up agin Sammy, and he shrinked back, 'fraid she was goin' kick un. He was glaazen hard to his ankle – li'l red mark there, but no blood. His hands was fumbling around the bottom of his pants. They seed that he was sweating streams, and no wonder. He'd never have believed it! Whatever could have took the maid he ded'n knaw. And she went on raging as if she was never goin' stop.

'So well for ee to knaw wot I'd be like to ee, then praps you woan't be so maaze to 'ave me. Aw yes, ole fella, you seemed to think I was a li'l worm to tread 'pon, but even a worm'll twinkle if you step 'pon un.'

'You bean't twinklin',' says Sammy, all gruff; 'you'm blaazin'.' He shuv'd his mouth fore quick bunk agin his knee, but that did'n stop the words coming out.

'Ess, I'm a blaazer all right, when I got to deal with sich idjits as you. Git up, do ee hear, or I'll slap yer chacks for ee!'

Slawly Sammy pulled up his sock and rised to his feet, shaking. He looked hard to Ginger for a tick or two, then to the dog what was eyeing of un all s'picious from in behind a fuzzy-bush. Ginger says, bottling up his feelings:

'You better go in I reckon. You've worked her up.'

''Twas your old dog what done it!' Sammy burst out, and he stooped quick, grabbed a stone in the road and drawed at the crettur. 'An I'm goin' report ...'

'You best not to!' shouts the maid, red in the face. 'You report Ginger's dog and I'll never spake to ee again so long as I live.'

Sammy tried to make a face at her, but couldn' manage it, so he turned around. 'You need'n,' says he, very low. 'I've found out wot you be, anyhow. I knaw wot fibs you've a-told me. You want Ginger, not me. Oall right; he's the wuss off. Good riddance to ee!' And he stanked away back the road, forgetting that his leg was bite.

He was in a proper mizz-maze all evening: did'n knaw what to do next. What was the good o' smashing Neale if Maria did'n want un? No cop 'tall – but Sammy mained to do it, if only to have his spite out on the both of 'em. 'Twas plain as a pike-staff that the maid had been making game of un all along; yet she'd seemed sincere 'nuff in it. Sammy was proper dithered and could'n make head nor tail o' the business.

Next morning he made sure to be in when Neale come with the milk. When Ginger knacked to door Sammy stride back, grim as granite.

'Here, I got some'ing to tell you,' says he, very curt. 'Our people's finishin' ...'

Ginger interrupted, talking 'bout something else. 'Well, Sammy,' he says, 'you got yer chance.'

'Wot do ee main?' ax Sammy, snapping his eyes.

'That there maid Blake ...'

Sammy waved the empty jug over his head. 'Doan't you mention her name to me,' he says. 'I've had 'nuff o' she to last me a lifetime.'

'You doan't want her then?' ax Ginger, and he burst out laffing. 'That's a clane swipe for her that is! She woan't have nobody now.'

'Wot – you've finished weth her?'

'Course I 'ave, arter seein' wot a gashly old temper she got. It opened me eyes. I bean't goin' let meself in fer that, not if I knaw it!'

Sammy glaazed down in the jug as Ginger tipped out the milk in un. His hand was shaking and when the jug got nearly full he beginned floxin' it out 'pon the doorstep.

'She've got paid out now, anyway,' says he, all savage. 'Spoase she screeched when you towld her and said she would never act like that to you; eh?'

'No, there wad'n very much fuss weth her; she took it sulky and said if I would'n 'ave no more to do weth her I could plaze meself – it did'n maake no difference to she! A touchy sort o' maid – I pity the bloke who *do* have her! Twon't be me ner you, anyhow.'

'No fear!' says Sammy, but he spoke all quavery, like if he was sorry 'bout something – and all of a sudden a tear come to his left eye and trookled down over his chack. 'Fore he could wipe un away ee'd splashed down in the milk.

Ginger turned and leaved un glaazen like a stewed owl in the jug.

That very evening, as Sammy was trudging home from the village, he seed Maria traapsing droo the fields jist ahead, making for a stile round the corner in front of un. He glowed for a croom, standing still in the roadway, in two minds whe'er to go on and face her or scoot back some other way. But it did'n take un long to decide. 'I woan't be bait!' says he to hisself. 'I'll go straight on and woan't look at her.' And on he went with his head cocked up, pouching out his mouth and trying to look at 'n.

Maria come out to the stile, and be time he got to the corner she was sticked up in the ditch, no hat on, smiling. Sammy did'n look – kipt his eyes turned down and stride along with arms flying. Next thing he knawed he'd bunked into something – not a dog this time, but a maid! Maria'd stepped for right in front of un.

'Wot be ee runnin' away for?' ax she, all husky.

Sammy glowed, red as a beet. 'An' wot be you comin' arter me for, I should like to knaw. I've had 'bout 'nuff o' you. Walking out with Ginger like you did ...'

The maid squeezed his arm. 'I could'n help it, Sammy, sure 'nuff,' says she, some anxious. 'I'd bin to A'nt Jaanie's all arternoon and was on me way back to the village when Ginger catched up weth me jist as I got in sight o' your housen. I could'n turn and go back and 'ad to go 'long weth un, cause he would'n leave me to meself. I 'oped as 'ow you would'n see me and was feeling some vexed over it.'

'Seems so, be the way you carr'd on,' Sammy says, all short. He was panting and could'n take his eyes off her face.

She laffed. 'Aw, you old silly, how ded'n ee see droo it?'

'See droo wot?' gasp Sammy, glaazen straight at her noase with one eye shut.

'Why, me acting like that. I feeld sure you'd be tickled. It come to me soon's I seed ee come around the corner. I tho't if I made outs to be some gashly Ginger'd 'ave a eye-opener and would'n want no more to do with me. An' it worked, did'n it?'

'You main – that was your way o'gittin rids of un? You done it all because you – you'm willin' to go with me?'

'That depend 'pon you, whe'er we'm goin' together or no,' says Maria, pulling his arm round her waist. 'One thing I can 'sure ee, Sammy – last night you 'ad all the jaw-in' you'll ever git from me – and I ded'n main it, even then!'

Denys Val Baker

The Outcast

The taxi called for them at half-past five. Anderson watched it crawling up the steep lane to the cottage, a fat black slug emerging from the misty world of the valley below. Up here the late sunshine still flooded the fields and slopes, the air was keen and crisp. Not for the first time he regretted having accepted the lecture invitation that was now to plunge him down into the grey mist and huddled streets of the nearby West Cornish market town. It was safer up on the moors, miles from anywhere, with a few scattered cottages and farms as the only neighbours. A man could think, a man could concentrate, a man could create. He looked round at his paintings hanging along the white-washed walls, at his latest canvas stretched tight upon an easel over by the window. Then he frowned. A man could also vegetate.

He picked up the black folder containing his talk and went down the narrow wooden stairway into the cottage parlour. He hardly noticed his wife, dressed for the occasion in a flower-pattern dress and a straw hat. She was a part of the over-familiar pattern of the room, with the blue chintz curtains, the worn leather ottoman, the black gleaming Cornish slab that was both kitchen oven and sitting-room fireplace. It was a cosy enough cottage, but he knew he would have died of despair if his spirit had been literally confined between its grey stone walls. Upstairs, like medicine in a cupboard, lay his escape: the strips of canvas, the potentialities of paint, the view out of the window over fields and hills – and the still wider view as he dreamed into space.

'Mr Anderson?'

'Coming.'

They locked the door behind them and climbed into the taxi. He stretched his legs and sank into one corner, trying to remember when they last enjoyed such luxury, instead of the usual mile walk to the cross-roads to pick up the twice daily bus. They would be doing that now, too, if the literary club's secretary hadn't provided the taxi. He smiled faintly, knowing the caution that lay behind the kindness. They had heard of his occasional descents into the towns, his heavy drinking bouts, the few but memorable outbreaks that were nevertheless mere shadows of the days in London when he had drunk hard and steadily, and all the time. He supposed they were terrified lest, left to his own motivation, he might never reach the lecture hall: worse, that he might arrive too drunk to give the lecture – or, still worse, to give the sort of lecture that might shock some of the club's more respectable members.

So they had neatly arranged for a taxi to deliver him to the secretary's house for an early dinner, thence to be escorted firmly and directly to the lecture hall. His spirits drooped at the prospect. He became conscious of a dry taste in his mouth.

'What's the time?'

'Quarter past six,' said his wife. 'We shall be in plenty of time.'

'I've got a terrible thirst. You know what it will be like … three-course meal and a cup of coffee. I think we'd better snatch a quick one now, while we can. God knows when we'll get away.'

She looked at him anxiously.

'Well, if you must … but do be careful.'

He leaned forward and directed the taxi to stop outside the King's Hotel.

The driver looked round worriedly.

'I was told to take you to Mrs Bennett's.'

Anderson flared.

'Well, I'm telling you different, see?'

The driver shrugged and pulled the car in. Anderson clambered out, muttering to himself. Did they think he was a little child or something? His wife suppressed a faint smile, and followed him out of the taxi into the hotel.

It was quiet in the bar. They had two quick beers, and he felt better. He had needed those. He took his wife's arm and they walked quickly along the promenade, and up the refined looking avenue to the secretary's house. He sighed as they rang the doorbell. Then, bracing himself, he went to endure the hour or so of soup and entrée, stewed fruit and coffee, and a stream of small town gossip.

*   *   *   *   *

The lecture was being given in a room at the local technical college. They arrived there five minutes before the advertised time, to find little groups of elderly ladies and a few sombre looking men, including two vicars, wandering around the large main hall, examining the uneven work of the art students. Anderson's heart sank.

'People always leave it to the last minute,' said the chairman, a little grey-haired doctor. 'No need for "alarm and despondency" – hah! hah! See, here come some more people now. Excuse me, will you?'

He pattered across to greet another continent of grey hairs. Anderson groaned and whispered sideways to his wife. 'They promised in their letter there'd be some of the art students here. Surely this isn't a college for old age pensioners?'

But the chairman, if he didn't produce young students, at least fulfilled another promise. He had said there would be about seventy people, and there were well over that by the time the lecture started. They gradually filled up the neat rows of chairs and clustered down the aisle. It was a full room, buzzing with faint conversation, when the doctor propelled Anderson to the end of the room and deposited him in a seat behind a table that was bereft of all except one lonely looking glass of water.

'Well,' said the chairman, coughing significantly. 'I think we might as well begin.'

He coughed again, this time the signal for the suppression of those final whispered conversations among the audience.

'Tonight, my friends we are to have the pleasure of listening to an address by one of our best known local artists, a man distinguished in the field of modern painting. Mr Anderson has chosen for his subject, "The Artist as Outcast From Society".'

Anderson gripped the black folder firmly, and got to his feet. He tried not to see the neat rows of faces, nor the strange uniformity of their expectant expressions. He tried not to notice that the few men all seemed to wear horn-rimmed glasses, that most of the women were rendered anonymous by neat little hats and sober coats. He tried to forget that the average age of his listeners must be somewhere in the fifties. He tried, in fact, to address himself to one lone student, a young girl, who had sidled in the doorway at the last moment, looking about as lost as he felt himself.

'I have come here tonight,' he began, 'from the outskirts of your town and the borders of penury ...'

That made them laugh, as he had intended. At least there was humanity in laughter.

'... to try to explain to you why, in my opinion, and that of many of my fellows, the Artist today has become an outcast from society – the first victim of the welfare state.'

He looked down at his notes. Well, he was embarked. There was a faint hush over the room. One or two murmurs of 'Hear – hear' had greeted his last remark. They would be with him, whatever he said. They were those sort of people: genteel, well meaning, cushioned against all the sufferings that had been so essential to his own development. They were that familiar species, the art lovers, who knew all about art but unfortunately very little about loving.

'Today the artist is faced with two choices ...'

Why not three or four or five? Why pretend there was a choice at all? For the artist, if they wanted to know, there was no real choice. If he found there was a choice, then he was no artist. It was as simple as that.

'Some artists of course, are in the fortunate position of being economically independent ...'

It was so irrelevant, if they only knew. What was it that forgotten writer, recently revived, Ford Madox Ford, had called one of his novels? *A Man Could Stand Up.* A wonderful title. It was like that for the artist, too. A man could eat, a man could sleep, a man could live – if he wanted to. He wouldn't starve, not these days. Those things were all questions of degree. It didn't matter whether you lived on the dole or in a mansion. It didn't affect your being an artist. You didn't take up art, like all these colleges tried to pretend. You were or you weren't, and it had nothing to do with the state of your bank balance.

'Some artists are forced to take up ancillary employment ...'

A good word, ancillary. He had looked it up in the dictionary. Indeed, he had gone to great pains to prepare this lecture. He had felt it mattered, to try and make these people understand something, a tiny fraction, about the artist and his life. Not about the artist and his dreams. He had known it wasn't any use trying to explain that. If they understood about dreams, they wouldn't have been there listening. They would have been dreaming, like he sat and dreamed day after day, up there in the cottage. You didn't have to be in a cottage on a moor to dream, though. He had dreamed and painted in a slum off Fulham Road just as well, if the truth be told. Only they wouldn't believe that, either. They liked it the romantic way, a cottage on the moors, long hair and corduroy suits.

Yes, he would have liked to make them see a little of the artist's problems. But looking at their faces – on the whole, nice, kind, pleasant faces – he felt so much like a man in a foreign country that he could have cried. But he knew even that would have registered upon them no more than the dry statements he was mouthing. They would have looked at each other, at first embarrassed, then – reassured he was not throwing a fit or anything – with amusement. These artists, a bit eccentric, you know … He could imagine the doctor hastily producing a large white handkerchief to mop up (no, hide away) the impolite tears. Someone, a little lady with a quakery grin, who would have rushed forward with a cup of tea. In a few moments they would have expected him, like a true blue Britisher, to have wiped away the last tear stain, gulped down his tea, and resumed his lecture. After all, hadn't they paid their two shillings?

'The artist is a living proof that all men are not equal.'

Someone clapped – someone else said 'Hear – hear!' – and they drifted into a genteel wave of applause.

How nice of them to sit back and vicariously associate themselves with words whose meaning had been cut out of life with men's blood and tears and sweat. He wondered how many of them had ever been possessed by that urge, that desperate compelling desire to create, to fashion out of nowhere an image of eternity. He wondered if any of them had paced the floorboards of lonely rooms, had sat through the long hours of night, had stared with intensity into the bewildering colours of the dawn – had sought and sought and sought, yet never found, yet still sought. He knew that none of them had (though it occurred to him as a tiny comfort that perhaps for the young art student at the back, perhaps for her, there was still the possibility).

And so he went on, reading his prepared statement that in so many ways announced so many profundities. And it seemed to him that the longer he talked, the further he removed himself from their comprehension. It seemed to him that the harder he tried to communicate with words, the deafer they grew. Indeed, once or twice he found himself shouting in an effort to force home his meaning, and the chairman gave him a worried look.

Better bring it to an end now, he thought, and for the first time that night he really panicked. For the words written on his manuscript seemed no longer valid: they left everything in mid-air. He had no conclusion to offer, no message to propagate.

Desperately he looked at their faces, scanning the rows, hoping in some muddled way to extract an idea, a phrase, a picture that would help him to formulate an ending to his address. But he found nothing, nothing but a faint flicker of hope in the pensive face of the art student at the very doorway, on the very brink of life.

And perhaps that faint glimmer of communication reached back into him and turned some tired wheel of thought, for suddenly he spoke.

'I have nothing more to say now. I have spoken for those who wanted to listen. For the rest of you – well, better than words, there are pictures. Better than phrases, there are canvases with paint upon them. They are here all around you, in this room. Take a good look at them.'

He waved his hands expressively at the rows of immature drawings and paintings, at the amateur images hacked painfully out of nothing, at all the scattered, confused, half-formed yet creative efforts of a new generation.

'Try to learn from them,' he said sadly. 'Try to learn. Try and see, not so much the picture, but what lies behind it. Think of the hopes and the ambitions, the days and the weeks, the lifetime's desires, that may lie hidden behind each picture. Try to understand.'

And then he sat down.

*   *   *   *   *

They applauded heartily. The chairman made a nice, neat speech that incorporated a graceful vote of thanks. There were a few questions, which he found it impossible to answer. Gradually, the meeting dwindled to a close. The chairman made another short speech, and it was over.

He looked at his watch, thinking of the nearby harbour pub, the atmosphere of smoke and brightness, the bubble of human voices … There was time to slip away. But first, cups of tea and biscuits, hand-shakes and conversations.

By the time they finally got away, it was too late for a drink. Too late. He sighed and took his wife's arm, and they walked along the promenade. It was almost deserted by this time of night, and only an occasional lamp lit up the straight roadway and the stone parapet. They leaned over the railings, staring out at the sea. Here and there bobbed the lights of fishing boats, like oases in some dark desert.

'Do you think they enjoyed it?' he said.

'Of course,' said his wife. 'It was different from what they're accustomed to hearing. It will make them revise their ideas. You'll see.'

'I wish I could think so,' he said. 'I wish I could.'

And he stared out to sea.

*   *   *   *   *

Later they were back in the cottage. The stillness of the night hung everywhere after the whine of the taxi had lost itself back into the mists of the valley. They were too tired too bother about a meal. They put the paraffin lamp out and took a candle with them upstairs. They undressed in silence, and got into bed. With a smile of goodnight, she blew out the flame and curled up beside him. Without commitment, he put one arm around her, making a pillow for her head. Soon, he knew, she would be asleep, with a strange look of innocence upon her face.

He lay quietly beside her, breathing evenly, and looked sideways at the moonlight falling through the window. Outside, in the great stillness, the fields shone with dew; on the hilltop old stones reared up out of the ground in gaunt shapes. It was so still and silent that he fancied he could hear the hum of the town that lay miles below them, could almost hear the babel of voices, chattering parrot-like voices. He closed his eyes and tried to re-enact the evening's scene, but it didn't make sense. He heard only the endless questions, the perpetual inquiry, and there was nothing he could say in answer. He opened his eyes again and stared at the unquestioning moonlight.

It was a beautiful silver light, that evening, pouring through the bedroom window in positive abandonment. He lay content to feast his eyes upon the precious sight, content to absorb, content to accept. It was wonderful there in the dark, with his wife sleeping in the crook of his arm; the great stillness all around, and the light from another world pouring itself at his feet.

In the morning, early, he was up and preparing a new canvas. All that day, and many days afterwards, he worked at a new painting. He forgot all about time and troubles, places and peoples. He felt completely cut off from the outside world, living in some trembling inner world of his own compulsion. He was the artist as outcast from society. A happy man.

Charles Causley

GOLDIE GOES WEST

As soon as Mrs Blood opened the door, Goldie knew that the sensible thing to do would be to run away, but that he wouldn't have the nerve. He picked up his cardboard suitcase, his dusty black overcoat, and followed her into the parlour. 'I can fit you nicely in my upper-back midear,' she was saying. 'You'm a gentleman, I can see.'

Nobody knew that he wasn't more than Goldie, and he felt his heart clang in his boots like a try-your-strength machine at the fair. She held open the baize-lined door, and Goldie walked hopelessly in: a condemned man approaching the gallows. He sank uncomfortably in a chair upholstered in grass-green velvet, and his eye took in the rubble of created china: presents from Looe, Bude, Polzeath; the dreadful oval portrait, like a cloud formation, of a 1917 sergeant-major; the unplayed cottage piano with the legs of the brontosaurus. But Mrs Blood was tapping his knee and looking anxiously at him. 'I beg your pardon?' he said.

She leaned towards him, black beads jingling. 'I thought you was going to faint. Blood used to look like it. It was the army done it.' She nodded vaguely towards the oval portrait and looked closely at Goldie. 'Thirty-six years,' she said, 'in the Duke's.' Goldie felt suddenly ill and closed his eyes, feeling in his waistcoat pocket for his tin of tablets. Damn! He had left them in the café where he'd had lunch. That was the third lot he had lost in a month. 'It's my inside,' he said. 'I was a p.o.w. Sorry.'

'You bide still, midear,' she said. 'I'll make a cup of tea.' And she drew the blind and disappeared somewhere to the back of the house. Goldie heard the clink of cups, the sound of the electric-light switch, the familiar noises of home. His shoulders shook, but not with tears. He laughed weakly; soundlessly. A damn fine salesman, he thought. The blokes on the boat were right. An ex-p.o.w. is no good; better off in the jungle.

Then there was that woman. She probably felt sorry for him. Curing the sickness of the soul with a cup of tea. Goldie wondered who she reminded him of? A tall, dark, bony woman in black: something of the gypsy in her. She was Cornish all right; there was that coal-seam glitter in her eye. Her hands strong, and her hair, although she must have been nearly sixty, ungreyed.

Goldie had been an actor before the war. Now all that was finished. He was thirty-seven, nerve gone, fit for what? This job, for instance: *Maddever, Male and Earle, Limited, Queen Square, Exeter. Coal, corn, manure, seed, wool and builders' merchants. Our representative in West Devon and North Cornwall: Mr A. E. Goldie, will have the pleasure of waiting on you in a few days.* Goldie tore the card in half and threw it in the empty grate. What did he know about corn or coal or manure? The sales manager knew it, too. They must have been pretty hard up to appoint him. Of course his uncle on the board, Albert Sprooge, had wangled it all for him. It'll settle you down, he had said; you must forget the war: forget the jungle, forget the stinking messdeck, forget the Japs. Albert Sprooge had never even seen a Japanese, and that son of his, Ivor, clever little Ivor who had suddenly got religion and agriculture in 1939, couldn't be spared from the farm. Goldie collected a mouthful of phlegm and swallowed it. Travelling about the country, Albert Sprooge had said, will do you a world of good. It'll bring colour to your cheeks, fill you out. Of course, the firm can't provide you with a car. But there are plenty of buses. And trains.

Yes, thought Goldie looking at his yellow hands, his thin demob shoes, there are: but not here. He thought of his weary ankles, the purple jungle sore on his leg. His head buzzed. He thought of the 'returns' that had to be made out tonight: Good Lord, Thursday again; the details of 'new business'; the cruel, tough, oriental faces of the farmers; the eternal rooms, the mountainous beds, the doubtful linen. And Ethel, in Exeter, hadn't written again. He wondered if his wife was still interested in him. Three years as a p.o.w. was a long time, and he always had been nervous of women. And what was it she had said the second night he was home? The truth, thought Goldie, at the price of five gin-and-limes. She had said that she was afraid of him. *That he looked like a Japanese.* Well, with his cropped hair, his steel spectacles, his jaundiced skin, he probably did.

Goldie suddenly came to a decision. He would walk out of the house. Damn Mrs Blood. Blast Maddever, Male and Earle. He would go home to Exeter, to his wife. There was always his pension. He picked the torn fragments of card from the grate, stuffed them in his pocket, walked silently across the room and quietly opened the door. Goldie nearly died of fright. That woman, Mrs Blood, was standing there.

'I've taken your tea up to your room, Mr Goldie,' she said. 'You can 'ave a nice quiet lie down, midear. Do your calls tomorrow. Forget 'em today.' She led the way upstairs and Goldie followed meekly after.

'*He hath led mee,*' thought Goldie, '*to darknesse, not to light,*
And against mee all day …'

'Did you say something?' said Mrs Blood.

'I was only thinking,' said Goldie.

All that was in 1946: Goldie's first year of peace. And, three years later, when he did his Dunborough round, he was still staying at Mrs Blood's. Twice a year he came: in the spring and autumn. Each time he stayed three weeks. The years were slipping, spooling away like a film: Goldie hardly seemed to notice. His uncle, old Albert Sprooge, had died. Another victory for the Allies, thought Goldie, and felt quite cheerful. Not that Goldie's position on the firm was at all secure with the old man gone: but he had ceased to worry. As a representative, he was neither successful nor unsuccessful. The only positive emotion he felt was one of acute distaste for his fellow reps. Their over-smart suits! Their jokes! Goldie couldn't imagine any of them in the background of a home, a wife, children. They seemed part of the scenery of the bar at the *Richard of Cornwall* or the smoke-room of Trelaw's Commercial Hotel: a place which, in appearance, always reminded Goldie of a brothel he had once visited in Bombay, except that Trelaw's Commercial Hotel was possibly not so clean. Goldie was glad that he had escaped Trelaw's, and felt thankful of his back-room at Mrs Blood's.

Curious, he thought, that he was always the only boarder there. Yet the curled, yellow card: *Apartments, Bed and Breakfast,* was never out of the window. He tried to recollect the face of the postman who had directed him there when he had first arrived at Dunborough, in the rain, with his cheap, shiny case in 1946. He often meant to ask Mrs Blood, but the opportunity never seemed to arise. She was a closed, shell-like woman. Barbed wire twinkled in her dark eyes. But, sometimes, there was the flash of kindness. Was it kindness? There was that cup of tea on his first day: when he had felt all in. It was good to have one friend in Dunborough.

Dunborough! Goldie looked up from writing his returns, looked across the valley to the little town: the houses climbing the steep hill like grey garden snails. The thin spire of the Wesleyan Chapel fingering the heavy sky. It rained in Dunborough almost as much as it had in the jungle. Goldie could see the green of the Saxon earth-works, the toothless mound that overhung the town and about which the locals were so proud. Green and grey: a town of slate. He could see, too, the white *Beau Geste* fort of the cinema; the red public library. He could hear the voices, those odd, sawn-off accents: neither Devonian nor Cornish, of the men working on the allotments along the side of the valley. A slate-blue rain began to fall. Goldie yawned, shuddered, got up.

He heard the front door close. A familiar figure was crossing the road outside. It was Mrs Blood; probably going to visit her sister. He watched her: tall, black, raven-like, moving through the dark, slanting rain towards the town. The curfew bell began to ring: a custom inherited from the days of the Normans. Eight o'clock. Goldie felt thirsty and decided to go down to the kitchen and make himself some tea. Mrs Blood liked him to make himself at home. Anyway, he was a 'good' lodger. He always washed up.

It was on the way downstairs that Goldie suddenly noticed the door. It was at the far end of the landing, on the curve. The stairway twisted in such a way that you didn't really notice the door until you were halfway down. With hardly a thought at what he was doing, Goldie turned in the stairs and climbed them again. He was going to take a look in the room. The key was in the lock; nothing could be easier. It might be a workroom; where Mrs Blood did sewing. Goldie wasn't by nature curious. In fact, his interest in other people was flat, negative. Usually, he just didn't care a damn. But he had a sudden feeling that the room held some clue to Mrs Blood's character. His heart thumping, his throat filled with a dry excitement he hadn't known since he was a boy, he put his hand on the door-knob.

'Looking for something, midear?' said a voice behind him. It was Mrs Blood. She had come back. What for? An umbrella? Goldie felt that he should have leapt in the air with fright, nerves, apprehension. But, surprisingly, he was completely calm. He felt delighted at his self-control. His hands were as steady as guns. It was thrilling. He felt capable of anything: even murder. He hadn't felt like it since Singapore. When was that? February, 1942?

'I wanted a clean shirt for the morning,' he said. 'I'm leaving early. I thought you kept the laundry ...'

'Down here, in the kitchen,' she was saying, anxiously. Goldie could see the rain on her dark face. She stood in the stairs taking off her coat. Goldie smiled. His voice was confident, clear.

'I thought you were going to your sister's,' he said. Mrs Blood shook her head. Yes, she seemed nervous. Goldie felt delighted. 'Come downstairs, midear,' she said. 'I'll make 'ee a cup of tea. You been workin'.' Goldie passed her on the stairs and went into the kitchen. Mrs Blood stayed a moment, shaking the rain from her coat in the stairs and spreading it on the banisters.

When Goldie came up to bed an hour later the key in the door at the bend of the landing was missing, and the door was locked. A thrill ran through Goldie. It's war, he thought. War. He was looking forward to his Dunborough trip next autumn.

In August Mrs Blood wrote and told Goldie that she couldn't put him up the following September. But Goldie arrived on the door-step just the same. Mrs Blood didn't seem surprised to see him.

'You'll be in your old room, then,' she said. ''E 'asn't turned up.'

'Who?' said Goldie, stirring his tea violently.

'My son,' said Mrs Blood. ''Ome from the army.' She looked at her watch: a gold one. 'It's too late now. Anyway, 'e'd 'ave bin on the same bus as you.'

'You didn't have that watch when I was here in the spring,' said Goldie. 'Your ship come home?'

'Per'aps,' said Mrs Blood. 'And I mus' definitely ask you to find fresh lodgin's as from this time, Mr Goldie. I'm leavin' Dunborough.'

'But you've lived here fifty years,' said Goldie, astonished.

'It's too long,' said Mrs Blood. 'I'm goin' to travel. 'Ave a look at that Mediterranean.'

'That gold watch has brought you luck,' said Goldie. 'Send us a picture postcard.'

'I will,' said Mrs Blood. 'Your room's ready when you want to go up.'

That night Goldie couldn't sleep. He heard the church clock on the other side of the river strike twelve, one, two. The light in Mrs Blood's room had gone out hours before. She was a sound sleeper; she had once slept through a thunderstorm, Goldie remembered. And the door to the room on the bend of the landing was still locked. He had tried it, gently, on his way to the bathroom. What was the secret behind it? Goldie's mind worked overtime. He tried to think of his seed samples, his cards of coloured cement, the calls he had to make the next day. He tried to concentrate on the firm of Maddever, Male and Earle. No good.

Goldie eased himself out of bed. He picked up the bunch of keys from his trousers; splayed them out like steel fingers. The chain glittered in the moonlight. He slipped on his dusty overcoat over his pyjamas. It was September, but Goldie was sweating. Had he had his malaria this year? He couldn't remember. *What was in that room?* Money? The old girl must have saved a bit in her time. There was that talk of going abroad. Going to the Mediterranean. Perhaps she was cracked. Goldie wondered if he was a little mad himself. Her husband, the whiskered sergeant-major, may have brought home some loot, some idol, from India. Or she may have an idiot son locked up there: to 'save' him from the asylum. On his calls in the countryside, the romantic countryside, he had heard of such things. Goldie crept along the landing.

His hand trembled as he tried a key in the lock. No good. Another. No good. Another. Impatiently, Goldie missed the keyhole and nearly rapped sharply on the door with the steel ring. He saved it with his knuckles, but pushed the door violently. To his amazement, it swung open.

In the moonlight, the room was bright as silver. There was no furniture save a camp-bed and a washstand in the far corner. The floor was bare, and the walls … Goldie looked at the walls. They were covered with pictures, oil paintings. Some in cheap frames, some with ragged edges: pinned on boards. A pile of them lay in rolls on the floor. Goldie picked one up, unrolled it and stepped towards the window.

Nervous as he was, and his feet were cold, he could not restrain a cry of astonishment. Even in the moonlight, Goldie could see that the painting was a masterpiece. It was a scene in a garden, it looked like an Italian garden. White walls, cypresses. Some girls, goddesses with long braided hair, were lying in the clear water of a fountain. He picked up another. Archers, wonderful men in strong, easy attitudes, were making bows, cutting thongs, under a thorn tree. He looked at another. A painting of the Last Supper. Goldie felt as though he had strayed into Aladdin's Cave. Nothing seemed real but these pictures. He wanted to see one in the light of day.

A sudden heavy sigh from the bed in the corner almost made Goldie gasp out in alarm. He pressed himself against the wall, in the shadow of the washstand. What he had thought was a rumple of blankets on the camp-bed was a young man, asleep. As he watched him he turned towards the moonlight, his bare arm resting on the dusty floor. He breathed deeply and fell into a heavy slumber again.

He could see the young man's face quite clearly. It was dark, heavy, Cornish. The eyes were too close together, and the long straight black hair had been combed viciously back from his brow. Two locks of hair, lay, Saturnine, like horns above his eyes. He must have been about twenty-six. A dull, even slightly idiot face with the mouth, in sleep, open. But unmistakably Mrs Blood's son. So he had arrived home after all! Goldie looked at the painting in his hand, at the paintings on the walls. He had a curious, overwhelming feeling that he was either in the presence of a lunatic or a genius. Who could have taught this young man, lying there in an army shirt like a man pole-axed, to paint like this? Goldie determined to find out. Obviously Mrs Blood had no idea of the value of the pictures. Or had she? This had happened before, Goldie thought excitedly, in painting, in music. He thought of Thomas Chatterton; of Alfred Wallis; of Clare. A dealer, an Exeter dealer: Andrew Simons, would tell him. The church clock banged out four as Goldie slipped the little painting of the Italian garden in his overcoat and stole back to his bedroom.

The next morning, at eight o'clock, Goldie was on the bus for Exeter. He lit a cigarette, and he suddenly noticed his hands. They were pink and white; yellow no longer.

Like everything else in Goldie's life, nothing happened as he expected. It was the dealer to whom Goldie showed the Italian picture who started everything off: Andrew

Simons. He was a little, grey man who looked rather like a teddy-bear made out of Harris tweed. He peered with interest at Goldie over his glossy counter.

'Is it – er – good?' asked Goldie.

'Very,' said the little man, not hesitating a second. 'It's not merely good, it's first-class,' Goldie swallowed eagerly. 'I can show you fifty more like that,' he said. Teddy-bear raised his eyebrows. 'Excuse me,' whispered the dealer, and hurried into the back room. Goldie wiped his brow with the dirty khaki handkerchief he kept in his hip-pocket. He always used a white one in front of his customers, of course. Khaki was bad for business. Goldie heard the ring of a telephone bell, a murmur of talk. Simons was on the phone to somebody. Presently the old man stepped down into the shop again. He looked warm too, thought Goldie; sweating.

'Well?' said Goldie.

'I'll be frank,' said the little man. 'It's not merely first-class. It's hot. Pinched.'

Goldie almost stepped back into a glass case of miniatures. And as he left the shop they arrested him. The old man had telephoned the police.

The young man in the camp-bed wasn't a lunatic or a genius: not even a painter. He was Alfie Blood, sometime army private, who had deserted after Cassino in 1944. Alfie was a wider boy than his narrow brow suggested. He had run a racket in tyres and stolen Naafi stores for two years in Rome. Then he had run a little personal side-line in *objets d'art*: especially Renaissance paintings, forty of which Alfie had looted from half-a-dozen Italian museums and monasteries from Salerno to Genoa. He had stowed home in a Danish butter-boat and Mrs Blood had hidden him for eight months. The police found their tickets, to Mexico City, in the washstand.

Alfie got four years. Mrs Blood got eighteen months. Goldie got a cracking headache. He made such a hash of his own defence, and the Bloods – cool as ice – spun such a yarn about him at the trial that people said it was lucky he got off at all. It was his war-service, of course, that saved him. But then, that was just the backhanded sort of good turn one might have expected, thought Goldie, from the Japanese.

Phyllis M. Jones

LOGAN ROCK

The field was full of cows. No one minded them, they were the buttercup and daisy cows, brown and white with soft beige faces and with udders full of fairy milk. One could imagine elves pulling at the long, clean teats on midsummer evenings.

Evenings when the sky spangled with starlight and the Plough, a clear saucepan, pointed over the Atlantic towards Wales. I could imagine, in spite of all this bright light, times when the black cloaked covens returned from night raids on the fields of Wales where they could bloat themselves with milk from Taffy's cows; instead of gulls' wings would be the whirr of broomsticks.

There was a concentrated accumulation of ancient activity in this small cove. But now it was afternoon and hot with summer. The Atlantic was like opal and laced with a spreading foam. Nearer inland we could see the sand under the water and long shelves of rocks.

If the scene was portrayed on paper by an artist, nobody would believe the colours. Green luscious grass, yellow flowers, white flowers, pea-green sea and rocks sparkling; patterns of foam over the shallows and, to the east of the bay, the threatening, rearing Logan Rock.

The car park linked us with this present tourist century. The attendant with his bag and tickets and guidebook commentary found all the world his stage and, finding an extra player that afternoon, fastened, ancient mariner-like, on my husband. With his sunglasses and camera, Ian tended to make the most of incidental characters and details to mould his own stories; I saw he meant to enjoy this conversation.

As I was the born-and-bred Cornish partner in our marriage, I guessed the car park gentleman had placed Ian in the 'up-the-country' white hat and easy tan brigade, and would patronise my husband with an oily charm. Still, we could explore without him – my mother, sister Cara and myself.

We were not out just to go beaching, but to enjoy a drive and a picnic. There was a small Methodist chapel nearby and we decided to enter.

It was one of those chapels which showed that people still cared. The pews were oak and had once been pieces of ships' timber. This was a part of Cornwall where smuggling was a way of life. The black-robed witches might even have raised the storms. The chapel made the link between past and present; the ships' boards on the floor were scrubbed and white, and protected by plain coconut matting. This also was right, simple and plain, as was the table altar, covered by a baize cloth and, apart from the visitors' book, supported nothing but a vase of fragrant, cottage-garden pinks.

The visitors' book was open at the current page. We all inscribed in it, Cara, Mother and myself. We looked back idly at the names on other pages. The chapel was solid and square and had a queer life of its own; it was not difficult to hear the old hymns ringing out across the cliffs on a winter's night nor to imagine the oil lamps shining through the dark.

Ian came to the door and waited for us to join him.

'Not too many cars,' I said.

'That's what the old chap was saying. Considering the weather's so absolutely perfect. But, as he said, it's not the sort of place for the usual holiday tripper.'

'No, I suppose not,' said Mother. 'It's a long walk right over there.' She looked towards Logan Rock with the cliff castle towering behind it.

'But that's what we came for. We must see it.'

'I don't need to see bits of Cornwall here or there.' Mother was searching for the warmest corner in the rocks. 'I just have to feel them.'

I knew what she meant; we felt the same way about this place.

'It's a long way. Do you really want to try it?' Cara was kneeling beside her bag and searching for her apples and a book. 'I'll stay with Mother.'

I wanted to be able to tell everyone I had been, and mentioned the way down to the beach looked difficult.

'It is,' said Ian. 'The car park chappie told me.' He was focusing his binoculars on the rock and when an elderly man, who seemed to be into some kind of professional research, passed, he said, 'Just look at that camera.'

We women looked around us. Cara nudged me. 'That's more in our line.' A couple were climbing down to the inshore rocks. They might have been on honeymoon. The boy was solicitous; she was a gypsy type in her long maxi-skirt and silly flip-flop sandals.

'Hardly the right climbing gear, even for small rocks.'

'Who cares when there's a helping hand.'

Cara had definitely settled herself by Mother and Ian was ready to begin. I waited, watching with female envy a mysterious woman on her own, who now came towards us. She carried painting materials and walked slowly as if absorbing every minute of this glorious afternoon. She seemed interested in the chapel too. She asked us about it, questions about Wesley and the Methodists. Home counties … to judge from her voice. She was wearing dark clothes with some of those folksy copper bracelets.

Mother was more interested in another couple we saw, a boy and girl who looked German. We all agreed on this, though no one knew quite why. I said, 'It's the arrogance in his walk.' Mother said, 'It's those shorts. I can see him dancing to their German bands in their beer gardens.'

Ian was studying the girl. 'It's her.' She was blonde and Nordic, wearing one of those embroidered blouses, traditional garments adapted by modern women with the same enthusiasm as their mothers or grandmothers before them.

Hot and drowsy, but utterly content in our speculative study of the few people visiting, we sorted ourselves among rocks which might have been carved for our purpose. Seats in stone with quartz-flecked slabs inlaid, the cliffs glittered with the chips of crystal when they reflected the sun.

Ian and I went to climb up to the Logan.

In the shadows of the rock the sun made little difference. It was cold and eerie; so easy to imagine the stormy nights and shrill screams above the sound of the waves, and the rattle of broomsticks and rustles of old women taking off over the spray into the wind. But there was a more sinister mystery here, a scent of fire and sacrifice and ominous hollows which had held frightening secrets.

When Ian was out of sight, I bared my behind and touched the rock in the manner of real witches. Not that I believed in anything like this, but that was the kind of place it was.

Ian took some photographs and we returned. The afternoon passed quickly. We drank tea, took more photographs and spoke a lot about the very distant past and witchcraft. There were many legends about this place which were easy to understand; it was a mixture of beauty and evil. There would be the old people singing their Sankey hymns so lustily, their feet on ships' timbers torn from wrecks ... if not by themselves, then with their knowledge. There was the green-yellow edge of sea and the drowning chorus from mermaids, the lost pool, and above all, the rearing, black toppling shape of Logan. Now there were even fewer people around and the sun was lowering. It was time to return.

The car park was almost empty when we passed the chapel. Ian said, 'I ought to see this before we go,' and I accompanied him into the building.

Some of the strength in the place seemed to have drained away since early afternoon. It was shadowy and the pinks in the vase were drooping. Ian insisted on signing the book. I opened it for him.

We both stared at the page which Mother, Cara and I had begun with our own names. There were foul drawings and crude remarks scrawled right across it. There were blots and curses and a couple of swastikas and the beginning of an obscene verse based on the Lord's prayer.

When we came outside neither of us spoke. Mother said, 'Wasn't it lovely in there?' Her smile faded when she saw our faces. Ian shook his head.

I scanned the cliffs and the headland. I saw the people we had seen. In the dimmed light against the western sky the figures were larger than life, darkened, evil and inscrutable.

It was as if a crazy artist had blotched the afternoon on grey paper. Each figure was grotesque. The cows loomed above us on a sinister green horizon.

Kenneth Moss

The Violin

The miners trudged homeward up the slope, their long shadows in front of them, sun and sea behind. There was sometimes laughter and banter on their way down in the mornings, especially among the younger ones, but rarely on the journey home; in their weariness, every faculty had to be concentrated on the walk. So in a long, straggling line, they dragged themselves up the hill in twos and threes, slowly and silently, oblivious to the magnificence of the sunset, deaf to the cries of the seagulls circling down over the sea behind them, aware only that, mercifully, the searing heat of the day was fading.

The yellow disc of the sun, dropping down towards the horizon, almost touches the edge of the sea. The evening air, shedding now the day's heat, is occasionally stirred by the very lightest of breezes, chilling suddenly the sweat on the foreheads of the miners, but failing to ruffle the sea that glitters flat and blue, motionless except for the gentle slapping at the foot of the cliffs. Everything stands out brilliant and sharp in the clear air, but the miners, broken by their day's labour, are conscious of none of it.

And now, from some vast distance, there begins to be heard a thin, high sound like a silver thread that stretches and curls upwards towards the sky. It is the sound of a violin. The thread seems to hover in the air for a moment, silvery against the blue sky, then it dances down, stumbling here and there, twisting and bubbling like running water before leaping up joyously again to the same high, pure plateau.

One of the men, lifting his gaze from the ground before him, turned towards his companion and smiled, but Zack made no response. Then the man looked behind at the three who followed. They smiled faintly back. Zack remained obstinately shut in to himself. The muscles in his face tightened but he gave no other sign that he had heard.

Disappointed by Zack's failure to respond, one of the men ventured a joke.

'Rome burning again, Zack?' he said.

Zack, too weary to organise his anger into speech and tired of the endless repetition of this same joke, only spat in disgust. His companions, satisfied now, exchanged smiles again and walked on in silence.

Somewhere on the cliffs, Eli was playing his violin.

Although Eli was Zack's younger brother, the two were opposites. Zack was firm, solid, and slow, like their father. Eli, on the other hand, with his quick, dancing eyes, was like an exaggerated version of their mother. Even as a child he had a gay, free spirit that rejected any kind of sustained effort, for it would have been like a prison to him and, like a wild bird, he refused to be caged. Although the father admired this quality of joy in the mother, he condemned what, in Eli, he only saw as a lack of application, and gradually he came almost to feel contempt for him. It was the father who, in his high seriousness, had insisted on giving biblical names to the boys. But even the father's stern animosity failed to dampen Eli's spirit; he remained carefree and devoted only to what pleased him, pursuing sudden whims, which he would follow only until diverted by some other brightly-coloured fancy, so that there was delight in all he did.

The mineworkers' families lived in stifling poverty, so as soon as he was old enough to work, Zack had to follow his father down the mine. When Eli reached working age, the father said he'd never be man enough to become a miner so he apprenticed the boy to a stone-mason in St Just. Eli hated the job. It was the only thing that could cramp his spirit.

The mother had come from a comfortably-off family in Penzance. They'd thought she was marrying beneath her and opposed the match, but her rebelliousness asserted itself and she went ahead just the same. She was never forgiven and so was surprised, when her widowed father died, to inherit a share of his estate. It did not in reality amount to very much, although to a miner's family it seemed a fortune. Each of the two boys was given a small sum by the mother and Zack, prudent and conscientious, put his in the bank. It remained there until he married, when it helped to set him and his wife up in their home. Eli, who years before had been fascinated by a travelling fiddler he'd heard in St Just on the St Just Feast Day, spent most of his on buying a violin; the rest went on trifles, of course. Eli, condemned vocally by the father, and silently by Zack, had at last found something on which he could lavish a sustained effort, and at every opportunity he would take his violin off to the fields to teach himself to play. To the father this was yet another sign of ungodly frivolity in his son. He felt a sharp sense of disgrace and came almost to hate the boy for frittering away his time instead of using it constructively, but Eli, who had never before stuck at anything, could not be deflected from his determination to master his violin. His will focused in a sharp, bright spot on one pursuit only; there was none left for any other task. The violin became the object of his life.

In time, he was able to play, but this considerable accomplishment only seemed to the father a fitting symbol of the boy's lack of seriousness. Zack had begun courting one of the village girls; Eli remained interested in nothing but the violin. On Sundays there was no working. The day was kept as a solemn religious festival, and the family trooped off dutifully to Chapel in their Sunday best – twice. Morning Chapel was followed by Sunday dinner, and the afternoons were meant to be an interval devoted to sober recreation until the evening chapel service. But Eli would sneak off on these afternoons to serenade the sad-eyed cows in the fields: at least *they* seemed interested. None of the father's thundering about his ungodliness and the disgrace of it all could prevail against Eli's determination. He would listen to his father's strictures, laugh gaily in agreement, and then slip off with his violin just the same.

The father died in what should have been his prime, worn out by the mine and finally broken and discarded. Zack, by this time a swarthy, thick-set young man, took on the responsibility for the family in his conscientious way; but Eli grasped the opportunity to give up his job. By now he had become a fairly accomplished violinist.

Although he could not read music he was able to play most of the popular tunes and even to improvise pieces of his own, which, it seemed, he could memorise effortlessly. He was now able to earn a few shillings as a travelling musician and would walk the Land's End peninsula in all weathers, perky as a rabbit, providing music wherever it was needed. Zack, who had never been as outspoken as the father, smouldered with resentment over Eli's failure to accept any responsibility for helping to support their mother, but she seemed secretly proud of Eli, and she defended him on the rare occasions when Zack did complain.

When she died, Zack, after a decent interval, was able to marry, and Eli, being unable to fend for himself, was taken in to live with Zack and his wife, Sarah. Zack still clung to his disgust with Eli, but over the years their mother's defence of her wayward son had formed in Zack a reluctant acceptance. To his friends and colleagues, Zack maintained the old contempt of his brother, but he found himself defending Eli when Sarah attacked him. Yet, for all the family solidarity and the habit of acceptance, Zack's disgust was still there, underneath.

The attitude of the rest of the village was one of amused tolerance for Eli. His happy, easy-going nature made him easy to get along with, despite his solitary habits, and though many also resented his lazing away the summer afternoons, his music was useful at celebrations, much more so than the St Just town band. So they accepted him in an amused, condescending way, much as they would the village idiot. Moreover, they were sometimes secretly enchanted by his playing, and having an accomplished musician in the village lent them a kind of distinction. The tolerance was not universal, however. There were still occasions when he was held up in chapel as an example of ungodliness, usually by implication, though on one occasion the preacher had compared him specifically to Nero, 'fiddling while Rome burned'. This comparison was taken up by Zack's colleagues, who liked to tease him with his brother, and when they heard Eli's violin they would ask, 'Rome still burning, then, Zack?' as they did this evening. The serious-minded Zack had never been able to see that this joke was as much at the preacher's expense as Eli's, for the comparison of Eli, sharp-faced, wide-eyed and puck-like, with Nero was so incongruous as to be ludicrous. Zack only felt it as a taunting criticism, and one that he had grown tired of. So this evening, too weary to respond in any other way, he merely spat.

When the line of miners reached the road it began to thin out as each man went his own way. Zack trudged on to where the road forked and took the left-hand turn, up past Trevorrow's farm, towards the little terrace where he and Sarah lived.

Theirs was the cottage at the far end of the terrace, and as he approached, Zack could see his wife picking flowers in their tiny front garden. Zack's marriage was a happy one and normally Eli was the only source of friction, though Sarah admired his musical gift and his reputation far more than she would ever admit, even to Zack – especially to Zack. Now, perhaps because of his weariness, it was Zack's solicitude for his wife that made him feel irritable towards her. She was eight months pregnant and he felt she should know better than to be bending down to pick flowers.

She stood up to greet him as he came through the gate, but Zack spoke before she could say anything.

'You shouldn't be doing that, Sarah,' he said, trying to disguise the exasperation in his voice.

'Why not? You know I like to have flowers about the place.'

'Yes, but the baby. It's not –'

'Now don't fuss so, Zack.'

'I'm not fussing. You know you shouldn't be –'

'Now never mind about that. What about that brother of yours?'

'What about him?' Preparing himself to defend Eli yet again Zack stopped to peck her on the cheek as they went inside. 'I heard him playing on the way home,' he said. 'Some handsome it was.'

'Yes, I heard. Mrs Pascoe's been here asking if he'll play next week at their Julie's wedding.'

'Well, that be better than having him here under your feet. And he'll make a few bob.'

'Yes, I know, but she wants to know if he's going to do it and I'm tired of carrying messages backwards and forwards for him.'

'Now come on, flower, why are you so upset about it? You can ask him when he comes in.'

'It's not only that. You know you can't rely on anything he says, anyway. He's quite likely to say yes and then not do it when the time comes – just because he don't feel like it! You know what he's like. Then I'll have Mrs Pascoe grumbling and groaning to me because he's let her down, and how he's spoiled Julie's wedding.'

'Well, that's Eli. You can't tie him down to anything. Never could.'

'That's the trouble. I don't know for the life of me why you don't make him get a proper job so he can pay his way here. I'm sure I don't know.'

'He does what he can,' said Zack.

'That's not the point. Gets away with murder, he do. Don't pull his weight nor nothing like it. Why should you have to go down the mine to keep him? If you ask me, you should make him do his bit so he can pay his way. It's not right.'

'He does pay. You said yourself Mrs Pascoe wants him at Julie's wedding. He'll pay us whatever she gives him.'

'Yes, if he manages to get himself along there, the lazy good-for-nothing. It's not right, Zack. Why should you be slaving down that mine, when he's wandering about all over the place, devil-may-care, just playing music? Why shouldn't he do his bit?'

'Because he's Eli,' said Jack.

'Well I don't know I'm sure. You're too soft by half. You should tell him. When the baby's born we'll need more money.'

'Perhaps when it's born I'll tell him.'

'Go on,' she said, affectionately now. 'I know you. Too soft by half, you are, Zack Thomas. Why he can't go back to being a mason again, I'd like to know.'

But Zack felt too tired to go back over all that old ground.

'Come on, flower, it's getting dark,' he said. 'I'll light the lamp.'

This was the way it went on. When the baby was born, they still continued in the same old way. Then a second baby, and still no change. Zack knew it was useless to try, anyway. Nothing would change his brother. Eli would only agree with all that was said to him, and cheerfully carry on as before.

Meanwhile, his reputation was spreading. One or two people had even begun to hear about Eli's playing as far away as Redruth, and once, when a conductor, famous among those who knew about such things, came from London to visit one of the Camborne mine-owners, Eli was invited to go along and play for them.

The news caused a sir in the village. Although they'd never heard of him, an invitation from Sir Edward Ferris to their Eli, who had always seemed more of a joke to them than a musician, must be an astonishing, major event, and for one moment, they could feel proud of their celebrity, though they were at a loss to know why he should be a celebrity. Then came the astounding news that Eli would not go. He didn't feel like it. He didn't want to go all the way over to Camborne to play. It wasn't that he objected to the long walk. He just saw no point in it. Why go to Camborne when he could play at Trewellard, or Lamorna, or Mousehole, or Sheffield?

To Sarah, this was just another sign of his waywardness. To the rest of the village it seemed unforgivable, looking a gift-horse in the mouth like this, especially when the gift was so undeserved, anyway. Their tolerance changed to disapproval. The prospect of their having cause for pride in Eli having been surprisingly held out to them, it was doubly frustrating to have it snatched away again by his capriciousness. He just didn't appreciate what was done for him. He'd never come to any good, hadn't they always said so? Even those who, on hearing of the invitation, had claimed they'd always said he was some handsome player, now remembered that instead they'd always agreed with the old man, and Eli was just an unappreciative, lazy good-for-nothing: here was proof of it.

But they'd got it wrong. It was true that Eli had told Zack he did not want to go all the way to Camborne to play and that he saw no point in it. It was also true that, when pressed, he said he saw no point in it. But the message he sent back to Sir Edward had been that he could not go because he only performed for money. These other objections had merely been his answer to Zack's complaint that such a reply was an insult to the conductor. Had they known that Eli proposed to *charge* Sir Edward for giving him an audience, the village would have been even more outraged.

Sir Edward's host shared the popular attitude that Eli was a presumptuous ingrate; but not the conductor himself. To everyone's surprise, he approved Eli's stand and a couple of days later a message came back that of course Eli would be paid a fee, and perhaps two guineas would be a suitable figure.

For once, Zack and Sarah were determined to prevail. Two guineas for an evening's playing was a princely sum in those days, and they were adamant that Eli should not miss it. On the appointed day, Eli was duly packed off to Camborne in Mr Trevorrow's pony and trap. Zack went along with him because Eli was not to be trusted, and also because Mr Trevorrow was certainly not going to let Eli go off in the pony and trap by himself.

Zack delivered his brother to the great house, then went off to wait in the Golden Lion.

Far from feeling honoured, Eli was amused by the whole affair. He could not take it seriously himself, and he found it funny that others did. To him it seemed to be all rather comic that everyone should suddenly be so solemn about his playing.

Eli began his recital with some of the popular tunes that he usually played. Then quite suddenly he broke off and launched into some of his own pieces.

Perhaps it was the sumptuous surroundings, perhaps it was the unusually attentive audience, perhaps it was Eli's sense of occasion, or maybe it was simply Eli's mood – whatever it was, he excelled himself. The violin became a living thing in his hands. It was as if he were the instrument through which some spirit of the violin poured out its ecstasy. An electrifying poetry possessed the air as the violin sang of its joy in trees and flowers and sky and its passions overflowed in cascades of brilliant-coloured sound. Now it hesitated, frozen in icy wastes, and the pure notes rang hard as steel, sharp as frost; and now, released again, it sang as if in some brazen Babylon with towers and palaces, where warriors hailed their king; and now some Egypt where Cleopatra's barge glided with purple sails and silvered oars; and now, through a long diminuendo, the vision faded and sombre colours held sway as the violin sang of ancient griefs amid the alien corn; until at last, softer now, and softer, the spirit of the violin passed quietly away into silence, and Eli's bow was stilled.

For perhaps half a minute the room was dominated by the silence of the violin, as though no one dared disturb the magic it had released. Then slowly, hesitantly, the applause began to break, but it seemed out of place, sacrilegious almost, breaking the spell of those dreams.

For Sir Edward, as for everyone else, it was a breath-taking performance. The violin had come to life, needing only to be held by Eli, it seemed, to play itself.

What could one do with a virtuoso like this, Sir Edward wondered, a virtuoso who was quite untutored and whose playing was all wrong, but yet with all his wrongness could transform a cheap violin into a Stradivarius?

He wanted Eli to come with him to London so that he could study Eli's unorthodox technique, the peculiar fingering, the strange bowing that could produce such tone from a third-rate fiddle. But Eli was his usual puck-like self, and Sir Edward could get nowhere with him. Eli only laughed gaily and gave his non-committal replies.

At the conductor's insistence, he played again, and once more, as he took the instrument in his hands and drew the bow across the strings, the violin quickened with its own life. This time it began plaintively with a sad, enchanting song, but gradually it gathered momentum until the wild melody was sweeping through dazzling arabesques, leaping and laughing through cataracts of sunlight, arpeggios glittering and splashing and diving and wheeling and dancing, whirling through mazes of dizzying sound until, with four quick, darting chords, the feverish dance came triumphantly to rest.

Tales of that performance spread back somehow even to the village, but when Sir Edward wrote to Eli repeating the invitation to London and Eli again refused, the village shook its head and gave Eli up as a hopeless case.

At first, Eli took pleasure in Zack's children. His own nature being childlike, he seemed to find more points of contact with them than with adults. But as the years passed, he grew more and more solitary, and had less and less to do with the two boys.

Everyone had stopped trying to change him, even Sarah. They accepted him now as he was, a free, elfin spirit.

Some felt that after the climax of that superlative night in Camborne, his playing had passed its best, but that was because the violin had taken on a purer sound. It still bubbled and gurgled, rippling like a silver river, but it was a purer river, the water now was distilled, and the sound had an edge of pure diamond.

Zack's elder boy, Peter, was eight now; the younger, Billy, five. Little Billy seemed to be entranced by Eli's violin. While still maintaining the distance that had grown between them, Eli would sometimes play little tunes for him while the boy sat giggling with delight at Eli's magic in making a voice come from some strings on a piece of wood. Then, when Eli stopped, he would cry, 'More! More!'

Surprisingly, Sarah took secret delight in Billy's attraction to the violin. What had always seemed reprehensible in Eli seemed like a gift, a precious talent, in little Billy, so she unobtrusively encouraged the affinity she thought she saw between Eli and her son.

That winter was unusually wet, and it was cold even in West Cornwall. Even so, Eli's familiar figure was still to be seen, walking the lanes, his pointed elf-like face nodding above the black, dishevelled clothes, the tattered violin-case under his arm. Sometimes he could be seen practising on some cliff, or sitting in a field, mesmerising the stones with his violin. A story went round that even the standing stones, the Merry Maidens, would come to life again, and resume their dance for Eli's violin where they'd left off one Sunday centuries ago.

Being out in all weathers, Eli had become hardened to the elements, but even he was not invulnerable. He came home early one drizzly day. Sarah wondered at this, for he would normally find shelter somewhere. He moped about the house that afternoon and even Billy could not persuade him to play the fiddle. He retired early to bed and never got up again. Within a few days he was dead. Pneumonia, the doctor said.

After Eli died, Sarah thought about young Billy. Perhaps if he were a little more stable than Eli, he could become a famous violinist and succeed where his uncle had failed. Besides, she missed the sound, for the violin had sat untouched on a shelf for weeks, mute now that Eli had gone. The instrument might be silent now, but if Billy were encouraged, who knows? So Sarah gave him the violin. And she gave him the bow and tried to encourage him to draw it across the strings. He tried once or twice, but the sound was excruciating, and Billy was so frustrated because the violin did not sing for him as it did for Eli, that in his temper he broke the bow.

Eli, who had once seemed so permanent a part of the West Cornwall scene, was occasionally spoken about for a few years after his death, and then he was forgotten. He was still in his thirties when he died, but when the boys grew up their hazy memory was only of a funny old man who was once their uncle.

As for the violin that for Eli had sung like Ariel, drawing its magic thread across the sky and touching the air with crystal, when the bow was broken Billy used it as a weapon to beat his elder brother Peter, and within a few days its back was broken. Then Billy cut himself on the E-string, so that finally what remained of Eli's violin, four steel wires and a few shards of splintered wood, was put in the dustbin.

And all along Tregeseal and Botallack, Trewellard and Boscaswell, Pendeen and

Morvah, Eli's memory died, and there was no more violin music in the lazy afternoons, and the Merry Maidens of Boleigh like the Nine Maidens of Boskednan resumed their eternal sleep.

Donald R. Rawe

The Deep Sea Dream

As a boy Neil was a funny little chap with shy secretive ways and probably too much imagination. He did not often join in coussers or conkers with other boys. He used to read a great deal, and books older than some people thought he should read. Queer books like Malory's *Morte d'Arthur*, Hunt's *Popular Romances of the West*, even *The Golden Bough* of Frazer.

Fortunately for Neil none of those around him at Hayle knew much about books, so they let him go his own way. In spite of his reading nobody ever called him clever. He might have been, but at school he was lazy; a proper dreamer. He had quick penetrating eyes and pointed pisky-like ears. A few tongues idly whispered he was a changeling.

It was near one Christmas when Neil had his deep sea dream. It was easy enough for him to piece together events and scenes which reappeared vividly linked in it so as to realize what had given rise to the dream; though these did not explain why it all stayed with him in accurate memory all his life.

They had been practising carols at school: mainly the normal ones that children sing from door to door, knocking after the first verse and vanishing in the middle of the second, once they had the coppers. But this year they had some that were new to Neil, and one of them – 'I saw three ships a-sailing' – delighted him with the Cornish simplicity of its words and tune. For no reason that he could see it made him want to cry; so he hardly ever sang it himself but sat listening to the others around him.

> I saw three ships a-sailing
> On Christmas Day, on Christmas Day:
> I saw three ships a-sailing
> On Christmas Day in the morning.

In the evenings he had been reading some ancient traditions and had been captivated by that series of conjectures, half hints and unproved assertions, about Lyonesse, the district between Land's End and Scilly and once part of Cornwall, which is supposed to have abruptly and inexplicably sunk or become flooded in the year 1099. Historians balanced and counterbalanced what evidence existed: some believed, some disbelieved there ever had been such a land. Nobody *knew*. It had not been proved that Lyonesse once flourished: but it had not been disproved. Neil only hoped the tradition was true.

And then the Sunday before at chapel there had been a sermon about Billy Bray.

The minister's eyes and voice seemed to glow with admiration, in rising revivalist fervour as he sketched the character of the miner evangelist who was born at Twelveheads, buried at Baldhu, and who built several chapels almost unaided. He used to work eight hours down the mine, eight building a chpel and four tilling his own plot of land. He would walk scores of miles in a Sunday to preach, dancing and jigging all the way for sheer joy of 'doing the Lord's work'. The last Cornish saint, the minister called him.

The deep sea dream that followed all this was so powerful that in his later life Neil could remember everything and see it all exactly as he had dreamed it. Other dreams leave mere threads of their stories with us on waking which stay in the memory for a month, a year or even several years, then suddenly seem to turn to dust like the golden hair of Guinevere when her body with Arthur's was dug up five hundred years after their deaths. But this vision (he could call it even that) was one of the memorable moments of Neil's life, and he treasured it intensely.

Sometimes he wondered whether it really had been only a dream.

He stood on Hayle quay very early in the morning, looking down at the mudflat and green seaweed. The tide was coming in, sweeping across the flats: grey, frothy, bearing scum.

There was only the sound of tiny hisses and crackles under the mud as the water seeped down into it. They were made by cockles opening. There was no one else to be seen; Hayle was a dead town. The only living creature was a heron standing like a verger some way out in the water, solemn and unmoving. The sun hovered over the hills toward Camborne and the red ruined engine houses of tin mines.

The tide mounted rapidly, becoming an opaque green; the seaweed on the walls waved hazily through it. And there Neil stood on the quayside, waiting.

He heard a flapping of heavy wings and a guttural call – Kronk-kronk! The heron had risen, unhurriedly but disturbed by something.

There was a ship coming up the estuary, without sails, yet noiselessly. A man leaned over the bulwark smoking a pipe. The heron fled up the river and nothing stirred except this black ship looming up, gliding soundlessly on the green water.

When she came near enough Neil saw a familiar figure-head beneath the bowsprit, and he recognized the schooner. A painting of the *Gipsy Maid* had hung on the wall at home for as long as he could remember. The master was his grandfather, whom he vaguely knew from his earliest recollections – he had died when Neil was six – but whom he remembered best as the subject of numerous stories. For years the *Gipsy Maid* had sailed from Hayle to Swansea taking tin over and coal back.

Alongside the quay came the schooner, his grandfather regarding him intently, smoking his pipe all the while. Neil felt shy of meeting the old man.

'Come aboard, me handsome,' said the captain at last.

Neil came aboard. They shook hands. Neither said anything more, and they both turned and regarded the town. The sun was high now and the shadows gone from the roofs. Yet it was deserted, with not even a dog in the streets. The tide was high and impassive. The captain knocked out his pipe on the bulwark and the sound seemed to echo across the empty quayside. Slowly he went aft to the wheel, still looking at the town and shaking his head cryptically.

The *Gipsy Maid* began to move, to glide astern without sail in the still morning air. The quay receded. Now the tide was ebbing, leaving a wet rim around the wall showing dank seaweed and rusty rungs of ladders.

The ship went ahead and started downstream to the open sea. A flag began to wave lazily on the mizzen-mast high above. There were no clouds.

Neil turned and glanced back at the town. On the quay stood a figure in white skirts and red petticoat. It was his mother: she was calling to him, but he could not hear her words. He was not curious to know what they were.

'Look,' he said to his grandfather. He said it without urgency, merely as a matter of passing interest. But the master stared straight ahead and would not look back.

' 'Tis mother,' Neil said. She was the captain's daughter: he ought to look. But he would not. The boy watched her growing smaller with the houses and the slipway. She waved farewell to him, timidly, reluctantly.

They heard a squawk above them: – Y-aak! – and looking up they saw a seagull perched on the foremast head.

'Ha!' said the old man approvingly. 'Good boy! Good boy!'

The gull looked around with wicked brittle eyes, poking its yellow beak from side to side.

'No storms with he up there,' remarked the captain.

Neil said nothing. There was still an awkwardness between the two; they were not behaving as grandfather and grandson should. But there was nothing he could do about it.

They were now well out in St Ives Bay and making for the outside ocean. Looking back towards Gwithian, Neil saw that the great sandy Towans had gone. There were now glowing fields and hedges sloping down to the water. He could see the village, the church spire, several fields of ripe wheat and green vegetable patches; there was even an orchard. These were fat and fertile lands; and yet they too seemed empty, forsaken: lonely fields on a lonely shore. Save for their brightness they were desolate.

It was not that he was surprised to see them, for he had heard about the rich meadows of Lelant and Gwithian, covered up by sand in a single night centuries ago. He looked across to port to see whether St Ives showed signs of life: but there was no St Ives as he knew it. Only a grey church, a few ancient cottages, and the long yellow beaches: and nothing stirred there either.

All this reminded him of the castle of Sleeping Beauty before the prince came. It was a day which the world was sleeping through and would never know existed. Perhaps each week actually had eight days, but the eighth day was unknown because everybody slept through it. It was probably the day reserved for the dead to walk on earth. Certainly grandfather took it calmly enough, as though he were used to sailing the *Gipsy Maid* around single-handed, having the earth to himself.

Suddenly and with something of a shock Neil became aware of two other schooners, one on each side of them. They were of the same type as *Gipsy Maid*; three-masted fore-and-aft. All three ships were now on the green ocean with the shore merely a vague blue line to port: they were sailing westward. They all had full sail now, and the great white canvases were taking the wind. But the seagull was still there on the foremast glancing around vigilantly.

The ship on their port side was full of men. Perhaps an emigrant ship going to Canada. Neil could see a small figure standing on the poop evidently haranguing the crowd on board. From time to time he heard a long drawn 'Aaah!' from them, and caught fragments of speech from the orator. Then perhaps the schooners came a little nearer each other or perhaps the wind changed slightly; at any rate he was soon able to hear whole sentences.

'You'm all workin fer the biggest company of all – the company of the Feyther, the Sonne, an' the Oly Ghost – an' brothers, I tell 'ee thet company wunt never go scat ...'

'Well now, look 'ere. Ef the Lord 'ad meant fer men to smoak, 'ed 've maade us all wid chimleys in our 'ades ...'

'Hess now, I do mind that there Prodeegal Sonne arunnin off 'ome from the far contry: I can see onn now, a-coussin over they moors with 'unger in the belly of 'n, an' 'is shirt tail 'angin out o' the hass of 'is trousies: and d'ye knaw, brothers, we'm all the saame as 'ee? I tell 'ee, we'm all of us Prodeegal Sonnes a-'ungrin an' athirsting fer our Evveenly Feyther. Then come in brothers, come in to the Kingdom uv Evveen, ragged hass or no!'

Neil heard another gasp of abasement and repentance from the listeners, and then the voice went on, speaking simply and not loudly over the waves.

'Well, the Lord put et into me 'ade to build a chapel: so me an me little sonne, us went to work an got some stawn ...'

The voice faded and became again unintelligibly removed. Still the little man on the poop talked and gesticulated, sometimes lifting his hands to the skies, sometimes bowing his head. He was not still a moment but jerked back and forth all the while. And still Neil watched, fascinated. The figure and some of the words were familiar to him, but who, who was it? He had the name rising like a fish in his mind but he could not catch it –

In desperation he turned to his grandfather.

'Who's that on th'other schooner, Grandad?'

The old man did not reply immediately. After a space he pulled off his peaked cap and said humbly, 'Why, now you mention it, thass Billy Bray.'

Of course: Billy Bray. Admiration and respect welled up in Neil; they were followed by something like remorse. He wanted to apologize, beg somebody's pardon for an error, a sin – some shadowy blunder he had made: what was it? He did not know, it had gone from him ... neither did it matter so long as forgiveness was given. O shrieve me hermit – O little missionary grant me grace – Saint Billy Bray pray for me pray for me, bring me to eternal –

The gull screeched and flew off the masthead. It did not go far but circled round the schooner making a kind of yodelling barking sound. The sky was stormy to starboard: big brown cloud masses hunching together, bearing across towards them. The wind was getting up, the canvas flapping and cracking like gunshots. Then the gull settled again on the masthead and though the atmosphere had become intense the clouds stood off to starboard, poised but for the moment only brooding.

At this point Neil noticed the schooner on that side. She was farther away than the other, an ill-defined black shape against the dark clouds, so that there was no opportunity to see who or what was on her. She was travelling with full sail and seemed to have no difficulty in encountering these splenetic seas: she slipped easily through them, loping along like a sea-panther. Neil knew there was someone on board her, someone powerful, possessed of a vibrant personality that made itself felt across this distance of rearing waves, through the enveloping air of inclemency. It was some giant or more than human creature; it was almost incomprehensible, yet something that lurked back there within the scowling clouds for a purpose ... it dared not be revealed, but could only be understood vaguely by being hidden.

Neil looked around. His grandfather was no longer with him. He looked upward; no seagull either. Across to port. Billy Bray's schooner – gone. And the other? He turned back to starboard.

The great bulk of cloud was turning slowly from brown to red, producing vivid gashes of purple and green that flared into the mass, mingled and were lost. The wrack swelled: it must soon disgorge violence. But still it went on spreading across the sky, Neil suffering in the suspense. He knew that one thing was certain: he could not escape the coming anger. The seagull had vanished and he was doomed.

There was no land in sight; he ran to the wheel. Acording to the compass the *Gipsy Maid* was sailing southwest. He was past Gurnard's Head and Cape Cornwall. He was beyond Land's End and the Scillies could not be far off. He was sailing above the sunken lands of Lyonesse.

The wind abated in an instant leaving a heavy brooding calm. The dark green ocean ceased chopping and clashing, and dropped into a thick turbid swell. The sky hung tremendous above like a precipice.

There was a faint rumble, then a yellow stab of lightning. Thunder. Rain hissed down, a million sharp furies on the green sea. Wind tore at the ship from all directions; she plunged and rose like a whale. The sails gave and the mizzen boom came flying around, kicking Neil overboard. He saw the foremast snap off as he struggled in the cruel water.

Then he was sinking slowly and restfully down through the green glassy sea; descending with relief in silence and coolness. Fish flicked past him through the greenness and faded. Peace, unbreakable peace.

A shape grew vaguely toward him. It had long hair swirling behind it; a white body and arms, a woman's smooth breast. A red-gold tail, a beautiful lazy tapering thing curving from side to side. Blandly, heedlessly she passed, swimming slowly with a dreamy motion. The beautiful tail receded into the gloom. Goodbye siren, goodbye merrymaid ...

Falling, falling gratefully, serenely, silently.

Lyonesse!

He remembered. By the rocks of Lethosow on a calm day you can see the houses of a sunken city below the waters.

Yes, but how many have seen it?

Fishermen have brought up pottery and slates from the bed of the sea.

But how long ago? Where are these things now?

A hundred and forty churches and parishes drowned in the storms of A.D. 1099 ...

A hundred and forty? After the Doomsday Book was compiled? Where are the records?

A man on a white horse escaped the flood and landed at Sennen to tell the tale ... The sea is too deep. The cliffs at Land's End are too old. All this happened too long ago.

St Michael's Mount: Caragclewse en Couze: the Grey Rock in the Woods. The Towans covered the meadows of Lelant. Submarine forests all around the coast. Languna too was lost ...

Sinking slowly, coolly, greenly. The sea bed is a long way but O when I touch it I shall know whether or not –

At first Neil considered that whoever had awakened him at this point had done him the greatest disservice they possibly could, and he wept a long time in his child's rage and disappointment. But later he was able to bear this fate well enough. After all, though he was so chagrined at being denied what he believed would have been the truth about Lyonesse, what would his feelings have been if it had been revealed to him that it had never existed? What was not proved was still not disproved.

He realized the truth about the third schooner when they next sang the Three Ships carol:

> Our Saviour Christ was in those ships,
> On Christmas Day on Christmas Day ...

As for the rest of the dream's events, he could connect them, account for having dreamed them. And as for Lyonesse – well, we all still dream about Lyonesse.

N.R. Phillips

BELLA VISTA

There was not much of a view from the windows of the Bella Vista residential home. By stepping into the large bay windows of the lounge and drawing aside the velvet curtains of the side sashes the guests could see the sea, across the promenade at the bottom of the wide tree-lined road in which the establishment was situated. Hardly any of them ever looked at it after a few days, so Mrs Harris, the proprietress, had no qualms about retaining the name after buying the property twenty three years ago with the settlement from that swine of a husband who had left her for a beaded hippy and gone off searching for himself in the East.

Sometimes, Miss Tidmarsh drew the curtains aside, to determine the state of the tide or weather, before going for her afternoon walk. But even she never looked through the window for the sake of the view. 'Seen it once,' Mr Ordish said, 'seen it enough. I didn't come here for the view. I came for the food.' He might have added that he also came in the hope that one day Mrs Harris, after twenty three years of sexual abstinence would succumb to his ardour and bring up his morning tea herself, instead of sending that scrawny chit of a girl with the bony legs. Like many older men, Mr Ordish was not yet dead, and he still had his desires. The thought that one so buxom in his bed might well see him off into paradise was a risk he would have taken gladly, and gone out in glory. Alas, it was always the girl, who, had he but known it, might well have done it with him because, before the Colonel came, Mr Ordish was the most youthful and virile of the Bella Vista's twenty residents.

The youngest of the ladies was Milly Crabbe, Millicent, as she insisted on being called, who hadn't been here very long and kept herself to herself. She had made a distant friendship with Miss Tidmarsh, and occasionally went for a walk along the promenade with her on fine afternoons. She was a nervous little woman who might have been quite attractive in her youth had she been blessed with a more gregarious personality. Miss Tidmarsh was no fool; she knew what went on in the minds of women like Milly Crabbe. Oh yes, if Miss Tidmarsh was anything, she was conversant with human behaviour. She had read *The Naked Ape* and books on body language, and had been astounded at what she had learned about apparently shy and reticent people like Milly Crabbe. They had every good reason to keep themselves to themselves, for what they were trying to do, albeit subconsciously, was to keep themselves from themselves. And no wonder, in Gertrude Tidmarsh's view.

On the morning that the Colonel arrived, Gertrude was sitting in the lounge, reading a further treatise on human behaviour; well, one aspect of human behaviour, to be perfectly honest, but Gertrude had come to the realisation that she had been a lifelong Freudian without knowing it, and in furtherance of her studies considered it essential to keep abreast of progressive thinking. She always took great care of her books, and wrapped them in brown paper, stuck down with sellotape. She had made a habit of reading in the lounge in the mornings, for experience had shown her that it was at this time of day that the home was at its most active. Things happened at other times of the day, of course, but here in the lounge of the Bella Vista residential home it was from breakfast, at eight thirty, to lunch at one o'clock, with morning coffee in between, that Miss Tidmarsh had found the greatest scope for her powers of observation in the subject of human behaviour. The powers of observation in most people, Miss Tidmarsh believed, were sadly underdeveloped, but what with her studies, and her birdwatching, she had a trained eye and an instinct for detail. She would have made an invincible detective. Of course, Miss Tidmarsh kept these things to herself, as people less gifted might have considered her powers of observation as mere prying, but people were like that.

When the skinny girl brought her morning coffee, Miss Tidmarsh laid her book aside and picked up a glossy magazine that Mrs Harris had left on the low table for the residents to read. Most of them were too poor, or too mean, to spend money on such trivia. Sitting in her vantage point behind the dusty plumes of pampas grass she turned the pages, glancing occasionally, with her shrewd, trained eye, at the comings and goings of the other residents.

There was Mr Ordish, going over to sit with Mr Thomas, where he would pretend to be absorbed in a game of chess while watching Mrs Harris behind her desk in the reception area at the end of the lounge. He was a Dirty Old Man, Miss Tidmarsh knew, and Mr Thomas a boring old, well, fart, actually, though she could never bring herself to even think such a thing. She turned the pages at discreet intervals, pausing at the pictures of country houses and flicking past the advertisements showing young women in brief and flimsy underwear. Some of them, she thought, even showed, but she would not wish to be seen looking at such things, the dark smudges of pubic hair through the diaphanous garments. Naked Apes, indeed! Gertrude wore respectable bloomers, as being symbolic of her chastity, and considered brassieres as disgusting sexist restrictions of the female body, allowing her own ample bosoms to sag and wander beneath her hand-knitted twin-sets as the Good Lord intended.

Here was Miss Crabbe! Such a restless little thing. Only been here three months, and already considering moving, going back to Torquay, of all places. There was absolutely nowhere to compare with Cornwall, in Gertrude's opinion. But Milly's restlessness was merely the manifestation of far deeper insecurity, there was no doubt of that, although one could never broach such a subject to one so close as Millicent Crabbe. Poor Dear. Those silly little chiffon scarves, with which she was for ever fiddling, were evidence enough of a life of frustrated coquetry. Probably wasn't allowed to flirt with the boys as a girl. These things were so obvious when one was trained in the matter. Gertrude came to the conclusion that she might even have made a better psychiatrist than a detective; they were much the same, really. Millicent, indeed. If ever there was a Milly hidden behind a prim façade, it was here, behind those restless eyes which never seemed to look directly into her own. Gertrude would have bet on it, had she been of the type to indulge in gambling.

'Good Morning? Millicent. Come and sit down. How nice to see you.'

Miss Crabbe sat down, and they discussed the possibility of Millicent moving on. 'Oh no,' she said. 'Goodness Me, No. Nothing wrong. I'm very comfortable here, but I like to have a change of scenery, you know. And I'm sure you must all be getting tired of my chatter by now.'

Silly woman had hardly opened her mouth, Gertrude thought. Keeping herself to herself. Afraid of some skeleton falling out of her built-in wardrobe, perhaps.

In her office behind the counter, with its plastic notice announcing 'Reception', Mrs Harris gazed out between a dejected rubber-plant and a sun-starved tradescantia as she waited for the new arrival. She regarded her residents as retarded infants, and ran the establishment quietly, efficiently, and with a rod of velvet-coated iron. She could never understand why so many of them wished to spend their retirement years here in Cornwall. Most of them had left their friends behind, buried a spouse soon after coming, and spent their days sitting about the place waiting for the next meal, never seeing the sea, the harbour, or the beaches they had so looked forward to living beside for most of their working lives. It was tragic, but she had no time to be involved in tragedies, with twenty of them to look after. Her own tragedy, she had learned to live with. It was not so much the fact that the swine had left her in her prime, but the fact that she had allowed it to make her bitter. Her bitterness had, she appreciated now that it was too late, been only too apparent, and had repulsed any other men who may otherwise have found her attractive. She was now coming to the even more bitter awareness that much of the frustration of the past years had been of her own origination. At forty seven she was approaching the time when it would be too late to expect the attention of any men except for the likes of Charlie Ordish, and she feared, more than anything in her life, ending up like the people who came to her in their lonely old age. This place was now worth in excess of a quarter of a million, and she was a rich woman. It frightened her. It was too much, all of it, to bear alone.

Look at those two over there. Hated each other's guts, but were firm friends, nevertheless. This kind of love-hate relationship Mrs Harris had learned to handle, along with all the other peculiarities of middle-aged, old, and lonely people. The new one coming today would present no problems. After a couple of days she would know his life history, as she knew the life history of all of them, for after a while the others became disillusioned with the newcomers and ceased to listen to them, regarding their own lives as of far more interest. It was to the staff, and particularly to Mrs Harris, especially if they could be seen by the other residents to be receiving an inordinate amount of her attention, that they told their most intimate secrets. When she had heard it all, and found it difficult to concentrate on them any more, they either became silent or moved on. The men were usually the loneliest beneath their hearty, boisterous, or detached exteriors, as Mrs Harris knew well, and she liked the men better than the women, as a rule, or rather, she disliked them less.

The new one, due to arrive at any minute, was a Mr Hammond. That much, but not much else, she knew from the letter she had received from his sister, presumably, two weeks ago.

'... he has asked me to find a quiet residential hotel where he may be afforded the facilities of a private room for answering correspondence. After spending so long in the East he may be somewhat reserved, but you will find him of little trouble, and not at all fastidious in his requirements. I enclose sufficent for a three month stay, but he may well be a permanent resident if your establishment proves to his satisfaction, as I am sure it will, as you have been highly recommended. Yours faithfully ...'

What was it? Alice Hammond? The signature was equally indistinct on the cheque, but it hadn't bounced.

They all said that, of course; may well be a permanent resident, and some of them were, or at least as permanent as old-age permitted. Mrs Harris knew how to organise a funeral better than any of the local undertakers. She looked at her watch. Ten forty five was his E.T.A as he had put it in his letter advising her of his arrival. It was that now.

Miss Tidmarsh looked over the top of her magazine as the hall porter struggled in with a large trunk. The hall porter was, as everyone knew full well, the somewhat grandiose title for the odd-job man, washer-up, second chef, and whatever else was needed about the place. Miss Tidmarsh had reason to believe that he was also something more than an eight hour a day employee to the manageress. She had seen him leaving very late at night, at times, and no blocked drain or light-fuse ever took *that* long to repair.

The trunk bore the legend, A.T. Hammond, Esq., for all to see, but Gertrude Tidmarsh, exercising her acute powers of observation, also saw, thinly painted over, the additional lettering, *Lt. Col.* A.T. Hammond, and what was it D.S.M.? She wasn't sure. But there were certainly letters, and letters, Gertrude was quite sure, gave a man, a person that is, status. The address was almost obscured, but the word INDIA was there as plain as a pikestaff. For those who used their eyes, that is.

'I wonder,' Miss Crabbe twittered, fingering her chiffon, 'what Mr Hammond will be like.'

Gertrude looked at her quickly from the corner of her eye with a glance of tolerant scorn, by far and away her favourite glance. She had several other glances, of course, like 'crushing irony' and 'amused indifference', but 'tolerant scorn' was reserved for those miserable wretches who struggled through life without ever exercising their God-given powers of observation.

'I feel sure,' Gertrude said, 'that *The Colonel* will be a perfect gentleman.'

She would be obliged to have a word with the poor man, or that Milly Crabbe would have her pinchy-paws into him before he knew what was happening. Shameless flirt! Lowered the whole tone of the hotel. Thank God she was soon to depart.

'Colonel? Gertrude,' Millicent asked.

'Of course,' Miss Tidmarsh said, off-handedly, placing the magazine on the coffee-table. 'Didn't you know?'

The wretched girl came in to remove the coffee cups, and Miss Tidmarsh changed the subject. This habit one found in people of discussing people behind their backs was not what she was brought up to. 'I am so sorry you will be leaving us,' she said, "just as we were becoming such good friends.'

'Well,' said Millicent, 'I haven't made my mind up yet. It all depends.' And she twittered softly, like a canary kept too long in a small cage, Gertrude thought. She knew the type.

He was nearly six feet tall, and all eyes were on him as he came through the main entrance, carrying a large suitcase without effort. So young, Miss Tidmarsh observed. And, though it was totally irrelevant, so handsome. Discreetly dressed, she noted, in lovat green, with a mustard waistcoat and soft-collared shirt. The tie, if Miss Tidmarsh was any judge, was hand woven. He wore highly polished brown brogues, and a gold ring third finger left hand, a widower, of course. His hair was greying at the temples. Gertrude's idea of the perfect man was a distinguished gentleman greying at the temples. The image of the perfect man had changed over the years, progressing from a Corsican bandit during a teenage continental tour with her parents, but he had always managed to elude her. Not that she was ever a man-chaser, far from it, and in any case, there was still time.

Standing at the reception desk, he signed in, talking quietly to Mrs Harris, his white teeth contrasting sharply with the tanned face and neat moustache. As he passed the ladies, on his way to the staircase, he smiled, and said 'Good Morning' in a deep, modulated voice. Public school, Miss Tidmarsh observed with satisfaction.

She reached for another magazine. Of course it is vulgar to comment on other people in their absence, but, when conversing with the likes of Milly Crabbe one was obliged to drop to their level, so to speak. 'Quite a gentleman,' she said, casually.

Millicent fingered her scarf. Gertrude turned a page, proffered a quick smile to her friend. Millicent drew the hem of her skirt down over her thickly bestockinged knees. If ever Gertrude saw the manifestation of suppressed desire in the body language of a woman, she was seeing it now. 'Do you know,' Millicent said, 'I think I've met him before.' She returned her friend's smile with an apologetic titter.

That *woman*, Gertrude thought. She was the absolute *limit*.

'Well!' she gasped, and turned the pages with a ferocious determination, half-expecting to see Milly's demi-nude photograph advertising some obscene undergarments.

Mrs Harris tidied some papers on her desk as she watched the retreating figure of Mr Hammond approach the stairs. He turned to take the first step and looked back at her. There was a slight, barely perceptible smile briefly on his mouth, and a knowing twinkle in his eye. She felt the blush on her cheeks, but returned the look. He may have seen the blush on her cheeks, but returned the look. He may have seen the blush, but the other, more intimate flush was known only to her. She pressed her hips to the counter as she watched him mount the wide, thickly carpeted stairs. It had been a long time, she thought, too damned long.

Over the next few weeks he established a regular routine. Always the first down to breakfast, he ate at a table alone, reading the morning paper. Then he returned to his room, where he could be heard clacking away on a portable typewriter for a couple of hours, after which he came down again, picked up his mail and went for a stroll along the promenade to the post box by the quay.

Although the careful observer had occupied her hide behind the pampas grass, she had not been able to engage him in conversation. He had gone out, after raising his hat with a polite 'Good morning', returned for lunch and spent the rest of the afternoon alone in his room. But Miss Tidmarsh, quite by accident, happened to be over by the desk when the postman came one morning, and there was no doubt that the Colonel was receiving a considerable amount of mail. There were several official-looking letters in brown envelopes, and one or two redirected items had foreign stamps on them. Miss Tidmarsh was intrigued. It just so happened that the Colonel came down and Mrs Harris appeared through the door that led to the kitchen behind reception.

'Good Morning, Colonel!' said Miss Tidmarsh, smiling sweetly.

'Good Morning, Madam,' he said, 'Good morning, Mrs Harris.' He looked at Mrs Harris, who smiled at him knowingly, but before she could speak Miss Tidmarsh said 'Miss. Miss Tidmarsh. Gertrude Tidmarsh.'

'Charmed to meet you, Miss Tidmarsh.' Now, an untrained ear might well have missed the astonishment in his voice on hearing that Gertrude was still a Miss, but not Gertrude's ear; she was as adept at identifying birds by their call-notes as by their eye-stripes and wing-bars. 'But it's just plain mister, you know. Plain Mister Hammond.' The deep lines etched a handsome smile around his eyes as he spoke.

'Ho Ho,' Gertrude said, 'You can't fool me!' Dash it! Why did her voice always crack like that whenever she tried to sound conspiratorial.

'Ha Ha,' said the Colonel. 'Well, I must beg you to excuse me Miss Tidmarsh, but I have to catch the morning post.' He bowed, very slightly, and turned to the proprietress. 'Good day to you, Mrs Harris.' And that twinkle in his eye was seen only by her.

'Hm hm,' Gertrude said as she watched him go through the door and pause on the step before striding briskly down to the road. 'What a charming man.'

'Yes,' Mrs Harris said. Charming indeed, she thought, but I hope there is a twinkle in more than his eye.

Gertrude retreated to her lair, and read the final chapter on human behaviour in her paper-covered book. All fascinating and highly informative material, she decided, and worth reading again. When Millicent appeared they exchanged the usual morning greetings and Millicent sat beside her dear friend.

'I had a word,' Gertrude said, during a lull in the conversation, 'with the Colonel this morning. Yes. Quite a chat, as a matter of fact. He is really a very charming man, when one gets to know him. Done a lot of travelling, you know.' She pursed her lips, until the lines radiating from the mouth looked like the lava flow from a tiny, extinct volcano, and complacently ran her tongue around her teeth. 'Been all over the world,' she said.

Miss Crabbe smiled a mirthless smile, and fingered her scarf. 'Has he?' she muttered. 'Yes, most interesting, I'm sure.'

Gertrude knew jealousy when she saw it. And she saw it now in the face of her friend, but things were come to a fine state if one could not have an innocent conversation with a gentleman friend and fellow resident without some people thinking the worst. She smiled at Millicent and turned her attention to the reception desk, and observed, with her usual alacrity, that things were apparently not running as smoothly in the administration of the Bella Vista residential home this morning. Mrs Harris was evidently having words with the thin chamber maid. Despite the training of her visual faculties Miss Tidmarsh was, as yet, unable to lip-read.

Mrs Harris led the girl back into the kitchen and into her office at the back, where all of the real work in running this establishment was done. She sat herself behind the desk while the dejected girl stood before her.

'I can not see,' Mrs Harris said, 'why it should take progressively longer to clean the Colonel's room.'

'It's very untidy, Mrs Harris.'

'That's what I mean. The place looks just the same when you come out as it does when you go in.'

'He won't let me touch none of 'is papers an' that.' The girl had omitted to mention when she applied for the job, that she had five 'O' and two 'A' levels knowing that she would have been turned down as over-qualified for a work experience scheme, but, so far, she had not forgotten to speak to everyone in the place with a broad Cornish accent and to act daft. 'He's braem particlar,' she said. 'I d' do me best.'

Mrs Harris couldn't make her out. She was the best worker she had ever had, never had to be told anything twice, never answered back with insolent remarks, and actually seemed to enjoy attending to the needs of the old people, especially the men, whom a lot of her staff had regarded as lecherous old scoundrels not safe to be alone with. Yet, despite being so good, almost too good, at her job, she seemed so thick. Just listen to the way she spoke! She had to admit, there was really no reason for ticking her off. But she had been in the Colonel's room for over half an hour yesterday morning, three quarters of an hour today. She had still managed to complete all the other rooms before leaving work, but that was not the point. 'Try to spend a bit more time on Mr Ordish,' she said.

'Mr Ordish,' the girl said.

'Yes. Mr Ordish. You know who Mr Ordish is.'

'He doan like me in 'is room, don't ee knaw. 'e d' fancy 'ee Mrs Harris.' She went off into a fit of giggles.

Mrs Harris ignored that, pretended she didn't understand the accent. 'I can't think what you do in the Colonel's room for so long,' she said, 'try and speed it up a bit.'

The giggles increased, and the girl's face became red. 'All right,' she said, 'I'll see what I can do wid 'n,' and she turned to leave.

'Just a moment,' Mrs. Harris said. But she changed her mind. It couldn't be. Not what she had briefly thought. With this bag of bones? No chance! 'Oh, never mind,' she said, repenting, 'just try not to neglect the other residents. The Colonel is no different from any one else in this home.'

Mr Ordish was only sixty-two. He had taken early retirement and come here while still young enough to adapt to new surroundings. When he looked at himself in the bathroom mirror he didn't see an old body. In fact he was quite fit, and what deterioration there was had occurred since coming here. In summer he swam in the sea every day, and in winter, when most of the residents dozed away the afternoons in the lounge, he went down to the local gym for a workout with the weights before going for a long walk along the coast. Whereas he was now described as 'sprightly', in his youth he had been 'slight'. That was the trouble, he told himself, he was still a young man who'd had too many birthdays.

He played chess with Mr Thomas with even less concentration these days. His mind wasn't on the game. Mr Thomas thought that his friend was getting old, unless his own game was improving. What he didn't know was that Mr Ordish had been letting him win for months. While Mr Thomas deliberated for ages on the permutations of every move, Mr Ordish directed his own concentration to the movements of Mrs Harris's body as she brought flowers and vases of water to place about the lounge. She had recently taken to wearing tight jumpers and hip-clinging skirts, which showed off her contours far more effectively than those dammed silly trouser suits women draped themselves in these days. He had been here two years, and not a single day had passed without him imagining the possible consequences should she come into his room in the mornings. He had taken to praying for it. Not praying, perhaps, more a sort of intimate conversation with whatever power controlled his destiny. 'Just one more sin, God, Old Man,' he said every night. 'Send her to my room tomorrow and give me something to repent. Make her randy for me and I'll send for the bloody Priest, I'll confess, I'll do penance, anything.' 'No chance,' the power said.

It was the girl who came, and she took even longer now, shoving the blasted vacuum cleaner into every nook and cranny as if the room hadn't been touched for weeks. Funny girl!

'That your wife,' she said one morning, 'in the photo?'

'Yes.'

'That you, standin' by her?'

'Yes.' He took the framed picture from the dressing table and sat on his bed. Her loss had nearly killed him, but he had overcome his grief, and now, he hardly ever thought of her. Not now.

The girl sat on the bed beside him. He handed her the frame, smiling at her.

'Good lookin'' she said. 'Got any more photos?'

He took a small album from his bedside cabinet and passed it to her. She turned the pages, slowly. Old wedding photos, some shots in a garden, seaside holidays – that one was taken here, before they built the concrete cubicles – Mr and Mrs Ordish at a party, – albino eyed and drunk. There was a recent one of himself emerging from the sea down by the prom. He looked lean and fit.

'Never look at them,' he said. The girl was wearing an evasive perfume, something barely perceptible. 'I'm not living in the past. Not yet.' He wondered if she was anorexic. 'You ought to be going to the Colonel's room,' he said.

'I'm gone off he.'

'Oh. Why's that?'

'Ohhh. You knaw.' Mr Ordish caught a quick flash of her grey eyes, and realised that he had never looked at her before. Not properly. She had long hair, drawn back into a coil at the back of her head.

'Like that, is he?'

'Bit,' she shrugged, resignedly, as if these tribulations were the skivvy's lot.

With eyes like that? 'Do you know,' he said, 'I've never asked your name.' She only nodded. So he had to ask directly. It made him feel unaccountably shy.

'Morwenna,' she said. 'It's Cornish.'

'Can you speak Cornish?'

'I've passed the examination of the Cornish Language Board.' She blushed. She had given herself away. 'Don't tell nobody, will 'ee?' she said laughing. 'You've got to be thick to get jobs down here. There was only this, or washing dishes, or working part-time in a supermarket for thirty five quid a week. I got thirty two on the dole.'

He laughed. 'You young devil.' With her hair down, and wearing something other than this shapeless wrap-around overall she would be quite a different person, he saw. She was the type who would improve in looks and figure as she matured. Those grey eyes, when their depths were scrutinized, revealed a sensitivity already beyond her years. She gave him the album, which he returned to the drawer. How was it possible that this girl had come into his room nearly every day for the past six months and he had never seen her.

'You've made yourself invisible,' he said.

'No I ab'm. You're damnee blind, 'cep for she with the big tits.' Despite the mischief, deep in the grey eyes, and her impudent smile, Mr Ordish blushed.

The Colonel's typewriter was clacking painfully when Mrs Harris approached his room. He could do with a secretary, he had so much correspondence. She tapped softly on the door.

'Come!' the Colonel bellowed. 'Oh, I'm sorry Mrs Harris. Quite forgot myself. Old habits die hard, don't you know.'

She was carrying a bunch of flowers. 'I thought you might like the room brightened up a bit,' she said, and began placing the stems, one at a time, in a vase on his mantelshelf. 'Do you like chrysanthemums?'

'Love 'em, Mrs Harris.'

She kept her back to him. Here goes, she thought. 'Rosemary. We need not be formal in private, Colonel.'

'Leonard,' he said, from behind her back.

She placed the last stem in place. Turned to face him, smoothed her skirt and backed to the door. 'I'll get some water,' she said.

In the bathroom, she did a quick renovation job on her make-up while the jug was filling, and dragged her jumper down, tight beneath her skirt. Forty seven she might be, but she was far from past it.

'There we are,' she said when the vase was filled, 'nothing like the feminine touch, Colonel.'

'Leonard,' he said.

She went over and stood close behind his chair at the desk. 'What are you doing? Writing a book?'

'Nothing as exciting as that, Rosemary, just answering letters, but my typing is dreadful.' He pulled a sheet of paper from the machine and threw it aside. Put a clean sheet in its place. He typed the address at the top right hand corner. She leaned forward to examine his typing, and her breast touched his shoulder. His hand slid from her waist, over the curve of her backside, down her leg to the hem of her skirt. She drew herself away from him, went to the door, and locked it. 'It's the girl's day off,' she said. 'We won't be disturbed.'

To Miss Tidmarsh's annoyance, several of the lady residents at the Bella Vista had taken to spending an inordinate amount of time hanging around the lounge in the mornings. Once or twice she had found her favourite seat occupied. 'They know darned well that I like to sit here,' she muttered to herself. 'It's disgusting. They were like a lot of … well, it only needed a red light over the reception desk!' She would have to leave, she decided. It was becoming impossible to live in such a sordid atmosphere.

As she happened to be near the desk when the Colonel came for his post, she had a few words with him, as usual, but he was evidently a very busy man, with little time for social intercourse. A little shy, too, she observed, but this was often the case with the masculine, outdoor types. When he had gone, she turned to Mrs Harris.

'The Colonel is certainly a very busy man,' she said, 'I hear he is organising the Poppy Fund.' This was true, but she had also heard that he was in charge of the War Graves Commission, and holidays for impoverished Officers (Retd).

'Well,' Mrs Harris said, 'that's not quite it.'

Private conquests are as hard to bear as public defeats, and she had the Colonel eating out of her hand. He said she drove him mad with lust for her, at a time when he had given up hope of ever finding love in his life. Quite touching, really.

'Actually,' she said, ceding a little of her conquered territory, 'the Colonel is an extremely kind, as well as a busy man. All the work he does is for charity.' She leaned further over the counter in order to confide in Miss Tidmarsh, who was obliged to look away, the things people wore these days. Frightening! 'You would be surprised,' Rosemary Harris said, 'if I told you he had sent a cheque for two hundred and fifty pounds to India only yesterday.' She watched Miss Tidmarsh's face for effect. '*Two hundred and fifty pounds* for a new well in a little village in the hills.'

'Really?' Gertrude had long since ceased to expect people like Mrs Harris to know the difference between 'surprised' and 'astonished', so she let it pass. 'How kind,' she said. 'As a matter of fact,' Mrs Harris said, 'I have been helping the Colonel with his correspondence.'

'How very kind of *you*,' she said, with a smile. So! There was no question about it now. Gertrude would leave with Millicent. This was no place for gentlewomen. Correspondence, indeed.

'I should imagine,' Mrs Harris said, 'that he is quite famous, in his quiet way.' She had ideas about a bungalow in the foothills of the Himalayas. Sell this place and go to India. 'Yes,' she said, 'people send him money from all over the place. And he passes it on to where the need is greatest. He sent thousands to Ethiopia.' There would be frangipani (or was it bouganvillea?) over the verandah as they sipped their sunshiners (was that what they called them?) as the shadows lengthened across the wadi. She pulled herself out of the daydream. 'Of course,' she said, briskly, 'he doesn't want it spread around.' She already regretted confiding in this silly woman. What business was it of hers. 'You must excuse me, Miss Tidmarsh, I have rather a lot to do.'

Miss Tidmarsh kept all this to herself. She watched from her lair with new respect for the Colonel. Once, he came over to her.

'Please forgive me, Dear Lady,' he said. How charming and Old Fashioned he was. 'But I am afraid I inadvertently picked up a letter of yours.' And he actually sat beside her for several minutes.

'Oh, it's from that silly nephew of mine,' she said, 'probably asking for money.' She was noticing, from the corner of her trained eye, that several of the ladies couldn't keep their own inquisitive glances from the direction of the pampas grass behind which she and the Colonel were enjoying their little tete-a-tete. Let them look!

Millicent Crabbe was among those who saw the two of them talking over in the corner, Gertrude noticed, and for some reason which was not hard to see, she kept herself apart from her friend for some days afterwards. Indeed she kept herself even more to herself, hardly ever being seen except when she scuttled through the lounge like a timid mouse, on the way to the promenade or the public gardens for her afternoon walk. How silly, Gertrude thought. There was absolutely nothing between the Colonel and herself. They were simply, good friends.

The Colonel had asked her to marry him. Rosemary Harris could hardly believe it. He was so handsome. And what a lover! She had asked him, to be honest, but he was too shy to broach the subject, so it amounted to the same thing. She had got him! He was going to take her to India, then the Sudan, where she would help him in his work. She was bursting to tell someone, but he advised discretion. 'Don't want the residents talking,' he said, 'I'm a private sort of chap, Rosemary, m'dear.'

She went to the estate agents in Fore Street. She wasn't far out, they said, Bella Vista was worth a quarter of a million – two hundred and fifty thousand pounds. They could sell it within three months. She was quite hard-headed with them, nobody's fool was Rosey Harris, after the struggle she'd had to build the place up. 'What about your commission,' she asked them, 'and the solicitor's fees? Make it two hundred and sixty thou' to cover costs, leaving me a quarter of a million clear.' 'Can do,' the man said. What with speculation on the government's intention regarding the care of the elderly, together with the local authority's reluctance to grant planning permission for any more old-people's homes, private nursing homes were at a premium in Cornwall. No problem, Mrs Harris. 'No boards,' she said.

'No need to sell the place if you don't want to,' Leonard said, 'I've got a fair bit put aside, don't you know. You can let it.' But she wanted to be clear of it all, not have the worry. 'We'll be quite well off, between us,' she said.

Would twenty do? Or should she make it thirty? With a determined flourish, Gertrude wrote the cheque for fifty pounds. It was her money, after all. A fine lot that nephew cared about her. The only time he ever wrote, it was to ask for something. All he was interested in was his filthy motor bike and that equally filthy, shameless thing he carried about on the back of it. Why should he have it all to waste? Far better, far far better, that the money should go to where it would be appreciated. When one realised that there were still villages in India without a well, to say nothing of the starving in Africa. She felt ashamed that she had not donated to such deserving causes in the past. There was so much good one could do in this world. Miss Tidmarsh would follow the example of the Colonel and become a philanthropist. She imagined all those dear little black faces queuing-up for water. The well might even bear the inscription 'This well was provided through the generosity of … '

At half past four she knocked on the Colonel's door. These things must be done in private.

'Why, it's Miss Tidmarsh,' he said. 'Do come in, Dear Lady. Please sit down. Rather untidy, I'm afraid.' The poor man was as embarrassed as a maiden. How touching. 'You know what we men are,' he went on, moving a pile of papers from a chair. 'There we are. Wasn't expecting visitors.'

Gertrude sat on the edge of the chair, while the Colonel sat once more at his table. An Angel passed overhead, Gertrude noticed.

'Would you care for a glass of sherry?' the Colonel said, suddenly.

'Oh, well, hmm, well, yes, just a teeny glass, if I may, please.'

He filled two glasses, and they sat sipping and talking until Gertrude quite forgot why she had come. It was not until she was leaving that she rememberd to press the envelope ino his hand.

'Now, Colonel, I have heard all about your wonderful work.' She checked the Colonel's protest. 'And I would like you to accept this little gift. Ah. No No!' She pushed his hand away and wagged a finger at him. 'It's a small world, you know. You can't keep things to yourself indefinitely.'

The Colonel was visibly impressed. 'Well well,' he said. 'I don't know what to say.' He was holding her hand.

'Good afternoon, Colonel,' Gertrude said, retreating to the door, 'and not a word to anyone about … you know what. Promise!'

'Promise,' he said.

She was smiling radiantly when she left the room. The two old dears sharing room ten nodded significantly to each other as she passed them on the landing.

There was now a glint of shared conspiracy in the Colonel's eye when he met Miss Tidmarsh in the mornings. They were sharing a secret, and she felt the stirrings of long suppressed emotions when those eyes wrinkled into a smile. Once, she saw Miss Ryder from room fifteen press an envelope into the Colonel's hand, but she had not been up for sherry, Gertrude was sure of that. Nevertheless, she was not too happy about it. Mrs Harris had said that the cheque he sent off for the well in India had been for two hundred and fifty. This induced some misgivings. She could see the inscription on the well as plain as daylight. It would be in granite. She knew a little man in Newlyn. In any case, she liked the Colonel's sherry, and he was almost an old friend. She would tell him tomorrow morning to expect her in the afternoon when that dreadful Harris woman had finished his typing, for she couldn't really invite him to her own room, not yet.

Now that Mrs. Harris had taken to cleaning the Colonel's room herself, Morwenna spent longer with Mr Ordish. She called him Charley.

'That bloody Hammond,' he said, one day when they were sitting on the bed together. 'He's queered my pitch.'

'With she with the tits?'

'Thought I had a chance before he came.'

Her grey eyes looked at him, and he returned her look with a wistful smile. 'Come here,' she said, and drew him down, on to the bed, 'what you need is a good cuddle.'

Gertrude rose from her seat and joined Miss Crabbe, who was going for a stroll. 'Thought I might join you, Millicent,' she said. 'It's a lovely day.'

They went along the prom, had a look at the boats in the harbour and finished up sitting on a seat in the public gardens. The leaves were just turning, and the autumn sun was warm.

'We might see the Colonel,' said Gertrude, casually, watching Millicent from the corner of her every-vigilant eye. There was no answer.

Millicent was being extremely quiet, even for her. The quiet ones were always the worst, as Gertrude knew full well. But as they watched the goldfish swimming in a tight shoal in the shallow water of their pool, Millicent said, 'Gertrude, you know we are not getting any younger.'

I'm well aware of that, thought Gertrude! She was also aware that when people said 'we' in such a context, they usually meant 'you' are not getting any younger.

'No,' she said, 'we are not, are *we.*'

Millicent pulled her gloves up her wrists, stretching the embroidered doggies beyond recognition as to breed, and almost to species. 'I have something to say,' she said. 'But I don't know whether I ought.' She was in a torment of indecision.

That was just the sort she was, Gertrude thought, tells you she's got something to say, and in the same breath tells you she can't say it. The people one had to put up with.

'Please, Millicent. We are friends,' she murmured.

'Yes. Well, it's about Mr Hammond.'

'Oh?' said Gertrude, icily.

'I. You. Oh dear! Don't do anything silly, Gerty. I mean women like us can make such fools of themselves.'

Gerty, indeed! 'I can assure you, Miss Crabbe, that I am perfectly capable of living my own life, and when I need advice, I shall be glad to ask for it.' She stood up in indignation. 'And as for the Colonel. Well!' She laughed, a little, carefree laugh.

Miss Crabbe was desperate. 'Oh dear,' she moaned, wrenching the gloves until the fingers were in danger of detachment.

'If you don't mind,' Gertrude said, sitting down again, 'I would rather the Colonel's name was omitted from our conversation in future.' She glanced around the garden with amused indifference, this, she felt, being the most appropriate glance for the occasion. What was the Colonel to her? Merely a very good friend. Make a fool of herself indeed! Dear dear. She was chuckling to herself most of the way back to Bella Vista.

It was a couple of weeks later that she was sitting by the pampas grass with a cheque in her handbag, waiting for the Colonel to come through the lounge, when two tall gentlemen came in and asked for Mrs Harris. Were they from the estate agent, she wondered, for there had been rumours about the town that the place was up for sale. No. They looked like Guardsmen, in mufti, or should one say civvies these days. Must get it right, now that she was moving in military circles. One thing she noticed immediately. They were kindred spirits in their powers of observation. One stayed by the reception-desk, talking to Mrs Harris when she appeared, while the other took a key and went up the wide stairs. Mrs Harris, unless Gertrude Tidmarsh was very much mistaken, had tears in her eyes, but the gentleman was evidently reassuring her.

Turning the pages of her magazine she came upon the illustration of a country house, the sort of house the Colonel should live in. And no doubt would, were it not for his charity work.

Presently the Colonel came down with the tall gentleman who had gone upstairs. What a handsome pair they made, Gertrude thought. The two strangers must be from the foreign office. One of them was quite dark, had Indian blood, perhaps, come to make arrangements for another well, possibly the one which her cheque would pay for. How exciting! The Colonel raised his hat as he passed. 'Good Day, Gertrude,' he said. 'Good Morning, Rosemary.'

The sound of her christian name from this handsome man was like a drug to Miss Tidmarsh, who watched with admiration as the Colonel, carrying a small valise, left the Bella Vista with a tall gentleman on either side of him.

Rosemary Harris suddenly burst into tears and rushed through the door to her private office at the back of the kitchen.

Outside, on the steps, the Colonel paused in the sunshine, and breathed deeply of the salt-tanged air.

'How did you do it?' he asked.

'We didn't, to tell the truth, Arthur. You did it yourself, by changing your name again. Little Miss Crabbe recognised you from Torquay. If you were still Major Smythe, you could have touched her for another hundred quid.

'Pity.' The Colonel smiled, a brief, wry smile. 'But there is no law against changing one's name, you know. And I've certainly never called myself Major, or Colonel, or anthing but "mister".' He smacked his lips thoughtfully.

'You chaps are wasting your time,' he said. 'I'll tell you what. None of that lot in there will go into court and give evidence, make damned fools of themselves. Even if you've got one or two, Miss Crabbe for instance, I've given more than enough to various charities, thousands of pounds, to cover what I've received from them.' He tapped his valise. 'Kept the receipts, too.'

'Besides,' he said, cheerfully. 'What's a man supposed to do when people keep shoving money into his hand, calling him "Colonel" for no reason at all, and rich women propose marriage.' He looked from one to the other of his tall companions. 'She asked me you know! I didn't suggest it.'

He straightened his back, and looked back at the Bella Vista. 'Very comfortable place,' he said. 'Recommend it.'

From the bedroom on the first floor Mr Ordish and his young friend watched the trio departing down the road.

'She's going to need somebody now, Charley,' Morwenna said.

John Branfield

MY IRISH TERRORIST

I have just been given a present. It's a sort of award, though not for being the most helpful member of the middle school, or anything like that. The reward for services rendered – and this puzzles and bothers me – was from the IRA.

I'm not one of those girls you sometimes see in news reports, wearing berets and anoraks and marching in military formation at the funeral of a gunman. I don't even live in Northern Ireland; I live in Cornwall, miles away from all the explosions and killings, the car bombs and mortar attacks, the armed soldiers patrolling the streets. I've only seen it on television.

I still can't believe that someone like me, Jenny Turner, fifteen years old, in the fourth year at the comprehensive school, preparing eight GCSE subjects and living an ordinary sort of life, could get involved in all that. I must be imagining it, I tell myself. It can't be true. And then I consider the facts …

It began a few evenings ago, soon after the start of the summer term. The school bus dropped my sister Clare and me at the roadside, and we walked down the lane. The trees had just come into leaf, an explosion of bright green which became more intense as we descended the valley. Our grey stone house, the old mill at the bottom, had disappeared from view. Only the 'Bed and Breakfast' sign showed clearly, freshly painted for the summer and newly hung.

'Oh no,' moaned Clare as she saw it.

We both hate having guests in the house. But with Dad in the United States and his maintenance cheques arriving only occasionally, Mum needs all the paying guests she can get.

'There won't be anyone yet,' I said. Mum is a great optimist. There aren't many tourists around between Easter and the Spring Bank holiday. And they never find their way down our unsignposted lane anyway. It's only when everyone else is full that they come to us.

We crossed the footbridge by the side of the ford. The white marker showed nine inches of water in the stream.

'And Mum's out,' complained Clare. Beneath the 'Bed and Breakfast' sign was another board saying 'No vacancies'. This didn't mean that the house was full; it was simply to stop anyone calling. I lifted it off its hook.

We walked down the drive between the mossy stone walls to the house. The key was under a stone at the back, and we let ourselves in. I changed and made tea. I called to Clare, asking if she wanted a cup. In my room, I started to look at my homework.

Through the open window I could hear a car coming fast down the hill, though I couldn't see it through the leaves. I heard the splash as it hit the ford, the change in the note of the engine as it revved up the slope. To my surprise, it turned into our drive. I caught a glimpse of red beneath the trees, the brakes squealed, and it skidded to a stop at the front porch. A moment later the bell rang.

The man at the door was in his thirties, with ginger hair and freckles. He had very blue eyes.

'Do you have any accommodation?' he asked. He had an Irish accent – it was very clear in the way he said 'accommodation', singing it up and down in a breathy sort of voice.

'Yes,' I said. 'What would you like?'

'Anything will do.'

'A double room?' I had noticed a female face behind the windscreen of the car.

'I'll take it,' he said.

I tried to think of what Mum would do. 'Would your wife like to have a look at it …?'

'No, that will be all right with her,' he said. 'We'll go and have a meal now, and come back later.'

He got into the car and drove off at speed, the gravel spurting from behind the wheels. Clare was standing behind me. 'That's odd,' she said, 'taking a room without even looking at it.'

When Mum came home I told her about the booking.

'Oh Jenny,' she said in dismay. 'You shouldn't have let him go like that. Did you ask his name?'

'No.'

'Did you take the number of his car?'

'No.' I was disappointed. I thought I had done well, making a booking so early in the season.

'You've got to get them to leave their luggage behind, to make sure they come back. They'll go to a pub now and have a meal, spend the evening there and find they can stay the night. We won't see them again.'

But Mum was wrong. We were still having our meal when the car returned, scrunching on the gravel. Mum rushed to the front door and ushered them into the kitchen. 'We were just going to have a coffee,' she said. 'Will you join us, Mr – ah?'

'You can call me Paddy Murphy,' he said.

Paddy Murphy! Clare and I looked at each other, and she suppressed a giggle. It was such a made-up name, he wasn't even trying.

'And this is Helga,' he said.

Helga was about five years older than me, and had close-cropped blonde hair. She wore a sort of track suit in black.

'Is that an Irish name?' asked Mum, knowing very well that it was not.

Helga looked at her uncomprehendingly, and then turned towards Paddy.

'She's German,' said Paddy. 'She doesn't understand much English.'

And Paddy, it seemed, didn't understand much German, because Mum wanted to know how they liked their coffee and he asked her and she didn't understand. I started German last year, and at least I can say 'mit milch oder ohne milch', so I translated. Then I made the black coffee for her and four white coffees for the rest of us. However did they get together, I wondered, if they couldn't even talk to each other?

Meanwhile Mum kept probing with questions. How much holiday did they have? Where were they making for?

'And where have you come from?' she asked, as I served the coffee.

'From Turkey,' said Paddy.

'My goodness,' exclaimed Mum. 'You *are* getting around. What were you doing in Turkey?'

'We were on our way here.'

'You went to Turkey to get to Cornwall?' she asked, puzzled.

'We spent the night there.'

'You spent the night in Turkey,' repeated Mum, completely bewildered. Clare and I were laughing into our coffee cups. 'Mum,' I said. 'He means Torquay.'

Soon she took them to their room, showing them where the television lounge was and telling them that if there was anything they wanted they had only to ask.

'I don't want you girls hogging the bathroom,' she whispered loudly when she came back. 'Just pop in and out quickly.'

'Guests first,' sighed Clare.

'And use the outside toilet.'

'Yes, Mum.' The season had begun.

I went up to my room to practise. I've been learning the Spanish guitar longer than I've been learning German. I played some studies to loosen my fingers, gradually increasing the tempo. There was a knock at the door. 'Come in,' I called.

It was Paddy Murphy. I thought he was going to complain.

'I heard you playing,' he said. 'You play very well.'

'It was difficult at first,' I said. 'My fingers weren't big enough, but they've grown now.'

'Will you play something for me?'

'What would you like?' I looked through some of the music. 'Do you like flamenco?'

He perched on the edge of the table at the low window where I do my homework. I played a Malaguena variation, a piece that I know well.

'Ah, that's lovely,' he said. 'It's the music of the people.'

'Do you play?' I asked him.

'I can strum a bit.' He reached out his hand for the guitar and I passed it to him. He played a few chords, getting used to the instrument. He adjusted his position and began. The sound was very Celtic.

'Are you Cornish?' he asked.

'I don't know,' I said. 'I was born in Cornwall.'

'Do you play any Cornish music?'

'There isn't any.'

'That's a shame,' he said. 'Because the Celtic races are full of music.'

He played a folksong. With his long fingers, he was a much better player than he let on. Then he returned the guitar. 'I mustn't interrupt your practice,' he said. 'I came to ask you a small favour. I'm having a spot of trouble next door. Do you think you could interpret for us again?'

'I'll try,' I offered. 'I'm not very good.'

'I'm hopeless.'

I followed him along the landing. I felt a bit awkward entering their room. The German girl was half sitting, half lying on the bed, with her feet on the counterpane. She had several books spread around her.

She looked up from her reading. Paddy stood by the window beneath the sloping ceiling. 'Ask her what she means to do tomorrow,' he ordered.

I translated, keeping it very simple. She said that she would stay there. Didn't she want to go with him? No, she was quite sure. She would leave it entirely to him. He was on his own.

At least, that is what I thought they were saying. But as I concentrated on how to put the words into another language, the meaning seemed to pass over my head.

They weren't at all like husband and wife. Well, I had never thought that they were, but they didn't even seem like friends or lovers. It seemed more of a business-like relationship, even military. It was as though instructions were being given, though who was ordering whom wasn't clear. I had the feeling that they were on some sort of mission.

Then Paddy was thanking me and I went back to my room.

I continued to practise, but all the time I was thinking of the couple on the other side of the wall.

I tried to put them out of my mind. If I was going to wonder about every visitor who came throughout the summer, I'd have no time for anything else. It was no business of mine. And yet, even as I was falling asleep in bed, I felt aware of them under the same roof.

When I came down in the morning there were the remains of a meal on the kitchen table. 'Paddy's up and away,' said Mum. 'He wanted an early breakfast and was out of the house by seven o'clock.'

'Where's Helga?'

'She's still in bed.'

I helped myself to cornflakes and milk. The window was filled with sunlight, and the garden beyond it shimmered green.

'They're staying on for another night,' said Mum, very pleased with the extra income.

I forgot about them all day at school, but when we got home Mum was indignant. 'Helga hasn't been out of that room all day,' she exclaimed. 'I left her breakfast on the table, but she didn't seem to want any. I wondered if she was ill, so I took her a cup of coffee at lunch time. The windows were closed and the room was full of cigarette smoke. I don't suppose she can read the notice.'

There was a sign which says 'Thank you for not smoking' in each of the bedrooms.

'She was lying on the bed, reading. What a way to spend a holiday, when it's been so lovely!'

'It's up to her,' said Clare.

'Oh yes, it's up to her,' said Mum. 'But it's an awful shame.'

I heard the red car come clattering down the drive when I was doing my homework, long after we'd had our evening meal. I heard it leave again almost immediately, and I was practising when it returned. I hoped Paddy would come in to talk guitars and play. But there was no knock on the door.

At nine o'clock I went down to the sitting-room to watch the news. Mum and Clare were already there, sitting in front of the electric fire. Paddy came in soon after the programme started.

There was an item from Northern Ireland, as there nearly always is. Earlier in the week an IRA man had been shot; his assassins were thought to have been members of another faction within the movement, that it was part of an internal power struggle. It had been reported each evening, and now the man's wife was interviewed, sitting in the same room where it had happened, in front of the television, with her little boy on her lap. She told how the three masked men had burst in and shot her husband, firing several times, while she and the three-year-old watched.

Mum tut-tutted and shook her head. Instinctively we all turned round to glance at Paddy Murphy. He was watching the screen, and showed nothing of what he thought or felt.

The programme moved on to another story. After the weather forecast – 'Another lovely day tomorrow,' hinted Mum – she switched off.

'That poor little boy, he'll have to live with that memory all his life,' she said. 'And the wife too. It must be terrible living in Northern Ireland.'

'It's tragic,' said Paddy.

'I've no sympathy with either side,' said Mum. 'The IRA or the para-military loyalist groups, they're as bad as each other,'

His pale face flushed. 'The IRA are fighting for their country,' he said. 'Ireland is one country, and part of it is occupied by a foreign power. They've a right to fight for their own land.'

'Hm,' went Mum. 'And so they shoot each other, even a man on the same side, in front of his wife and child.'

'Things like that happen in wars. It's the fault of the British government.' Paddy Murphy was now bright red. 'They must take their troops out of Ireland.'

Clare was looking at the television page of the newspaper. 'Hey, we're missing –' she began.

'Oh no,' interrupted Mum sharply. 'No more television, it's time you were off to bed.'

I couldn't sleep. I couldn't help thinking about Paddy Murphy. What were they doing in Cornwall?

He was a supporter of the IRA. Perhaps he was one of the gunmen who had shot dead their rival in front of his wife and child. Perhaps he was on the run, with Helga as his minder. Or perhaps he was on the run from the IRA, one of the breakaway faction, a friend of the dead man.

It seemed incredible. It seemed too much of a coincidence, that someone in the national news would end up in our lost little valley. But if someone was on the run, he had to end up somewhere, it had to be a coincidence for someone.

But then, if he was in hiding, why would he draw so much attention to his Irishness? Why wasn't it Helga who went out, while he remained hidden at the mill? And yet if he wasn't hiding, what was he doing?

'They aren't staying on,' said Mum, when we returned the next afternoon. 'They came down late this morning and Paddy said he'd like to settle the bill. I told him how much it was, and he said he didn't have any cash, he'd have to go to the bank. He's coming back later.'

'That's the last you'll see of him,' said Clare.

'Oh no,' said Mum with a smile. 'They've left their luggage in the porch.'

We had our tea and washed up. Clare went out into the hall, and a moment later gave a shout. 'Hey, Mum1 Have you *seen* their luggage?'

We followed her. She had opened the door to the porch, and there, placed right against the inner door where it was least visible from the hall, was a battered old cardboard case. It was tied together with a piece of string.

'Hard luck, Mum,' said Clare, putting her arm around her. 'I bet it's empty … You've been had.'

But Mum and I glanced at each other, and the same thought occurred to us both. What *do* you think if an Irishman, a self-professed supporter of the IRA, leaves a suspicious-looking case on your front doorstep?

Clare moved forward, to prove that it contained no more than old newspapers. 'Don't go near it!' screeched Mum. 'It might be a bomb!'

We huddled together, staring at the case on the floor. It looked pathetic, harmless. 'How can you tell?' I asked in a low voice.

'Ssh,' said Mum. 'See if it's ticking.'

We remained deathly quiet. There was the rustling of leaves outside, the trickling of the mill stream. There was no sound from the case.

'I don't think bombs tick any more,' I whispered. 'I think they are more sophisticated nowadays.'

'Oh my God,' said Mum. 'What are we going to do?'

'Phone the police.'

We crept back to the kitchen, stepping as quietly as we could. Mum went to the phone, and then withdrew her hand. 'I can't,' she said. 'I can't tell them I think the IRA have planted a bomb in our house, it's too ridiculous.'

'They won't mind.'

'But why us?' asked Mum. 'Why would they choose us? We're not the grand Hotel at Brighton, for heaven's sake.'

We went to the scullery, to be further away from the suspected bomb. 'It can't be,' said Mum. 'It couldn't happen to us, we're not important enough. I'd feel too foolish, telling the police.'

'You could report that they had left without paying.'

'I'll give them until seven o'clock,' Mum decided. 'If they haven't come back by then I'll ring the police.'

We went into the garden, to be away from the house. Everything was bursting into leaf, growing wildly, and we set to work with shears, scythe and mower. We were alert to every sound, our bodies tensed for the flash of the explosion, the roaring noise, the house collapsing in ruins.

'I'll give them another five minutes,' said Mum, 'and then I'll phone.'

At three minutes to seven we heard the car, roaring fast down the lane, the splash as it shot through the ford. It turned in at the gate and came down the drive, squealing to a stop in front of the porch.

Paddy had put the case in the boot by the time we were there. He took out of his hip pocket an enormous wad of ten-pound notes, peeling off several for Mum and refusing any change. He leaned into the car and Helga passed him a large flat parcel. With a flourish, he presented it to me. 'It's a little token of appreciation,' he said, 'for all the help you've given us.'

Then he got into the car and accelerated away, scraping the side on the stone wall as he went. He turned into the road, there was a glimpse of red through the trees at the ford, and then the noise of the engine faded away on the hillside.

Mum breathed out a great sigh of relief. We all felt light-headed, as though we had had a narrow escape. I opened my present on the kitchen table. It was a record of Julian Bream playing Malcolm Arnold's guitar concerto. A note said that it had been composed in Cornwall.

'How silly we were,' said Mum, 'to think that they would plant a bomb here. We thought they were terrorists!'

And yet, despite my pleasure in the record, I still thought there was something very suspicious about Paddy Murphy. 'If he wasn't a terrorist, what was he?' I asked.

'He was just a man who had picked up a girl.'

'Then what was he doing yesterday?'

'I don't know.'

Was he just an amorous Irishman? Or was he an IRA man, even if he was not one of the splinter group that they were trying to kill? Perhaps he had come to Cornwall to make contact with the extreme nationalists who want, like the IRA, to break away from England. Perhaps he wanted to meet an arms-dealer, or arrange for the smuggling of arms into Ireland through Cornish ports.

I went into the sitting-room and wondering whether I should have accepted it, put the record on the turntable. The music and the performance were perfect. How could anyone who liked such music, and who was understanding enough to know that I would like it too, be associated with the murderers who shot a man dead, as he sat watching television with his wife and child? How could anyone who played the guitar so well, with his long sensitive fingers, have anything to do with the handling of weapons and explosives?

The music brought him clearly to mind, with his red hair and bright blue eyes.

How could he accept the killing and maiming of people, the destruction of their homes by bombs? How could he do it?

That is, if he really was a terrorist. And I think he was.

Liz Harman

MRS TREMAIN'S CRISIS

It was the buttocks that started it off. Rounded, muscular, straining against his tight blue jeans. He was a young man, in his early twenties perhaps, sun-tanned with a shock of dark wavy hair. Where his yellow t-shirt parted company with his jeans the skin showed smooth and tanned, a gold earring glinted in his ear. He leaned on the railings of the harbour wall, obviously enjoying the sun on his face. As if sensing her looking at him, the young man smiled and then raised his arm and waved. Mrs Tremain instinctively started to raise her arm in reply, then realised that he was not smiling and waving to her, but to a long-legged, long-haired honey-skinned beauty behind her. The girl ran past her, and threw herself into the young man's arms. They kissed, and with arms entwined around each other's waists, they ran off towards the harbour. Mrs Tremain thought enviously, 'When was the last time that happened to me?' She was depressed; it was her 60th birthday, and no longer could she look on herself as being in her fifties and middle-aged – from then on she was entitled to draw retirement pension and to apply for a senior citizen's bus pass.

Mrs Tremain had always looked after herself; she was as smart and trim as she had been in her thirties, her skin was good, pampered by creams and potions, and her hair owed only a little to the expertise of her hairdresser. In short, she looked good for her age. There was the rub: always that qualifying statement, 'for her age'.

Disconsolately Mrs Tremain returned home. Her husband Steven was waiting for her.

'I thought,' he said, 'that as it is a lovely day, and it's your birthday we would go out for a drive and try that new restaurant down to Sennen for lunch.'

'I wish you wouldn't go on about my birthday,' snapped Mrs Tremain. 'I want to forget it.'

Later, as they sat in the restaurant at Sennen, looking out at the wide, golden sweep of the bay, the great Atlantic waves, the exuberance of the black-wetsuited surfers as they rode the tops of the rollers, Mrs Tremain thought of the young man she had seen that morning, and visualised those long, hard muscled limbs encased in a figure-hugging wetsuit. When they returned home, they found their elder daughter Jane waiting for them.

'Happy Birthday, Mum,' she said.

'Don't talk about it,' her mother replied. 'Look at those cards, all reminding me.'

She indicated the row of birthday cards on the mantelpiece, each emblazoned with a golden 60.

'How about a cup of tea, Jane?' said Steven. 'I'll give you a hand.' Together they went out into the kitchen. Mrs Tremain felt on edge and very unsettled.

Next day dawned just as fine and sunny. Sixty plus one. Now I am really into my sixties, she thought.

'I know what we'll do,' said Steven. 'We'll take the car and have a whole day out, just going where we feel like going.'

'What about the shopping?' said Mrs Tremain.

'That can wait. They're open 24 hours a day in any case, so come on, don't let's waste the fine weather.'

They set off, and Steven drove the car on to the St Just road. 'Be lovely down Cape Cornwall today,' he said.

'I don't mind where we go, it's all the same to me,' said Mrs Tremain, determined that she would not enjoy herself. As they approached the old mining town of St Just, Steven suddenly turned left on to the Land's End road.

'I thought we were going to Cape Cornwall,' she said.

'Sorry, my love, I wasn't thinking. But it's nice this way,' replied Steven. As they approached the tiny St Just airport, they could see the sun shining on the toy-like aeroplanes sitting on the green runway.

'Be nice over Scilly today,' he said. Then he made a sharp turn and parked in the airport car park.

'What on earth are you thinking of Steven?' said Mrs Tremain. 'This is for people who are going to Scilly.'

'That's right,' he answered. 'We're catching the 10 o'clock flight.'

'We're going to Scilly for the day?' she asked.

'Three days actually. I thought you'd be surprised.'

They hadn't been to the Isles of Scilly since their honeymoon 38 years earlier. Then, they had stayed in a small guesthouse in Hughtown. 'What are we going to do about clothes, we can't go with just what we stand up in?'

'All sorted,' said Steven. 'Jane packed our suitcases when we went to Sennen yesterday.'

'But my toilet things, what about them?'

'Jane went to Peasgood's and bought duplicates of everything you use,' said her husband. 'So don't argue. Come on.' Not knowing whether to be pleased or cross, Mrs Tremain followed her husband into the airport. After a somewhat bumpy take-off, Mrs Tremain allowed herself to relax and think that perhaps she might enjoy herself. The magic of Scilly started working its spell as soon as they spied the jewel-like islands surrounded by jade-green water.

'I don't suppose Mrs Jenkin is still doing bed and breakfast after all these years, do you?' said Mrs Tremain.

'I've booked somewhere else this time,' said Steven. 'They say you shouldn't go back to the same place – in case you're disappointed.' At St Mary's they got into a taxi, and Steven directed the driver to take them to the Star Castle Hotel, the best on the island. At once Mrs Tremain started worrying whether Jane had packed the right clothes for them – and she thought about jewellery? Why had Steven been so impetuous?

Thirty-eight years earlier they had looked with envy at the Star Castle. After checking in at reception, a young man stepped forward, saying: 'I think you will find all is in order in your room, sir, and may I on behalf of the hotel, wish you a very happy stay.'

Glancing at Mrs Tremain, he said: 'Please accept our heartiest congratulations.'

The door had barely closed on the porter who had carried their luggage to the room, and furiously, quite ignoring the luxurious bedroom, the bowls of scented island flowers, the pink roses on the dressing-table and the champagne standing in the ice-bucket, Mrs Tremain rounded on Steven. 'You told them, didn't you – you told them that it is my sixtieth birthday. How could you, when you know how I feel about it.'

'No, I didn't,' said Steven, mildly. 'I said we were on our honeymoon.'

Mrs Tremain was speechless. 'Everyone will be looking at us, smirking, thinking we are honeymooners at our time of life.' There it was again – age. 'What will they think?'

'They'll think that I am the luckiest man in the world.'

Putting his arm around her shoulders, he went on: 'I'll tell you this much, Rosie Tremain, if you live to be ninety, to me you will always be the eighteen-year-old beauty I fancied that night at the Bonfire Social at the church, the one I fell in love with and married.'

By now she had noticed the pink roses on the dressing-table. 'You remembered, after all this time, that I carried pink roses on our wedding day.'

'Don't think I'd forget, do you? After all, I had to pay for them.'

Turning to him, Mrs Tremain saw a handsome sixty-four-year-old man with a gentle teasing look in his eyes. Suddenly Mrs Tremain saw the humour of the situation; she smiled and then burst out laughing. They spent the day happily exploring old haunts, reliving old memories. Mrs Tremain stood in the window of their bedroom, gazing out over the darkening sea. She had enjoyed being wined and dined, Jane had had the foresight to pack her smartest dress and the new earrings that Steven had given her for her birthday. The jade-green sea was turning black, the lights of the fishing boats twinkled like stars on the water. The lighthouses were flashing signals as if having a conversation. She thought, as she watched the light from the Bishop Rock lighthouse: 'That's what Steven is like – a rock, solid and secure, and always there,'

Steven stood behind her. He put his arms around her. Content, she leaned against him, and for a moment she thought of the golden couple of the previous day.

'I hope they will be as happy as we have been.'

Steven rested his chin on top of her head.

'Love you Rosie Tremain.'

'Love you Steven Tremain,' she replied. And she did. He was the only man she had ever loved, or ever would.

For a little while they stood in silence. Then she said: 'What shall we do tomorrow?'

'Let tomorrow look after itself,' replied her husband. 'We haven't finished with today yet.' He gave her a hug and said: 'After all, we are on our honeymoon.'

E. V. Thompson

THE DAY THE CUP CAME TO TRESCOPPA

Trescoppa is typical of many surprisingly large villages to be found tucked away among the china clay workings around the St Austell area of Cornwall. Drab stones, a working men's club – and a chapel or two. Of course the village has its choir too, but overshadowing even life itself are the white waste heaps which stretch away beyond the hills, an inheritance from generations of china clay workers. In other words, you might say, just another working village which has known better days.

But Trescoppa has something else – a rugby football team. Not a run of the mill rugby team, but the best in Cornwall. The small community is inordinately proud of its team. During the rugby football season the progress of the fifteen brave men is virtually the sole subject of conversation. Almost all the arguments on a Saturday night in the working men's club are heated discussions on such subjects as whether Cap'n Hunkin should have kicked for the line or taken the ball through the centre in the last match, or whether Jimmy Trecarrow should be retained for the next one.

On Sunday, in the chapels, both Wesley Spargo and Harry Hooper, two fiery preachers, might be heard fervently calling for divine guidance on the tactics the team should adopt in their next game. The service might end with a call for forgiveness for the full-back who missed an easy drop-kick on the previous day.

So it is easy to imagine the fever that gripped the villagers the year the team reached the finals of the National Amateur Rugby Cup.

The semi-final had been a hard match. It was eventually won by nine points, two broken noses, a fractured collar bone and a twisted knee. All the opponents could muster were five points, a broken thumb, a suspected fractured ankle and a sent off the field for punching a linesman. Everyone agreed it was one of the best games they had ever seen. The final, to be played in London, promised to be even better. The other finalists were a tough Lancashire team, who, so rumour would have it, had included a karate course in their training curriculum.

For weeks the village fairly buzzed with plans and counterplans to ensure that victory would be theirs. China clay production in the local pits dropped to a record low, while old Oggie Williams, the butcher – generally acknowledged as being the meanest man in all Cornwall – had taken to adding a free steak to orders placed by the wives of the team members.

'Just to build up his strength, mind,' he would say, 'Not to be considered a regular occurrence.'

There were some arguments as to who would take responsibility for the supporters' travelling arrangements. Colum Jago had offered, but someone was quick to say: 'No way! You'd have us travelling in an open lorry while your racing pigeons sat in their loft getting fat on seed that we'd paid for.'

A sharp operator was Colum.

Eventually, after it was agreed that any surplus money should go into chapel funds, Wesley Spargo said he would take on the task.

The team went to London a week before the match was due to be played and every day the local daily paper carried pictures of the team 'outside Buckingham Palace', 'at the Tower of London', and one morning with arms draped about the shoulders of chorus girls from one of the London shows.

This brought forth disgusted grumbles from Oggie Williams.

'To think I wasted good steak for all that gallivanting. I thought they were going to London to play rugby football.'

At last the great day arrived. Early in the morning all the able bodied men in the village, plus a few of the not-so-able ones, were at St Austell railway station to board a special train that had been organised for them. They were in a very happy mood, reinforced, no doubt, by the numerous crates of beer that boarded the train with them.

The womenfolk who were left behind had serious misgivings about the occasion. Not at the prospects of the team, you understand, but at the thought of their men being let loose in London.

It was left to Loveday Mitchell to voice their feelings.

'It's not the match I'm worried about, it's what they might get up to afterwards that bothers me. A terrible wicked place is that London, with all those brazen hussies, and their goings on. I should hate to see my David's name in the Sunday papers.'

As her David was a wizened little man of about 75, the possibility seemed extremely remote. But all the other women knew how she was feeling.

The train pulled jerkily out of the station and, as the strains of *Trelawny* faded away in the distance, the wives and sweethearts who had gone to the station returned to their homes, taking their misgivings with them. The supporters enjoyed the journey to London. As the train sped through sleepy English country stations, the few waiting passengers were startled to hear the well-sung strains of partisan songs coming to them through open carriage windows, occasionally accompanied by an empty beer can.

Eventually the train pulled into Paddington Station and the supporters arrived in the great metropolis. For some it was their first glimpse of London and the rush and bustle of life slightly overawed the more timid among them. However, once on board the coaches which were to take them to the rugby ground, this feeling soon evaporated. They began pointing out places of interest with all the excitement of schoolboys.

Once at the ground, Wesley Spargo called them together and went over the arrangements he had made for them.

'Right,' he said. 'Do you all have your tickets?'

He looked around the crowd of Cornishmen and was satisfied with the number of nodding heads.

'Good. Now, mind you give our team plenty of support. We want to take that cup back to Trescoppa.'

He held up his hand to silence the loud cheer that went up at his words.

'Don't forget, I want there to be no trouble between you and the Lancashire support – not unless they start it,' he added, in a manner that reminded his listeners that he had been a champion boxer and Cornish wrestler before becoming a preacher.

'Now, when the game is over we will meet back at the coaches to go to a West End hotel, where they are holding a reception for the teams and their supporters. After that you must make your own way to the station – and don't get lost. Remember the train leaves sharp at midnight. Away you go lads – and have a good time.'

The men broke off and made their way to the various entrances of the rugby ground.

With a wisdom gained from many years organising rugby finals, the officials had arranged for the Cornish supporters and the Lancastrian counterparts to be on opposite sides of the ground. It was a wise precaution. Long before the match was due to begin, cheers and a great deal of bantering echoed back and forth across the green turf. Out on the pitch there was a fine display of marching and playing from a female bagpipe band. Then, to thunderous applause from the huge crowd of supporters, both teams of finalists trotted on to the field.

Trescoppa won the toss and elected to play into the wind for the first half, a decision that met with the noisy approval of their supporters.

Then the whistle blew – and the game was on. From the very first minute it was apparent that both teams were evenly matched and both played hard rugby. By half-time both teams had scored five points and each had lost a man, carried from the pitch. The excitement among their supporters was at fever pitch and it took a few pints of good beer to restore their voices.

The second half was equally exciting. Trescoppa were actually in the lead when they received a major setback. Their star right-winger, Ross Curnow, was brought down by a tackle accompanied by a punch that went unseen by the referee and linesmen and Ross was carried from the pitch. During the exhibition of high feelings that followed the incident the Trescoppa captain was ordered off for threatening the offending Lancastrian.

The Cornish team was unable to overcome the handicap imposed upon them by the loss of such valuable men and when the final whistle sounded they had lost by the narrow margin of fourteen points to eleven.

All the way to the hotel where the reception was being held, the Trescoppa supporters replayed the game time and time again – and the same conclusion was reached each time. Had it not been for that foul tackle, Trescoppa would have won the cup.

Inside the huge hall in the hotel a platform had been set up on which stood the tables reserved for the teams and various dignitaries from the world of rugby football. In the centre of the platform was a smaller table with a green baize cloth. Upon it was the trophy for which both teams had given their best. The Amateur Rugby Cup.

It was unfortunate that the organisers of the reception lacked the experience of the rugby ground officials. As the supporters entered the hall they were casually directed to tables set around the platform – Cornishmen and Lancastrians mixed.

Their error became apparent during a speech made by a senior official of the Rugby

Football Association. He had just mentioned the high principles of the game and was praising the sportsmanship displayed by the players seated on the platform when a voice from the body of the hall shouted: 'Yes, but only from the Trescoppa team.'

This brought forth jeers from the Lancashire supporters and a chant of 'Dirty play! Dirty play!' from the Cornishmen.

Afterwards, nobody could say with certainty which side threw the first punch, but within seconds the hall had erupted into a seething mass of battling supporters.

The speaker on the platform, himself an old-time rugby player of no mean prowess, valiantly called for order. However, when the brawling crowd spilled on to the stage, memories of past glories overcame him. Recalling the old adage 'if you can't beat them join them', he took a swing at the man closest to him.

Unfortunately, this happened to be the Trescoppa preacher, Wesley Spargo, who was himself trying to restore order. Both men crashed into the Trescoppa team's table. They went down, swapping punches, amidst jelly, ice-cream and assorted broken crockery.

Before a victory could be claimed by either side, the police arrived on the scene, blowing whistles and wielding batons. The instant the cry 'Police!' went up combatants forgot their differences and made a concerted rush for the doors.

Later, as the supporters' train sped through the night towards Cornwall, the rugby fans happily recalled dinner.

'It was memorable,' said Jimmy Trecarrow, fingering a bruised right eye. 'If only we were taking the cup back to Cornwall with us it would be the end to a perfect day.'

Colum Jago, sitting in the corner of the carriage, spoke for the first time.

'If that's all you need then you can stay happy. The cup is going back with us.'

There was a sudden silence and the occupants of the carriage looked at Colum.

'What do you mean?' asked Jimmy. 'We lost the game didn't we? The other team has the cup.'

'Lost the game indeed,' snorted Colum. 'All of us know that if it hadn't been for that foul tackle we would have won.'

He cast a fierce glance about the carriage, daring anyone to disagree with him. Nobody did.

'Right then,' he said. 'While all you non-thinking men were doing your best to knock each other's silly heads off, I was up on the platform, taking what's rightfully ours.'

As he spoke, he stood up and, taking his old raincoat from the luggage rack, he unwrapped it with a flourish and held its contents up to show the astonished men.

'Here it is ... we're taking the cup home with us.'

The cheering and stamping of feet that accompanied the production of the cup brought the occupants of the adjacent carriages running to see what was happening. In no time at all word had gone the length of the train.

'We're taking the cup back to Trescoppa!'

The police made extensive enquiries, of course, but the non-rugby playing detective inspector in charge of the investigation had no hope of gaining the confidence of the Trescoppa villagers, and he was not the type to go crawling around in Colum Jago's pigeon loft in search of a missing cup.

They still play rugby football in Trescoppa and although they have never again reached the national finals, they do not mind overmuch. They still have the cup. It is not shown to strangers, of course, but if you happen to be in the village on a certain day in May and hear the sounds of riotous celebration taking place behind locked doors at the working men's club, you know what is happening. The men will be celebrating the day that ranks next to St Piran's Day in their calendar. The day the cup came to Trescoppa.

Michael Morpurgo

'Gone to Sea'

William Tregerthen had the look of a child who carried all the pain of the world on his hunched shoulders. But he had not always been like this. He is remembered by his mother as the happy, chortling child of his infancy, content to bask in his mother's warmth and secure in the knowledge that the world was made just for him. But with the ability to walk came the slow understanding that he walked differently from others and that this was to set him apart from everyone he loved. He found he could not run with his brothers through the high hay fields, chasing after rabbits; that he could not clamber with them down the rocks to the sea but had to wait at the top of the cliffs and watch them hop-scotching over the bounders and leaping in and out of the rock pools below.

He was the youngest of four brothers born onto a farm that hung precariously along the rugged cliffs below the Eagle's Nest. The few small square fields that made up the farm were spread, like a green patchwork between the granite farmhouse and the grey-grim sea, merging into gorse and bracken as they neared the cliff top. For a whole child it was a paradise of adventure and mystery, for the land was riddled with deserted tin miners' cottages and empty, ivy-clad chapels that had once been filled with boisterous hymns and sonorous prayer. There were deserted wheel houses that loomed out of the mist, and dark, dank caves that must surely have been used by wreckers and smugglers. Perhaps they still were.

But William was not a whole child; his left foot was turned inwards and twisted. He shuffled along behind his older bothers in a desperate attempt to stay with them and be part of their world. His brothers were not hard-souled children, but were merely wrapped in their own fantasies. They were pirates and smugglers and revenue men, and the shadowing presence of William was beginning already to encroach on their free-dom of movement. As he grew older he was left further and further behind and they began to ignore him, and then to treat him as if he were not there. Finally, when William was just about school age, they rejected him outright for the first time. 'Go home to Mother,' they said. 'She'll look after you.'

William did not cry, for by now it came as no shock to him. He had already been accustomed to the aside remarks, the accusing fingers in the village and the assidu-ously averted eyes. Even his own father, with whom he had romped and gambolled as an infant, was becoming estranged and would leave him behind more and more when he went out on the farm. There were fewer rides on the tractor these days, fewer invitations to ride up in front of him on his great shining horse. William knew that he had become a nuisance. What he could not know was that an inevitable guilt had soured his father who found he could no longer even look on his son's stumbling gait without a shudder of shame. He was not a cruel man by nature, but he did not want to have to be reminded continually of his own inadequacy as a father and as a man.

Only his mother stood by him and William loved her for it. With her he could forget his hideous foot that would never straighten and that caused him to lurch whenever he moved. The talked of the countries over the sea's end, beyond where the sky fell like a curtain on the horizon. From her he learned about the wild birds and the flowers. Together they would lie hidden in the bracken watching the foxes at play and counting the seals as they bobbed up and down at sea. It was rare enough for his mother to leave her kitchen but whenever she could she would take William out through the fields and clamber up onto a granite rock that rose from the soil below like an iceberg. From here they could look up to Zennor Quoit above them and across the fields towards the sea. Here she would tell him all the stories of Zennor. Sitting beside her, his knees drawn up under his chin, he would bury himself in the mysteries of this wild place. He heard of mermaids, of witches, of legends as old as the rock itself and just as enduring. The bond between mother and son grew strong during these years; she would be there by his side wherever he went. She became the sole prop of William's life, his last link with happiness; and for his mother her last little son kept her soul singing in the midst of endless drudgery.

For William Tregerthen, school was a nightmare of misery. Within his first week he was dubbed 'Limping Billy'. His brothers, who might have afforded some protection, avoided him and left him to the mercy of the mob. William did not hate his tormentors any more than he hated wasps in September; he just wished they would go away. But they did not. 'Limping Billy' was a source of infinite amusement that few could resist. Even the children William felt might have been friends to him were seduced into collaboration. Whenever they were tired of football or of tag or skipping, there was always 'Limping Billy' sitting by himself on the playground wall under the fuchsia hedge. William would see them coming and screw up his courage, turning on his thin smile of resignation that he hoped might soften their hearts. He continued to smile through the taunting and the teasing, through the limping competitions that they forced him to judge. He would nod appreciatively at their attempts to mimic the Hunchback of Notre Dame, and conceal his dread and his humiliation when they invited him to do better. He trained himself to laugh with them back at himself; it was his way of riding the punches.

His teachers were worse, cloaking their revulsion under a veneer of pity. To begin with they overburdened him with a false sweetness and paid him far too much loving attention; and then because he found the words difficult to spell and his handwriting was uneven and awkward, they began to assume, as many do, that one unnatural limb somehow infects the whole and turns a cripple into an idiot. Very soon he was dismissed by his teachers as unteachable and ignored thereafter.

It did not help either that William was singularly unchildlike in his appearance. He had none of the cherubic innocence of a child; there was no charm about him, no redeeming feature. He was small for his age; but his face carried already the mark of years. His eyes were dark and deep-set, his features pinched and sallow. He walked with a stoop, dragging his foot behind him like a leaden weight. The world had taken him and shrivelled him up already. He looked permanently gaunt and hungry as he sat staring out of the classroom window at the heaving sea beyond the fields. A recluse was being born.

On his way back from school that last summer, William tried to avoid the road as much as possible. Meetings always became confrontations, and there was never anyone who wanted to walk home with him. He himself wanted less and less to be with people. Once into the fields and out of sight of the road he would break into a staggering, ugly run, swinging out his twisted foot, straining to throw it forward as far as it would go. He would time himself across the field that ran down from the road to the hay barn, and then throw himself at last face down and exhausted into the sweet warmth of new hay. He had done this for a few days already and, according to his counting, his time was improving with each run. But as he lay there now panting in the hay he heard someone clapping high up in the haystack behind him. He sat up quickly and looked around. It was a face he knew, as familiar to him as the rocks in the fields around the farm, an old face full of deeply etched crevasses and raised veins, unshaven and red with drink. Everyone around the village knew Sam, or 'Sam the Soak' as he was called, but no-one knew much about him. He lived alone in a cottage in the churchtown up behind the Tinners' Arms, cycling every day into St Ives where he kept a small fishing boat and a few lobster pots. He was a fair-weather fisherman, with a ramshackle boat that only went to sea when the weather was set fair. Whenever there were no fish or no lobsters to be found, or when the weather was blowing up, he would stay on shore and drink. It was rumoured there had been some great tragedy in his life before he came to live at Zennor, but he never spoke of it so no-one knew for certain.

'A fine run, Billy,' said Sam; his drooping eyes smiled gently. There was no sarcasm in his voice but rather a kind sincerity that William warmed to instantly.

'Better'n yesterday anyway,' William said.

'You should swim, dear lad,' Sam sat up and shook the hay out of his hair. He clambered down the haystack towards William, talking as he came. 'If I had a foot like that, dear lad, I'd swim. You'd be fine in the water, swim like the seals I shouldn't wonder.' He smiled awkwardly and ruffled William's hair. 'Got a lot to do. Hope you don't mind my sleeping awhile in your hay. Your father makes good hay, I've always said that. Well, I can't stand here chatting with you, got a lot to do. And, by the by dear lad, I shouldn't like you to think that I was drunk.' He looked hard down at William and tweaked his ear. 'You're too young to know but there's worse things can happen to a man than a twisted foot, Billy, dear lad. I drink enough, but it's just enough and no more. Now you do as I say, go swimming. Once in the water you'll be the equal of anyone.'

'But I can't swim,' said William. 'My brothers can but I never learnt to. It's difficult for me to get down on the rocks.'

'Dear lad,' said Sam, brushing off his coat. 'If you can run with a foot like that, then you can most certainly swim. Mark my words, dear lad; I may look like an old soak – I know what they call me – but drink in moderation inspires great wisdom. Do as I say, get down to the sea and swim.'

*   *   *   *   *

William went down to the sea in secret that afternoon because he knew his mother would worry. Worse than that, she might try to stop him from going if she thought it was dangerous. She was busy in the kitchen so he said simply that he would make his own way across the fields to their rock and watch the kestrel they had seen the day before floating on the warm air high above the bracken. He had been to the seashore before of course, but always accompanied by his mother who had helped him down the cliff path to the beach below.

Swimming in the sea was forbidden. It was a family edict, and one observed by all the farming families around, whose respect and fear of the sea had been inculcated into them for generations. 'The sea is for fish,' his father had warned them often enough. 'Swim in the rock pools all you want, but don't go swimming in the sea.'

With his brothers and his father making hay in the high field by the chapel William knew there was little enough chance of his being discovered. He did indeed pause for a rest on the rock to look skywards for the kestrel, and this somehow eased his conscience. Certainly there was a great deal he had not told his mother, but he had never deliberately deceived her before this. He felt however such a strong compulsion to follow Sam's advice that he soon left the rock behind him and made for the cliff path. He was now further from home than he had ever been on his own before.

The cliff path was tortuous, difficult enough for anyone to negotiate with two good feet, but William managed well enough using a stick as a crutch to help him over the streams that tumbled down fern-green gorges to the sea below. At times he had to go down on all fours to be sure he would not slip. As he clambered up along the path to the first headland, he turned and looked back along the coast towards Zennor Head, breathing in the wind from the sea. A sudden wild feeling of exuberance and elation came over him so that he felt somehow liberated and at one with the world. He cupped his hands to his mouth and shouted to a tanker that was cruising motionless far out to sea.

'I'm Limping Billy Tregerthen,' he bellowed, 'and I'm going to swim. I'm going to swim in the sea. I can see you but you can't see me. Look out fish, here I come. Look out seals, here I come. I'm Limping Billy Tregerthen and I'm going to swim.'

So William came at last to Trevail Cliffs where the rocks step out into the sea but even at low tide never so far as to join the island. The island where the seals come lies some way off the shore, a black bastion against the sea, warning it that it must not come any further. Cormorants and shags perched on the island like sinister sentries and below them William saw the seals basking in the sun on the rocks. The path down to the beach was treacherous and William knew it. For the first time he had to manage on his own, so he sat down and bumped his way down the track to the beach.

He went first to the place his brothers had learnt to swim, a great green bowl of sea water left behind in the rocks by the tide. As he clambered laboriously over the limpet-covered rocks towards the pool, he remembered how he had sat alone high on the cliff top above and watched his brothers and his father diving and splashing in the pool below, and how his heart had filled with envy and longing. 'You sit there, with your Mother,' his father had said. 'It's too dangerous for you out there on those rocks. Too dangerous.'

'And here I am,' said William aloud as he stepped gingerly forward onto the next rock, reaching for a hand-hold to support himself. 'Here I am, leaping from rock to rock like a goat. If only they could see me now.'

He hauled himself up over the last lip of rock and there at last was the pool down below him, with the sea lapping in gently at one end. Here for the first time William began to be frightened. Until this moment he had not fully understood the step he was about to take. It was as if he had woken suddenly from a dream: the meeting with Sam in the hay-barn, his triumphant walk along the cliff path, and the long rock climb to the pool. But now as he looked around him he saw he was surrounded entirely by the sea and stranded on the rocks a great distance out from the beach. He began to doubt if he could ever get back; and had it not been for the seal William would most certainly have turned and gone back home.

The seal surfaced silently into the pool from nowhere. William crouched down slowly so as not to alarm him. He had never been this close to a seal. He had seen them often enough lying out on the rocks on the island like great grey cucumbers and had spotted their shining heads floating out at sea. But now he was so close he could see that the seal was looking directly at him out of sad, soulful eyes. He had never noticed before that seals had whiskers. William watched for a while and then spoke. It seemed rude not to.

'You're in my pool,' he said. 'I don't mind really, though I was going to have a swim. Tell you the truth, I was having second thoughts anyway, about the swimming I mean. It's all right for you, you're born to it. I mean you don't find getting around on land that easy, do you? Well, nor do I. And that's why Sam told me to go and learn to swim, said I'd swim like a seal one day. But I'm a bit frightened, see. I don't know if I can, not with my foot.'

The seal had vanished as he was speaking, so William lowered himself carefully step by step down towards the edge of the pool. The water was clear to the bottom, but there was no sign of the seal. William found it reassuring to be able to see the bottom, a great slab of rock that fell away towards the opening to the sea. He could see now why his brothers had come here to learn, for one end of the pool was shallow enough to paddle whilst the other was so deep that the bottom was scarcely visible.

William undressed quickly and stepped into the pool, feeling for the rocks below with his toes. He drew back at the first touch because the water stung him with cold, but he soon had both feet in the water. He looked down to be sure of his footing, watching his feet move forward slowly out into the pool until he was waist-high. The cold had taken the breath from his body and he was tempted to turn around at once and get out. But he steeled himself, raised his hands above his head, sucked in his breath and inched his way forward. His feet seemed suddenly strange to him, apart from him almost and he wriggled his toes to be sure that they were still attached to him. It was then that he noticed that they had changed. They had turned white, dead white; and as William gazed down he saw that his left foot was no longer twisted. For the first time in his life his feet stood parallel. He was about to bend down to try to touch his feet, for he knew his eyes must surely be deceiving him, when the seal reappeared only a few feet away in the middle of the pool. This time the seal gazed at him only for a few brief moments and then began a series of water acrobatics that soon had William laughing and clapping with joy. He would dive, roll and twist, disappear for a few seconds and then materialize somewhere else. He circled William, turning over on his back and rolling, powering his way to the end of the pool before flopping over on his front and aiming straight for William like a torpedo, just under the surface. It was a display of comic elegance, of easy power. But to William it was more than this, it became an invitation he found he could not refuse.

The seal had settled again in the centre of the pool, his great wide eyes beckoning. William never even waited for the water to stop churning but launched himself out into the water. He sank of course, but he had not expected not to. He kicked out with his legs and flailed his arms wildly in a supreme effort to regain the surface. He had sense enough to keep his mouth closed but his eyes were wide open and he saw through the green that the seal was swimming alongside him, close enough to touch. William knew that he was not drowning, that the seal would not let him drown; and with that confidence his arms and legs began to move more easily through the water. A few rhythmic strokes up towards the light and he found the air his lungs had been craving for. But the seal was nowhere to be seen. William struck out across to the rocks on the far side of the pool quite confident that the seal was still close by. Swimming came to William that day as it comes to a dog. He found in that one afternoon the confidence to master the water. The seal however never reappeared, but William swam on now by himself until the water chilled his bones, seeking everywhere for the seal and calling for him. He thought of venturing out into the open ocean but thought better of it when he saw the swell outside the pool. He vowed he would come again, every day, until he found his seal.

William lay on the rocks above the pool, his eyes closed against the glare of the evening sun off the water, his heart still beating fast from the exertion of his swim. He lay like this, turning from time to time until he was dry all over. Occasionally he would laugh out loud in joyous celebration of the first triumph of his life. Out on the seal island the cormorants and shags were startled and lifted off the rocks to make for the fishing grounds out to sea, and the colony of seals was gathering as it always did each evening.

As William made his way back along the cliff path and up across the fields towards home he could hear behind him the soft hooting sound of the seals as they welcomed each new arrival on the rocks. His foot was indeed still twisted, but he walked erect now, the stoop gone from his shoulders and there was a new lightness in his step.

He broke the news to his family at supper that evening, dropped it like a bomb and it had just the effect he had expected and hoped for. They stopped eating and there was a long heavy silence whilst they looked at each other in stunned amazement.

'What did you say, Billy?' said his father sternly, putting down his knife and fork.

'I've been swimming with a seal,' William said, 'and I learnt to swim just like Sam said. I climbed down to the rocks and I swam in the pool with the seal. I know we mustn't swim in the sea but the pool's all right isn't it?'

'By yourself, Billy?' said his mother, who had turned quite pale. 'You shouldn't have, you know, not by yourself. I could have gone with you.'

'It was all right, Mother,' William smiled up at her. 'The seal looked after me. I couldn't have drowned, not with him there.'

Up to that point it had all been predictable, but then his brothers began to laugh, spluttering about what a good tale it was and how they had actually believed him for a moment; and when William insisted that he could swim now, and that the seal had helped him, his father lost his patience. 'It's bad enough your going off on your own without telling your Mother, but then you come back with a fantastic story like that and expect me to believe it. I'm not stupid lad. I know you can't climb over those rocks with a foot like that; and as for swimming and seals, well it's a nice story, but a story's a story, so let's hear no more of it.'

'But he was only exaggerating, dear,' said William's mother. 'He didn't mean ...'

'I know what he meant,' said his father. 'And it's your fault, like as not, telling him all these wild stories and putting strange ideas in his head.'

William looked at his mother in total disbelief, numbed by the realization that she too doubted him. She smiled sympathetically at him and came over to stroke his head.

'He's just exaggerating a bit, aren't you Billy?' she said gently.

But William pulled away from her embrace, hurt by her lack of faith.

'I don't care if you don't believe me,' he said, his eyes filling with tears. 'I know what happened. I can swim I tell you, and one day I'll swim away from here and never come back. I hate you. I hate you all.'

His defiance was punished immediately. He was sent up to his room and as he passed his father's chair he was cuffed roundly on the ear for good measure. That evening, as he lay on his bed in his pyjamas listening to the remorseless ker-thump, ker-thump of the haybaler outside in the fields, William made up his mind to leave home.

His mother came up with some cocoa later on as she always did, but he pretended to be asleep, even when she lean over and kissed him gently on the forehead.

'Don't be so unhappy, Billy,' she said. 'I believe you, I really do.'

He was tempted at that moment to wake and to call the whole plan off, but resentment was still burning too strongly inside him. When it mattered she had not believed him, and even now he knew she was merely trying to console him. There could be no going back. He lay still and tried to contain the tears inside his eyes.

Every afternoon after school that week William went back down to the beach to swim. One of his brothers must have said something for word had gone round at school that 'Limping Billy' claimed that he had been swimming with the seals. He endured the barbed ridicule more patiently than ever because he knew that it would soon be over and he would never again have to face their quips and jibes, their crooked smiles.

The sea was the haven he longed for each day. The family were far too busy making hay to notice where he was and he was never to speak of it again to any of them. To start with he kept to the green pool in the rocks. Every afternoon his seal would be there waiting for him and the lesson would begin. He learnt to roll in the water like a seal and to dive deep exploring the bottom of the pool for over a minute before surfacing for air. The seal teased him in the water, enticing him to chase, allowing William to come just so close before whisking away out of reach again. He learnt to lie on the water to rest as if he were on a bed, confident that his body would always float, that the water would always hold it up. Each day brought him new technique and new power in his legs and arms. Gradually the seal would let him come closer until one afternoon just before he left the pool William reached out slowly and stroked the seal on his side. It was gesture of love and thanks. The seal made no immediate attempt to move away but turned slowly in the water and let out a curious groan of acceptance before diving away out of the pool and into the open sea. As he watched him swim away, William was sure at last of his place in the world.

With the sea still calm next day William left the sanctuary of the pool and swam out into the swell of the ocean with the seal alongside him. There to welcome them as they neared the island were the bobbing heads of the entire seal colony. When they swam too fast for him it seemed the easiest, most natural thing in the world to throw his arms around the seal and hold on, riding him over the waves out towards the island. Once there he lay out on the rocks with them and was minutely inspected by each member of the colony. They came one by one and lay beside him, eyeing him wistfully before lumbering off to make room for the next. Each of them was different and he found he could tell at once the old from the young and the female from the male. Later, sitting cross-legged on the rocks and surrounded entirely by the inquisitive seals, William tasted raw fish for the first time, pulling away the flesh with his teeth as if he had been doing it all his life. He began to murmur seal noises in an attempt to thank them for their gift and they responded with great hoots of excitement and affection. By the time he was escorted back to the safety of the shore he could not longer doubt that he was one of them.

*   *   *   *   *

The notepad he left behind on his bed the next afternoon read simply, 'Gone to sea, where I belong.' His mother found it that evening when she came in from the fields at dusk. The Coastguard and the villagers were alerted and the search began. They searched the cliffs and the sea shore from Zennor Head to Wicca Pool and beyond, but in vain. An air-sea rescue helicopter flew low over the coast until the darkness drove it away. But the family returned to the search at first light and it was William's father who found the bundle of clothes hidden in the rocks below Trevail Cliffs. The pain was deep enough already, so he decided to tell no one of his discovery, but buried them himself in a corner of the cornfield below the chapel. He wept as he did so, as much out of remorse as for his son's lost life.

Some weeks later they held a memorial service in the Church, attended by everyone in the village except Sam whom no one had seen since William's disappearance. The

Parochial Church Council was inspired to offer a space on the Church wall for a memorial tablet for William, and they offered to finance it themselves. It should be left to the family they said, to word it as they wished.

*   *   *   *   *

Months later Sam was hauling in his nets off Wicca Pool. The fishing had been poor and he expected his nets to be empty once again. But as he began hauling it was clear he had struck it rich and his heart rose in anticipation of a full catch at last. It took all of his strength to pull the net up through the water. His arms ached as he strained to find the reserves he would need to haul it in. He had stopped hauling for a moment to regain his strength, his feet braced on the deck against the pitch and toss of the boat, when he heard a voice behind him.

'Sam,' it said, quietly.

He turned instantly, a chill of fear creeping up his spine. It was William Tregerthen, his head and shoulders showing above the gunwale of the boat.

'Billy?' said Sam. 'Billy Tregerthen? Is it you, dear lad? Are you real, Billy? Is it really you?' William smiled at him to reassure him. 'I've not had a drink since the day you died, Billy, honest I haven't. Told myself I never would again, not after what I did to you.' He screwed up his eyes. 'No,' he said, 'I must be dreaming. You're dead and drowned. I know you are.'

'I'm not dead and I'm not drowned, Sam,' William said. 'I'm living with the seals where I belong. You were right, Sam, right all along. I can swim like a seal, and I live like a seal. You can't limp in the water, Sam.'

'Are you really alive, dear lad?' said Sam. 'After all this time? You weren't drowned like they said?'

'I'm alive, Sam, and I want you to let your nets down,' William said. 'There's one of my seals caught up in it and there's no fish there I promise you. Let them down, Sam, please, before you hurt him.'

Sam let the nets go gently hand over hand until the weight was gone.

'Thank you Sam,' said William. 'You're a kind man, the only kind man I've ever known. Will you do something more for me?' Sam nodded, quite unable to speak any more. 'Will you tell my mother that I'm happy and well, that all her stories were true, and that she must never be sad. Tell her all is well with me. Promise?'

' 'Course,' Sam whispered. ' 'Course I will, dear lad.'

And then as suddenly as he had appeared, William was gone. Sam called out to him again and again. He wanted confirmation, he wanted to be sure his eyes had not been deceiving him. But the sea around him was empty and he never saw him again.

William's mother was feeding the hens as she did every morning after the men had left the house. She saw Sam coming down the lane towards the house and turned away. It would be more sympathy and she had had enough of that since William died. But Sam called after her and so she had to face him. They spoke together for only a few minutes, Sam with his hands on her shoulders, before they parted leaving her alone again with her hens clucking impatiently around her feet. If Sam had turned as he walked away he would have seen that she was smiling through her tears.

The inscription on the tablet in the Church reads:

WILLIAM TREGERTHEN
AGED 10

Gone to sea, where he belongs

Les Merton

Winter Harvest

Almost all that remains of the wall built in the reign of Henry VIII around the Cornish town of Launceston is Southgate, which spans the main street. This was once one of the entrance gates to Launceston, and, some say, the entrance to Cornwall itself. The historical facts of the grand Southgate did not interest Dingo Pepper. He slunk into the shadows of the pavement passage under Southgate arch. His cynically pessimistic mood blended with the deepening darkness of the winter afternoon.

The inner knot of tension that had gripped Dingo Pepper like a vice when he stepped out of his car, eased. The aura from the former debtors' prison above the Southgate arch was vaguely familiar. It emphasised Dingo's need for money, and provided the conviction needed.

Dingo peered out. He saw the fat figure of Charlie Walton waddle out of Race Hill Bookmakers to make his customary visit to the Cornwall Bank in Southgate Street. Dingo Pepper exposed his canine teeth in what passed for a smile.

Charlie Walton was blissfully unaware he was the subject of Dingo Pepper's attention. In fact he had never seen or heard of the lurking figure. The Launceston bookie was gloating. His betting shop had made a profit of over £6,000 this week. Only £1,000 of this would go through the accounts of his business. The rest of the money, Charlie had in his briefcase to lodge in his safe deposit box at the Cornwall Bank. Later, he would move it by dubious means to an off-shore account.

'Bloody bookies,' Dingo Pepper muttered, hugging the threadbare coat to his wiry frame. The gun in its shoulder holster bulged more solidly than muscle ever could.

Pale blue cigar smoke, filtered by deep inhaling, drifted through Charlie Walton's obese lips as he approached the Southgate arch. Dingo Pepper smelt the aroma and eased the gun out of its shoulder holster.

Charlie Walton saw the glint of metal as Dingo Pepper moved out of the gloom. The cliché, 'don't approach this man, he is armed and dangerous,' flashed through the bookie's mind. He turned with amazing agility for such a fat man. It was not quick enough. The pistol was already against his ribs. 'Walk over to the white Ford parked across the street, and get in the car by the passenger door,' Dingo hissed.

Charlie Walton was no hero. He felt a sudden need for the toilet. With the embarrassment and discomfort of a wet crotch, he did exactly what the gunman requested. Dingo Pepper got into the car's driving seat and Charlie babbled his first words.

'Take the briefcase, it's full of money. I won't say anything. Honest!' Charlie Walton crossed his heart with his free hand and then undid the briefcase safety chain from around his wrist.

Dingo Pepper smirked, revealing the pointed edges of his teeth. 'Undo the combination locks and put the case on the back seat.' He prodded the bookie in the ribs with the barrel of the gun.

Beads of sweat stood out on Charlie Walton's face. His podgy fingers fumbled with the combination locks and the briefcase clicked open.

'There's over six grand here.' Charlie turned and pushed the unlocked briefcase through the gap between the front seats of the car. The fat man struggled, but managed to lift the case of money onto the back seat of the car. Thinking it was time to go, Charlie went to open the passenger door. The pistol jabbed his ribs again.

'Not yet, we are going for a little drive,' Dingo growled. He felt in control of the situation, and smirked.

The canine teeth and staring eyes of the unknown perpetrator unnerved Charlie. The bookie's bladder emptied of its own free will for the second time that day.

'Good job this isn't my car,' Dingo snapped. He slipped the gun back into its holster, turned the starting key and accelerated into the traffic. He drove through the town and out the other side, then turned off into a housing estate and stopped the car near a police station.

'It's always safer to do things near a police station,' Dingo explained, taking the pistol out of its holster and pointing it at his passenger's head. He continued, 'I'm going to walk around to your side of the car and open the door. You will get out, open the back door of the car, then put all the money into this holdall and hand me the holdall. Do you understand?'

Charlie nodded. Dingo nipped immediately around the car and opened the passenger door. The gun menacingly waved the bookie out of the car. Charlie closed the front car door and opened the back car door quickly. He bent forward and scrabbled the bundles of notes out of the briefcase, and into the holdall. He straightened up and handed the bag full of money to the watchful gunman.

'Can I go now?' Charlie whimpered.

Dingo sneered and displayed the canine teeth that earned him his nickname. 'Guess what? We're going for another drive. Walk to the red Austin parked in front of us. Open the passenger door and get inside.'

Charlie did has he was bid. When Dingo started the Austin, he did a three-point turn and headed the car towards the A30 road, and the heart of Cornwall.

Dingo pushed the car up to eighty miles an hour, until he was forced to slow down because of patches of thick fog. When they reached Five Lanes, Dingo turned the car off the main road and drove towards Altarnun. He stopped outside the Cathedral of the Moor.

Dingo wasn't a church lover and wouldn't have appreciated the splendour of the building dedicated to St Non, even if it were not obscured by the swirling mist.

Charlie Walton was ordered out of the car at gun-point. He started to protest. Dingo snarled and cocked the pistol. The fat man heaved himself out of the passenger seat and stumbled into the churchyard.

'That's far enough,' Dingo hissed. He put the pistol to the bookie's ear and pulled the trigger. The fat man's bowels opened, and blood, carrying fragments of bone, gushed from the gaping bullet hole as Charlie Walton crumpled into a heap at his killer's feet.

The stench from the corpse and the copper odour of blood made Dingo urge. He deposited his fish-and-chip lunch over a headstone, without a single thought of respect for the delicately carved design by a young Neville Northey Burnard.

Dingo went back to the car and got into the driving seat. He opened a small panel on the dashboard, took out a flask of whiskey, raised it to his lips, and took a large swig. He wiped his mouth with his hand and replaced the flask of whiskey.

Dingo cursed the mist that was getting thicker, and drove out of the village back onto the main A30 road, and headed south.

*   *   *   *   *

The car was crawling along at a speed that didn't exceed ten miles an hour. The killing of the Launceston bookie seemed a lifetime ago. Dingo had the window down and was driving with his head stuck out of the window opening trying to get better vision. It was impossible. Mist clung to the car like a shroud.

The car went over several bumps. Dingo braked. The car stopped, and he applied the handbrake and got out of the car. He left the lights on and the engine running. Dingo walked around the dark shape of the car, felt underneath and around all of its wheel areas, and realised he had driven off the road onto moorland.

Dingo cursed, 'Bloody fog, bloody countryside!'

He stood up and looked around helplessly. He dare not drive any further, and he dare not leave the car. Dingo Pepper smoked only on the odd occasion. This seemed like an appropriate time. He opened a packet of Capstan full-strength, put a cigarette into his mouth, struck a match to light the cigarette and inhaled the full strength deeply. At first he thought it must be a reflection of the burning cigarette end, but every so often a yellow glow seemed to appear in the distance. Dingo inhaled again before dropping the cigarette and stubbing it out with his shoe. The mist seemed to shift in the distance, and he was sure he could see a light. The killer edged carefully forward, and every step he took, he moved his forward foot to the left and to the right, feeling the ground. Another step and he felt the ground harden. He bent down and touched the surface.

Tarmac! Dingo turned and looked back. The light from the headlights could be seen. The mist was lifting. Dingo Pepper retraced his steps to the car, opened the driver's door and got in. He turned the lights off, and waited.

Within minutes he saw the light in the distance more clearly. After a quarter of an hour, Dingo could make out the shape of a building with two lights shining from downstairs windows. He put the car into first gear, turned the lights on and edged forward. The windscreen wipers kept the window free of the damp mist, and through the arcing wiper-blade Dingo could see he was getting closer to the lights.

*   *   *   *   *

The Harvester was once a 13th century thatched cottage on the wagon trail running from Roughtor, across the spine of the moor, and down to Fowey. The isolated cottage became the haunt of highwaymen and smugglers in the 15th century. The low-beamed-ceiling parlour was used as a meeting place for moorland dwellers and farmers, who eked a living from the harsh landscape. They called it the Kiddley Wink, and if they wanted a drop of smuggled brandy, they would wink at the kettle in the corner. Slowly, the cottage became an inn that kept its character, but changed its name to The Harvester in the 19th century.

The Harvester still had a thatched roof. The cob wall between the kitchen and parlour was knocked down to make the present-day low-beamed-ceiling bar. Cheery warmth was provided by an open log fire, and an olde worlde atmosphere was enhanced by the hooks, sickles, scythes, pitch forks and fading photographs of horse-drawn hay-wagons that decorated the walls.

The last sheaf of corn cut at nearby Tor Farm for the yearly end-of-harvest ceremony, 'Crying the Neck', was always displayed behind the bar of the pub on the moor until it was replaced with the next year's last-cut sheaf.

*   *   *   *   *

The Harvester had been in the Treloar family for generations. Bessie Treloar, the current landlady, was the last of the Treloars. She had never married. However, Bessie had enjoyed the company of many of the local farmers over the years, and despite numerous attempts by one and all, including the highly fertile, she failed to get pregnant. Bessie always said she would keep trying with any man that came from good Cornish stock.

At forty-five, Bessie was very attractive. Her plump figure with its ample bosom was most becoming. Her long, jet-black curly hair high-lighted sparkling eyes, and an ever-ready smile that dimpled round rosy cheeks.

Bessie sat in an old armchair enjoying her customary smoke from a clay pipe. She always said it was one of the best times of the day – a touch pipe with a drink of cider before the customers arrived, in front of a fire that inspired day dreams.

Dingo Pepper slowly and quietly opened the front door of The Harvester. He slipped inside and surveyed the bar. It appeared empty. Dingo wiped his lips on the sleeve of his coat, drew his lips back, and sniffed the public house aroma.

'Anybody home?' Dingo asked loudly. Turning to a sound of movement coming from the far side of the room, he exposed his canine teeth in a forced smile. Bessie stood up, placed her clay pipe into an ash tray, and frowned with disappointment before she put on her greeting-the-visitor look.

'Come in me 'ansum,' she said in a welcoming Cornish accent. 'What would you like to drink?'

'Pint o' bitter.'

Bessie went behind the bar and took down a beer mug. She bent down, and filled the mug with a pint of bitter straight from a large wooden barrel resting on a strong shelf built about a foot above the floor. Dingo stared at the curve of Bessie's buttocks through her long, black, clinging skirt.

'Looks good,' Dingo hissed, as Bessie put the pint on the bar.

'What? My bottom, or the beer?'

Dingo exposed his pointed teeth in what passed for a smile. 'Both, now you mention it. How much?'

'One 'n' fourpence for the beer, if you please. The other is not for sale,' Bessie replied with good humour in her voice.

Dingo sorted through his loose change and put the right money on the bar.

'Got any grub?' he asked abruptly.

'Would you like a 'ome-made pasty? 'Tes still warm.'

'Sounds good,' Dingo nodded and displayed his canine teeth. 'What about a room?' He picked up the holdall. 'I wanted to make Falmouth, but I won't in this mist.'

'No rooms, but you can sleep in the armchair if that's any help, and I'll just charge you for breakfast in the morning.'

Dingo nodded, 'It'll be warmer than the car.'

''Tes sorted, then,' Bessie said. 'I'll go 'n' get you your pasty.' She entered the kitchen behind the bar and came back with a pasty that hung over the side of the dinner plate.

'Christ!' Dingo exclaimed. 'That's one hell of a pasty.'

Bessie smiled. 'I'll only charge you a shilling for it. You can pay for the food when you settle up in the morning. Just pay for the drinks as you go. Sit over there at the table, 'tes more comfortable than trying to eat at the bar. I'll finish me smauke before the regulars come in.' She moved from behind the bar to sit in her chair by the fire.

Dingo took his pint and the pasty over to the indicated table and sat down. He took a bite from the pasty and realised the holdall was at the bar. He got up and walked across and picked it up.

'Must have the crown jewels in there, the way you are guarding that bag!' Bessie said, turning to look at Dingo.

'No, no, just like to keep me stuff safe,' Dingo said with a snarl, then realised he was the only customer. He saw Bessie looking at him. He gave a hard, forced smile. 'Force of habit. London you know.'

Bessie smiled, put a taper in the fire, took it out again, sat back, and lit her clay pipe and inhaled the essence of deep rich tobacco.

*   *   *   *   *

Dingo pushed away his empty plate and moved towards the bar. He turned to Bessie, who rose from her chair in front of the fire and made her way behind the bar.

'Nothing like a bit of home-made grub. I'll round it off with a drop of whisky,' Dingo smirked and continued, 'Tell you what, make it a double. I'm having a good day ...'

Bessie poured a generous double whisky and placed it in front of her only customer. 'Cash or Harvest?' she asked, and quickly corrected herself, 'Half a crown for cash.'

Dingo put a coin near his glass on the counter. Bessie bent forward to pick up the silver half-crown piece. Dingo tried to sneak a look at the landlady's cleavage which the low-fronted top revealed.

'Home grown,' Bessie remarked proudly, stepping back and thrusting her bust forward in a provocative manner, 'but not available.'

Dingo licked his lips. He ran his tongue around his pointed teeth. 'Everything is available for the right price,' he stated, and went back to sit at the table.

The front door of The Harvester opened and a tall, well-built man in his early forties entered briskly. He had a hessian sack over his shoulders to keep him dry.

''Ansum weather for ducks!' the newcomer exclaimed, as he hung the hessian sack on a peg behind the pub door. He wore a tough and durable Cornwall rugby jersey tucked into a pair of corduroy trousers.

''Usual, Alfred?' Bessie asked, and started to draw a pint before Alfred had a chance to answer.

Alfred, who had the look of a farmer and the build of a rugby player, balanced on one leg and then the other as he pulled off his wellington boots. He walked to the bar in a pair of home-knitted socks. 'One of these nights, I might demand something different, Bessie Treloar, and make you throw the pint you've poured, down the drain.'

Bessie smiled. 'Cash or Harvest, Alfred?' she inquired. 'Harvest, maid, – you know that by now. I'm only a poor farmer, struggling to survive the elements Bodmin Moor throws at me.'

Alfred took a long sip at his drink. He turned and looked at Dingo. 'Your health, sire!'

Dingo nodded and curled his lip back to reveal the points of his teeth.

'Time for introductions. This is Alfred. He owns Tor Farm. I'm Bessie and you're ..?'

Dingo scowled. 'Smith, Mr Smith.'

At that moment, the front door of The Harvester burst open, and a female in her early twenties rushed through the door. She bent forward and shook her head. Water sprayed from her hair.

'God!' she exclaimed, 'it suddenly pissed down!'

'Doc!' Bessie protested loudly.

'Ah! I'm bloody soaked,' the girl said, and looked up. 'Sorry!' She gaped open-mouthed at Dingo. 'I never realised we had company.' Her face lit up. She smiled, and walked towards Dingo holding out her hand in a greeting of friendship. 'Sorry about that. I'm Angela ... They call me Doc ...' She paused, her hand still outstretched. She lowered it, slowly. 'And you're ...?'

'This is Mr Smith!' Bessie intervened.

'Alright,' Dingo said abruptly. He looked at the girl referred to as Doc, undressing her with his eyes as he looked her up and down, before his look lingered on the wet shirt clinging to her shapely breasts. 'Another double whisky landlady,' Dingo demanded as he turned and walked towards the bar.

The other two customers looked at each other and raised their eyebrows.

Bessie placed the ordered drink in front of Dingo.

'Half-a-crown please, Mr Smith,' Bessie said politely. Dingo put a coin on the bar and moved slowly in the direction of the open fireplace.

'What would you like, Doc?' Bessie asked the pretty, but bedraggled, young girl, as she handed her a towel to dry herself.

'I'll have a drop of whisky,' Doc answered as she rubbed her hair with the towel. 'I don't want to catch a cold. A vet with a cold is no good to man or beast.'

'Cash or Harvest, Doc?' Bessie asked, placing the ordered drink on the bar.

'Harvest, I'm skint till the end of the month.'

'What's all this cash or harvest?' Dingo asked with a scowl as he moved back towards the bar. 'Am I the only one paying in cash?' he said menacingly, and asked sharply, 'Is harvest some kind of country bumpkin tick, like a slate is up north?'

Alfred laughed loudly, and the two females smiled.

'It's right the reverse, my 'ansum,' Alfred said, and chuckled before he continued, 'we don't go into debt around here. Harvest is money we've already got behind the bar!'

Bessie nodded. 'As landlady, I can honestly say, harvest is money everyone here has got put back to see us through the lean times.'

'How much you got put back then ...?' Dingo inquired innocently, and looked away so they couldn't detect the look of interest in his eyes.

'That's only for us to know!' Doc said in a firm, quiet voice, 'and Bessie, I'll have another whisky on the strength of a good harvest.'

'And I'll have another pint,' Alfred said, and laughed. His large shoulders shook with mirth.

'I'll join you.' Bessie put the two ordered drinks on the bar and poured herself a large whisky.

The three locals raised their glasses. 'Harvest!' they said in unison, and all laughed.

'Come on!' Dingo exclaimed. 'Come on, you can't leave me in suspense.'

Bessie, Alfred and Doc looked at one another and smiled. The silence was broken by a clock chiming out the half-hour somewhere in a room behind the bar.

'Time!' said Bessie.

'Time!' exclaimed Dingo tensely. 'It's only half past seven!'

'Time!' Bessie repeated more loudly. 'Time ... to tell you about Harvest.'

Dingo relaxed his wiry frame as he realised he had been had. He tried to smile, but the face he pulled looked more like a dog snarling, and it made Alfred chuckle again.

'I'll tell you what Harvest is,' Alfred said when he had regained his composure. 'Every summer we get hundreds of visitors here, who all want to know about life on the moor. They all buy us more drink than we can ever drink in one session. Bessie keeps tally, and at the end of the season we have a harvest of plenty to keep us watered through the long winter.'

Dingo looked in amazement and said with awe in his voice, 'You canny lot of buggers.' He put his hand in his pocket and put two five pound notes on the bar. 'Put that in your funds and tell me about life on the moor.'

Dingo's eyes never left the five pound notes, and his disappointment was plain to see when Bessie scooped them up and placed them down her top in the care of her ample bosoms.

'Well ...' said Doc, 'cheers, first of all. One of the many things I get asked is, why everyone calls me Doc. Most assume it is because I'm the local vet, but I've been called

Doc, since I was ten years old. Whenever I found an injured creature, I always tried to help it, even down to putting sticky tape on broken snail shells.'

'That's true. I remember,' Alfred said with a chuckle, 'you even tried to revive a dead goldfish with the kiss of life!'

'For that,' interrupted Doc, 'I've got to tell Mr Smith about the night you slept with the ghosts that haunt that ramshackle old farm house you call home!'

'You mean, the night I slept with the goats!' exclaimed Alfred, who chuckled again.

'Hang on a minute!' Dingo said, 'I've got to have a slash ...'

'Through the door, turn right ...' Bessie informed Dingo who was looking everywhere but the right direction.

Dingo went to pick up his holdall. He hesitated, picked it up, and headed for the door Bessie had indicated.

'I'll have a quick wash while I'm out there,' Dingo said by way of explanation for taking the holdall with him, as he went through the door that led to the convenience.

'Funny chap,' said Bessie quietly.

'What do you reckon ...?'

Before Alfred could finish what he was going to say, the pub front door opened and a young, good-looking policeman hurried in.

'Bobby! Bobby!' Doc exclaimed, and ran over and put her arms around the young policeman and kissed him passionately.

Bobby, the local policeman, gently pushed away the attractive girl who was his fiancée.

'Doc, I'm on duty ... Bessie, Alfred ... whose car is that outside?'

'Some up-the-country fella – got lost and is sheltering from the weather for the night ... I think he's heading for Falmouth.'

'Where is he!' Bobby asked with an intense urgency in his voice.

Bessie pointed towards the toilets. The policeman breathed in and took out his truncheon.

'Leave this to me,' Bobby stated and moved towards the toilet door.

Dingo entered with a gun in one hand and his holdall in the other. He pointed his gun at the young policeman. 'Back off, copper!' Dingo snarled, and edged into the room. 'All of you – back against the bar!' Dingo indicated with the gun.

'Put the gun down, you fool!' Bobby said, and bravely stepped towards Dingo.

'I'm arresting you on suspicion of murder ...!'

Doc screamed, 'No! Bobby, stay back!'

Dingo was distracted. The four locals all seemed to move at the same time. He tried to cover them all. Bessie ducked down behind the bar. Doc staggered from the push Bobby gave her, before he tried to grab Dingo's gun arm with his free hand.

In the commotion, Alfred dived to the nearest wall and snatched down a scythe. Dingo stepped aside to avoid Bobby's wildly swinging truncheon, and in the very same moment, Alfred made a low sweep with the scythe. Dingo screamed like a tortured animal. The long sharp blade cut through his trousers into the backs of his legs, slicing into his calves. The merciless scythe ripped through the muscles, and cracked shin bones, before glancing off and tearing a strip of flesh into a flap that hung with torn muscles. Blood from the hideous wound sprayed everywhere. Dingo's lean body was like a toppled tree, and he started to fall backwards. The gun in his hand went off, firing a bullet into the ceiling.

'I 'ave 'un! I 'ave 'un! I 'ave un!' Alfred shouted triumphantly, above Dingo's screams of agony.

Dingo's body crashed to the floor. He was still screaming. He fired the gun again without aiming, and the bullet tore a piece out of the front of the bar. Dingo was in agony. He knew it was a fight to the death and tried to stand. Bobby, the young policeman, grabbed hold of a handful of Dingo's hair and pulled his head back. Dingo was weakening quickly from the loss of blood, and the pain. His arms flayed about aimlessly. The gun dropped from his hand and fell to the floor. Dingo howled like a cornered beast that couldn't defend itself.

Bobby yanked Dingo's head back again. The vicious killer's neck went taut. It was taut long enough for Bessie to take aim. With all of her might, she made a sweeping blow with a razor sharp machete she had taken from behind the bar.

The one powerful blow, with a tool being used as a lethal weapon and wielded in total defensive anger by the Harvester landlady, was enough to sever Dingo's head from his twitching body. Blood spurted from the headless corpse like a fountain, covering the four attackers who descended on the body as one.

Bobby the policeman pulled clear, dragging Dingo's detached head with him.

Alfred shouted triumphantly again 'I 'ave 'un! I 'ave 'un! I 'ave 'un!' The blood-soaked women staggered to their feet.

'What 'ave 'ee?' they asked wearily in unison.

Bobby held the severed head at arm's length.

'A neck! A neck! A neck!' they all shouted.

*   *   *   *   *

Bessie and her three regular customers worked into the night cleaning the blood-stained bar. Dingo's body and severed head had been wrapped in tarpaulin and lay on the back seat of his car, still parked outside the front door of the The Harvester, with the young policeman's bike leaning against the car door.

Bessie filled four glasses with whisky and sat down with her exhausted customers around one of the tables.

'I need this!' Bessie raised her glass.

'Down the hatch,' Alfred replied, and emptied his glass.

'What are we going to do with the body?' Bessie asked.

Alfred stretched his arm across the table and put his hand on Bessie's hand.

'I'll push the car with the body in it down Bal Tor mine shaft before it gets light.'

'Will anybody ever find it?' Doc asked with a worried look on her face.

'No one ever found the other three cars and at least six bodies I've tipped down that shaft over the years.'

'Just make sure you're not seen from the road,' the young policeman added, to voice his concern.

'How much did you find in his pockets?' Doc asked turning to look at Bobby.

'Just over twenty quid,' Bobby replied. 'I gave it to Bessie for the Harvest fund.'

'Bloody hell!' exclaimed Doc. 'We forgot about his bag.'

'I'll get it,' Alfred stated.

He walked across the room. The bag must have got pushed into a dark corner, near the toilet door, during the activity earlier. Alfred picked up the holdall and walked back to the table. He placed the holdall on his chair and undid the zip.

'Bloody hell!' Alfred exclaimed, as he pulled out wads of £5 notes.

'He must have robbed that bookie before he murdered him,' Bobby remarked in an official-sounding police voice.

'Never mind that,' said Bessie with a smile, 'this looks like the best harvest we've ever had, and to top that, it's a winter harvest!'

'I'll drink to that,' Alfred chuckled.

They all raised their glasses and clinked them with the toast:

'Winter Harvest!'

Myrna Combellack

FAMILY

'Whites? You want the Whites? I d'knaw the bleddy Whites. Not much more you do wunna knaw 'bout the Whites … like fresh air, they do … oldest, craftiest bleddy antiques outside Trura museum.

I tell 'ee … after the las' war, 'Murrikuns pulled out … 'ansome 'uts, they 'ad … greet pianas brawke up, campbeds, chairs, all the bleddy lot went down the shafts … then after they done that they chucked the choppers down after um. Nothin' was bleddy left, time we lot got out there … bleddy Whites got there first … live out on the downs, see. Bin campin' f'r generations … don' notice rain an' wind … got leather skin, they 'ave. My fam'ly now, we wus pioneers … Klondike … Mexico … we wus there. But the bleddy Whites … gippos … common bleddy diddiguys, my hansome.'

He spat on the ground where he stood.

'Whites … lived under canvas … coupl'a waterproof clay sheets an' a singin' kettle. 'Appy? 'Appy as san'boys, 'r san'flies more like … dozens a kids … Lena, Sophie, Roma, Selina, Sonia … an' then there was Sam. They bleddy Whites got the bikes. 'Murrikuns got too tired when it come to the bikes. Whites said they'd do it for um. Don' knaw whose bleddy bikes they put down the shafts, but 'twasn' mine. Next thing, they got a caravan … bleddy greet rusty thing … still there on the downs. Put un behind a' ol' engine 'ouse f'r shelter. Smoke used t' rise from th' ol' stack on a summer's day. Men, standin' at the corner a the rawd used to look up at th' 'ill at un, like lookin' at starvation … bleddy gippos …

I brung up my fam'ly … better times … bus service thro' the village. Got work in the docks … walk four miles … walk four miles back … think nothin' of ut … french polishin' in th' evenins. Won a lot of prizes through the years with bantams … 'es … bantams … Scotch greys … my daughter Julie was born March 25th … same night as they Whites 'ad the boy Sam. Course, midwife come to we first, then went to she … ol' woman White, same night.

Never mixed with the village, I didn'. Village never mixed with the Whites … well you couldn'. When I 'ad ol' Key, the dog, I used t' goo up th' 'ill f'r a walk an' a bit of sport. Alwees came back that way, too. Never seen nobody 'roun' … one ur two of theys kiddies. Oldest one was what they do call "in care". They 'ad a lot of caravans be now … seemed t' collect the bleddy things …'ad 'em all in a circle like somebody wus gwoin attack 'em ur somethin'. All mixed up with slag an' earth, they was … washin' dryin' on the bare rock 'longside the rawd. Ess … we 'ad some fine dry days, they days. My wife use t'ave ol' Missus White 'ere sellin' clothes-pegs an' flowers an' whisperin'. I wish I never let she inside the door. Nothin'll graw on minin' land ... bleddy flowers don't graw on minin' land, thas f'r sure. One day my wife was dryin' clothes by the fire. "Gwoin t' Lunnun," she said, "gipsy said I was gwoin t' Lunnun." So she went. I wus s'mad ... I c'n remember now.., like 'twas yesterdee ... hollow, clear ride ... sharp new rawd ... the sound a the tyres of me bike grindin' up the 'ill to the bleddy gippos. I was feared t' let un go in case they pinch un fr'm under me eyes an' sell'n where I stood. S' bleddy mad, I was, I went right in the middle a they caravans ... greet circle a caravans ... jes shouted. No answer ... jes the crackin' a metal shrinkin' in the dark. Gippos.

They 'ad angers on, too ... people, you knaw, like themselves. Then they 'ad a lot of fights an' another lot come. I never knawed who wus there an' who wasn'. Not inner-ested. Other people was ... used t' spend their time thinkin' about ut. Not me ... not innerested. But see ... scrap metal was the thing ... scap metal ... dirty bleddy business an' fit f'r the Whites. Wouldn' think they Whites 'ad a 'ead f'r business. But there 'tis ... they got on in life ... started stringin' clotheslines between the caravans. Scrap metal ... they maids was 'ansome too. One night ... got up an' moved ... *all* the bleddy lot of um. Straight through the village in the middle a the night ... scrap metal an' all. Never made a soun'. Settled down beside the quarry ... more room ... less windy, see. Well ... settled down there. Bleddy cheek. Poor ol' Buddle used t' keep 'is motor-bike down there. "Aw Mr White," ee' said ... thas me ... I got the name ... no relation you unnerstan' ... "Aw Mr White, I'm in some trouble, but bugger that, bugger that, ol' bike can stay where 'ee is." Left un all down there, 'ee did ... tar-barrel garage, bike an' all.

Then I 'ad a bit of a tragedy. My daughter, Julie, fourteen year old ... never come back from dancin' class. Went down a shaft. When they brung 'er up, she was small as a baby. Nobody didn' knaw nothin'. But then, I used t' see somebody 'angin' 'roun' the 'ouse 'ere. Used t' stand in the porch of May Palminter's, opposite. All weathers ... used t' jes lean on the doorframe an' look in 'ere. Sam. I used t' feel 'im creepin' roun' the 'ouse. One Saturdee afternoon, I opened the back door quick an' stared the bugger straight in the eye. Jes stood there. Next day, Sundee, 'ee let 'isself down in the quarry on a rubber bed an' let th' air out. Didn' knaw 'ow t' swim.

Insurance men come roun'. Village gone mad all of a sudden f'r life insurance. Whites was insured f'r Sam ... fancy that ... Crafty Bleddy Whites. I never 'ad no bleddy insurance f'r Julie ... tidn' decent.

Next thing you knaw, they'm buildin' ... concrete sheds. wood 'uts ... an' a greet illiterate bleddy sign all in blue an' white ... WHITE'S BLEDDY CAR SPARES.

Missus alwees seem the same. Got a 'lectric cooker now ... you c'n see un through the winda a that fancy garden shed they do live in now. I do still see Mister in that yel-low mac some council workman left be'ind on the rawd ... bicyclin' roun' the lanes pickin' up bits an' pieces a things ... I don't nod to the bugger ... nobody do.'

Helen Dunmore

THE LIGHTHOUSE KEEPER'S WIFE

She'd gone. She hadn't waited for him.

Nancy always waited for him. She believed that there would always be a good reason if he was late. Not like his sister May. May thought disaster had come if she had to wait ten minutes for Jack to meet her outside the Stores. She'd look at her pocket-watch, glance up the street, shake her watch busily, as if it might not be working. May believed the worst, then drew it to herself. She'd had money since she married Jack, and she lived in town as she'd always wanted, but it made no difference.

He thought all those thoughts as he went up the stairs. There would have been time to live through a whole life while he climbed. He put his hand on the round curve of the plaster, as he always did. Its little prickling points were invisible to the eye, but he felt them. The door to the room was open and the room was full of sun. Fear prickled him, like the plaster. People had said Nancy would never stand the life, but she had stood it. She was everything he was not, light and graceful, laughing out of a crowd. She would stand with her sisters at the street corner, her skirts blowing, her face whipped with laughter. No one else could dream of belonging in that tight circle.

He loved to watch her. He would rather watch Nancy dancing than dance himself. He would sit very upright, his eyes sharp and distant, his body planted in the chair so that little by little the room felt its presence, and the girls would glance at him as they went by.

They said she would never stand the loneliness of the life, with him gone for his twenty-eight days' duty six times a year. He had moved her ten miles down the coast from her sisters. She'd slept with them every night of her life, she told him. Nancy and Liza together, Hester in the truckle, then Sarey in her cot-bed behind the door. She'd stared round their bedroom the first night they were married, and then she'd taken a run and a jump and landed in the middle of their big bed and let herself fall back with her arms wide, feeling all that space, laughing.

The bed was too big when she lay alone in it. He was an off-shore lighthouseman and she knew that when she married him. If the lighthouse tender couldn't land to change crew on relief day, Nancy might be waiting for him another week. Often the weather was bad when it came to changeover. He'd watch the wall of white foam crash against the glass and know he wasn't going to get off. But Nancy stood it. She had her little garden. She didn't flinch. She knew all the fishing boats and would stand to watch them go out around the point, her skirts blown back against her legs, moulded to them by the wind. He was glad there was no one else to see her like that. She fed her garden with fish-meal and rotted-down seaweed, and when salt-storms burnt off the leaves of her spinach and lettuces, she planted again. He would see her kneeling on the path, skirts bunched under her, tamping the seedlings in with her quick fingers.

Sometimes she would walk the ten miles to Carrack Cross to see her sisters, but she would never stay more than one night. When he asked her why, she shrugged and said, 'This is my life now.' He would watch her scrambling over the black, sharp rocks, picking mussels at low tide with her skirts kilted up. If she climbed the cliff he knew she could look westwards as far as the grey tumble of houses that was Carrack Cross. When she set off with her basket to pick blackberries or early mushrooms, he had to fight the fear that she would never come back home again, and that the prints of her stout black boots on the wet fields would be the last thing he would ever see of her.

Slowly, methodically, he would climb the lighthouse tower, towards the light, thinking of her. A mound of sea thudded against the tower, then fell back and weaselled at the foot of the rock, getting its strength. Nancy said she did not mind thinking of him in the lighthouse, no matter how bad the storms, but what she kept out of her thoughts was the moment when he was brought off the landing-platform, with the sea hungry for him and the lighthouse tender pitching. Sometimes the sight of it came into her mind at night, before she could push it away. It made her sick to think of it, she said, though he knew she could walk to the edge of the cliff and stand there without a moment's dizziness.

He was standing still, not on the steps of the lighthouse tower, but on his own staircase, at home, one hand on the plaster wall. He must go on up to her, where she was waiting for him.

She was there, as he'd known she would be. Her toes pointed up through the sheets and she looked like a child waiting to be kissed goodnight. They'd often thought of when Michael would be old enough to talk to them and have a story at bedtime. Would they teach him to say his night prayers? Nancy thought yes, Blaise no. He knew she already said a prayer over Michael when she put him in his cot. He had no faith in it himself, but believed there was no harm, if Nancy did it.

He stood in the doorway and stared at her toes, because he was afraid to follow the white sweep of her body up to her face. He had seen terrible things done to the faces of the dead, when the sea got them. Nothing must touch her eyebrows that flexed like two fine black wings when she laughed. Nothing must touch her mouth. He'd noticed her mouth before he noticed anything else about her.

The sunlight was strong. It made him blink. But those windows were dirty. It made you realize what had been blowing on to them all winter. All that salt. It had made a crust on the panes. He would clean them for her. She'd lain there and listened to the rain, all night long sometimes. She never told him that she lay awake, but he knew it from the way the skin under her eyes was dry and sunk with sleeplessness. It had been a dark, long winter, but now it was over.

'Winter's over.' She'd said that yesterday, hearing a scuffle of starlings in the roof-space. He'd wondered if he should smoke out the birds for her. Starlings were filthy things, full of mites. And then she'd said the sun was reaching higher on the wall opposite her bed.

'Look, it's up to that mark on the plaster now.'

She'd pointed. This was a world of her own, in this room. The rest had shrunk away from her, and she no longer asked about it, or even noticed the wood-anemones and celandines her sisters brought her, their stems packed into wet moss. The baby sounded far off, though he was only downstairs. These past two weeks she'd stopped asking for Michael. She couldn't hold him any more. Michael was too strong for her. He kicked, and she cried out. It was just weakness, she said, her lips white.

He'd unlaced his boots at the top of the stairs, ready. Now he took them off so there'd be no noise to trouble her. He went over to Nancy and touched her feet. The darn on the counterpane ran up the side of the little tent her body made. She had darned that darn. It was her own fine stitching. He might have watched her do it, but when? Suddenly he saw her, sitting opposite him through the evenings of his off-duty, her polished head moving just a little with each stab of her needle. She didn't look up. Didn't look at him.

He had his hand round her feet, holding them tight. Why hadn't they flopped to one side as they did when she relaxed into sleep? When she was deep into her sleep she seemed boneless. She turned away from him, one fist up to her face, dreaming into it.

The bottom stair creaked. Someone coming. There'd been people all the time since they sent Nancy home from the hospital, not able to do any more for her. Her sisters most of all. He put out his hand to fend them off but the next stair creaked, and the next. Someone was walking up, slowly, steadily. As quick as thought he crossed to the door and shut it. There was no bolt, just the latch. No key he could turn. He called out in a voice that was unfamiliar to him. 'Wait. I'll be down.'

There was no answer. Whoever it was stood still, then creaked away, heavily. Maybe it was the doctor. He flushed, alone behind the door, because of his incivility. The doctor was old. He knew Nancy. He didn't whisk in and out, he sat with her. He never left her without making sure that she would be able to hold down the pain until his next visit. You could never pay enough for treatment like that. Blaise would not let her suffer like they'd let her suffer on the ward. He had used up all the money Nancy'd begun to set aside for Michael when she first knew she was pregnant.

All his thoughts turned in him like a cloud of gulls, disturbed. He couldn't bear to let them settle. What if he looked at her again? Which way had they turned her head? Or did it lie as she had turned it?

She was lying with her face turned toward the window. He almost laughed in relief. After all his thinking, it was easy enough to look at her. What was she doing turned that way, instead of facing the door as she always did when she heard his tread on the stairs? He could see her now, up on her elbows in her white nightgown, with a rosy bruise of sleep on her face where she'd crushed it into the pillow.

But she was turned to the window. Maybe she didn't expect him. She couldn't hear how still the air was, or see how calm the water lay in the bay. In her dreams she thought he was still out at the lighthouse, waiting for the storm to be over so that he could be taken off. When the sea was calm she would always be there to meet him, on the exact day, at the exact hour. She'd have Michael on her hip, shading his eyes against the sun.

A noise burst from his throat. He stumbled back across the floor to her, and knelt at the side of her bed. Her hands were smooth at her sides, outside the bedclothes. Her face was white, but no paler than she'd been many other days. Nancy'd never had much colour even before she was ill. Her hair was a bit untidy on her forehead. So close, he could see tiny grey strands in it. He'd never noticed them before. She was only twenty-nine. In her family they went grey young, but it looked right on them, even youthful. All her sisters had those clear faces and large, beautiful eyes, but he couldn't see the beauty in any of them except her. It was strange to see them in ranks, staring out at you from a photograph. It made Nancy look less herself.

Her eyes were shut. Of course they would be. But he'd seen this closure before. This sunkenness, a gap left by something suddenly gone. Her lids didn't lie lightly over her eyes, cushioned by flowing blood. They seemed to stick to the round globes of her eyeballs. He put out a hand, but against her face it only showed how she had no colour, none at all. He cupped the side of her face. *She's not cold*, he thought triumphantly. Not cold at all. Let them get out of that. He glanced behind him but there was no one there. His breath came lumpily, as if he'd been running. He'd been a good runner, a fine runner once. No use now. She'd seen him pass them all in the men's eight-hundred-yard dash. She'd smiled then. Let them dare say that she was cold.

He felt her again. He snuggled her face against his hand. There was his thumb against her cheek. His thumb looked dirty, though he always scrubbed his hands before he came up to her. He was afraid of the way she felt now. Always before when he'd touched her, he'd believed he could feel her blood moving. Her blood ran faster and more brightly than other people's, and closer to the surface of her skin. She had bled a lot when Michael was born. They'd had to throw the mattress away, even though she'd wadded it with newspaper under her. Maybe she was ill then, before they knew it. Nancy might be pale but her fingers were warm in the coldest winter, and she never needed to wear gloves. Sometimes she'd put her hand in his pocket, while they were walking.

Her body lay like a basin of cooling water, neither cold nor hot. He bent over as if to kiss her cheek, but he did not touch her. He was afraid to make a dent in her flesh and see it stay there. Her lips were slightly parted and there was a bubble of saliva on the corner of her mouth. If she'd known it she'd have knocked it away quickly, before he saw it, with the back of her hand.

'Nancy,' he said, quietly, not to embarrass her, the way he'd once pointed out wordlessly that she had a splotch of blood on the back of her pink summer skirt. But she lay still.

From downstairs he heard the noise of a baby crying. Angry, frustrated crying. He listened for a minute before he realized that it was Michael. He'd have been trying to get into the cupboards again. He liked to bang the cups together and smash them. If Nancy'd been downstairs the baby wouldn't have cried. He remembered suddenly how he'd been in the kitchen once when Michael tried to stand against a kitchen chair, then he'd slipped and knocked the corner of his eye as he came down on to the floor. A splash of the baby's blood hit the cardinal-red tiles. It was only a little cut but it was deep. Before the baby knew he was hurt Nancy had swooped down and picked him up.

In a minute he was smiling, with a clean white handkerchief pressed over his eye. The cut stopped bleeding almost at once, but it left a mark, a thin white line over the eye. That mark was there now.

Downstairs the crying rose to a pitch. The baby would be bucking in the arms of the sister who was holding him, straining his head back and screaming, his face patched red with rage. Then he'd close in and bite, then cry again, frightened at what he'd done. He never used to be like this. Only since Nancy went away to the hospital.

'My wife,' he said aloud, staring at Nancy. It seemed a long time since he had said those words. They were as awkward now as they'd been those weeks after the wedding, when he'd had to shape his lips to it before he could say 'my wife' with an air of ease. And then from one day to the next he'd got used to it, and stopped saying it. He called her Nancy sometimes, but mostly 'you'. He'd said to her this morning, 'Will you be all right? I'm going now, to fetch you the Bengers Food.'

She needed building up. She could not take solid food, and that was what was weakening her. He had ordered the Bengers Food for her, and it would be delivered by Trelawny's cart, as far as New Hayle farm. It was only three miles to walk. He would be back before she knew it.

And she'd said 'Yes', without smiling, not seeming to pay much attention to him or what was said. He knew she was dull from the stuff the doctor had given her. He hated it, but he knew it was better for her that way. So that was it, he thought now in amazement. That was her last word to me. That flat 'Yes', about nothing at all.

Tim Saunders

BLUE MURDER

The Bards meet in the face of the sun, the eye of the day. And in the face of the sun, the eye of the day, a bullet will set out on its journey. The men and women in blue robes gather in the Bardic Circle. This year, it's in Truro's lovely old piazza. Three times the Grand Bard, Map Mordarth, asks if there is peace. His name means 'Son of Surf'. He bestrides the Logan Stone as if he were curving in towards Fistral Beach. His day job is in an accountant's office.

Three times the Bards and the vast crowd answer 'Peace!' The Horner, suave jazz saxophonist Gwas Bylk, makes the four corners of Cornwall ring. The Herald Bard, fiery petite Guhyen, calls those quarters to order. Celtic delegates greet and are greeted, each in their own language. The crowd waits, breathless, for the heart of the ceremony. Only one watcher knows that a heart will stop.

The Lyonesse Crystal Cup goes to the year's most beautiful new poem in Cornish. Some say the cup was made by Merlin himself. Some say the cup is the Holy Grail. Some say you'll gain immortal life if you drink dry whites from it on Saint Piran's Day.

How do you versify your way to immortality? Write a poem, and sign it with a pen-name. Put your real name and address in an envelope, seal it, and write your pen-name on the outside.

When the Bardic High Council choose the winner, they don't know who wrote what. No bias. No sweat. At the Gorseth, the Grand Bard calls for the winner by their pen-name. Map Mordarth asks 'Trepollpen' to come forward. The crowd falls silent. Thousands of poetry fanatics hold their breath. Will the Bodmin Boy make a Triple Crown of it? Will the so-called Free Bards try it on from their base in Scilly?

Then the thousands gasp as one. A tall, blue-robed figure strides into the middle of the Circle. A hubbub of astonishment surges through the crowd as they recognise the triumphant Bard. Excitement explodes into hysteria as the tall Bard approaches the Logan Stone. He bows smugly to the Grand Bard. The murmur explodes into a roar.

A Bard's heart is a subtle thing, full of visions. A bullet is a subtle thing, finely machined from lead and alloys. They meet. They debate for a millisecond or two. The heart concedes that the bullet has the better argument. Ten thousand throats shriek with astonishment as the winning Bard crumples into a crumpled blue heap.

Map Mordarth wishes he hadn't asked about peace. The Bards want new answers. The shocked officers of Truro Metropolitan Police Department want answers.

Bardic paramedics, their wipe-clean green robes swirling, rush to the crumpled blue heap. They tap, prod, and tweak. They identify the deceased as Trellis Lambswool Unwin, the Bard Cos Kelyn. Life is found to be extinct.

'Stand back, you sillies,' barks burly Commissioner O'Rowse, chief of TMPD, 'or I'll ban ice-cream for a week.'

He waves his arms. He barks orders. His men bark at the crowd. They throw a cordon round the corpse. And round the Bards. And themselves.

'Nobody move!' barks the Commissioner. 'You're all suspects. You're very, very silly suspects indeed.'

'Chieth, the nurderer nay ge getting ayay yhile ye're all stood yere like lenons.' Superintendent Hamilton Jenkin speaks without moving his lips. You need to if you want to get on in the TMPD.

'Arrest anybody who moves!' barks the Commissioner.

'Tan ye nove to nake the arrest, Chieth?' Inwardly, Jenkin sighs. The Commissioners's approach to routine policing can make helping old ladies over the road more complicated than a gig race in a Force 6. When Jenkin retires, he will set up as a ventriloquist.

'You're such a fool, Jenkin,' O'Rowse groans. 'Nick him, you morons.'

Nobody moves. Nobody nicks anybody. O'Rowse throws his hat on the ground and jumps up and down on it. He yanks Map Mordarth off the Logan Stone and drags him over to the corpse. His mirror-bright toecap prods the expired Bard.

'One of you fatuous Druidical fellows did this. You're all under arrest.'

'Hold it, O'Rowse.'

A heavy hand clamps down on the Chief's beefy shoulder. 'You'm outside your jurisdiction, boy.'

The Bards grin. The TMPD men try not to grin, as a bleary-eyed Bard in the most crumpled Bardic gown ever emerges from a hatch in the Logan Stone and waves a Bardic warrant card at the Commissioner.

'Galar's the Bardic name,' he says. 'Galar Pen.'

'Galar Pen?' Commissioner O'Rowse scratches his head. 'That means "Headache", doesn't it?'

'Don't ask.'

The weary, unshaven Bard shows his badge. The triple-sunbeam of the Gorseth gleams like a robot's exudate.

'I'm the Keeper of the Mistletoe.'

'Not …' O'Rowse turns paler than a bottle of Tippex in a Hayle care home.

'Not …the Keeper of the Mistletoe.'

'Yes, sure enough,' gloats the Grand Bard. 'I have the pleasure of introducing the Keeper of the Mistletoe – in other words, Head of the Gorseth Security Service.'

The Keeper of the Mistletoe, in fact, constitutes the entire security service of the Gorseth in himself. This can render life complicated. Galar Pen scans the crowd, trying to remember why his Bardic robe is inside out and why his left hand has turned green and his right has turned purple. He looks at the Redruth boogie-woogie man in a mauve jump-suit, the chubby spiritualist in camouflage trousers, the identical triplets in Cornish Duck-Hunting Tartan, the old lady in Dolly Pentreath costume and biker boots, the woad-wearing Hevva-crier, the jug-eared saffron-gatherer …

'Biker boots!'

Galar Pen whirls round, but the old lady and her basket of fish has disappeared. 'Which way did she go?'

'Up Lemon Street,' splutters an innocent bystander. 'I think. Or not. Which way did who go anyway?'

'What about searching the body for clues?' Guhyen's voice is drowned in the roar of a 12-cylinder Harvey-Davidstow engine as Galar Pen leaps astride his official Bardbike. Bards and bystanders alike leap aside as the Bardbike screams out of the elegant Piazza and up the hill. Galar Pen is half-way to Saint Agnes before he wonders whether, well, whether today was worth the effort.

He stops the bike, ducks his head in a stream a few times, and wonders why he's wearing odd shoes. Then he turns round and drives back to Truro. He's almost there when he sees a handsome maid with a cat-carrier trying to hitch a lift. A bit of a cat person himself, Galar Pen slows and pulls over.

'Going far, are ee?' he asks in a polite tone that would have made his Granny proud.

'He's a very fine cat indeed,' says the young woman in a voice that would charm a restaurant critic. 'His last owner took him to the vet. I'm taking him back to have it undone. Or done. Or whatever 'tis I mean. Come and see.'

Galar Pen gets off to view this fine feline, although later he can't recall why. What he will remember, though, is just happening to notice that the girl is wearing biker boots. Then it all goes blank.

It's a very sad security Bard who reports to the Bardic Council that evening. He started off with a handsome murder, made Commissioner O'Rowse stamp his tiny foot and burst into tears, and lost the only suspect. He's also lost the Bardbike.

'It's bad enough the so-called Free Gorseth threatening to wipe us all out,' moans the Grand Bard.

'They haven't done yet, though,' squeaks Galar Pen. 'They'm still out on Scilly.'

'No thanks to you!' booms the Deputy Grand Bard.

Galar Pen wishes he wouldn't do that.

'And thanks to your blundering, Bardic stocks have fallen 15.5 eurobezants. What is the point of you, boy?'

'We'll decide that after 48 hours.' The Grand Bard doesn't know the Deputy Grand Bard is toying with the idea of a Bardic coup. It wouldn't surprise him, though. 'That's how long you've got to solve this filthy foul murder.'

Lemon Street at night is the wrong place for a man tired of his own company. The prosperous ranchers from Blisland and Stithians show off their mink-coated wives here. Tanker captains from Bude and Gorran Haven spend the profits of entire voyages here. Hard-nosed oilmen from Trematon and Mount Hawke come here to get a bit of kulcha in the sophisticated nightclubs and the avant-garde theatres.

And there are the girls – gorgeous, deliciously arrogant creatures whose cast-offs will be snapped up next week by designers in Paris, Milan and New York. If they cry into a lace handkerchief, your heart warms like Hayle Power Station. If they smile, your heart shatters. And one of them watches Galar Pen as he stumbles into Dolly's Dive in the shadow of the neon-lit Lander Memorial. And as he slumps up to the bar, she slides on to the stool by him.

'Mine's a Pilchard's Neck,' she murmurs, 'with ice.'

Galar is a thinking in terms of a double Alka-seltzer, with a Ribena chaser. A swift and painless death would be an acceptable alternative. Rich the bartender grins, his saffron-dyed moustache glinting in the soft lighting.

'The lady wants a Pilchard's Neck with ice.'

Rich's gleaming pate looks wider than Mount's Bay at high tide.

'What's yours, me handsome? Bacardi Benjamin? Poncemeor Julep? *Cointreau a la crème de Rodda*? Zephaniah Zuzube?'

'He'll have a double Alka-seltzer.' As well as being a mind-reader, the lady has a familiar voice. 'And pour a Ribena chaser.'

Old crone, cat lady, nightclub siren – Galar Pen's got every right to be surprised.

'Make that a treble Alka-seltzer.' Her voice is even lower and sweeter and more familiar. 'And I'm paying.'

'No you bain't ma'am, if you please.'

Galar Pen scrabbles in his kevlar Bardsporran and slaps a few dynars on the counter. 'Tidden fitty for a lady to disburse funds for her own refreshment.'

'I'm no lady,' she murmurs, and the coins clink back into Galar's Bardsporran. Galar's head swims as she guides him to an alcove. A band somewhere is playing numbers from *West Downs Story*.

'And I'm not quite a gentleman.'

He manages to swivel his head g-e-n-t-l-y. Take away the golden cascade of hair brushing her shoulders, add Ordnance Survey-type wrinkles to the warm, smooth skin, wrap a shawl and a Demelza-style frock round the silk top and designer jeans. The biker boots are a giveaway, of course. So what's her game?'

'So what's my game, that's what you're wondering.' She guides him into his seat, and hands a Didymus Bank credit note to a waitress in a Bal Maiden micro-dress. 'Keep the change.'

'Tidden fitty to be reading a man's mind all the time.' Galar begins to wish he'd joined the Pan-Cornubian Naval Service so he could spend his time trying to catch Free Gorseth speedboats trying to implement amphibious Bardic ceremonies in the coves of Penwith. He sips his drink. *Le Nouveau Paraquat* est arrivé. It will do him good. His head will stop aching. He will keep his job. 'You want to apologise.'

'Now who's reading minds? But yes, I'm going to apologise. But they were right behind me. I had to get away. You were my only hope.'

'Who were right behind you?' Why doesn't he just make an arrest, and go back to bed?

'They know I've found out how they did it.'

'Who did what?' His tongue feels like a carpet off-cut. 'If …'

'The people who – oh no! quick, it's him – quick, under the table.'

'It's who?' What's he doing under the table? Galar can put up no resistance as the Dolly-Pentreath/Bikerette shoves his drink into his hand. But he squeaks as she forces him under the table. 'Look, Miss, it's –'

'Shut up!' she hisses, as the upper world disappears from his view. Suddenly, her voice is high and relentlessly jolly. 'Tesen Gales, darling, how wonderful to see you.'

'Desidora, baby.'

A diminutive pair of boots swims out of the shadows. They are unmistakably Bardboots, scaled down. Above them rises no Bardic robe, but neatly-rolled yellow socks and a pair of hairy legs.

'I got your message. How –'

'Tesen Gales, sweetie, I've got you the stuff. Now, Tesen Gales, you naughty boy.'

A shapely biker's boot is kicking Galar Pen into a corner. He scrunches himself into a wretched bundle under the seat. He finds his nose squashed into the front page of yesterday's *Kerrier Morning Advertiser*. A picture of a squad in shorts and baseball caps accompanies the headline 'Free Bards Regroup'. The mysterious triple-personality woman – crone, biker, nightclub habitué – is talking to the new arrival.

'You must come and sit by me.'

'Desidora, can't you call me just Tesen?' The Bard's feet don't quite touch the floor. 'I knew you'd be there for me.'

'I always am … Tesen. When I saw that little advertisement for Montacute's Cattle Cake on the Advertiser, I just knew.'

'You've saved my bacon, Desidora.' The teeny Bardic bottom shuffles up closer to the geometrically elegant configuration of the Lason-Straze designer jeans. 'What'd I do without you?'

'I bet you say that to all the Muses.'

'No, no, Desidora, you're the only one.' A nail-bitten hand reaches into a camou-flaged Bardsporran and pulls out a thick brown envelope. 'And the … stuff?'

'Isn't it a bit more than stuff?' The low, soft voice quivers as a smooth hand reaches into the Praah handbag and draws out a gold-sealed envelope.

'Oh yes, oh yes, so 'tis!' Tesen Gales' ankles lock tight together. 'This is the genuine honey-smooth Bardic nectar, so to speak.'

'To speak?' Her voice raises a semi-tone or two.

'So to recite, Desidora, so to declaim, so to … sing in perfect ecstasy.'

Galar knows he's heard that voice before. The blurred memory of a noisy evening up to Launceston flits across his memory. Last year, yes, when he was investigating that cross-border traffic in unlicensed hooklines.

'That's *much* better, sweetie-pasty.' Her voice is smooth again. 'Just a moment, I must powder my eyebrows.'

'Eyebrows?' The little Bard's voice shoots up a squeak. Yes, it was that gig in Coppinger's Dive, when a mistimed raid by Launceston Vice Squad ruined weeks of effort.

Tesen's feet flail in agitation. Galar Pen tortures himself round under the cross seat for fear of having his teeth kicked out.

Yes, that farce in Launceston. He remembers reaching the Gents just as Tesen Gales climbed out the back

Five minutes, ten minutes, she's not coming back. Galar Pen wonders if he can hold out. If only –

'Tesen Gales, as I live and breathe,' booms a big red voice. A pair of Gurney shoes topped by Altarnun designer slacks appears at the end of the alcove table. 'Mind if I join you?'

'Join me?' Tesen's voice shoots up an octave.

'Me join?' Join? Me? Me join? Yes – join! Me, that is.'

'I see that your glass is empty, you splendid old Bardic person.' Galar Pen hears the snap of a huge forefinger and thumb as the newcomer sits down.

'But I'm some glad I ran into you, my dear sweet Bard, because I'm in the process of putting my books in order.'

'Got enough room on your shelves, haaaaaaave –' Tesen Gales' voice shoots up even higher and evaporates. Galar Pen watches his feet twitching in agitation.

'My account books.'

This other voice is soft, and full of silky menace. The elegantly-tapering limbs of the waitress glide into view, the hem of her Bal Maiden micro-dress just visible beneath the edge of the table.

'What's your poison, my fine Druidical polymath?'

'Swift and painless, ah, ah, no, joke, joke, well since you are so kind –'

'You'll have an *Original Famous Chough* with ice. And mine's a double *Redruth Boogiewoogie.*'

The waitress clicks away as Galar Pen wonders whether he might just resign now, crawl out, apologise to the two men, and go home. But then … the newcomer has legs like tree trunks.

'A rouble Dedbuth Roogiewoogie.' Tesen's voice is as bright as a canteen of cutlery in a wedding at Crackington. 'Handsome. Nery vice. Joper prob. Yes.'

'And we can discuss your arrangements for paying your saffron bills, my delightful Bardic comrade in arms. I've had a hard day – the Gorseth security service is still breathing I'm led to believe, and I take that as a personal affront. The sooner the Free Gorseth takes over, the better.'

Galar's an obliging sort of fellow, so he tries to stop breathing for a bit. No, it's a habit he won't manage to get out of for a bit. But he's tired, so *very* tired, and his eyelids have discovered a mysterious, quasi-magical attraction for one another. All this rushing about is catching up with him. Bards, bullets, balloon tyres, exotic blondes, extraneous ballads, aching bones, brainwaves, it's all too, *too* much.

It's dark. It's quiet, too, apart from the ticking of a grandmother clock and the screaming of his joints and his muscles. This chorus makes the Redruth supporters sound like a string quartet at Saint Endellion. The clock has ticked a whole bucketful of tocks before he's managed to crawl out from under the seat. It's tocked a whole bucketful of ticks by the time he's reached the window. The window, apparently, is alarmed. Is it, now? Nothing as alarmed as it'll be if he has to throw this chair through it. The window keeps mum, not the slightest bit alarmed, as Galar unlatches it. It keeps mum, dad, and the darling kiddies as he gracefully falls out on to the pavement. It slides shut again, knowing what's good for it, as Galar staggers away. Galar Pen wonders if it mightn't be time to wake up again. Getting out alive must have been a dream. But his muscles, joints, and odd squelchy bits he hadn't realized were there assure him that he's awake. This is no dream. And that is his Bardbike, standing demurely at the kerb and sporting a TMPD ticket. This is a jurisdictional outrage. Any other time, he'd have Commissioner O'Rowse grovelling. Bardvehicles are exempt, but a Bardbike is as good a place as any to recover from too much reality. Carpeting the Commissioner can wait. Galar drags himself on to his lovely, welcoming Bardbike. He cushions his head on his arms as he slumps over the handlebars. Ah, what joy to be one of the Bardic Bards of the Barded land of Kernow.

'Wake up!'

Why is the entire cosmos rocking and shaking?

'Galar Pen, you Bardic bonehead, wake up this very instant!'

So he does, especially as a pair of slender arms are wrapping themselves gently round him. An agreeably warm personage seems to have seated itself on the pillion

'Now then, you handsome great hunk of Bardhood.'

Galar knows that voice, so he does.

'You're going to shake your head twice, switch on the engine, shake your head thrice, kick away the stand, and drive off.'

'Am I?'

He is. He does. Desidora yells directions into Galar's ears as he roars down Lemon Street. He weaves through the cultural quarter, dodging the rush of taxis outside the theatres. This time, he's travelling westwards, but he's not going west. Grimacing at such a 70s rock-journalist turn of phrase, he lets the mystery woman direct him over the border and into Penwith. They stop for petrol and a pit-stop, both literal and figurative, at Long Rock. While a sleepy mechanic tweaks various bits of the Bardbike, Desi slips into the Ladies.

'Handsome maid,' observes the semi-somnolent mechanic.

'Handsome enough.' Galar hears himself sounding smug. 'If you like that kind of thing.' Which he does.

'Sure enough.' The mechanic bends down to the rear wheel. 'Check your tyres?'

'Why not?'

Yes, why not? Why not go zooming off into the night with a handsome maid? Why not brush up on lepidoptera, attend beetle drives, take up the controversial Dip & Sigh Diet? Why not, why not, why on Earth, on Mars, on Alpha Centauri? It dawns on Galar that the mechanic's jaw is dropping. It's dropping so far it'll hit the concrete soon. The fellow's eyes are the size of beer mats. Galar Pen follows the direction of his gaze.

'You'll have to dress.'

'I am dressed.' Galar looks down to check, though. His voice seems to be coming from somewhere else. 'But ... not *properly* dressed.'

Dressed. So she is. Yards and yards of sheer magical mist hover round her, rippling in the moonlight as she glides over the forecourt. Her hair is a copper waterfall splashed into gold. The softly-sheened pearls round her neck, the subdued sparkling of emeralds at her ears, the modest dusting of diamonds in her hair, seem almost irrelevant in comparison. Almost, that is.

'You'll find a few odds and ends in the panniers.'

Penzance is two towns. To be more precise, it's three towns. Or four. Depends on your angle. But if you find yourself in the exclusive Heamoor quarter, with its tree-lined avenues, elegant squares, statues, marble fountains, and high-walled mansions, then it's one town. Heamoor is the only Penzance that matters. And the Heamoor Opera Festival is the height of the Penwith social calendar. The great, the good, and the Very Wonderful stroll, smile, bow, kiss – mwah! mwah! – stroll again. Sip, nibble chat, wave – yoohoo, Montague Dahling! Oh look, there's His Imperial Majesty Napoleon IV – what a whirl, what a delight. The musicians scrape, puff, strike and tinkle away in their orchestra pit, dug into the lawn in Daniel Square. There are some singers on the stage, dressed up in silly clothes and wishing they were in Port Stanley. They think of the cheque that will not be in the post, because the Master of the Revels will pay them in cash. One day, they will have an intelligent and appreciative audience. But not today. To the assembled social climbers, music is just wallpaper. That's why the lead tenor nearly undergoes an infarct when he notices that somebody is listening.

Giuseppe Verdi's *Doride* doesn't often get an airing nowadays. Its tale of a simple peasant girl who, with the aid of her fairy godfather, becomes princess of the legendary land of Cornovaglia, is too incredible for today's sophisticated tastes. The lead tenor is singing Bertoldo, who's been dying for most of Act 3, from unrequited love for Doride. He will die of a broken heart, and return from the grave to find that the wicked enchanter Biscotto plans to turn her into a butterfly. She will, but that is for Act 5. The chorus of Vaporetto captains will swell their tune, the singers glance round, wondering wherefore the silence. The conductor recovers, frozen with shock as the chorus slips out through the gaps in the scenery. He keeps the orchestra trilling away on that top chord. Trill, trill, trill. The crowd carries on swirling round – mwah! mwah! Dahling! – and keeps smiling. The lead tenor remembers who he is, where he is, and who he's pretending to be. The conductor semaphores furiously, and launches into the aria *Ohimè! Che purgazione linguistica!* He gathers speed, the orchestra catches up with him, and soon the orchestra and the remaining cast are zipping through the rest of Act 3 at four times the tempo. The beautiful lady nods, and leads her companion off in the direction of the nearest refreshment tent.

The refreshment tent is cool and spacious, like the mind of a Regional Assembly member. It is also elegant, lit by high glowing globes round which moths biff and baff and buffet. They'd prefer to be somewhere else, nibbling mulberry leaves or avoiding choughs. But destiny calls. This is a romantic scene. Moths are required. A moth's got to do, etc. Flit, flit. How do, fellow-moth? Biff, baff. Not so bad. Buffet, buffet, flit, flap, hey, mind your left wing … too late. Looking from moth-level, you see a loose pattern of colour where ladies and gentlemen cluster round tables. And in one corner, there is a great splash of blue where Bards gather. And around the edges, in the shadows, you notice a line of Vaporetto captains. Of course, if you were a bright moth, you'd have noticed the hungry sparrow that's found its way into the tent. This sparrow has flown all the way from Essex, and it's ravenous. But you have the compensation of knowing that your last moments afforded you a moth's-eye view of the Duchy's finest.

'Gentlemen.' Desidora's gaze sweeps over the assembled geniuses. 'And Ladies. Oh yes, Ladies. Permit me to introduce my research assistant.'

'Research assistant.' Galar Pen's voice springs from somewhere, and he's not sure where. In fact, he's not sure of anything. He knows these Bards. The Bards know him. Why doesn't anybody say anything? Why doesn't he? Is it because he's dressed in a fox doctor's parka?

'Dear lady, let me offer you a seat.' Fiery little Mars Malow, defender of flower beds and railway halts, leaps to his feet. He beckons to a waiter, flaps his arms, grimaces. 'You shall have refreshment, you shall have every attention.'

'Every attention.' Galar Pen takes his station behind Desidora as she settles gracefully into a sedentary posture. He knows that none of this will make any sense. He won't even try to understand.

'You'm all some kind,' she coos, 'accepting my little invitation.'

'Little invitation,' Galar hears himself say.

'Well, it read "I know everything. Be there or else. A Friend".' Pen Hicka speaks in his deep, gravelly, singing-the-blues voice. Desidora ignores that last tasteless remark, and smiles gracefully as she accepts a bubbling glass of Bolingey '78. Her head turns a little, and Galar senses her gaze on him. Perhaps he'll tell his voice to go back whence it came and stay there.

'We'm a little family – well, a family, now, aren't we? How many years' most poetic Bards have we got here?'

'An average of 163,712, Most Gracious Lady.' Small, chirpy Dywedhor an Yst bounces up and rattles out his statistic.

'This makes allowance for multiple winners counter-calibrated in parallel, with reallocation of runners-up as cross-compensated miniature variables. We've also preterselected for all winners of the Lyrical Ballad category who've gone to the Great Bardic Circle in the Sky, older Epigrammists who're indisposed, Pons-A-Bowt who's in traction after performing one of his performance poems too performingly, and –'

'And,' Desidora smiles sweetly enough to ice an entire wedding cake. 'We'm one down.'

'We'm one down,' chorus the Bards and their Ladies, the Bardesses and their Gentlemen, and all other possible permutations.

'Some of us are well down anyway.' Her radiant gaze falls on Tesen Gales, trying too hard to look inconspicuous behind a glorious display of exotic grigglans. 'But being low in altitude doesn't mean a Bard's going to be low in poetic ambition. The opposite, if anything. Am I right, delicious little Bardikins. Or … am I right?'

'Both!' Tesen Gales' voice comes out like a bat squeak with extra vibrato. 'I'm already big in Ladock, Lanyon, and Launceston. This time next week I'll be big in Amalveor, Arwennack and Altarnun. I may be inaltitudinous, but my ambitions are sky-high.'

'Doesn't it inspire you?' Desidora's gaze sweeps over to the Bardic crowd. 'And some of you need inspiration, so you do. One or two of you can be very hard work indeed. Carer Vavrogow Byghan, my lovely boy, where are you?'

'Prescient and contexted, O Muse of Fire.' A very tall, very thin Bard in wraparound Dame Edna-style shades unwinds himself somewhere towards the back of the of the crowd. By the time he's finished standing up, he seems to stretch almost halfway up the nearest tent-pole. His voice is thin and reedy. 'And grateful, deeply grateful, more than grateful.'

'More. Than. Grate. Ful.' Desidora sighs. When she sighs, all but one of the few surviving moths are so whelmed over by melancholy that they faint. Over the next few seconds, they plop into wine glasses, teacups, and Bardic drinking horns. 'How long did it take me to coax that prize-winning epic on the love life of Henny Jenner out of your bubbling Bardic brain?'

'It took …' The elevated Bard seems to have lost two or three feet of his height. '… six weeks.'

You are a moth. You are, in fact, the sole surviving moth in the refreshment tent. You know you haven't got long. You're not going for that old moth trope of flying into flames. But you can see three hungry choughs circling amongst the ropes and pegs and pins and cables at the top of the tent. Any moment now, one of them will spot you.

As moths go, you are a film buff. You're a great fan of John Wayne and the 'Hell-I-will-gotta-do' school of cinematography. You think of *The Sands of Iwo Jima*, and decide to take one with you. You flit upward into the light, do several barrel rolls, and loop several loops.

A flurry above, and hungry choughs are diving towards you. Throttle back, an upward glance to make sure they're still with you, then full ahead at the central tent pole. They'll impact between eight and thirteen seconds after you.

You are a puff of wind. You have wandered the breadth of the Atlantic. On your way, you filled the sail of a round-the-world yachtswoman. She shouted several words to you you hadn't heard before because she was trying to sail the other way. You weren't going to hang around where you weren't appreciated, so onwards you blew. You found a cruise liner, where an unhappy man was trying to clear litter from the deck. You helped him by blowing it all overboard. The 'litter' was, in fact, his definitive epic poem. It treated of certain aspects of life, particular regions of the universe, and almost everything. This was the masterpiece that would establish him as the greatest living poet in his language. Now he cannot even remember what that language is. But now you've seen a cluster of huge tents and pavilions.

You are a chough. Being a fully-fledged national icon is a hard life for an avian. Standing perfectly still on badges, buttons, flags, coats of arms, and book covers takes it out of a bird. Still, you get a good adventure flight now and then. Eeeaoww! Zoomm! Whoosshh! Digging up a lawn is fun, too. Peck, peck. Spling. Splong. Splatter. It's also fun to terrorise the odd moth. There he goes, over by that lamp in the big tent. Flitter, flitter. Glitter, glitter. Go on, get him! Whoosh! You are *most* put out to be tangled up in some guy ropes inside the top of the tent. Your friends are no help at all. Where are they when you need them? Exactly. So you struggle, flap, flail, and struggle again. A small shiny metal thing goes ping! It tumbles, sparkling by on its way downwards. You struggle some more. Struggle, struggle. A couple more sparkly little couplings and fastenings uncouple and unfasten. Why is everything shaking? Why are all these huge canvas sheets starting to flap?

'Unbearable, I tell you, *unbearable.*' Desidora snaps her fingers. Out of the shadows step serried ranks of Vapoetto captains. They whip off their boatcloaks and their nautical hats, and are transformed into a company of men in Royal Blue shirts and shorts, bezant-yellow baseball caps, and black-and-white ski masks. It occurs to Galar Pen that something small, round and hollow is resting against his spine, about halfway up. Or down. There are several issues to be considered here. First of all, these desperate villains are obviously the so-called Free Gorseth, who've established a reign of poetic terror in Scilly. You might have guessed that *they* were involved in the Bardic murder. After all, they were behind the Great Morwenstow Cheese Heist, the Downderry Counterfeit Tartan Scandal, the Herbal Pasty Quota-Hopping Affaire and the Camborne Architectural Feature Swap. Yes, you might have guessed. But you'd have needed to be a bit brighter. The next problem is that one of the self-styled Free Bards may be toying with the idea of bringing Galar Pen's earthly existence to an end. On reflection, this may in fact be the first problem.

The third problem is that Tesen Gales is rising from his place. He hurries over to Desidora, and bows low before her. She gives him a gracious little nod. He blushes, and rips off his Bardic headdress, and with a twonngg! of tuneful vibration the peak of a baseball cap thrusts itself forward. Grinning wolfishly, he tears off his gown to reveal the shirt and shorts of a Free Bard. The Grand Bard's jaw drops. The Deputy Grand Bard's jaw drops. The jaws of past Grand Bards, the Sword-Bearer, the Harpist, the Piper, the Mistress of the Robes, the Crimper of the Pasties, the Saffroner of the Buns, the Lady of the Flowers, the Attendants of the Lady of the Flowers, the Flower Girls, the Flower Boys, the Shakers of the Cocktails, the Movers of the Motions, the Lighters of the Lamps, the Feeders of the Cats, yes, all their jaws drop, drop, drop.

Galar Pen is feeling even more occipitally dolorous than usual. It occurs to him that Desidora is no longer standing anywhere near him. She has, in fact, joined Tesen Gales over with the Free Bards.

'I'm sorry about this, Galar, my dearest Galliepoos.' Her head tilts engagingly, appealingly, delightfully. 'I did my best to throw you off the scent, so I did.'

'But the scent was too divine, Desi, Desidora, what should I call you?' Galar decides that he doesn't greatly care for the smooth, simultaneous way in which the Free Bards are raising their weapons. It's all too much like lion-taming to be altogether nice, and too much like synchronised swimming to be interesting.

'You should call her "Divine One", you nasty little heap of wombat's doo-doos,' snarls Tesen Gales. 'And you should call me "Towering Genius" because that's what everybody will call me after tonight. Everybody, do you hear. *Everybody!*'

'Glowering Tedious?' Yes. Exactly. Galar notices that his tongue is taking its own view of what sounds it might enunciate. 'Glamorous Teetering? Yes.'

The quasi-divine being is changing, and so is her shimmering, shifting, shapely appearance.

'Early this morning, my dear little Tessiekins set up a clockwork-operated Angove and Nossew in the helmet of King Montague IV's equestrian statue in the Piazza. It was trained on the exact spot where the prize Bard would go up to collect his prize. The Gorseth ceremony runs like clockwork, and the gun would go off at precisely the right moment. Bard and bullet would arrive at the same spot before the Logan Stone at exactly the same time. That was the signal for the Free Bards to mobilise ... and Act!'

'ACT!' they cry.

'I will be Empress of all the Cornwalls. There will be no muse but me.' She seems to have slipped into something more comfortable, a sort of coronation robe combined with a crystalline diving suit. Her hair is flickering brightly like ethereal flames, rippling through every shade from Letterbox Red to Sunflower-Seed Spread Yellow. 'And this lovely, loving, loveable Free Bard will be my favourite, my acolyte, my Potemkin.'

'They'll name of battleship after me.' Tesen nods his baseball cap vigorously. His eyes are bright with the burning light of a hundred bright horizons. 'Her Imperial Majesty will walk Her realms, from Hugh Town up to Launceston, from Penryn to Morwenstow, declaiming the divine verses that She will inspire me to compose.'

'That I will compose through you, Tesen,' snaps the fair Goddess of Song. 'It's not too late for you to be chewed up and spat out, remember.'

'That you will compose through me.' Tesen goes pale and corrects himself in a quavering voice. 'No longer will I merely rhyme and scan. You will rhyme and chime, scan and span through me.'

'I am the fellow-poet of all poets,' chants the Muse, drawing herself up to greater and greater heights.

'She is the fellow-poet,' chants Tesen.

'She is, she is,' chant the Free Bards.

'I am tired of lurking in the background.'

'She is tired,' responds Tesen.

'She is, she is,' trill the Bards.

'There is only so much legalized metaplasm that a tutelary deity can take. I am Inspiration. I am Beauty. I am Niceness.'

'She is Niceness.' Tesen's voice is like the pipe of a great cathedral organ.

'Nicenes-s-s-s,' flows the simpering chorus.

'Yes, I am Song.' Her voice is mutating into the Fifth State. 'I am Verse. I am the Walrus. Koo-koo-ka–'

'Is this death?' muses Galar Pen as the thick whiteness enfolds him. The enveloping thicknesses are wrapping round him, drawing him down. The feeling in his outer extremities is confused and confusing. He seems to be smothering in this thick draping heaviness. It is just like a thick, weighty fabric, he reflects, as consciousness drifts away. It is, as it happens, a thick, weighty fabric. There are muffled voices, there are aches and pains, flashing lights, itching, scratching, bumping and whistling. Galar Pen gathers that people are stumbling over him, prodding, pushing, and one or two are even cutting him free.

As the dashing lads of Penzance's gallant Fire Brigade lift him up and hand him over to the dedicated lads of Penzance's equally gallant Ambulance Service, who carry him off to their state-of-the-art Saffron II ambulance, Galar tries to remember why there are acres and acres of canvas here. Why are entire squadrons of ambulances nosing around? Why are officers and men of the Cornubian Carabineers handcuffing comical chaps in blue shorts and shirts and silly hats?

Later on, he asks Sister Short of the Royal Peninsula West Infirmary what's going on. She tells him not to be silly, turns him over, and sticks a needle in his left buttock.

The next person that Galar Pen sees is the Grand Bard. His Grandness is accompanied by the entire Gorseth Council. They bear gifts. They bear grapes. They bear bottles of nutritious drinks, they bear improving magazines, and they bear hygienically-wrapped packets of nutritious minibuns.

''Tis like this, see …' begins the Grand Bard.

'You'm probably thinking …' says the Deputy Grand Bard.

'Well done, boy,' cry the Gorseth Council. 'Hurrah! Hurrah! Hurrah!'

'Yes, boy, you saved us. She was going to wipe out the Gorseth, and take total control of Cornish poetry. Thanks to you, boy, leading her into that brilliant trap, her evil plot was foiled.'

'I don't know …' Galar Pen thinks of all the blunders and disasters. 'I feel sort of guilty.'

'We'm all guilty, boy.'

'We'm all guilty,' agrees Galar Pen in a shaky voice. 'That's what my job depends on.'

Simon Parker

WILD OATS

'Porridge, love?' Frank called to his sleepy son. 'I've made plenty.' He always made plenty. He always made the same amount in fact. One mug of pinhead oats, three mugs of water and a good pinch of salt. Frank was a porridge eater – and a champion of its various qualities and delights – by circumstance, not by birth. He hadn't always made porridge. But since marrying Maire he had embraced those aspects of her Scottish culture he took a fancy to. Porridge, square sausage and single malts were eagerly welcomed into his life. Jimmy Shand, midges and mutton pies he never quite got used to.

Frank had always lived in a bustling, scruffy fishing port on the toe of Cornwall. It was his home all right, but that didn't stop him from yearning to turn his back on it for a bit and to see a little of the world.

Maire had sailed into his life on a mist-heavy sea, and he immediately fell for her mane of jet hair as she climbed the granite steps of the harbour when the boat she was helping to crew put into port for repairs en route from the Clyde to the Azores. She never completed that journey, choosing instead to wave off the rest of her shipmates from the pier, her other arm firmly clutching Frank's calloused fist.

'Porridge?' he called again.

Laurence shuffled in, half dressed, half asleep and still half drunk from the night before.

'Porridge?' his father repeated.

'Is that all you've got, my man?' snapped Laurence, feigning the accent of an upper class English gent. 'How's a chap expected to enjoy a good day's shooting with just a bit of gruel in his gullet? Where are the devilled kidneys, you scoundrel?'

Father and son laughed, embracing gently and comfortably.

'Porridge it is then,' said Laurence, settling down to read the jobs page of the local newspaper.

This ritual, or one very similar, was acted out nearly every morning; for Frank and Laurence it was as much a part of waking as yawning. Maire had become oblivious to their antics, quietly drinking her tea and listening to the radio news as her two 'boys' sniggered at their own performances, which became more elaborate and theatrical by the day. Maire's contribution to the daily drama, meanwhile, was to suddenly transform from a silent, calm and near-motionless creature into a dervish, jumping up, crying something about the time, rummaging about in a desperate search for keys, purse, shoes, kissing Frank and Laurence and flying out of the front door.

Maire worked in a bookshop. She was assistant manager, though the title meant little. But she enjoyed her work, meeting other enthusiastic bookworms, avid children, and elderly self-educated gentlemen. Finding and ordering a title to replace a lost and cherished memory from someone's childhood was a regular request, and her particular joy. Every hour spent poring over catalogues, telephoning publishers and speaking to antiquarian dealers – and they were usually as antiquarian as their wares – was worth it just to see a customer's face as he or she was transported back decades to a perfect day at a time when their lives were simpler, less cluttered.

Frank had worked for years as a harbour odd-job man. His was the lot of many Cornish men with few qualifications but nevertheless a fierce determination to resist the well-trodden route of so many of his peers, forced to leave the land of their birth to find employment up the line. So he picked daffodils and broccoli in the season, mended stonework, collected port rents, helped in the café and generally kept the quayside tidy and ticking. Poorly educated and poorly paid, he was treated as an ignorant dogsbody by some of the wealthy sailors who now used the quay and whose presence was beginning to become as important to the port as the long-liners, crabbers and trawlermen whose forebears had built the harbour.

But despite a lack of prospects, Frank always had his dream. He'd had the same consuming ambition for almost as long as he could remember. He'd had it in fact since his own father had given him a copy of Laurie Lee's *As I Walked Out One Midsummer Morning* when he was eleven years old. His father said he'd found it floating – actually floating – in the harbour amongst a raft of flotsam.

'The darnest thing,' his father had said, as he handed it to Frank. 'The darnest thing.' And he shook his head, smiling in a kind of wonder and disbelief.

Frank read it over and over until the pages became frayed and the cover had to be repaired with Sellotape. And as he read it, his dream was born, to one day save enough money to travel to a distant port, and there wander freely and poetically on foreign soil.

But it wasn't to be, and Frank had his dream roughly snatched from him on a squally July afternoon when an untidy Force 8 was making conditions in the bay difficult for sailors and fishermen alike. He was busy making fast everything along the South Pier, tying down tarpaulins and securing mooring ropes, when a rich but inexperienced 'yacht yob' with 'money aplenty but shit for brains', as Frank put it, lost control of his rig and let the boat's boom swing wide of the quayside. All its weight and force, boosted by a 60ft gust, smashed Frank's legs against a granite mooring post.

Of course, he could have been killed. That's what the yachtman's smart lawyer argued, as if it were some consolation to a man who for a while thought he'd never walk the length of the quay again, let alone wander freely and poetically on foreign soil. The compensation seemed quite fair at the time. But Frank was two years without work and they couldn't go another winter without replacing the linhay's old corrugated iron roof. In no time those precious few thousand pounds were gobbled up. And with it Frank's dream of seeing the world.

And then there were Laurence's violin lessons. They had to be paid for – Frank wouldn't have it any other way. Laurence didn't actually want violin lessons, but Frank was insistent. It was simply a case of 'my son's going to have all the things I never could'. Maire thought it unwise to persist with the argument that even though Frank felt deprived as a child because his parents were too poor to be able to afford music lessons, Laurence would feel similarly aggrieved, or even bothered. As it turned out Laurence, to the silent disappointment of his father, never took to the instrument. Even he had to admit – to himself at least – that there was very little one could describe honestly as musical in the scrapings Lawrence made as he dutifully undertook his nightly practice. Frank didn't protest when these sessions began to get shorter and shorter until the forlorn little fiddle – and with it another of Frank's dreams – was left to gather dust on a shelf in the parlour, while Laurence went off and practiced his 'tailflips' and 'fakeys' with the other skateboarders.

A couple of summers drifted by and before Frank realised what was happening, Laurence was no longer his little boy. He was a year out of school, and despite reasonable exam results, had no job. And with unemployment running at nearly sixty per cent of the male population in the area, there was little hope of one.

Frank knew Laurence was at that age when anything seemed possible and life stretched out before him like a long thin road, edged with trees in blossom, bathed in sunshine, full of promise. Frank could remember feeling like that when he was seventeen. There was no rush to get stuck into anything. Just let it happen. Laurence wasn't idle; he'd surf and swim and cycle. Sometimes he'd spend a whole day dangling a couple of hooks off the end of the South Pier, bringing home enough mackerel and pollack to give everyone in the terrace a good tea. And on warm summer nights, he and a few friends might light a fire in the dunes and just talk about nothing much until dawn.

Frank knew that carefree feeling, and saw so much of himself in the boy. Sometimes he'd sit and watch him when he knew Laurence was oblivious to his presence. He'd watch him lovingly wax his surfboard as the sun lit up his hair just before it slipped into the ocean. And at those moments he knew for sure that he loved him like no father had ever loved a son before. It was for that reason that he set about plotting Laurence's future, a future full of adventure, of dreams fulfilled.

Where was that old copy of *As I Walked Out…*? Those tales of little Lolly Lee, who'd strolled away from his home and family with hardly a backward glance and found love and romance and poetry in Spain, still captivated Frank. He asked Maire to get him a new copy. She knew he kept the one his father had given him by the bedside, knew how important it was to him, knew in her heart that this fresh copy must be for Laurence. Knew he must be dreaming again.

The first morning after it arrived Frank rose early. Into the pot, as usual, went one mug of pinhead oats, three mugs of water and a good pinch of salt. Then, as the familiar brew began to bubble, Frank sprinkled in Page One of Laurie Lee's epic tale, which he had carefully chopped into fine dust with his best gutting knife.

'Porridge, love?' he called, and his son responded in the usual way before sitting down to his steaming bowl. On that first morning, Laurence unknowingly ingested '*the stooping figure of my mother, waist-deep in the grass and caught there like a sheep's wool*' and was quite unaware of the potency of each spoon as its contents slipped down between mouthfuls of sweet tea.

On Day Two Laurence's intestines were '*affronted by freedom*' and on Day Three they met '*an old hag with a tooth like a tin-opener*'. On Day Four he was serenaded with '*tunes of sober zest*' and '*rewarded with silver*' while on Day Five '*a fluid young girl of sixteen hugged him steadily throughout one long hot day with only a gymslip on her sea-wet body*'.

And so it went on. Each breakfast-time Laurie took Laurence on a journey of discovery from Zamora to Valladolid, Segovia to Madrid, Toledo to Malaga – and all to the impassioned accompaniment of a gypsy fiddle.

Frank, meanwhile, waited and hoped for any small sign that his son was experiencing an awakening; some portent that a wanderlust was being kindled from within.

And sure enough, one February morning – when Laurie had been '*in Manolo's Bar muttering about civil war*' – Laurence told his father, quite casually, that 'a few of us are thinking 'bout buying a round-the-world ticket, do a bit of surfing and stuff; there's too many local maids whispering 'bout marrying and settling down'.

Frank smiled gently. Inside he was dancing.

'Home's not going nowhere, son,' he told him. 'It'll all still be here when you get back.'

After a summer saving every last penny earned slogging in hotel kitchens at all hours, pulling potatoes, and taking holidaymakers on boat trips round the bay, Laurence packed a single bag, strapped his surfboard on his back, and was gone. That night Frank read to Maire: '*She stood old and bent at the top of the bank, silently watching me go, one gnarled red hand raised in farewell and blessing, not questioning why I went.*'

They both held each other and wept. Happy for him, aware that he had to go, but brimming with the anxiety felt by all parents.

After almost thirty years of 'bumming around the world' as he put it, Laurence finally wandered home for good. Frank was long dead. But he'd had one last dream. It concerned the letters Laurence had sent him each week without fail from the places he visited – New Zealand, South Africa, Cambodia, Guatemala and, of course, Galicia, where Laurie Lee first landed and where the Atlantic breakers pound the northern Spanish coast in such a way as to create the most perfectly formed waves Laurence had ever surfed. Frank's dying wish was that Laurence's letters should be cremated with him and that the ashes be scattered to the four winds when the first Force 10 blew into the bay after his funeral service.

'You see me travel then, boy,' he'd said.

Laurence took over the running of the bookshop, which his mother had bought a few years earlier. In old age, on winter days when no one came to buy, he liked nothing more than to sit by the paraffin stove in the back of the store room and to turn the pages of a novel set in a foreign land. He read avidly, for the first time in his life. Everything from Hemingway to Yevtushenko, Rushdie to Rulfo, Lampedusa to Rivas. He liked most writers ... though strangely enough, Laurence found he never could quite stomach Laurie Lee.

Annamaria Murphy

BELOW

As Mary Robartes panted through the sweat, the memory of previous pain visited her limbs, her fingertips, the tiny hairs on her arms, the innermost chambers of her heart. She swore to the flaking ceiling that this one would not go below.

She prayed for a girl, but didn't expect to be heard as she was not a church-going woman. Sure enough it was another boy. The child shot out past the midwife and on to the kitchen floor. This was a good sign to Mary. It meant that the child was eager to get into the light, out from the darkness of her.

She named him 'Lughes', which means lightning.

'That's how he came out, like lightning,' said Mary. 'He's dark like a storm cloud. The effort of him almost split me in two. Like a boulder, covered in black moss. Only a man could've designed a woman.'

'That's true,' said Jim.

And as she laughed, her milk came, and so did the tears. In later years the boy favoured salt on his supper.

Jim, her husband, could sing. His voice was as deep as Cook's Kitchen, where men sweated rivers 240 fathoms below. She first heard him sing in a concert up Trewirgie. She was doing the teas. His voice wrapped around her like a mist. When she served him his tea in the interval, she made the biscuit soggy from nervous spillage. His eyebrows, like black caterpillars, came just below the serving hatch. They married three concerts later. Lughes grew tall. His brothers had joined Jim down at Crofty.

'If you think Lughes is going below, you can think again.'

'What else will he do?'

'He can work at the petrol station, go to college, open a shop, anything. Don't go filling his head with buccadhus, and ghosts and underground caverns. There's plenty to look at up here.'

'Ah Mary, you don't mean it,
Soft in the night Mary,
Hard in the day Mary,
Mary who sheds no tears,
Mary who has no fears,
Mary whose eyes twinkle like Galena.'

'I've got fears Jim Robartes.'

'Mary who can read a man's thoughts
Through the fug of pipe smoke,

Through closed eyelids,
Under the sheets,
Only place she can't read them is down below. Fifty fathoms, a hundred fathoms. I've got me own thoughts there. Some I leave on the surface though, some words too explosive for a hundred fathoms. What else is the lad going to do Mary?'

Mary dreams of fast waters and tunnels, and men's voices. She wakes in a sweat most nights and can't remember why. She recalls that her father couldn't swim, nor her brothers.

'It's like you've been below,' says Jim, 'the heat of you.'

Mary shivers, and Jim sings her a quiet song.

Lughes never went below, because Crofty closed, and flooded, and opened, and closed, and flooded again.

'Brimming over with tears,' as Jim said.

Church-going or not, Mary thanked the Lord.

Lughes loved to surf, to catch the wave and shoot out from it.

For a while he had a job in a light-bulb factory, to pay his way to Australia. He loved the delicate filaments that captured the light. He loved the way they flickered in a storm.

Stacey Guthrie

DOUBLED UP AND BAKED LIKE FATE

Vicky Trembath glanced nervously at her watch, wondering if the helicopter was going to be late again. In the ten years she'd been working on the mainland she had never got used to the stomach lurching flight that got her there and back. To ease her nerves she picked up a discarded copy of *The Cornishman* and flicked through the accommodation pages. Jim had been talking about moving for a while now but with the property market the way it was Vicky didn't hold out much hope of anything turning up.

They'd been in their unit on platform 42 since they got married. She was happy enough; they were on the 24th floor so they had a good view but lately Jim had seemed more agitated than usual. She put it down to stress from his job at the new pasty factory but maybe he was just fed up with her. She glanced at the date on the paper – 23rd June 2096, it was only four months until their 10th wedding anniversary. Ten years. People had thought they were an odd match, Jim so vocal and her so timid.

A voice blasting from the tannoy jolted Vicky from her thoughts. 'Flight 3521 is now landing on pad 72. Would all passengers present themselves to be scanned.' Vicky laid the paper on the seat, rolled up her sleeve, passed her arm under the scanner and made her way to the helicopter. Five minutes later she was in the air and on her way to work.

Jim watched as Terry added a fourth spoon of sugar to his tea.

'Take it easy Terry. Your teeth'll fall out.'

Terry grinned, flashing a set of sparkling white, if rather large, teeth.

'They did years ago boy, made myself this new set when I was working in the butchers department at Pasty Hut.'

He tapped his teeth with his spoon.

'Let's just say it was neeeeigh problem finding the parts.'

Then he laughed so much he went puce and nearly fell off his chair. Jim sighed. He was happy in this new job and the money was very good for factory work, though there was something he couldn't quite put his finger on. For a start no one had ever met the boss. Every Monday morning all the workers gathered under the giant screen in the processing room for a pep talk by the owner of the factory. Strangely, after the broadcast Jim could never quite remember the owner's name or what he looked like. Talking to his colleagues about it revealed that it was the same for everyone. No one seemed bothered by it though.

'Matter do it Jim? Long as we get paid on time I don't care if ee's the Queen o' bleddy Sheba.'

He guessed they were right. Vicky was always telling him he thought about things too much. The bell signalled that tea break was over and Jim heaved another sigh and went back to work.

Vicky carefully opened the door of the first holiday home and stepped over the threshold. She savoured this moment every day. Such beautiful houses, it took her breath away. She loved her job and felt so lucky to be able to spend time cleaning in such lovely surroundings. Sometimes she pretended this house was hers. She imagined pottering around the garden, spending the afternoon preparing a meal for Jim and the two curly-haired, dark-eyed children who invariably crept into her daydreams. Vicky flushed pink at the silliness of her fantasy and shook herself. Houses like this weren't for people like her. She remembered in history class at school how they'd discussed the Great Cornish Housing Crisis and the government's brilliant idea of building afford-able housing units on offshore platforms and shipping what they called the 'Indigenous Population' on to them. Apparently there were some people who didn't like the idea but then there were always people who didn't like progress. Vicky liked her little unit on platform 42. It was small but that made it easy to heat and she found it comforting to be so close to her neighbours – all 5000 of them. Just then the postman arrived and as she picked up the letters and placed them on the growing pile by the telephone, Vicky realised she hadn't seen or heard from Mr & Mrs Swinburne in ages. They were probably just busy in London and they always came down for Mrs Swinburne's birth-day in September. As long as her wages were still going in by direct debit, who was she to be so nosy?

The weeks went by as they usually did and life was good for Vicky and Jim. Jim had been promoted to the export section and was now working preparing meat for the spe-cial pasties which were sent to London to be sold at outlets which were cropping up with increasing frequency at mainline train stations. He wasn't quite sure what made them different from the normal ones or why they had to be made in a separate area, but his wages had increased considerably and Vicky had been talking about babies again so for once in his life he wasn't going to ask questions.

One evening in late September Jim arrived home from work to find Vicky looking pensive. She was standing by the kitchen sink, peeling potatoes and frowning. Jim went up behind her and slipped his arms round her waist.

'A'wright maid? You were miles away there.'

Vicky put the potato she was peeling down and turned to him.

'Oh it's probably something and nothing Jim,' she said, 'it's just it's Mrs Swinburne's birthday today and they always come down without fail. I've just got a bad feeling about it, tid'n right.'

'Well, it in't nothing to do with us, bird. They come and go as they please.'

She sighed and wiped her hands on the dishcloth.

'No, you're right Jim, I shouldn't go getting ideas. They're very important people. They don't have to answer to the likes of me.'

Jim grunted.

'Dunno 'bout important, but they definitely in't short of a bob or two. You seen that geet diamond ring she wears? Bet that cost as much as our unit.'

Vicky changed the subject swiftly, she wasn't in the mood for one of Jim's rants about second home owners. The Swinburnes were lovely people and they'd been very good to her. They even paid her a pound an hour more than the minimum wage and they didn't have to do that. She wondered whether she should tell Jim that she hadn't seen or heard from any of the other second home owners for ages either but he'd probably just call her daft. And he was right, she was being daft. Wasn't she?

Tuesday 23rd October 2096 at 6.15pm found Jim on the horns of a dilemma. It was their 10th wedding anniversary and he'd spent his lunch hour buying a beautiful necklace for Vicky. He'd put it in his locker for safe keeping ... and that's where he'd left it. There was a strict rule that all employees had to be off the premises by 5.30pm sharp. No one had ever been let back in under any circumstances and anyone not on the night shift even attempting to get back into the special export section after 5.30 was sacked on the spot. Jim briefly pondered on the fact that he'd never met anyone from the night shift but the thought was quickly superimposed by a picture of Vicky's face as he told her he hadn't got her a present. Poor Vicky, she'd be really upset if she thought he'd forgotten their anniversary. She already thought he was going off her, when in reality he was just distracted by this new job. There was nothing else for it: he'd have to break into the factory.

Jim waited by the gates trying to figure out how on earth he was going to get in. At 6.30 he heard an engine and looked down the track to see what looked like a meat lorry approaching. In the six months he'd worked there he'd never seen a meat delivery, they always happened at night. He quickly hid behind a gorse bush as the lorry pulled up to the gates and the driver stated his business through the intercom. Jim gave a silent prayer of thanks to whoever was listening and jumped on the ladder at the back of the truck. He couldn't hear what was being said through the intercom but the driver guffawed and the truck slowly moved through the now open gates. The truck made its way to the loading bay at the back of the special export section and came to a halt. Jim jumped off the back of the truck and sprinted over to the door which, thankfully, was open. He ran to the staff room and keyed his security number into the locker, breathing a sigh of relief as he grabbed the necklace and ran out the way he had come in. As he sneaked past the delivery truck he caught a glimpse of the meat being unloaded. There was something about it that didn't quite look right. Did beef usually come in large, zipped bags? He pushed the thought from his mind as he manoeuvred his way past the truck and down to the gates. The gods were definitely with him and he managed to sneak out as the lorry was leaving. He thanked his lucky stars as he ran all the way to the flight pad to catch the last helicopter back to the platform.

Vicky loved her necklace and they'd spent a very romantic evening planning their future in a bigger unit, with the two little tackers that Vicky had been dreaming of for the last eight years. They talked briefly about the political group who'd made it to the local news with their claims of wanting 'Cornish Homes For Cornish People' but that was just a pipe-dream. Locals hadn't been allowed to live on the mainland for more than 70 years and there was no way they'd ever be able to afford the houses there anyway. Jim and Vicky laughed at the protest group's naivety and set to practising making those babies Vicky so desperately wanted. All in all Jim was a very happy man.

Next morning Jim sauntered into the factory without a care in the world. He was still basking in the rosy glow of the night before and was happily whistling as he reached over for the next slab of beef. He placed it in front of him and picked up his filleting knife. As he started to cut into the lean, sinewy meat something caught his eye. It was sparkly and metallic and the incongruity of it against the soft, red flesh caught him up short. He reached down to pick it up and found it was a ring, a very large, diamond ring. There was something familiar about it, something that brought back a memory of annoyance, like the wearer of it had patronised him at some point. The realisation hit him like a brick and the blood drained from his face. The recognition of who it belonged to coursed through him like ice through his veins. That ring belonged to Mrs Swinburne. His head swam as he remembered the meat delivery the previous night, the odd shape of the bags, the fact that the Swinburnes had never once missed Mrs Swinburne's birthday in the 10 years Vicky had worked for them. Jim felt sick as he looked down at the lump of meat in front of him. It was definitely very pale for beef but he'd just assumed it was some special cut saved for the Londoners. How right he'd been. His memory turned to the signage on the sides of the meat lorry.

Kernow Arta Pasty Company
Delivering Quality Pasties To London
Tastes Like One Of Your Own

Notes on the authors and texts

Anon (1618) *The Bohelland Tragedy.* This early chap-book narrative draws on some of the central tenets of European narrative: wicked stepmothers, disguise, greed and over-ambition. Set in Penryn, the story tells of how a father kills his own son. The narrative has remained in the Cornish imagination for a number of centuries. In 1736 the playwright George Lillo (1693–1739) completed a famous stage version of the tale, which he titled *Fatal Curiosity.* Dramatic interpretations have also been completed by Donald R. Rawe (*Murder at Bohelland,* 1991) and by the Cornish Theatre Collective (Bohelland, 2003).

Nicholas Boson (1624–1708), born Newlyn, Cornwall, merchant, short story writer and Cornish literary and language scholar. Boson was forbidden to speak Cornish at home, and it was only when he had to negotiate business with local fisherman that he learnt to speak Cornish. Between 1674 and 1708 he wrote *A Few Words about Cornish,* and sometime in the 1660s, *The Duchess of Cornwall's Progress* in both English and Cornish. His version of *John of Chyanhor, or The Three Points of Wisdom* was published by Edward Lhuyd in 1707.

Robert Hunt (1807–1887), born Devonport, Plymouth, scientist, antiquarian, poet and folklorist. Originally studying for the medical profession, Hunt became Keeper of Mining Records at the Museum of Geology and lectured at the School of Mines on mechanical science and experimental physics. He also helped to found the Miners' Association, his contact with miners giving him insight into the folklore of Cornwall. He published the two volumes of *Popular Romances of the West of England* in 1865.

Anthony Trollope (1815–1882), born London, novelist and short story writer. Originally a post-office surveyor, Trollope is most famous for his series of comic novels based around the imaginary English county of Barsetshire. These include *The Warden* (1855) and *Barchester Towers* (1857). Trollope travelled extensively to Australia and Ireland, setting four novels in the latter country. Many of his novels have been adapted to the television mini-series format.

William Bottrell (1816–1881), born Rafta, near Land's End, Cornwall, folklorist, and short story writer. Bottrell was educated at Penzance Grammar School and Bodmin

School. As a young man he travelled to France and Spain, becoming interested in Basque folktales. He worked as an English teacher in Quebec, and later travelled to Australia. After the death of his wife, Bottrell returned to Cornwall to live at Lelant, assisting Robert Hunt with his collection of folktales. His folklore writings were then complied into three volumes.

Thomas Hardy (1840–1928), born Higher Bockampton, Dorset, novelist and poet. 'A Mere Interlude', which is set in Penzance and on the Isles of Scilly, first appeared in the *Bolton Weekly Journal* in October 1885, twelve years after the publication of *A Pair of Blue Eyes*, Hardy's first and only Anglo-Cornish novel. It was later collected into *A Changed Man, The Waiting Supper and other tales* (1913) which Hardy himself called 'a dozen minor novels'.

Mark Guy Pearse (1842–1930), born Camborne, Cornwall, Methodist preacher, West London Missioner, poet and prolific writer of stories and religious texts. The best-selling *Daniel Quorm and his Religious Notions* (1874 and 1875) was read by all levels of society and was much admired by Queen Victoria. Although the religious message was paramount in his writing, his wit and humour and his understanding of his fellow-Cornish and their speech patterns resulted in beautifully-crafted and entertaining stories.

Joseph Henry Pearce (1856–c.1930), born Penzance, Cornwall, novelist and short story writer. Working as a clerk in London, he devoted his leisure time to literary pursuits, producing such novels as *Jaco Treloar* (1893) and *Ezekiel's Sin* (1898) and two volumes of short stories. The *New York Times* described his Cornish short stories as being 'written with exceeding strength and somewhat with a Hawthorne coloring', while Brendan MacMahon finds them 'laconic, almost minimalist'. His use of dialect is masterful.

J(osiah) Henry Harris (c.1848–1917), born Plymouth, journalist, novelist and short story writer. Having lived in Mevagissey as a child, Harris returned when he retired from his post as chief reporter for *Central News*. In a house overlooking the harbour, he produced such works as *Our Cove* (1900), *Cornish Saints and Sinners* (1906) and *The Luck of Wheal Veor* (1901) from which 'Souls for Gold' is taken.

Arthur Quiller-Couch (1863–1944), born Bodmin, Cornwall, lecturer, essayist, critic, poet, novelist, short story writer and Liberal politician. Anthologies such as *The Oxford Book of English Verse* (1900) and collections of essays such as *On the Art of Writing* (1916) enhanced his reputation as a man of letters in England, while his numerous Cornish novels and collections of short stories made him pre-eminent amongst Cornish writers. The stories in *Noughts and Crosses* (1891), from which 'These-An'-That's Wife' is taken, he described as being 'composed in country walks, on railway journeys between Cornwall and Fleet Street, and some under the stars over Plymouth Hoe in night-pacings through an interval thoughtfully provided for me by the Great Western, breaking trains on the way home'.

John Baragwanath King (1864–1939), born near Penzance, Cornwall, landscape painter and writer. He exhibited professionally during the first decades of the twentieth century in London, Paris, Brussels, Florence and Berlin. He was a bard of Gorsedh Kernow and President of St Austell Old Cornwall Society, his interest in the legends and folklore of his homeland being reflected in *Arthur and others in Cornwall* (1925).

C. A. Dawson Scott (1865–1934), born Dulwich, poet, novelist, short story writer and playwright. 'Sappho', as she was known for much of her life, was part of the lively literary scene that was a feature of 1890s' London. Her family's links with Cornwall – Henry Dawson Lowry was a first cousin – were strengthened when she and her husband had a holiday home built at Constantine Bay just before the First World War. *Wastralls*, the first of her seven novels with a Cornish setting, was published in 1918. As well as founding P.E.N., the international association for writers, she was well-known in the 1920s for her interest in psychic phenomena and established The Survival League.

H(enry) D(awson) Lowry (1869–1906), born Truro, Cornwall, short story writer, novelist, poet and journalist. He moved to Camborne while still in his teens and studied chemistry at the School of Mines before graduating in the subject at Oxford in 1891. His first book, *Wreckers and Methodists* (1893) was followed two years later by *Women's Tragedies*, both being collections of stories in which Camborne – as 'Tallywarn' – features prominently. *Wheal Darkness* (1927), a novel of Methodist life in the Camborne-Redruth area, was completed some years after his death by his cousin, C. A. Dawson Scott.

Charles Lee (1870–1956), born Stockwell Green, London, novelist, short story writer and poet. He attended Highgate School and received a BA Honours from the University of London in 1889. For health reasons, in 1893 he went to live in Newlyn, and became friendly with the artistic community there. He also stayed at Cadgwith and Portloe, and wrote *Paul Carah Cornishman* (1898), *The Widow Woman* (1899) and *Cynthia in the West* (1900). In 1907, Lee left Cornwall for good. His novellas and short stories are compiled in *Cornish Tales* (1941) and *Chasing Tales* (2002) edited by Arthur Quiller Couch and Simon Parker respectively. A one-act play version of *Mr Sampson* was performed for television, just before he died.

Phyllis Bottome (1882–1963), born Rochester, novelist and short story writer. The daughter of an American clergyman and a Yorkshire woman, she studied acting in London before establishing herself as a prolific writer of feminist novels and works of non-fiction in which personal freedom was a recurring theme. Her friend Daphne du Maurier edited her collected stories in 1963. 'An Awkward Turn' was published in *The Century* in December 1916 before being included in *The Derelict* five months later.

D(avid) H(erbert) Lawrence (1885–1930), born Eastwood, Nottinghamshire, novelist, poet, dramatist and short story writer. His major novels include *Sons and Lovers* (1913), *The Rainbow* (1915) and *Lady Chatterley's Lover* (1928). Between 1916 and 1917, Lawrence and his German-born wife Frieda lived at Tregarthen near Zennor. Both were persecuted as German agents. His experiences in Cornwall are fictionalized in the novel *Kangeroo* (1923). 'Samson and Delilah' was published in *England, My England* in the United States in 1922.

Anne Treneer (1891–1966), born Gorran, Cornwall, teacher, poet, biographer and short story writer. Best-known for her autobiographical trilogy *Schoolhouse in the Wind* (1944), *Cornish Years* (1949) and *A Stranger in the Midlands* (1952), she also produced *Happy Button and other stories*, in which the sparing, yet telling use of Cornu-English dialect confirms her as one of Cornwall's best exponents of the genre.

A(lfred) L(eslie) Rowse (1903–1997), born Tregonissey, near St Austell, Cornwall, poet, short story writer, historian and literary scholar. Rowse was the son of a china clay worker, who was educated at St Austell Grammar School and won a scholarship to Christ Church College, Oxford in 1921. He was then elected a Fellow of All Souls College in 1929. Rowse travelled extensively, especially to America, and after a distinguished lecturing career at Oxford, he retired to Trenarren House, near St Austell. Rowse wrote over one hundred titles in his lifetime, including *Tudor Cornwall* (1941), *A Cornish Childhood* (1942) and *The Cornish in America* (1969). His *A Life: Collected Poems* was published in 1981.

Mary Williams (1903–2000), born Leicester, romantic novelist, ghost-story writer and poet. Although she studied illustration and remained a busy artist for the rest of her life, it was as a writer of children's books and newspaper columnist in Wales that she first made a name for herself. Moving to St Ives, she developed her lifelong interest in ghosts and Cornish folklore and, thanks to publisher William Kimber who shared her great love for Cornwall, began a hugely successful career as a writer of supernatural tales at the age of 72. She continued to write and paint up to the time of her death.

Daphne du Maurier (1907–1989), born London, novelist, biographer and short story writer. For over forty years, historical romances and adventure stories such as *Jamaica Inn* (1963), *My Cousin Rachel* (1951) and *The House on the Strand* (1969) made her one of the most popular writers of the twentieth century and her work has become synonymous with Cornwall. Her narrative skills and strong visual sense resulted in hugely successful film adaptations of many of her novels and stories, including that of 'The Birds' by Alfred Hitchcock.

J(ohn) C(ourtney) Trewin (1908–1990), born Plymouth, of Cornish parents, journalist, short story writer and drama critic. Trewin spent his childhood holidays on the Lizard peninsula, eventually writing *Up from the Lizard* (1948) as a memory of his time there. Initially a journalist for the *Western Independent*, then at the *Morning Post*, he eventually served as drama critic on the *Observer* newspaper for over sixty years. He published several volumes of literary and theatrical criticism.

Winston Graham (1908–2003), born in Manchester, novelist and short story writer. His first Poldark novel, *Ross Poldark*, was published in 1945, and was followed by a series of eleven further titles, the last of which was *Bella Poldark* in 2002. The Poldark saga was made into a highly-successful television series in the mid-1970s. Graham also wrote a number of thrillers, writing some thirty novels in addition to the *Poldark* series. He lived in Perranporth from 1925 until 1959, before moving to East Sussex.

Jack Clemo (1913–1994), born at Goonamarris, St Stephen-in-Brannel, Cornwall, poet, novelist, and short story writer. Clemo's breakthrough novel was *Wilding Graft* (1948), followed by an autobiography, *Confessions of a Rebel* (1949). His first poetry collection, *The Clay Verge* was published in 1951. Clemo often fused his visionary Christian beliefs onto the china clay landscape of mid-Cornwall. Italy, and Venice in particular, formed a thematic concern in his later poetry.

Denys Val Baker (1917–1984), born Poppleton, near York, editor, novelist and short-story writer. During the 1940s he founded and edited several literary magazines, one of the most well-known being the hugely-influential *Cornish Review* which he famously described as 'born originally in 1949, prematurely retired in 1952, resurrected in 1966 – finally buried … [in] 1974'. Having settled in West Penwith in 1946, he remained an integral part of the Cornish literary and artistic scene until his death.

Charles Causley (1917–2003), born Launceston, Cornwall, poet, playwright, editor and short story writer. Often using forms such as ballads, popular songs and hymns, and simple and large themes such as death, innocence, truth, and love, Causley's poetry made him one of the foremost writers in Cornwall and Britain during the second half of the twentieth century. Following the publication of his first poetry collection, *Farewell Aggie Weston*, in 1951, a book of stories that same year entitled *Hands to Dance & Skylark* drew on his experiences in the Navy during the Second World War.

Phyllis M. Jones (1923–), born Truro, Cornwall, novelist, poet and short story writer. Although she has lived in South Wales since 1945, she remains deeply attached to Cornwall, which features in such autobiographical volumes as *The Bells of Truro* (1994) and *No Harbour Lights* (2007). Her work has appeared in such magazines as *The Cornish Review, An Baner Kernewek* and *Cornish Scene. They Gave Me a Lamp* (1992), which was based on her experiences as a Colliery Nursing Officer at Cynheidre Colliery, was widely acclaimed. A collection of short stories, *New People in an Old World*, was published in 2009.

Kenneth Moss (1928–), born East End of London, short story writer. He moved to Cornwall in 1960, living at Sennen Cove and later at St Ives. There he helped establish

The Cornish Review, a magazine to which he contributed a number of stories and articles. He later worked as Principal Lecturer in English at Liverpool's Central College. *Encounter in St Ives and other stories of Cornwall* was published in 1980.

Donald R. Rawe (1930–), born Padstow, Cornwall, poet, dramatist, novelist, folklorist and short story writer. Rawe has lived in Cornwall since 1960, after a time teaching in Australia. In 1970 he founded Lodenek Press, the Cornish publishing house. Among his many publications are *Looking for Love in a Great City* (1956), *Petroc of Cornwall* (1970), *The Trials of St Piran* (1971), *Padstow's Obby Oss and May Day Festivities: A Study in Folklore and Tradition* (1971) and *A Prospect of Cornwall* (1996).

N. R(oy) Phillips (1930–), born St Ives, Cornwall, naturalist, novelist and short story writer. Phillips first came to prominence with the novel, *The Saffron Eaters* (1987). The characters of this novel are also explored in *The Horn of Strangers* (1996) and *Apocalypse Dreckly* (2005). Phillips has also written extensively on ornithology.

John Branfield (1931–), born Burrow Bridge, Somerset, novelist, short story writer and art and local historian. He and his young family moved to Cornwall in 1961, a year after the publication of his first novel *A Flag in the Map* (1960). He taught in grammar and comprehensive schools before becoming a full-time writer. He has published twelve novels and two collections of short stories, most of them for older children. The best known are *In the Country* (1966), *Nancekuke* (1972), *The Fox in Winter* (1980), which was commended for the Carnegie Gold Medal, and *A Breath of Fresh Air* (2001).

Liz Harman (1931–), born Newlyn, Cornwall, short story writer, storyteller and poet. A regular entertainer throughout West Penwith and across her homeland, she was made a bard of Gorsedh Kernow in 2008 for services to Cornish dialect and literature. *Now 'Ark To Me* (2006), her first collection of stories and poems, was followed by *Now 'Ark Some More* in 2009. Her Newlyn Passion Play, *This I Did For You*, was performed locally at St Peter's Church in 2009.

E(rnest) V. Thompson (James Munro) (1931–), born Oxfordshire, novelist and writer of books on various aspects of Cornwall and Cornish life. Having spent a number of years in the Navy and working with Bristol police, in 1970 he moved to Cornwall where he developed a very successful career as a writer. His first novel *Chase the Wind* won the Best Historic Novelist Award in 1977 and has been followed with a host of other titles, including *Ben Retallick* (1980), the first of the nine-volume Retallick series and three volumes featuring the Jagos (1983–1993). His latest novel is *Churchyard and Hawke* (2009). He is a bard of Gorsedh Kernow.

Michael Morpurgo (1943–), born St Albans, novelist, poet, playwright and librettist. Initially, he trained for the British Army at the Royal Military Academy, Sandhurst, but later became a primary school teacher. Morpurgo began writing in his late twenties, and has written many children's titles, several of which are set in Cornwall and on the Isles of Scilly. These include *Why the Whales Came* (1985), *Arthur, High King of Britain* (1994) and *The Wreck of Zanzibar* (1995). Morpurgo held the title of Children's Laureate from 2003 to 2005. Nick Stafford's acclaimed adaptation of his novel *War Horse* (1982) opened at the National Theatre in 2007.

Les Merton (1944 –), born Helston, Cornwall, short story and Cornish-dialect writer, poet, editor and publisher. Merton has lived in Cornwall all his life and, after a variety of jobs, has found his niche in the contemporary literary scene. He is editor of the highly regarded *Poetry Cornwall*, runs Palores Publications and was made a bard of Gorsedh Kernow in 2004 for services to Cornish literature. His own output has included *Dark Corners: a return to Cornish noir* (2005), *There's an 'F' in Phoenix in Redruth* (2007, a selection of award-winning English and Cornish dialect writing, and (as editor) *101 Poets For a Cornish Assembly* (2006).

Myrna Combellack (1948–), born Carharrack, Cornwall, academic, novelist and short story writer. Combellack studied English and Literature at the universities of York, Leeds and Vassar College, New York, working as Academic Secretary at the Institute of Cornish Studies, and later as a teacher. The writer of a number of studies on Medieval and Tudor drama, she completed an acclaimed English language verse translation of *Bewnans Meriasek*, titled *The Camborne Play* (1988) Her *Playing Place* series of novels (1989 onwards) reflect a changing landscape and people in a fictional inland Cornish parish.

Helen Dunmore (1952–), born Yorkshire, novelist, poet and short story writer. Having graduated in English from the University of York, Dunmore taught English as a foreign language in Finland before conducting poetry and creative writing courses for the Arvon Foundation. While in Finland she began to write the poems which formed her first collection *The Apple Fall* (1983). *Zennor in Darkness* (1993), her first novel for adults, won the McKitterick Prize, while *A Spell of Winter* three years later won the inaugural Orange Prize for Fiction. Her acclaimed, Cornwall-based Ingo quartet for children was published between 2005 and 2008. Her latest novels are *The Betrayal* (2010) and, for children, *The Ferry Birds* (2010).

Tim Saunders (1952–), born Northumberland, poet, essayist, translator, editor, short story writer and broadcaster. Saunders was brought up in Cornwall and studied Celtic Studies at the University of Aberystwyth. He is the editor of two major collections of poetry in Cornish: *The Wheel: An anthology of modern poetry in Cornish 1850–1980* (1999) and *Nothing Broken: Recent Poetry in Cornish* (2006). Co-editor of the collection, *Looking at the Mermaid: A Reader in Cornish Literature 900–1900* (2000), his collected poems in Cornish, *The High Tide,* appeared in 1999. His latest work (with Alan M. Kent) is the Cornish-language poem cycle *Awen, Aval* and *Awedh* (Muse, Apple and Watercourse) due to appear in 2011. He is a bard of Gorsedh Kernow.

Simon Parker (1959–), born Redruth, Cornwall, journalist, editor, short story writer, playwright and publisher. He is a founder member of Scavel An Gow and editor of both *Scryfa*, the well-known Cornish literary review, and of *The Western Morning News'* 'Living Cornwall' supplement. He was made a bard of Gorsedh Kernow in 2003 for his promotion of all things Cornish, especially Cornish literature, and his work has been awarded its Henry Jenner, Sybil Pomeroy and Holyer An Gof cups and been broadcast on BBC Radio 4 and BBC Radio Cornwall. His latest play, *Gonamena*, was performed at Sterts Theatre near Liskeard in 2009.

Annamaria Murphy (1957–), born Polperro, Cornwall, dramatist, poet and short story writer. A teacher, Murphy is well known for her work with Kneehigh Theatre, including (with Carl Grose) *Tristan & Ysuelt* (2003), and *The Bacchae* (2004). She has written for C-scape Dance (including an adaptation of 'Below'), and for Rogue Theatre. Most recently, she has completed a dramatisation of the life of Mary Bryant titled *Oh Mary* (2009), and completed *Scummow*, her third play for Radio 4.

Stacey Guthrie (1965–), born Penzance, Cornwall, short story writer. Educated at Penzance Girls Grammar School and Cornwall College, Guthrie works as a textiles artist from a 5 acre smallholding in west Cornwall. She is also a singer and an actor and has appeared in Pauline Sheppard's play, *Tin & Fishes*.